By a Silver Thread

DFZ Changeling Book 1

Rachel Aaron

Series Information

By a Silver Thread

With a Golden Sword

To the Bloody End

Other series set in this world

The Heartstrikers

The DFZ

See the back for more details!

Copyright and Publishing Info
By a Silver Thread

Aaron Bach
"Writing to Entertain and Inform."
Copyright © 2023 Rachel Aaron

ISBN Paperback: 978-1-952367-21-2

Cover Illustration by Luisa Preissler
Cover Design by Rachel Aaron
Editing provided by Red Adept Editing

Prologue

Good Samaritan's Children's Hospital Long-Term-Care Facility
Detroit Free Zone
65 years after the return of magic

The nurses didn't enter the monster's room unless they had to.

Every morning, they had a fight in the hall about whose turn it was to go in. The monster could hear them arguing through the vents in the steel door that separated her from the rest of the hospital. Eventually, someone would admit defeat and stomp over to the medicine cabinet. This was the monster's signal to scramble into her bed and hide under the sheets, burying her furry head under the flat pillow in the hopes that her horns wouldn't be so obvious.

It always took the nurse at least five minutes to count the pills. No one seemed to know what they all did anymore. The doctors hadn't come to see the monster in months, but their directions still had to be followed.

When all the pills had been doled out into the little plastic cup, the nurse stomped to the monster's room and unlocked the heavy door, calling out as she entered.

"Lola?"

That was the name on the chart taped to the wall: Lola Daniels, age seven. But the monster hadn't been a little girl for a long time now, and she didn't answer. She just hid silently under the sheets as the nurse bumped the heavy door open with her hip.

"Med check."

The woman said it like a threat. Like all the nurses who braved the monster's room these days, though, she didn't actually check anything. She just dumped the medication tray with its plastic cups of water and pills on the counter by the sink and got to work. She gathered the dirty towels, returned the donated book of fairy tales to its place on the windowsill, wiped down the tiny, child-sized toilet, and mopped the linoleum floor, all without ever once glancing at the far-bigger-than-child-sized lump trembling under the bedsheets.

The whole process took less time than the argument over whose turn it was to do the chores. Once the room met the minimum definition of clean, the nurse banged back out the door and locked it behind her. Even so, the monster waited for her slapping footsteps to fade all the way down the hall before emerging from her hiding place.

She slid out of the bed like a lump of black hair pulled out of a drain. Her claws clicked on the freshly mopped floor as she shuffled over to the medication tray the nurse had left behind. Moving slowly so she wouldn't knock anything over, she grabbed the plastic pill cup, turning it over so the tablets fell out onto the leathery pad of the massive paw that had once been her left hand.

Her beady little eyes no longer saw in color, so the monster arranged the pills by size, moving the smaller, easier ones to the front while saving the bigger, harder ones for last. Then, using her claws like chopsticks, the monster picked up each pill and wedged it through the wall of her dagger-like fangs into her mouth to choke it down.

It would have been easier with water. Picking up the soft plastic water cup was beyond her these days, though, and her square-shaped head no longer fit under the faucet. She supposed she could have skipped it altogether. It wasn't as if the pills had ever helped, but the nurses still checked every night to make sure she'd taken her medicine. Their muttered "good job" was the only nice thing anyone said to the monster anymore, so even though it made her gag, she choked down every one, wedging pill after pill through the wall of her teeth until the plastic cup was empty.

She'd just finished swallowing the last one when she saw something flashing in the fluorescent light. It was getting harder and harder to see these days, but the monster knew what it was. It was her thread. A beautiful, silver thread, thin as spider silk but stronger than steel and shiny as a new promise. One end of it was tied around the bulge of fur and scales that used to be the little girl's left wrist. The other ran off toward nothing, vanishing into thin air just a few inches away from her body.

The sight of it glittering made her forget about the choking pills. The monster didn't know what the thread was, but for as long as she could remember, it had been tied around her wrist. Sometimes it danced like a fishing line with a big catch on the end. Other times, it lay still for weeks, but it was always there, shiny and beautiful.

The monster loved that thread. She wished sometimes that other people could see it so she'd have something to show off. Most of the time, though, she was glad she didn't have to share. The thread was her treasure, the one lovely thing she had left. She was running her claw down the bit she could see just for the pleasure of feeling how smooth it was when the lock on her door clicked again.

The monster dove for her bed with a squeal, her scrambling claws leaving huge gouges in the linoleum floor. The nurses would yell at her for that later, but the monster was too frightened to care at the moment, because the person who stepped into her room wasn't a nurse or a doctor. It was a man she'd never seen before.

The monster keened pitifully through the unruly forest of her teeth. She couldn't let the man see her. The nurses had learned to ignore the thing under the blankets, but strangers always gawked, and it made her feel terrible. Not just the normal hurt of being stared at, either. This was real, physical pain, as if her whole body were melting like ice cream in the sun.

The monster didn't know why it happened, but she feared the melting like nothing else. Just the possibility made her cry under the blankets, covering her face with her paws as she pushed her hairy body against the cinder block wall. She was praying to her silver thread to make the stranger go away when his hand landed on top of her blankets, ripping them off her like a magician revealing a trick.

She howled when the light poured in, lashing out with her claws, but the stranger didn't jump back or scream. He just stood there, staring at her, his blue eyes taking in her claws and fangs as if he was measuring them.

The howling monster went still. She didn't know what the stranger was doing here, but he was the first person who'd seen her like this and hadn't run screaming. His staring didn't make her body feel like it was melting, either.

That was odd enough to make the monster lift her shaggy head, which was how she saw that the stranger wasn't looking at her anymore. He was staring at the silver thread tied around what used to be her wrist. The same shining thread that was looped like a wire around his own gloved palm.

"Found you," he said, his deep voice triumphant as he gave the thread a tug.

The force yanked the monster out of her bed. She landed sprawling on the floor, yowling in surprise and rage. How dare he touch her treasure! But greater than her anger was her awe.

Even back when the monster had been human, no one but her had ever been able to see the thread, much less grab it. Even she could only touch the silver line, never move it, but the man didn't seem to realize he was doing the impossible. He simply yanked again, hauling the monster across the floor like a landed fish.

"You've given me a great deal of trouble," he scolded, his

refined voice growing testy. "Do you know how hard it was to track you?"

The monster didn't. She had no idea who he was or how he'd gotten here or what he wanted with her, but her mouth was too full of teeth to ask. Even if her voice had still worked, the monster didn't know if she'd have been able to speak. Now that she was close enough for her dim, beady eyes to make out his face, the monster realized that the man looming over her was quite possibly the most perfect-looking person she'd ever seen.

It was as if a movie star had stepped straight out of the television. The stranger was tall, with perfectly symmetrical features and slick black hair that was just starting to go gray at the temples. He was easily the handsomest person who'd ever set foot in the hospital. Too handsome to be real, actually, which was how the monster realized who he must be.

He was the hero. And he'd come here to kill her. Because she was the monster.

She slumped at his feet in a furry heap. Of course. That must be how he'd been able to touch her thread. It probably wasn't even *her* thread but someone else's lost treasure, which was why he'd tracked her down. She'd read the stories in her book, so she knew how it worked: slay the beast, retrieve the treasure, and then everyone lived happily ever after. Except for the monster, who was dead.

She hid her hideous face at the thought, whimpering into the hero's shiny shoes. Maybe it was better this way. If the hero killed her, she wouldn't have to swallow pills anymore, and it wasn't as if she had a reason to hold on. She clearly wasn't getting better, and her parents didn't even visit anymore now that they'd had another baby who wasn't a monster. But even though she was already lying defeated at his feet, the hero didn't pull out a sword or lop off her head. Instead, he leaned down to grab the thick tuft of black fur at

v

the nape of her neck, lifting her off the ground like a kitten.

Once again, the monster shrieked in pain and surprise, but the hero didn't even flinch. He just batted her flailing claws aside and grabbed her massive jaw, forcing her head up until her black, beady eyes were looking straight into his blue ones.

"You're more degraded than I feared," he said, twisting her from side to side as he examined her jagged fangs. "Another week, maybe less, and you'll be so far gone that even the slatternly staff who run this place will be forced to admit you don't actually have *cancer* or whatever idiot fantasy they've concocted to hide your inhumanity from themselves. They'll finally realize you're impossible, utterly unbelievable. When that happens, the magic constituting your body will destabilize, and you will cease to exist."

He stopped there, waiting for her answer, but the monster just stared at him, uncomprehending.

"You will die," he said, enunciating each word like the doctors did when they thought she was being a very stupid child. "Lost. Gone forever. You won't even be a memory."

That didn't sound so bad. If no one remembered the monster, then they wouldn't hate her anymore, and she was tired. So, so tired of the pills, of hiding, of always being alone. Tired of being a monster. It might be nice to just vanish and—

The hero yanked her thread so hard she squealed. He ignored the sound, stretching the silver thread taut between his hands as he leaned down to shove it in her toothy face.

"Do you know what's at the end of this line?"

The monster shook her head.

"A child," the elegant man told her. "A *human* child." He paused, arching an eyebrow. "You *do* understand that you're not human?"

The monster hung her head in shame, which the man apparently took for a nod, because he kept going.

"You are a changeling," he explained, his voice taking on a lecturing tone. "A product of the parasitic fairy magic that has recently begun creeping back into this plane."

He paused as if he expected her to apologize for this. The monster just kept staring, though, and eventually, he continued.

"Seven years ago, one of these fairies stole a human child and left a pile of gossamer magic—you—in its place. This"—he yanked on her silver thread again, making the monster whimper as the sharp wire cut painfully into her hairy flesh—"is your connection to that child. If you die, that innocent little girl—your sister by magic, closer than your twin—is lost to the fairies forever. Do you want that to happen?"

The monster gaped at him, awestruck. That was why the hero was here! He hadn't come to take her treasure. He was here to save a child! Her *sister*.

Just the word made her shiver. She'd been living in hospitals for as long as she could remember. Even back before she'd started growing fangs, she'd known her parents hated her for being sick and costing them money. She'd always been a monster and a burden, but if her life was what kept her sister safe, that changed everything.

She looked again at the silver thread shining more preciously than ever in the hero's gloved hand, and the handsome man's lips curled into a smile.

"Do you want to save her?"

The monster nodded her head wildly.

"Then you must pay the price," he said. "For her and for yourself."

The monster slumped. She couldn't pay. She had nothing, no money or valuables. Even her room here was paid for by a charity.

But the man wasn't finished. "You will pay with your service," he said. "If you continue as you are, the magic that forms your body will degrade further and further until you are no longer able to hold yourself together. When that happens, you will die, and your human sister will be forever lost. But it doesn't have to be that way."

He reached down to lay his hand fearlessly on the monster's furry shoulder. "I can save you," he said, his blue eyes burning in his handsome face. "Both of you. My name is Victor Conrath, and I work miracles."

He was telling the truth, for no sooner had he spoken than the miracle occurred. Where his hand rested on the monster's shoulder, the fur and scales began to vanish. Skin, smooth and human, rippled down her arm, which was no longer huge and misshapen but small and thin: a little girl's human arm.

The sight of it brought tears to the monster's beady eyes. But even as she went to raise her fingers—her tiny, clawless, *human* fingers—in praise, the miracle ended. The hero took his hand away, and the monster came back as quickly as it had gone, leaving her sobbing on the floor.

"I can make you human forever," he promised as she cried on his shiny shoes. "You can keep on living, an anchor for your sister, and all I ask in return is your obedience. Swear your life to me, changeling. Become *my* monster, and I will save you both."

I swear it! the monster tried to shout, but all that came out was a high-pitched whine. The silver thread bucked on her wrist, tearing into the scaly skin beneath her fur. She knew it was her sister begging her to save them, so the monster bent her head all the way to the floor at the hero's feet, trusting him to understand that she'd pay any price. She'd be a good servant, a good monster. The hero would not be sorry!

That must have been enough, because his face broke into a cruel smile.

"Then the contract is made," he said in a voice full of magic, though the monster didn't know it as such yet. She did, however, see the knife he pulled out of his jacket pocket.

The monster stopped begging when the blade came out. Not because she'd changed her mind but because her body was no longer her own. An invisible force was pushing her down, pinning her to the floor so that she could not see, only smell the leather and blood as the man peeled off his glove to slide the knife across his palm.

"Bound to me in blood and service, the changing flame is fixed," he whispered as his blood landed like burning rain on the back of the monster's head. "Your life for mine, your power to me, now and ever more."

He leaned down to slash her next, sliding the silver knife along her back as if he was trying to skin her alive. The monster wailed as the blade bit in. She knew she had to be brave for her sister, but it hurt so much. The wound bled like a waterfall, covering her in so much blood, his and hers, she didn't know how either of them was still alive. But while she definitely felt light-headed, she didn't faint. What she did was *change*.

Everywhere the red blood flowed, the monster washed away. Fur vanished, claws retracted, crooked limbs straightened and shrank. Her beady eyes turned back into human ones, letting her see in full color for the first time in months. Her jagged teeth pulled back into her skull, which was no longer thick and square but small and covered in soft, human hair, not coarse fur.

The whole process couldn't have taken more than a minute, but when it was over, she wasn't a monster anymore. She was a person. A little girl, barely seven. There were her hands—her *human* hands—pressing down on the linoleum, which she could see for the first time was lemon yellow beneath the scarlet smears of her blood. And on her wrist—her tiny, human wrist—the silver thread lay so still that she could easily imagine her sister on the other end, calm and happy and safe, because of her.

"I'm human."

The words, the first she'd spoken to anyone in almost a year, came out as a whisper, but the hero shook his head.

"No," he said sternly, wrapping the silver thread around his bloody palm to haul her back to her feet. "The girl at the end of this line is human. *You* are a monster."

He said it with such conviction, the girl couldn't do anything but bow her head. She was still staring at the ground when the man threw something at her.

"Put that on."

The girl scrambled to pull whatever it was off her head. It felt like a blanket, but when she got it in her hands, she saw it was a boy's coat, brand new with the tags still on, and far too large.

"Why do I—"

"You can't walk around without clothes," the hero snapped, cracking the door so he could watch the nurses outside. "Now do as you're told, and be quick about it. We need to go."

It'd been so long that the girl hadn't even realized she was naked until he told her. Her hands were shaking so badly she could barely get her scrawny arms through the sleeves. The fuzzy lining soaked up the blood that still covered her like a sponge, making things even more difficult, but she got it on in the end. She still needed pants to be truly decent, but the coat was long enough to be a dress on her, which must have been good enough.

"Here," the man said, taking an orange prescription bottle out of his pocket. "You'll also need one of these."

"No!" the girl cried, shying away. "No more pills."

The look on the hero's face made her feel one inch tall. "You do not speak back to me," he told her coldly, opening the cap and shaking a pill into his hand. "This is no ordinary medicine. I made them to reinforce the spell I just cast on you. If you do not take these pills precisely as instructed, you will revert to your monster form, and your sister will die. Do you want that?"

The girl shook her head.

"Then do as you're told," he snapped, grabbing her hand and pressing the pill into it.

It was much smaller than the other medicines she'd taken, but her throat still closed at the sight. She especially didn't like the pill's color, which was the same shiny red as the fresh blood that still coated her fingers. The hero was glaring, though, so she popped it into her mouth. Like everything else he'd done, it tasted like blood, but she got it down somehow, opening her mouth to show the hero, who was still watching, that she'd done as she was told.

"Good," he said, dropping the pill bottle into the pocket of her coat. "You'll take one of those every twelve hours to start, though we might need to increase the dose as your powers expand."

"Powers?" The girl's face split into a smile. She liked the idea of powers, but her excitement faded when she saw the hero's glare.

"Don't get ideas," he warned, grabbing the door handle. "You belong to me now. My monster to use as I see fit. You will address me as Master at all times, and you will obey every order I give immediately and without question. Do you understand?"

When she nodded, his face grew deadly.

"Yes, Master," the girl corrected, scrambling to get the words out fast enough.

He gave her a pat on the head for getting it right before turning back to the door. "Let's get out of here."

The girl didn't see how. Even with the door unlocked, the hallway outside was full of nurses and cameras. They might not care enough to check on her more than twice a day, but surely, they'd notice a stranger taking her out of the building. When the hero led her through the door, though, all the nurses were lined up in front of the nursing station, faces blank and eyes closed as if they'd fallen asleep on their feet.

"Excellent," her master said when he saw them, tossing the head nurse a set of keys. "Go start my car."

The woman nodded and rushed to do as he'd said, leaving the girl gaping.

"You'll see I'm not like other mages," the man explained, pausing to examine the chart taped beside her door. "Lola," he read with a frown. "I was going to call you Emily, but I suppose Lola will suffice." He glanced down at her again, then turned and started down the hallway. "Come, Lola. We have much to do."

"Yes, Master."

His handsome face split into a grin at her obedience. As they walked by the sleeping nurses, Lola saw that each one had a bloody fingerprint pressed over their lips. The girl didn't know what it did, but the security guard had one on his mouth as well. He jumped to open the key-locked door that was supposed to protect the chronically ill children of Detroit. He even pulled off his hat to bid her master a very good day as the hero led his new monster out into the dark, sticky heat that was the DFZ Underground in summer.

20 years later

Chapter 1

Halloween in the Detroit Free Zone was madness.

The moment the summer heat gave the faintest hint of weakening, the streets—both the looping elevated bridges of the Skyways and the gridlocked, shadowed underpasses of the Underground below—were saturated with flashing advertisements for Halloween-themed everything. There were costumes, candy, special-edition vampire-themed sodas, full-immersion VR horror experiences, rolls of preprinted spellwork tape that would illusion your apartment to look like a haunted graveyard complete with howling ghosts that flew through your guests on command. Anything and everything you wanted for the holiday, and a bunch of stuff you didn't, could be yours for a low, low price, provided you didn't ask any questions about what went into making it.

Even the wealthy neighborhoods weren't spared the capitalistic bonanza. The bedroom community of Windsor, Canada, was more restrained—and safer, since, unlike the DFZ, Canada had laws against virtual advertisements popping into drivers' faces or through people's windows—but even here, the mansions were decked out in the best horrors money could buy. There were flights of witches cackling through the sky, zombie hands that sprang up from the perfectly manicured lawns whenever a car drove by, even a skeletal dragon that roared green fire from the top of the Great Yong's riverside mansion—a gift, raved *Dragon Watch Weekly*, from his human daughter, who was famous for her love of kitsch.

Many a cutting op-ed had been penned in the various magical journals about the backwardness of decorating with ghouls and witches when there were real dragons and spirits flying through the skies. But holidays were about tradition, and Windsor *loved*

1

tradition. This was where all the rich people who wanted to be near the money explosion that was the world's most capitalistic magical city—but didn't want to deal with the DFZ's lawlessness and perpetual disasters—lived. Cowards, Victor called them. But cowards with money and clout, which was why Lola had been sent here tonight.

Teetering on the sky-high heels of the rail-thin model body she'd been assigned for this job, Lola strode up the walkway to the only house in the neighborhood that wasn't lit up with three figures' worth of professionally installed Halloween decorations. The were no lights on inside, but the etched-glass door opened before she could touch it, snatched out of the way by a wild-eyed man wearing a dirty designer suit six months out of style.

"Do you have my pills?"

Lola pulled an orange prescription bottle out of the ridiculously tiny purse that had gone with tonight's body. The man dove for the container the moment he saw it, but Lola dodged away, using the model's superior height to lift the pill bottle out of his reach.

"Payment first."

The man's unshaven face collapsed into a look of utter fury. He looked a decade older than the last time Lola had seen him. She didn't know if that was the stress or if he could no longer afford to visit the mage who put on his rejuvenatory illusions, but he looked like hell. Very, very desperate hell.

"I don't have it," he said, raking his fingers through hair that used to look thick and golden but was now greasy and thinning. "And I'm not going to be able to get it unless you give me the pills. If you could just give me a few, I—"

"That's not how this works," Lola reminded him, resting a hand on the model's hip, which was so tiny even she didn't know how it was holding up her printed designer pencil skirt. "You

2

know the rules, Frank. Our master doesn't make exceptions after the deal's been struck."

"He's no *master* to me," Frank snarled, baring his yellowed teeth. "You tell your bastard boss that I know what he is. He's no miracle worker. He's a blood mage, a mind controller! That's illegal even in the DFZ. I breathe one word of what he's doing to the right people, and the Paladins will string him up before he can smirk."

"You think it's that easy?" Lola asked, her picture-perfect model poise falling away as she hunched farther into the doorway, speaking in a whisper even though there was no one but them to hear. "I've been under Victor's boot a lot longer than you. If getting rid of him was as simple as calling the Paladins, none of us would be in this situation. But outside authorities aren't welcome in the Free Zone, and Victor's too good to get caught even if they did get in. You can't threaten him, and trying will only bring him down on you harder."

"Then what am I supposed to do?"

A fragile smile flickered across Lola's impossibly red lips. "Walk away."

Frank scoffed. "Like I'm going to just give up and—"

"Don't be stupid," she snapped. "This is your chance. Victor's already gotten what he wants from you. Now he's just milking your addiction for profit, but you don't have to let him. There's a lot of us who can't escape, but you can. You can leave this place! Go anywhere you—"

"I don't want to go," Frank snarled, glaring at her with watery eyes. "Don't you get it, sweetheart? I had it all! Every studio in town was begging me to work for them because my ideas sold, but I can't have those ideas without my pills!"

"Yes, you can," Lola said desperately. "Even Victor can't make something out of nothing. You said it yourself: he's a blood mage.

3

His magic monkeyed with your brain to supercharge your creativity, but they were all still *your* ideas. His pills didn't make you a genius. You had that brilliance inside you the whole time! All Victor's magic did was make it easier to grab, but you don't need—"

Frank's cracked lips curled into a sneer. "If I could do it without him, you think I'd be standing here, talking to you?" He stepped to the side so Lola could see past him into his dark, empty house. "You think I'd have sold all my furniture and let my face go to hell if I could just 'try harder' and get the same results? I need my damn pills, and you're going to give them to me."

Lola shook the model's perfectly coiffed head. "You know I can't do that."

"You might want to think again," he said, pulling a pistol from his pocket.

Lola heaved a long, sad sigh. "You don't want to do this."

"Don't tell me what I want!" Frank roared, shoving his gun square at the center of her chest. "You think I'm scared of your boss? He may act like the devil at the crossroads, but he's human just like the rest of us." He cocked the hammer with a final-sounding click. "Now hand over that bottle, or your master's gonna have to find himself a new puppet."

Lola looked Frank dead in the eyes as she slid the pill bottle back into her tiny purse. "Pointing a gun at me might make you feel better, but it's not going to change a thing. I'm actually glad you don't have the payment. Me walking away tonight might just be the best thing that's ever happened to you."

"You're not going anywhere."

Lola was opening her mouth to keep arguing when he pulled the trigger. The *crack* of the gunshot echoed through Frank's empty house, followed by the wet sound of splattering liquid.

Frank shrieked, his bloodshot eyes going huge as the woman

4

he'd just shot shook her head at him, and not because he'd missed. There was a gaping, quarter-sized hole in her chest right above where her plunging neckline ended, but the stuff oozing out of it wasn't blood. It wasn't even red but rainbow iridescent and shimmery as a beetle's wing.

More of it was splattered on the floor behind her where the bullet had passed through. It crawled back to her as Frank watched, sliding up her tall heels like drips of paint going backward.

"What the—" Frank scrambled back into his empty house as the rainbow glop melted into the model's legs. "*That's not possible!*"

Lola winced harder at the words than she had at being shot. "Come on," she cajoled, scrambling to salvage the situation. "You take magical creativity-enhancing pills made by a blood mage, but me being bulletproof is where you draw the line?"

"You're not bullet*proof*," Frank said wildly, gesturing at the hole in her chest that was already closing. "It went right through you!"

"I've got an implant."

"No way," he said, shaking his head. "I've seen every body mod on the market, and none of them do *that*. Even dragons don't heal that fast!" He stared at her, body shaking. "What the hell are you?"

"Your last chance," Lola said, dropping the model's sultry, sophisticated voice for something much harsher. "I never liked you, Frank, but no one deserves the trouble you've just brought down. Victor doesn't care about me, but I guarantee he already knows you just shot one of his representatives, which he'll see as an attack on himself. He doesn't take those well. He also doesn't like threats to turn him in to the Paladins, so if you want to live past tonight, I suggest you forget the pills and go. Just get in your car and drive away from the DFZ as fast as you can."

That was the best advice Lola could have given anyone. Advice she would have taken herself if she could have, but Frank was too scared to hear it.

"You're not human!" he cried, his voice cracking as he dropped the pistol on the floor. "*Get out of my house!*"

Again, his words hit Lola harder than the bullet. The hole in her chest that had been closing reopened at his shout. Her face was also having trouble, the photo-shoot perfect features melting like wax. This only made Frank panic worse, which meant it was time to go. She'd tried her best, she really had, but you couldn't force a horse to drink, and Frank was a very stupid horse.

The sight of her melting face had already sent him screaming into his empty living room, so Lola gathered what was left of her body and made her own exit, tottering through the dead grass of his neglected lawn on what was left of her rapidly softening heels. The stilettos had dissolved completely by the time she made it to the sidewalk, but that actually made it easier to run down the tree-shaded street to the armored black sedan idling at the corner. The tinted rear window rolled down as she approached, and then a smooth, hateful voice spoke from inside the dark car.

"You look a mess, my monster."

"This whole thing's a mess," Lola replied, or at least she tried to. Frank's stubborn disbelief had done a lot more damage than she'd expected. The fairy gossamer that formed her body was melting so quickly that her jaw felt like soup, and the rest of her wasn't doing much better. Her limbs had gone so soft that she looked more like a kid's jelly toy than a person as she struggled to open the car door.

It wouldn't have been a problem if the man sitting in the back seat had helped. He had a driver, a handsome man whose mind had been so invaded by blood magic that he couldn't do anything but smile and slavishly obey. Her master could have ordered the man to stab himself, and the poor thrall would have done it in a

6

heartbeat. Telling him to scoop Lola off the ground would have been nothing, but Victor Conrath didn't believe in help, so Lola had to improvise by squishing her body through the open window.

"I can't believe you let Frank do this to you," Victor said as she landed on the leather seat beside him. "The man doesn't have an ounce of conviction in his body."

The melting puddle gurgled back, causing Victor to smirk as he pulled an orange pill bottle stamped with the name LOLA out of the pocket of his crisp gray blazer.

"You're going to have to do better," he said as he opened the cap and tapped a bright-red pill into his palm. "If you continue to be this fragile, you'll be right back to the state I found you in."

He smiled and tossed the pill at the melted woman. It landed in her softening body like a drop of fresh blood. As it sank in, her melting body grew rigid again, churning and changing until she was the perfectly made-up blond once again, right down to her too-tall stilettos.

"*Ugh*," Lola retched, scrubbing her chest where the pill had landed. "I hate melting."

"Then don't do it," Victor said coldly. "Frank Grimes is a hack who never had an original thought unless I showed it to him. He shouldn't have been able to touch you."

"It's *because* he's a hack that he hurt so much," Lola argued, examining her fingers, which were still a little noodly at the edges. "Gossamer only works when people believe what you're showing them, and anyone would have a hard time buying a woman who doesn't die when you shoot her through the chest. A more creative person could have come up with some sort of explanation, but Frank's mind is as set as a cement brick, which is why his disbelief hit me like one."

"Not if you'd given him a better show," Victor scolded. "Why

7

didn't you throw out some blood or pretend you had an antibullet ward sewn into your clothes? Anything would have been better than letting him see the truth. Honestly, have I taught you nothing?"

"I was upset," Lola muttered, which wasn't an excuse. She could and should have done any of those things, but she'd thought maybe she could get through to Frank if she showed him what he was really dealing with. She also hadn't expected him to panic so hard.

"You were an idiot," Victor said, glaring at her with those blue eyes that still made her feel one inch tall. "That's a very dangerous thing for a monster to be. Do I need to re-educate you?"

"No," Lola said, dropping her head.

"No?" he repeated expectantly.

"No, Master," she whispered.

"Better," he replied, pulling out his cell phone. "I take it Frank Grimes won't be making his payment?"

She shook her head. "You want me to put on a different shape and try again?"

"You've done enough," Victor said, his elegant fingers moving through the air as he tapped a message into his smartphone's augmented-reality field. "I'd hoped to get a bit more blood out of that stone, but he's clearly all squeezed out. I'll take care of things from here."

The way he said that sent shivers through Lola's still-firming body. "He can still be useful," she insisted. "Frank's an idiot, but he knows people. You could—"

"Why are you arguing his case?" Victor asked, his eyes sliding back to hers suspiciously. "I thought you hated him."

Lola didn't *hate* Frank. He was like all of her master's clients: a sad, selfish man willing to do anything to get what he wanted, even if it meant taking a deal from the devil. No one deserved to

8

be under Victor's thumb, though, and Lola would eat a bullet any day if it kept even one more drop of blood off her hands.

"I can still fix this," she told him. "Frank said he was going to call the Paladins. I could take the shape of one! Everyone's afraid of those zealots, even nonmages. I could use that to convince Frank to—"

"My decision has been made," Victor said crisply. "Frank's contract is over, and I have other work for you."

Lola's gossamer began to sink. "Another job?"

He nodded, twitching his fingers at his thrall. The smiling man in the driver's seat leaped to obey, tripping over the pavement in his rush to open Lola's door.

"Go get yourself back together," Victor ordered as she got out. "I'll call when you're needed."

She wasn't ready to give up, but while Victor had enchanted his face to reveal nothing, not even his true age, twenty years as his monster had taught Lola to read his signs, and she could already tell that it was hopeless. Fighting past this point would do nothing but make him angry, so she backed off, lowering her head obediently as Victor's thrall shut the door.

"I'm headed back to the house to take care of a few things," he told her through the gap in the tinted window as his brainwashed driver got back into the front. "Keep your phone handy."

"Yes, Master," she said, eyes going to the orange pill bottle he was still holding in his hand. "Um, I'm going to need..."

Her voice trailed off as Victor tossed the bottle out the window. Way harder than necessary, but that was how it always was. Her master was never happier than when he was making her scramble, even if it meant he'd have to make her a new batch of pills because he'd thrown the old bottle down the storm drain. As she dove to snatch her pills out of the air, Lola realized she was giving him too much credit. Victor wouldn't give her new pills.

9

He'd make her climb into the drain after them while he watched, the hateful bastard.

"I can see you thinking things you shouldn't," her master said from the car. "Even after all these years, I'll never understand how a changeling can have such a transparent face."

"Just lucky, I guess," Lola said, clutching the pill bottle in her fist. "Good night, Master."

Victor's eyes narrowed at the implied dismissal. Punishing her for it must have been too much bother, though, because all he did was roll up the window, sitting back in his seat as his driver started the car and pulled them off down the dark street.

Lola watched them go impatiently. That Victor bothered with a driver when all cars were self-driving these days never ceased to astonish her. Even with his mind turned to jelly by blood magic, the thrall was still alive. One would think a man who made his living doing illegal blood magic would care more about potential witnesses, but Victor loved nothing so much as showing off his power. He kept dozens of the brainwashed servants, sometimes for years, and Lola had never heard any of them speak, so perhaps it was a moot point.

When the sedan's taillights finally passed out of sight behind Frank's neighbor's insane haunted graveyard display—complete with skeletal hands bursting out of the sidewalk and a headless horseman that rode in circles, throwing illusionary pumpkins at anyone who came within twenty feet of the property—Lola shifted out of the rail-thin model body with a groan of pure relief. Changing her shape out in the open like this was risky, especially after what had just happened with Frank, but it was *so* uncomfortable having to cram all her gossamer into such a slender package, not to mention unbalanced. How anyone actually walked in heels that high, Lola had no idea, but she was willing to risk another hit to ditch them.

Thankfully, no hits came. Frank's mansion-lined street was so full of crazy decorations—both the augmented-reality kind that required a cell phone or other mana-ready device to see, and real made-by-an-actual-human-mage illusions that anyone could touch and feel—she probably could have turned into an elephant and no one would have noticed.

Lola quite liked being an elephant, actually. It always got her good reactions, especially from kids. Sadly, an elephant trundling through Windsor's most expensive zip code would probably earn her some painfully disbelieving looks, so Lola settled for something more practical, letting her gossamer spread out into a much more relaxed, curvier body with baggy jeans and a red T-shirt. Also sneakers, because stilettos were murder even when you made them yourself.

She did her face next, swapping the model's striking features for a far more approachable beauty that Lola called her "yogurt lady." The face was so named because she'd stolen it off a yogurt ad last year. With its warm smile, thick black hair, and advertiser-approved light-brown skin tone, Yogurt Lady blended perfectly into the multiethnic DFZ. The face was a new enough addition that Lola still had to check herself in her smartphone's camera to make sure she hadn't forgotten any details, but her ears didn't look lopsided, so she pronounced it good enough.

Such a drastic, full-body transformation would have taken her hours back at the beginning, but Lola had been changing under Victor's exacting eye for two decades now. She had her new body ready to go in less than twenty seconds, which turned out to be just fast enough not to get caught by the next car that came around the corner. The driver looked straight at her, but Lola didn't even feel his attention, yet more proof of how great this face was.

For all that it could look like anything, gossamer worked best when it looked like nothing at all. Humanity's magic had only reawakened eighty-five years ago. But while just under half the population were mages who could actually use their magic, every human alive could move it subconsciously, and they flung that power like rocks at things they didn't like.

A few hurled opinions wouldn't bother the bigger, scarier fae, but Lola was a changeling stretched far beyond her time. Without Victor's blood to hold her gossamer together, she'd fall apart like a snowman in spring. Or worse, fall into something else.

Even after so many years, Lola didn't like to think about the monster. She'd never changed back completely, but she'd had enough close calls to learn the value of being unremarkable. The easier people's eyeballs slid over her, the better her magic held up. Just switching from the attention-grabbing model to the blandly pretty yogurt lady had freed up enough gossamer for Lola to make something else, like the car she spun next.

Again, it was nothing fancy. Exciting as they were to drive, flashy rides drew a *lot* of attention. Too much to handle in her current state, but old junkers were everywhere. Even out here in the rich suburbs, there were ratty cars tucked away down side alleys and behind fences for all the staff who kept the big, fancy houses running. All Lola had to do was pick one and spin a copy for herself, crafting her gossamer into a perfect match, right down to the dented fender.

Satisfied that no one would look at her twice now, Lola slid behind the wheel of her new car and started it up, remembering at the last second to make the engine hum like an old-model electric rather than a new one. When everything sounded good, she pulled through the field of illusionary skeleton hands and drove out of Frank's fancy neighborhood toward the far less decorated—but much less distracting—four-lane artery road that would take her over the Ambassador Bridge and back home to the DFZ.

Being made of gossamer, her car didn't have a computer on

board. It could have driven itself if she'd been willing to give it that much autonomy. But constructions made from gossamer tended to match themselves to people's expectations if she didn't keep a close eye on them, and Lola wasn't keen on having her car break down just because some know-it-all in the car next to hers thought her ride looked like a junker. She didn't mind driving in any case, especially once she got out of the fiddly small streets by Frank's and onto a major roadway. Once all she had to do was match her speed to the rest of the traffic, Lola took her eyes off the road to get a better look at the pill bottle Victor had thrown at her.

There'd been thirty pills inside when she'd gone into Frank's house, but for some reason, there were only fourteen when she opened the lid now. That was pretty typical. Victor's magic wasn't like hers in that his pills didn't dissolve if you thought about them too hard, but they still weren't real. They were miniature, encapsulated versions of the spell he'd cast when he'd found her. If Lola didn't take two every day, she'd turn right back into the monster she'd been back then.

There was nothing she feared more, not even Victor, which was why Lola made sure to keep a full bottle with her at all times. Her master didn't like her feeling so secure, though, which meant her pills tended to go missing whenever he touched the bottle. That said, fourteen wasn't a bad number. He'd left her with far fewer before, and he'd already said he'd be calling on her again soon, so Lola wasn't too worried. She was much more scared that she'd have to take another pill tonight.

For someone who wasn't even a mage, Frank's freak-out had sure packed a wallop. Even with the pill Victor had dropped into her, melting into a puddle had left her gossamer feeling softer than Lola was okay with. She'd thought she could head it off by changing her shape to something easier, but even the familiar yogurt lady face was feeling slippery, and her car was riding much

13

lower than it should.

That wouldn't fly. Even in the DFZ, people noticed a car riding on four flat tires. All it would take was one helpful soul insisting on taking her to a mechanic, or worse, looking under her hood, and Lola would be right back to melting.

One big hit she could handle, but two in a row would send Lola right back to her true, monstrous form no matter how many of Victor's blood pills she choked down. She swore she could already feel her fangs poking through the gossamer that formed her teeth. Lola *really* didn't want to take another pill so soon, but she also knew better than to play chicken with the monster. Safe was always better than sorry, so she steered her car into the slow lane and pulled out her phone to find something sweet enough to cover the pill's bloody aftertaste.

Good thing she was headed back into the DFZ. Lola had lived in the city all her life, and she'd never had to go more than three blocks to find somewhere that sold dessert. Sure enough, her phone popped up a Tim Horton's just on the other side of the river. She took note of the directions and steered her car onto the bridge ramp, sticking to the slow lane to avoid the gauntlet of constantly route-optimizing self-driving cars. She'd just squeezed her little junker into the pocket between two party buses with parties currently going on inside them when she spotted a flash of blue light on the road ahead.

Her first thought was the police, which was enough to make her swear. True to the "free" in its name, the Detroit Free Zone didn't have cops unless someone paid for them, but it wasn't unusual for the Canadian government to run checks on their half of the bridge. Usually, they did it on cars going the other direction, but this blue light was on the "Entering the DFZ" side, which meant Lola needed to be somewhere else.

She started shifting lanes at once. Even if it was just a routine traffic stop, human scrutiny melted gossamer always, and no one looked harder than a freaking cop. That was the last thing Lola needed when her magic was already messed up, but no matter how hard she lane jockeyed, there was nowhere to go. She was already in the pipe for the bridge with traffic on all sides. She was about to say screw it and take her pill dry right here in the car when she realized the light she'd seen was just blue, not flashing blue and red. It was also coming straight at her.

Lola slammed on her brakes, nearly causing a wreck. Horns blared as drivers leaned out their windows to curse her in multiple languages, but while Lola felt their anger like barbs in her gossamer, she couldn't spare them a glance. She was too busy staring at the black motorcycle with the ghostly blue headlight roaring down the Ambassador Bridge ahead of her, weaving back and forth through the lanes of oncoming traffic like a salmon swimming upstream.

Other people had started to notice as well now. The angry drivers forgot all about her as everyone began leaning out their windows to take pictures of the black-dressed motorcyclist roaring up the road as if laws—both those of the Dominion of Canada and of physics—didn't apply to him. Within seconds, the whole DFZ-bound half of the bridge came to a standstill as everyone watched the motorcyclist weave his speeding bike through gaps it never should have fit between.

Just the thought of all those eyeballs sent a shiver up Lola's spine. The man on the motorcycle didn't seem to notice or care, though, because he wasn't a changeling. He wasn't even human. She should have realized who he was the moment she spotted his iconic blue headlight. Everyone else on the bridge had, but it wasn't until Lola saw the shiny black helmet completely obscuring his face that she knew him for certain.

It was the Black Rider, the specter. That was how he was able to ride his bike through places no human should, because he wasn't human at all. He was an urban legend.

Humans didn't just throw their magic at fairies. They shoved it into concepts too. Get enough people all believing in the same thing, and the magic they pushed at it took on a life of its own. That was how powerful spirits like the one that ruled the DFZ were born, but the idea worked on a smaller scale as well. All those stories kids used to tell about Bloody Mary had eventually birthed a real entity that killed fourteen people before the Merlin Council got it under control.

That was the difference. Unlike actual spirits, who were intelligent and had control over their actions, urban legends were slaves to their stories, and the Black Rider's were pretty terrifying. The DFZ tourism pamphlets claimed he was an unkillable man who rode a silent motorcycle through the Underground, hunting for victims. They said he ate the people he cornered, that his bike bled when you cut it, and that he made no sound at all, even when he crashed into you.

Lola didn't know about all of that, but the silent part seemed true, at least. Despite zipping between three lanes of traffic, his motorcycle made no sound at all. Even when he shot straight past Lola's window, all she heard was the wind whooshing behind him. She wouldn't have known he was there at all if he hadn't made such a scene, but even that didn't last long at his speed. People had barely gotten their phones up for a photo before the Black Rider was gone, his taillight leaving a ghostly blue trail as he vanished into the gnarl of traffic on the Windsor side of the bridge.

That didn't seem right. All the stories Lola had heard pinned the Black Rider to the DFZ Underground. She hadn't realized his range extended to Canada and apparently, neither had anyone else. The crowd around her was already vanishing back into their cars to update their social media with this new, rare sighting. Some

16

people actually started vlogging the incident right there in their vehicles. Lola was just happy their attention was focused on something else as she inched her way through the traffic jam, squeezing the doors of her junker slightly closer than its frame really should have allowed to slip into the gap the rider had left in his wake and book it up the bridge to her destination.

Ten minutes later, life was *much* better. She'd made it to the coffee shop and bought herself an iced vanilla latte in a cup so big, it could have doubled as a bucket. The traffic from the Black Rider incident had cleared up, and Victor hadn't called her about the new job yet. That didn't mean it wasn't going to happen, but Lola was happy to take her rare moment of peace as she plopped on the hood of her car to drink her trough of sugar-caffeine and stare at the sunset, which was actually visible for once since she was near the river.

Normally, the only place you could see the sky in the DFZ was on the Skyways: the bridge city that had been built over the ruins of Old Detroit back when the city was ruled by Algonquin, Spirit of the Great Lakes and big-time hater of humanity. The Lake Lady had eventually been forced out by the rise of the new Spirit of the DFZ, making Detroit the only city in the world that ruled itself. Algonquin's Skyways were still there, though, leaving seventy percent of the DFZ's population basically living under a bridge.

Lola normally didn't mind living in the dark. People kept their eyes to themselves in the Undercity, which made it heaven for her. It was nice to see the sky sometimes, though, even if her view was partially blocked by giant flashing advertisements for a special blood-red coffee Tim Horton's was offering as a Halloween collaboration with *Fenrir*, the mega-hit monster movie of the summer that was still going months into fall.

Lola turned away from the animated poster in disgust. Shocker to no one, but she *hated* monster movies, and whoever was

17

running *Fenrir's* advertising was pushing it hard. She couldn't drive down the street without seeing that stupid giant wolf's unnecessarily realistic fangs snapping at her from every bridge and wall. Even after she turned off her phone's augmented reality, Fenrir's hairy face was still snarling down at her from paper posters plastered all over the giant, building-sized supports that held up the Skyways.

There was no escaping the ads, so Lola crawled back into her car to grab the prescription bottle she'd left on the passenger seat. Taking a huge gulp of her coffee, she popped the plastic cap with her thumb and shook out a pill. Just like the first one back at the hospital, it was the size of a baby aspirin, glossy and red as a drop of blood against her palm. It smelled like blood, too, which was why Lola chugged as much of her too-sweet coffee as she could stomach before popping it into her mouth.

As ever, the little tab went down like a fresh garden slug, leaving a trail of heavy, metallic, bloody slime down her throat that no amount of vanilla syrup could cover. She sucked frantically on the straw anyway, chugging the sweetness like she was doing a keg stand to make the awful taste go away faster. It took half the giant cup, but eventually, the bloody flavor vanished, leaving only the comfort of tight, firm, well-controlled gossamer.

Sighing in relief, Lola recapped the bottle and settled into the driver's seat to enjoy the remaining half of her drink. She took another sip just for the taste and waved her hand, nudging her gossamer aside to reveal the silver thread that was still tied around her left wrist.

"Hello," Lola greeted her sister with a smile. "Guess what? We made it through another day."

She turned her arm as she spoke, making the silver thread glimmer in the neon light of the signs outside, which were all starting to come on as evening fell.

18

"Do you think we should wait here for Victor's call or take a chance and drive home?" she asked her sister. "He said he was going back to his house, so we've probably got at least an hour before—"

A clatter interrupted her one-sided conversation as her phone began vibrating wildly on her dashboard.

Lola rolled her eyes at the racket and dropped her giant drink into the car's cupholder. "So much for a break."

Nudging her gossamer up to cover her thread again, she leaned forward to grab the dancing phone. When she slid her finger over the screen to see who the old man wanted her to be this time, though, the number in the caller ID wasn't Victor's. It was a text from his automated security system, the one on the other side of the wards that surrounded his house. There was no explanation, just the highest-level emergency code.

Dropping her phone with a curse, Lola started her gossamer car with a thought and peeled out of the coffee shop parking lot. She turned her phone's augmented reality back on between traffic lights, flicking her fingers through the floating menus to call Victor on every device he had, but nothing got through. The lines just rang and rang.

After her third unsuccessful attempt, Lola tossed her phone into the passenger seat and just focused on driving, weaving between the other cars toward the highway as fast as she dared.

Chapter 2

13 pills

Even driving like an absolute lunatic, it still took Lola thirty minutes to get to Victor's mansion. Part of this was just the reality of driving in the DFZ. It wasn't merely a crowded mess of ten million people with zero public transit. The double-layered city itself was alive.

The Spirit of the DFZ was the newest and most active of all the gods that had come back with the return of magic. She was *constantly* rearranging her buildings and streets, including the elevated highway Lola was attempting to race down. Nothing had actually closed—nothing *ever* closed in the DFZ—but even in a city this crazy, there were few people willing to drive on a highway that was undulating like a snake. Traffic had come to a standstill while the road slithered into its new position, leaving Lola tapping her fingers nervously against the wheel.

At least there were no dragons. In addition to being a living city, the DFZ was also home to the Peacemaker. Lola didn't know the details, but twenty-five years ago, he'd convinced the DFZ to let him claim her as his territory. Once the city was his, at least as far as his own kind went, the Peacemaker had turned it into a sort of Dragon Switzerland, banning all fighting, murdering, and eating of humans.

The bubble of safety this decree created had turned the DFZ into the world's biggest hub of dragon dealmaking since it was the only place two dragons could talk without worrying about one eating the other. Lola loved the sentiment, but she wished the Peacemaker had chosen somewhere else. Moving roads were bad enough, but nothing clogged a street faster than a hundred-foot dragon flying overhead.

Thankfully, traffic cleared up once she reached the north side of the city. She pushed her car hard, lane jockeying to make up for lost time. Victor *still* hadn't answered any of his phones, and the house alarm was texting her every three minutes now, pushing her faster still as she zoomed down the ramp to Victor's.

Her master lived in the old University Heights neighborhood. It used to be a dump back when it'd been magically toxic as part of Algonquin's Reclamation Land. That project had ended when the Spirit of the DFZ took over the city, and the old lots had rapidly regained value since, with no Skyways overhead, University Heights was one of the only places inside the city limits where you could have a house on the ground that wasn't under a bridge.

It was too far out for the really rich people, most of whom lived on the Skyways or across the river in Windsor, but it was a pretty fancy neighborhood by DFZ ground-level standards. There were trees and parks and schools, no gun vending machines or pawn shops. It was a nice area, definitely not the sort of place you expected to find a blood mage, which was exactly why Victor had chosen it.

Lola slumped in relief when she finally turned onto the main road through the neighborhood that would take her to Victor's house. She was waiting at the light to turn onto his block when a streak of blue shot past her.

It happened so fast, she almost missed it, but when Lola turned around in her seat, there was the Black Rider. He was dark as ink save for his lights, which burned ghostly blue in the orange glare of the streetlamps. One look was all she got before he vanished again, disappearing up the ramp behind her like the figment of humanity's collective imagination that he was.

Lola turned back around with a shudder. She wasn't usually superstitious, but seeing the DFZ's most famous urban legend twice in the same hour felt like a bad omen, *and* the Black Rider had come from the direction of Victor's house. The Rider's stories often had a vengeance vibe, and her master did have a lot of enemies in the city. Maybe the alarms were going off because he'd finally met a monster he couldn't leash.

The possibility haunted her all the way to Victor's house, which was on the fourth hole of what had once been the Detroit Golf Club. Some enterprising developer had turned the whole course into a tiny-house community with a putt-putt theme. It would have been adorable if Lola hadn't had so many bad memories associated with the place.

Victor's unit was definitely the most boring of the bunch: a simple red-brick square with a high-pitched roof to shed the snow that still fell thick and heavy despite the ravages of global warming. Everything looked normal when Lola pulled into the tiny driveway. Through the house's window, she could see Victor's latest batch of human thralls watching TV with matching euphoric expressions on their faces. The tiny yard was mowed and trimmed, the little porch swept and clean, porch light off as always.

Nothing looked alarm-worthy, but then, it wouldn't from out here. The charming little cottage all the neighbors assumed was being rented to a rotating set of happy but strange young professionals was entirely a fabrication. Victor's real house only existed beyond the back gate.

Prying her hands off the wheel, Lola cut the illusion of her engine and bolted out of her conjured car. It was dark enough now that she probably could have pulled the gossamer back in, but she didn't want to risk another hit to her magic, especially when she didn't know what was waiting inside.

Stuffing her phone into her pocket, Lola crept past the window with the creepy thralls toward the gate that led to the house's tiny backyard. From the front, it looked like a swinging block of wooden fencing surrounded by overgrown holly bushes. The moment Lola pushed it open, though, it became something else.

The wards hit her first. Lola shivered as dozens of layers of Victor's bloody magic broke over her in rapid succession. There were Look Away enchantments, alarm spells, and several much nastier creations of his own design. Any of the attack spells could have cooked her if she'd failed to pass muster, but after twenty years of twice-daily pills, Victor's blood was as much a part of Lola as her own gossamer. She passed through the protections without so much as a blip, stepping off the paved path onto a carpet of pillow-soft emerald grass.

No matter the situation, her master's home never failed to steal Lola's breath. Victor had won it from a fairy—an *actual* fairy, not a changeling—long before he'd found her, and it was beautiful in the way only a place made without care for the constraints of reality could be.

The cute, upwardly mobile neighborhood with its tiny, kitschy houses was nowhere to be seen. In its place was a bowl of white-peaked mountains surrounding a forested valley. Waterfalls poured from cliffs at picturesque intervals, and the deep-purple night sky glittered with thousands of stars, all perfectly visible despite the full moon riding high overhead.

Lola didn't know how it was still so lovely. Fairy barrows were famous for rotting without constant upkeep from their makers, but she'd never seen so much as a bent blade of grass. The whole valley still glowed like a jewel in the silvery moonlight, quite literally. All the trees here were made of jade and silver, their delicate stone leaves clacking musically in the gentle night breeze.

The emerald meadow she'd emerged into was right at the jade forest's edge. From this side, the fence gate looked like the

23

entrance to an ancient temple: a towering stone door covered top to bottom in Victor's bloody spellwork. In the dark forest ahead of her, Lola caught a glimpse of Victor's tigers, security enchantments that stalked like shadows between the forest's silver trunks. The cat she spotted didn't look as if it had made a kill tonight, so Lola kept her distance, creeping across the feather-soft grass toward the stone stair that was the only safe path through the woods.

She stopped at the bottom, cupping her hands over her ears, but she didn't hear anything alarming. Just the usual night breeze and the sweet song of the golden nightingales. Like the tigers, the birds were also enchantments, yet another component of Victor's multilevel security system. They only sang when all was well, but *something* had triggered the alarms.

Lola went up on her tiptoes, scanning the dark path for any sign of the emergency. Yet again, though, she didn't spot anything out of the ordinary, nor did she see anybody else. Apparently, she was the first one here.

That made no sense. Lola was hardly Victor's only monster. Jamie's absence wasn't surprising since she lived on the Skyways and traffic was awful, but Simon was Victor's apprentice. He had a fairy door in his closet that went straight to the front gate. He should have been here seconds after the alarm went off.

Maybe he'd already gone up to the house? Keeping her gossamer ready, Lola took out her phone and tapped the second name on her contact list after Victor's. As always, Simon picked up by the second ring, but Lola didn't even give him a chance to say hello.

"Where are you?"

"At my house," Simon replied in his calm, deep voice.

"*What are you doing there?*" she hissed, moving away from the tiger that was eyeing her from the edge of the forest.

24

"I *was* working," the mage said irritably, but his annoyance vanished when he caught her panic. "What's wrong?"

"You didn't get the alarm?"

"What alarm?"

From anyone else, Lola would have called that a bad joke. Simon wasn't the joking type, though, which just made this all the more confusing. Why would Victor's alarm system call her instead of someone who could actually *do* something? It made no sense, but no way was Lola dealing with this alone.

"You need to come to the mansion right away," she said, craning her neck as she tried to look in every direction at once. "Something triggered the alarms half an hour ago, and Victor's not answering his phone."

The line went very quiet, and then Simon said, "I'll be there in five minutes."

Lola ended the call and shoved the phone back into her pocket. She considered waiting at the gate until Simon arrived, but there was still a chance this whole crisis was one of Victor's loyalty tests. Lola feared his anger more than anything that might be lurking ahead, so she forced herself to move, creeping up the stone steps toward the house as fast as her trembling legs would carry her.

Like the valley of jade trees that surrounded it, Victor's mansion was straight out of a fairy tale. It looked like a miniature castle: a pure-white fortress sitting at the mountain's foot next to the pool where the biggest of the waterfalls spilled from the cliffs above. Its heights were crowned with a golden tower as spindly as a sheaf of wheat, and the slope leading up to it was covered in roses that perfumed the air.

It was incredibly beautiful in the moonlight, but it also looked just like it always did. Given the urgency of the alarm, Lola had expected a war zone, but the house actually looked more peaceful than usual when she stepped out of the jade forest. There was no movement, no sounds save for the roaring of the waterfall and the nightingales' song. She didn't even see any lights flickering behind the castle's stained glass windows.

Gossamer jumping at the eerie silence, Lola dove off the flagstone path into the wall of roses. The thorns tore at her as she went. If she'd been made of actual flesh and blood, she would have been shredded. Being gossamer, though, Lola's body just popped back together like jelly as she pushed through the thicket to peer through the window that looked into the main hall.

As with everything else in his life, Victor's house began with his magic. The castle's front doors opened straight into his workshop: a cathedral-like stone hall honeycombed with stained glass windows to let in the light. It was practically where he lived since Victor preferred to work every hour that he was awake. When Lola peeked inside now, though, what she saw killed her last hope of a false alarm.

Victor's workshop looked as if a bomb had gone off inside it. His equipment, delicate antiques from magical traditions most people had forgotten existed, lay smashed against the stone walls, and the marble floor was covered in a layer of black soot from the seven interlocking magical circles, all of which had been scorched beyond recognition. There was so much wreckage, Lola couldn't actually tell if the moonlit room was empty or not. She huddled by the window for a solid minute, waiting for movement. When nothing stirred, she wiggled out of the bushes and ran back to the front, pushing the gigantic wooden doors out of the way until she was standing at the threshold of what had been her master's sanctum.

"Victor?" she called.

No reply. Her shaking voice didn't even echo in the huge, dark room. Worried that was due to the second set of private wards, Lola moved another inch forward, sliding her sneaker over the bloody line that was supposed to keep everything but her master out.

"Victor!"

Again, nothing.

The persistent silence shook Lola's gossamer harder than Frank's bullet. She gave it a shove, forcing her magic to behave as she shaped a big flashlight into her hand and ran across the blasted room to the main circle beneath the glass dome specifically positioned to harness the light of the full moon. She dropped into a crouch when she reached it, running her free hand over the melted golden inlay for a trace, a clue, anything she could use. This was the heart of Victor's power, his safest haven, where he worked his greatest magic. It wasn't possible that something could wreck it and then just vanish without a trace. This *had* to be a test, one of his stupid power games. He couldn't really be—

Lola's frantic searching was interrupted by her phone buzzing in her pocket. She dropped her flashlight to grab it, convinced it must be her master calling to yell at her for ever doubting him. When the screen flicked on, though, Simon's number was shining back at her.

"Where are you?" she hissed the moment the call connected. "The workshop is trashed, and I can't find Victor anywhere!"

"I can't get in." Simon said. "All the wards are on emergency lockdown. The whole compound's sealed tight."

"I got in!"

"You're a changeling," he reminded her. "Magic doesn't work right on you."

That was true, but... Lola looked down again at the scorched casting circles. She'd watched Victor work great magic here. Even helped with some of it, much to her shame. No matter how ambitious his spells got, though, he'd never come close to overloading the inlaid metal rings. Whatever had done this, it'd

27

been bigger than anything he'd cast before. Maybe even bigger than him.

"Simon," she whispered, her voice warbling as her gossamer began to buck with fear. "You don't think he's—"

"No," Simon said firmly. "You'd know if Victor was dead. We all would."

He was right. Even with her magic churning like a whirlpool, Lola could still feel the blood he'd poured over her all those years ago. It stuck to her like a film under her skin, making Lola feel sick as she clutched her phone.

"What are we going to do?" she whispered. "Victor's the only one who can make my pills. Without him—"

"It won't come to that," Simon said firmly. "You keep searching the house. I'll call Jamie and we'll meet at her place since she lives closer to the mansion than I do. Bring anything that looks remotely useful, and we'll figure this out together."

"Okay," Lola breathed, forcing herself to stay calm. "See you soon."

The moment Simon hung up, she dropped her phone and shoved her hand into her gossamer to bring out her prescription bottle. She popped the white plastic cap and dumped the pills into her shaking, ash-streaked palm. Not counting the one she'd taken right before she got the alarm text, she had thirteen left.

Lola's hand began to shake even harder. Thirteen pills. If she took them like normal, that was a six-and-a-half-day supply, which meant she had less than a week to find and retrieve Victor before her monster went out of control. Assuming they *could* save Victor from whatever had been strong enough to take him.

That bleak thought made her gossamer go wild. Lola didn't have the pills to waste on a panicked transformation, so she forced herself to get a grip, squeezing her quivering magic until her body felt stiff as a board.

28

She held herself like that until she'd forced the change all the way down. When her gossamer was stable again, Lola slid her pills back into the bottle one by one. She was stowing the prescription bottle deep, deep inside her gossamer when she felt a familiar tugging on her arm.

Lola waved her left hand, removing the veil of gossamer to reveal the silver thread tied around her wrist, which was jerking like a kite string in a storm. "Shh, shh, it's okay," she whispered, bending down to kiss the twitching thread. "Don't worry. We'll find him in time. I won't let us turn back into the monster."

Her shushing did nothing to stop the thread's wild movement. Lola didn't know if that was because her sister couldn't hear her or if she simply didn't believe. Honestly, Lola was having a hard time buying the words herself. Even kneeling in the ruins of his exploded workshop, the idea that something could have gotten the better of Victor still felt unreal. He was the hero and the villain combined, the master of monsters, all-powerful miracle worker. He couldn't be defeated any more than he could be escaped.

Whatever had happened, though, she wasn't getting any closer to figuring it out sitting on her knees. The clock was already ticking, so Lola forced herself to get to work. She spent the next half hour searching the castle from top to bottom. Other than the workshop, though, nothing appeared damaged.

The stone cottage out back containing Lola and Simon's childhood bedrooms, the grand library, the kitchens, and the warded underground gym where Victor had taught Lola how to spin gossamer were all untouched. She couldn't check Victor's private rooms at the top of the golden tower because the magic that teleported people up there only worked for him, but everything looked fine from the ground. Whatever had happened, it seemed to have been confined to the workshop, so that was where Lola went back to.

She cased the entire hall from end to end, examining what was left of each burned-out circle before reaching down to scrape up a bit of the ash with her fingernail. Then, bracing herself, Lola put her finger into her mouth.

The ash dissolved instantly on her tongue, filling her gossamer with smoke and the heavy, bloody taste of Victor's magic. There was quite a lot of Victor, actually. He must have been casting something enormous when the intruder caught him. The explosion might even have been caused by his own spell going awry, but that didn't feel right. Lola had been forced to endure Victor's company every day since she was seven, and she'd never seen him lose control of anything. That said, she'd never seen anyone get the better of him, either.

She tasted the ash three more times from three different places around the room, but it was hard to get a fix on anything through Victor's overpowering magic. The best she managed was an aftertaste of something familiar mixed with the blood. A faint, subtle sweetness tinged with bitter walnuts.

Lola scowled and spat. The spittle hit the ground with a golden flash before vanishing in a puff of woodsmoke, and she wiped her mouth with a grimace. Fairy magic. Just a trace but fresh enough to mean no good.

Fairies were magical parasites. They'd attached themselves to this world ages ago to feed off humanity's magic. Then the Drought had hit, the thousand-year span when the world's magic had fallen so low, it was practically nonexistent.

The Drought had sent all of Earth's magical creatures into hibernation. Many starved to death waiting century after century for the power to return, which it finally had eighty-five years ago when a meteor had struck the Canadian shield rock, sending magic rocketing back into a world that had forgotten about it. But while the resurgence had been enough to bring back human mages, manticores, chimeras, dragons, and everything else that required a certain level of magic to function, fairy gossamer was different.

Lola was an extreme example, but every fairy needed a certain amount of superstition to exist. Dragons could eat you no matter what you thought of them, but even the most powerful fairy queen couldn't so much as tweak the nose of a person who didn't believe she existed.

That hadn't been a problem eleven hundred years ago when magic was common and people everywhere had lived in terror of the unknown, but the modern age of science and reason had hit the fairies hard. Of the few courts that survived the Drought, several decided to abandon the human realm entirely, and those that did stay kept themselves strictly hidden.

This seemed to have worked out pretty well for them. Not only did hiding protect the remaining fairies from humanity's new insistence that everything make rational sense, but it was a lot easier to hunt prey that didn't know you existed. Real fairy gossamer wasn't nearly as delicate as Lola's, but anyone with a reason-based education could still pierce through it if they knew what they were looking at, which meant there was absolutely no reason for modern fairies to reveal themselves. That didn't explain what one had been doing here, though.

Lola rolled the bitter-walnut flavor around in her mouth. She hadn't tasted enough fairies to identify which one the magic belonged to, but its presence boded nothing good. Fairies were skilled at slipping through human defenses and, aside from dragons, were one of the few things powerful enough to threaten her master. That didn't necessarily mean a fairy had done this, but it wasn't looking great.

Scraping up another tablespoon's worth of the ash with the fairy's taste, Lola spun her gossamer into a plastic baggie and slipped the sample into it. She took photos of the wreckage with

31

her phone next, especially the burned-out circles. When she'd recorded everything she could think of, Lola tucked the plastic baggie into her gossamer next to her pills and strode out of the towering workshop and back down the forest stair toward the front gate.

She already had her new car pictured by the time she reached the emerald clearing. A fast one this time. Usually, Lola liked to take her time and do her research whenever she made vehicles she knew would attract attention. Accuracy was critical when it came to making sure people believed in the things she made, and few humans were as picky about details as car nerds. There was no time for fussing around with reference photos tonight, though, so Lola just went with the car she knew best: a classic Ford Mustang in bottle green.

Classic cars were always a risky move. *No one* was a bigger stickler for detail than car fans. But Lola needed to be fast tonight, and a Mustang going eighty actually drew less attention than a no-name junker going the same speed. She had the whole Mustang perfect in her head by the time she opened the garden gate, popping out of Victor's secret world to find her new ride ready and waiting.

If any of the neighbors noticed her car's Cinderella transformation, Lola didn't feel it. She opened the driver's door with a tug of magic and jumped into the bucket seat, spinning her tires as she threw the Mustang into reverse and peeled off down the quiet street.

And unseen above her, on the roof of the decoy house where Victor parked his thralls, a small, child-like figure sat in the dark, watching the flash of the Mustang's red taillights all the way down the road until they vanished around the corner.

~~~

Lola must have already used up her bad luck for the night, because she made it all the way up to Jamie's place on the Skyways without hitting a single traffic jam. She parked on the street below the all-white high-rise, doubly glad now that she'd chosen the Mustang. The collector car fit right in with all the other fanciness people who lived on the DFZ's upper story liked to drive.

She changed herself to match when she cut the headlights, taking advantage of the sudden darkness to swap out her yogurt-lady for the far less comfortable—but far more appropriate for the area—male fitness model on the billboard for the gym across the street. But while the initial change took less than three seconds, getting the details right took a lot longer.

As a changeling, Lola was technically a fairy spell without gender, but she'd still spent her entire life thinking of herself as a girl. Victor had spent years trying to break what he called her "complacent delusion," but even after he'd forced her to spend five months living as a different man every day, Lola had never achieved the same mastery over men's bodies that she had with women's. Picture references helped enormously, though, and after a few minutes of staring at the ad through her window, Lola had the model's strong jaw, muscled arms, and stylishly tousled hair down pat.

She did her clothes next. Again, Lola wasn't nearly as good with men's fashion as women's, so she kept it simple: dark jeans, loafers, and a tight white T-shirt that hugged the fitness model's rock-hard abs. She was opening the door to head out when she caught sight of herself in the Mustang's rear-view mirror.

Lola stopped with a jerk. Her face was a perfect copy of the model's, but the eyes looking back at her were an electric green that could not possibly exist in nature. Cursing the blight of image-enhancement filters, she toned down the color and lowered her cheekbones for good measure. When she was certain she'd gotten rid of all photo-manipulated weirdness, Lola climbed out of her car and jogged up the steps to the high-rise's gilded entrance.

As Victor's longtime personal assistant, Jamie got paid more than anyone else in his organization. Her condo was in a lovely, artistic building with a view of Lake St. Clair and a twenty-four-hour security desk staffed by an actual person. The guard arched his eyebrow as Lola used Jamie's entry code to open the lobby door, and she felt her gossamer soften slightly. She must have passed muster, though, because he didn't say a word as she walked by. She flashed him the fitness model's blindingly white smile and headed for the brass-caged elevators, slamming her finger on the call button rapid-fire.

It seemed to take forever for the doors to open and even longer to actually make the trip all the way up to the twentieth floor. Lola tapped the model's huge foot impatiently, dashing into the carpeted lobby the moment the elevator doors opened. She sprinted down the silent hall to Jamie's door. When she raised the model's huge fist to knock, however, the white door opened before she could touch it.

As always, the sight of Jamie caught Lola by surprise. You simply didn't expect to see people that beautiful in real life. Even tied up in a messy bun, her silver-blond hair was shampoo-commercial perfect. Her eyes were a striking shade of light lavender above a perfectly symmetrical face that still somehow managed to look interesting and nongeneric. Her skin was golden, with no trace of artificiality, and her body was even more perfectly toned than Lola's fitness model's, without the magic of photo editing.

It was a good thing Jamie wasn't made of gossamer, because it was hard to believe someone that perfect was human, especially since she still looked exactly the same now as when Victor had first introduced her to Lola twenty years ago. At the time, Lola had been too shy to ask what kind of miracle Victor had worked on her, and afterward, it hadn't felt necessary. One look at Jamie was enough to guess exactly what she'd sold her soul for.

"Is that you?" the perfect woman asked, her manicured eyebrows drawing into a suspicious scowl as she looked Lola's male body over.

Rather than answer a question that loaded in a public hallway, Lola dug her phone out of the model's skin-tight jeans and showed Jamie the number for Victor's private line: a magically protected string of thirteen digits that only the people he owned could copy, write, or make sense of.

"About time," Jamie said, grabbing Lola's muscled arm to drag her inside. "Simon's already here."

Lola sighed in relief, vanishing the model's shoes so she wouldn't track dirt onto the spotless white carpet.

Jamie's condo looked nothing like the ornate mansions that surrounded Frank's place in Windsor, but it had the same overbearing aura of money to burn. Everything inside was minimalist and white: white walls, white rugs, white couches. Even the kitchen was pure, shocking white, making the usually stylish Simon look almost scruffy by comparison.

A black man in his early thirties, Victor's one and only apprentice was rangy and remarkably tall. With his smart black clothes and thick-rimmed glasses, he would have looked more at home reading in a coffee shop than leaning on Jamie's obviously-never-meant-to-be-actually-used breakfast bar. He certainly didn't appear happy to be waiting in a kitchen that looked like a morgue, but his expression softened considerably when he saw Lola.

"You made it," he said, his face breaking into a smile, which made him look much younger than the scowl. "I was starting to get worried."

"You told me to search," Lola replied in her normal voice, which sounded ridiculous coming out of the burly fitness model.

Too ridiculous, apparently. Even though Jamie and Simon were both well acquainted with her changeling tricks, Lola still felt their disbelief kick in when she spoke. It was just a small nudge, but with only thirteen pills in her pocket, it didn't feel like a smart time to be taking risks.

She dropped the model body at once, shifting back into the yogurt lady they were all more familiar with. She also switched out her T-shirt for a sweater. Jamie's apartment was arctic.

"Now that we're all *finally* here," Jamie said, covering her eyes with a perfectly manicured hand to shield herself from Lola's change, which she'd always described as "gross," "you want to explain what this is about? Simon's been tight-lipped as a sphinx."

"I thought it best to avoid establishing any preconceptions," Simon replied tersely. "I also hardly know more than you do. Lola's the one who was actually there, so go ahead."

Lola smiled gratefully. She'd always found Jamie intimidating. Despite not being a mage, she'd worked for Victor the longest and considered herself superior because of it. She was also surprisingly intolerant of Lola's magic. You never knew what was going to set off her disbelief, which made talking to her feel like walking through a minefield. Simon was much more accepting, so he was the one Lola focused on as she told the story.

"The mansion was attacked. Someone or something got through the wards and blew up the workshop. Every casting circle's been burned to a crisp, and Victor is missing."

"You're *sure* he's just missing?" Jamie asked, her tanned face going pasty. "Not—"

"He's not dead," Simon said with iron certainty.

Jamie scowled. "How do you—"

"We'd know," he told her, tapping a finger against his temple.

36

"We'd *all* know."

"Right," Jamie muttered, placing her own hand against the column of her swan-like throat as she turned back to Lola. "How did you find out?"

"I got a text from the house's emergency system," Lola said, handing Simon her phone. "By the time I made it to the mansion, though, whatever did this was gone."

She almost told them about seeing the Black Rider but decided against it at the last second. This business was mysterious enough without throwing urban legends into the mix, and Lola had no actual reason to suspect he was involved. Jamie was already looking at her suspiciously, leaning against her spotless white fridge as she pulled out her own phone.

"Why would the security system message *you?*" she demanded, scrolling through her messages. "I didn't get anything."

"Neither did I," Simon said. "I wouldn't have known anything had happened if Lola hadn't called. Victor must have wanted her specifically."

"At least we know he's alive," Jamie said, stroking her shiny hair possessively. "Thank God for that."

Simon didn't look thankful. He'd been Victor's apprentice since he was eleven. Like her, Victor had scooped him up and shaped him to be useful, but unlike Jamie with her beauty or Lola with her pills, Simon's ties to Victor were in the past. Where their master's death meant Lola's doom, to Simon, it would have meant freedom, which was probably why the security system had called her instead of him.

"Did you find anything when you searched?" he asked, handing Lola's phone back.

"Nothing useful," she replied. "Victor's magic was so thick, a whole circus of mages could have been casting in there and I wouldn't have picked them up, but I did taste a hint of fairy

37

magic."

Simon's scowl deepened. "Do you know whose it was?"

"No, but it had to be someone big to leave a trace through that much blood."

"Could it have been the queen?" Jamie asked. "She's been gunning for Victor ever since he took over the barrow."

Simon shook his head. "Alva can't even keep her own people in line. It'd take her and her entire court to defeat Victor in his workshop, and I'm pretty sure that would have left a lot more than a hint of fairy magic."

"It didn't taste like her, either," Lola added. "Alva's magic is sour as an unripe peach. This was more…"

She trailed off, trying to think of how best to explain. Tasting magic was a fairy power, which made it difficult to describe to humans. Simon probably wouldn't be able to use the information even if she did manage to pass it on, but Lola knew who could.

"I'm going to ask Tristan."

"Absolutely not," Simon said sharply. "We can't go spreading news of this around until we have an idea who's behind it, *especially* not to the fairies."

"We're never going to get an idea unless we start asking questions," Lola argued. "Tristan knows every fairy in the US. If anyone can tell me whose magic I tasted, it's him. He's not bad as fairies go, and he's no friend of the queen."

"He's no friend, period," Simon insisted. "No fairy is, and you're certainly not going to see him this late. He'll be in his barrow for sure by now. There's no way I'm letting you meet a fairy in the heart of his power while Victor is M.I.A."

Lola narrowed her eyes. She loved Simon dearly. He'd been all she had back when they were growing up together under Victor's boot. But they weren't kids anymore, and this was not the time.

"I don't trust Tristan as far as I can throw him," she said, glaring Simon down. "But you know what happens to me if we don't find Victor." She set her arm on the cold counter, turning it over to show him the wrist where her sister's silver thread was hidden.

"I'm not going to lie down and wait to die, Simon. We need answers, and I'm the only one of us Tristan's going to talk to."

"Fine," he said, rubbing his hands over his face. "Just don't forget what he is."

Lola never did. No matter how beautiful or friendly they might appear on the outside, every fairy earned their power by killing and eating other members of their own species, and Tristan was a very powerful fairy.

"Well, someone had better do something," Jamie snapped, typing frantically on her phone. "The changeling's not the only one who needs pills. Fairies are one thing, but Victor's got a lot of clients who will do *very* bad things to us if they don't get their meds on time."

Lola sighed bleakly at the truth of that. Victor was the only one who knew the full extent of his empire, but she'd made enough of his deliveries to know that most of the people he'd sold miracles to weren't washed-up has-beens like Frank. Keeping people in line with scarcity only worked if you were there to dangle the carrot just out of their reach, and while Simon wasn't a bad blood mage, Victor was the only one skilled, ruthless, and cruel enough to run the empire he'd built.

"We have to get him back," Jamie said in a tight voice. "I can stall his clients for a day or so, but Victor was paying off someone to keep the Paladins off his case, and I don't know who it was."

"How do *you* not know?" Simon demanded.

"Plausible deniability," Jamie snapped back. "He keeps a lot of stuff from me in case the office gets raided. It's worked fine for decades. We never planned for him to just *vanish*."

39

"If the Paladins get involved, we're dead," Simon agreed, clenching his hands. "I'm kill on sight since my soul's already stained with blood magic, but they won't spare the two of you, either. Just being associated with blood magic's enough to warrant a death sentence in their eyes."

Jamie's face went white as her kitchen at that. "I'll look through the account to try and find which Paladin he was paying off," she announced as she strode into her office. "You two find Victor before we all end up on a Paladin's sword."

"Are they really that bad?" Lola whispered as Jamie stormed away. "I mean, I know they hunt blood mages, but Victor never seemed too worried about them."

"Victor's Victor," Simon whispered back, staring at his clenched fists. "He could take them if they attacked. We can't." His dark eyes flicked up to hers. "Be *very* careful out there, Lola."

"Isn't that my line?" she said, giving him a smile.

Simon didn't return it. Not being a psychopath, he didn't revel in blood magic like their master did. He didn't use the stuff at all if he could avoid it, but just once was enough to stain the soul. Good illusions could hide the mark from most people, but the Paladins were blood mage hunters. They'd sniff Simon's truth out in a heartbeat if they caught him.

"Hey, it's going to be okay," she whispered, squeezing his hand. "Even if the Paladins did decide to bust us while Victor was out, they'd never get past the city limits. They're a foreign military organization. The DFZ hates those."

"She also hates blood mages," Simon reminded her. "We'll just have to hope we find Victor before the Paladins convince the city that we're the greater evil. Fortunately, I've already got an idea on that score."

She wasn't surprised. Simon was always the one with the plan. "What have you got?"

"I'm going to use a finding spell."

Lola frowned. "Do those work on Victor?"

"Not normally. I'm sure this comes as no surprise, but Victor was extremely paranoid about being tracked. He invested a lot of his magic into making himself difficult to locate, which is working against us right now. But difficult doesn't mean impossible, especially since I helped make all of his security wards. To get around them, though, I'm going to need a material link."

Not being a mage, Lola didn't follow. "What's a material link?"

"A piece of his body," Simon explained. "Hair, skin, stuff like that. Material links are the strongest magical connection there is, which is why Victor and I designed his personal wards to burn any biological materials he might drop."

"Ew," Lola said.

"Hey, no one said being an illegal blood mage was pretty."

She stuck her tongue out at the thought, and then her face grew serious. "So how are you planning to track him if Victor's paranoid security automatically destroys the only thing you can use?"

Simon gave her a nervous look. "I'm going to need one of your pills."

"But I've only got thirteen left!" she cried.

"It's our only chance," he insisted. "Victor made those pills out of his own blood. You can't get a stronger material link than that."

That was true, but... "Can't you use somebody else's?"

"I would if I had any, but you know as well as I do that Victor makes all his pills on demand and keeps them on his person at all times. Whatever extras he might have had vanished with him when he was snatched."

Lola dropped her head onto the tile with a groan. She hadn't been paying attention at the time, but now that she thought back, she'd left Frank's pills behind in Victor's car after she'd melted.

41

Stupid move in hindsight, but how could she have known she'd need them? It wasn't as if the pills worked for anyone other than the person they were made for.

"Even if I had someone else's, yours would still be better," Simon said. "Victor put more of himself into your pills than he ever did for his clients. Just give me one, and I should be able to find him anywhere on the planet."

Lola understood what he was saying, but it still felt like signing her own execution papers as she pulled out her prescription bottle and tapped a pill into Simon's hand.

"I'll use it well," he promised, tucking the precious red tab into his jacket's inside pocket. "Don't look so nervous, Tinkerbell. I'll have a bead on him long before you're in any danger."

Lola rolled her eyes at the old nickname. Simon smiled and started gathering his things to go now that he had what he needed. Jamie was already frantically moving her hands through four AR displays in her pristine white office, so Lola took her cue to leave as well, changing back into the male fitness body as she started toward the door.

"I'll walk you out," Simon said, hurrying to her side, but Lola shook her head.

"Victor was a cruel teacher, but all those lessons he drilled into us about security weren't wrong. Whatever took him might already be moving on the rest of his organization. We arrived separately, so that's how we should leave. It's the safest way."

"You're right," Simon said, though he didn't look happy about it. "I'll call you as soon as I find something. Be careful at Tristan's. And Lola?"

She looked at him quizzically, and Simon pointed at his eyes. "They were green, not blue."

Lola blinked, changing the model's eye color as she did. Simon smiled and opened the condo door, letting her back out into the hall.

Leaving behind a perfectly good pill she hadn't even taken felt like cutting off a finger, but Lola forced herself to keep walking. Simon might not be a savant like Victor, but he was no slouch. He'd have their master located in no time. Meanwhile, Lola would keep working on the fairy angle. Between the two of them, they should be able to get Victor back before any of his many, *many* enemies closed in.

Shivering at the thought, Lola waited impatiently as the elevator took her down the twenty stories to the street. The security guard was still eyeing her suspiciously, so Lola picked up the pace, using the model's ridiculously long legs to carry her swiftly out of the building. She shifted the moment she got into her Mustang, dumping the troublesome muscle body for her comfy yogurt lady as she plopped into the bucket seat. She'd just gotten the car started when something appeared in her headlights.

The Black Rider was right in front of her.

Chapter 3

12 pills

He was an inky blot in the blinding glare of the Mustang's halogen lamps, the blue gleam of his own headlight flickering like a ghostly fire. He was standing beside his bike with his arms crossed over his chest, the tinted visor of his black helmet reflecting Lola's headlights back at her like two giant eyes. For a moment, they both just stood there, and then the Black Rider stepped forward.

Lola didn't give him the chance. The second his boot hit the asphalt, she gunned the engine and shot down the street, missing running over the Black Rider by a half inch. She sped down the side street and whipped left at the first intersection she saw. The turn was sharp enough to roll a taller car, but the Mustang's low body held her to the road. She peeled around the corner with a rubber screech, sending the elegantly dressed Skyway locals fleeing out of her way.

She was too panicked to feel their angry attention. Her thoughts were spinning as fast as her wheels with every horrible thing she'd ever heard about the Black Rider. How he killed the people he cornered and fed them to his silent bike. How he could rip you apart without touching you and never make a sound.

The next corner came up faster than she expected. Lola spun the wheel, scraping her bumper on the curb as she raced through the maze of elevated bridges back toward the highway. One nice thing about urban legends: their slavish adherence to the terrible stories that birthed them cut both ways. The Black Rider's stories were as grisly as they got, but in all his legends, he only attacked people in empty, quiet places. It was late now, and Jamie's fancy neighborhood was deserted, but if she could get to a busier part of town, there was no way he could—

Her thoughts cut off like a knife as she caught sight of a ghostly blue flash in her mirror. The Black Rider was right behind her, matching her Mustang easily. He sped up as she watched, threading his bike into the narrow gap between her car and the sidewalk.

He was so close now that Lola could hear the utter silence of his bike. The unnatural quiet was scarier than any roaring. She hit the gas with a curse, throwing her car down the road as fast as the gossamer would go, but the Rider's blue light was still shining in her mirror.

She leaned forward in her seat, urging her car even faster. Why was he chasing her? Jamie had said Victor's enemies would be coming out of the woodwork, but surely the Rider wasn't one of those. Even her master couldn't sell a miracle to an urban legend, right?

Her whirling thoughts were interrupted by the Rider's light getting bigger in her mirror. Despite her breakneck speed, he pulled up beside her quiet as a fish. For a second, he was right outside her window, and then his arm went out to grab the handle of her door.

Lola shrieked and veered hard, smacking him with the side of her car. At least, that was what she meant to do. The Black Rider swerved at the last second, nearly hitting a parked van. Lola scrambled to straighten out before she hit something herself, hurtling down the street with her speedometer pinning the red. For a beautiful moment, she thought she'd gotten enough distance to get away. Then her whole car lit up blue and red as a police car whipped out of an alley behind her.

Lola almost screamed in frustration. One of the best parts about living in the DFZ was that there were no cops, but this was the Skyways. Folks up here could afford nice things like speed limits and private security, and this rent-a-cop had apparently taken issue with her doing a hundred in a twenty-five zone. The Rider cut his lights the second the cop appeared, fading back into the darkness like the ghost he was, but Lola didn't believe for a second that he was gone, putting her in a bind.

If she stopped for the cop, the Rider would probably kill them both. If she kept driving, though, the cop would call for backup, and then she'd *really* be screwed. One cop she might be able to fake her way through, but a whole squad would melt her magic into soup.

Her options were getting worse by the moment, so Lola decided to take a risk. She hit her brakes and started to slow down, making it look like she was preparing to pull over. Then, when she'd drifted back down to a speed at which she could take some of her attention off the road, Lola closed her eyes and *pushed*.

The invisible magic that formed her body clenched in response. The intensity of it was almost painful, but the brief discomfort was instantly overwhelmed by a flood of pure potential. Gossamer was the stuff of imagination, dreams made solid. It gained stability from belief, but it could be whatever she desired, and right now, Lola was willing to dream big.

It was amazing how quickly her magic could work when she wasn't being careful. No sooner had the image of what she wanted crossed her mind than the finished illusion tore out of her, and another car careened into the street. It was a rigged-up lowrider, solid black and expensive. It slammed on its brakes when it saw the flashing lights, then a shotgun barrel slid out of the tinted passenger window and plugged three slugs into the back of the cop car. The man inside swore and ducked as his rear windows exploded, and the lowrider shot away with a chorus of hollers and taunts echoing off the buildings.

The rent-a-cop forgot all about Lola after that. He slammed his car into reverse and took off after the bait, screaming into his radio for backup. The moment his flashing lights winked out of sight around a building, Lola hit her own gas, shooting away down the street. As if he'd been waiting for his cue, the Black Rider shot out of his hiding spot on the shadowed sidewalk and zoomed after her, his blue headlamp dancing like a will-o'-the-wisp in the dark.

He caught up even more quickly this time, his silent motorcycle matching her acceleration effortlessly, and Lola slammed her palms against her steering wheel. Just how fast was the bastard? With the cop still chasing her phantom car, she was running out of options. Two cars plus her body was the limit of what her gossamer could sustain, but Lola couldn't dissolve her decoy while the cop was still fixated on it. She needed to take the illusion down easy, dissolving the car only at a point where the cop could realistically believe he'd lost it. First, though, she had to lose the threat behind her.

Silent as a shadow, the Black Rider zoomed up beside her, and then a loud bang went through her car as he slammed the flat of his open hand against her window. Lola hit her brakes in pure panic, filling the air with the stench of burning rubber as her tires lost traction on the pavement. The Black Rider shot past her only to turn on a dime, his bike coming around effortlessly twenty feet down the street. Then he stopped, boots planted firmly on the pavement, and waited.

Even as she struggled to get her skidding car back under control, Lola saw what he was doing. He knew she was going to crash, and he'd positioned himself to take advantage of it. The burst of anger that came with that thought cleared her panic away, and Lola seized control of her car. Prying her foot off the brake, she wrenched the wheel straight and hit the gas. When her car was aimed straight at the Rider, Lola took a deep breath and let it

47

go.

The speeding car dissolved into pure, shimmering gossamer in an instant, dropping Lola through the driver's seat onto the pavement. Her body softened on instinct to cushion the fall. It was still going to hurt, but Lola forced her focus to stay on the remnants of her car, shaping the flying gossamer into a solid slug of high-speed steel that hit the Black Rider like a train.

Lola caught a glimpse of the Black Rider's head coming up in surprise before her transformed car slammed into him. That was all she had time to see before she hit the road herself.

Even with her magic softened to jelly to absorb the impact, it wasn't a fun time. She slammed into the pavement like a lump of rainbow putty, splatting nearly flat before rolling into the side of a parked SUV. For a terrifying moment, the color vanished from her vision, flicking back to the old black and white of her monster. Then, like a camera coming into focus, the world snapped back.

Lola came back together with it, collapsing onto the asphalt in more or less human form. She lay stunned for a moment, and then, with a low moan, she pushed up onto her elbows to examine the damage.

There was a lot. She didn't see any cuts or bruises because gossamer didn't do that, but every part of her was throbbing. She felt like an egg that had just been scrambled in a blender. She also still felt very oozy and soft, which scared her far more than the pain.

Terrified, she whipped her attention back to the car she'd used to draw the cop away. Gossamer constructs were little better than robots if she didn't control them, but the lowrider had done surprisingly well. It was still racing down the roads, firing its guns like a maniac, only now, it had about ten Skyway Security Corp cop cars behind it.

Lola closed her eyes with a curse. Of all the nights for hired security to actually earn their pay. Hitting the road had scrambled her gossamer, but it was the cops' intense attention that was really putting her in danger. She could already feel herself melting like a popsicle on the pavement. If this escalated any further, she was done for.

Cursing again, Lola tucked herself against the SUV she'd crashed into and closed her eyes, shifting all her attention to the decoy car. For a sickening moment, she lurched between the gossamer she thought of as her body and the car she'd created. Then, all at once, Lola *was* the car, flying down the road with ten cops right behind her.

Since she wasn't a real fairy, the objects Lola made didn't have true minds of their own. Their reactions were governed by perceptions of those around them. The cops thought they were chasing a maniac, so the black car drove like a maniac, which was how things had gotten so out of hand. It still wasn't too late to salvage the situation, though, so Lola took control, leaning hard on the tricked-out engine.

The burst of speed let her outpace her pursuers long enough to whip the lowrider into a parking deck. She crashed through the toll booth and turned again, flying down the ramp to the underground levels. The second she left the cops' line of sight, Lola dissolved her creation, and the black car vanished like a shadow. Just in time, too. The cops were already roaring down the ramp with sirens screaming as her vision faded, flitting back to her main body as her gossamer returned.

Lola collapsed onto the pavement below the dented SUV, her body bubbling like a cauldron as all her parts came back together. Fortunately, being human was the first illusion she'd learned. She popped back into her yogurt-lady body after less than ten seconds, then closed her eyes and braced for impact.

Somewhere to the south, ten patrol cars were realizing that the car they'd been chasing with single-minded intensity had vanished, just poofed out of existence in a parking deck that had only one way out. That couldn't happen, and the combined backlash of their disbelief hit Lola like a cartoon hammer.

The blow struck every part of her at once, turning her back into jelly on the pavement. As she tried and failed to stabilize, Lola wondered if this was it: the hit that dissolved her for good.

Luckily for her, humans were fantastic rationalizers. As fast as their disbelief had kicked her in the teeth, the pressure faded as the cops realized the idea of a disappearing car was utterly ridiculous. And as their brains began thinking up all sorts of explanations for what must *really* have happened, the instinctive lash of their subconscious magic fell away.

Lola gasped as it released her, flopping on the ground like a landed fish. But while every part of her was throbbing like a finger slammed in a car door, she was still alive and, more importantly, still human, or at least human-ish. Parts of her were definitely looking a little wonky, but she'd pass for a person in the dark, which was good enough. Bracing her only slightly melty hands against the pavement, Lola crawled out from under the SUV to look around.

She immediately wished she hadn't. Her transformed Mustang was still there, a smoking wreck almost fifty feet away, but something was moving beneath it. A leather-clad arm emerged as she watched, and then the Black Rider began to pull himself out of the wreckage.

Lola grabbed the SUV's dented door. By the time she'd pulled herself to her feet, the Rider was up and moving. He turned toward her next, his black helmet glinting under the streetlamps without so much as a scratch.

Fear hit her in an icy wave. She let go of the SUV and tried to run, but her legs weren't as firm yet as she'd thought. They gave out on the first step, dropping her back to the pavement.

She scrambled back to her knees with a string of curses, dragging her soft body along the pavement like an unfired clay doll. And behind her, slowly, the Rider kept walking.

Just like his bike, his boots made no sound on the pavement, but it didn't matter. Lola could feel him getting closer like an icy wind on her neck. She swore again and tried to hobble faster, but the Rider just kept silently advancing like the villain in a teenage horror movie. He was only a few feet away now, close enough to lurch forward and snatch her. Lola was wondering why he didn't just get it over with when a miracle happened.

The block they'd crashed on was lined on both sides with towering, overpriced office buildings. They were empty at this time of night, but not entirely. The Black Rider was practically on top of her when the door of the building in front of the crashed Mustang burst open, and an elderly man in maintenance coveralls ran into the street.

"God almighty!" he shouted, running toward the wreckage.

Lola and the Black Rider both froze. From where he'd come out, the man apparently hadn't seen Lola yet, but he must have been able to see the Black Rider just fine. The old man shrieked at the sight, and the Rider stiffened, his body going tense under the inky black of his motorcycle suit.

Lola didn't know why an urban legend cared who yelled at him, but she knew a chance when she got one. The moment the Rider was distracted, she made a break for it, cutting the flaming pile of gossamer that had been her car loose in the process.

It was a desperate, painful thing to do. The gossamer she'd used to make the car was as much a part of her body as her human shape, but she couldn't dissolve it in front of a witness without taking another disbelief hit, *and* she couldn't leave it behind without risking another situation like the one with her distraction

51

car. If she cut it free, though, the gossamer could persist in that state for days unless someone looked too hard at it. Even if it dissolved in front of an entire crash forensics team, the gossamer would no longer be tied to her, which meant she wouldn't be hurt. That wasn't much of a consolation, but it was the best option Lola had at the moment, so she ripped it free.

It hurt a lot more than she remembered. Cutting off gossamer was a lot like cutting off an arm, but while the pain was enough to bring tears to her eyes, the loss wasn't permanent. Fairy magic was fluid by nature. Even a big chunk like this would come back eventually, and less gossamer meant stronger control over the magic she had left.

The moment she severed the burning wreckage, her body stopped melting. Gathering what was left of her magic tightly around her, Lola scrambled under the parked cars to the sidewalk on the other side and spun herself a new ride.

She didn't have enough gossamer left to make another car, so she took a page from the Rider's book and conjured up a motorcycle. She shifted her own body to match, switching out her trusty yogurt lady for a big tough biker with sideburns long enough to braid. The moment both changes were finished enough, Lola hopped onto her new bike and raced back the way she'd come, leaving the Rider eating her dust with the still-shrieking janitor.

She looked over her shoulder a half dozen times as she flew down the street, but the monster didn't follow. He didn't seem to be murdering the old man either, thank goodness. He just stood next to the flames of her severed car, watching her go.

Lola didn't know what part of the Rider's legend had made him act like that, but she was delighted to finally get a break. She turned the first chance she got, making a beeline for the ramp down to the Underground so she could lose him properly.

Lola drove through the neon-lit darkness for a good twenty minutes before she finally convinced herself that she wasn't being followed. She then spent another ten minutes looking for a convenience store that didn't have a clerk. The moment she spotted one, she darted inside, leaving her bike idling on the sidewalk as she purchased a jug of OJ and a box of donuts from the auto-vendor using the account on her phone.

Food in hand, Lola sat back down on her bike and started shoving donuts into the biker's mouth, washing each one down with big gulps of juice. After a huge expenditure of gossamer, nothing helped like sugar. She polished off the dozen donuts and the half gallon of juice in seconds, then went back in for a bag of gummy worms, but it wasn't working.

Cutting the car had given her enough control to get away, but the damage was still severe. Even after a pound of sugar, her gossamer was runny and weak, causing the biker's extensive tattoos to ooze like syrup down her hairy, muscled arms. She kept eating anyway, cramming fistfuls of gummy worms into her mouth in a desperate attempt to avoid taking yet *another* pill tonight. When her bike handles started drooping, though, Lola knew there was nothing else for it.

Letting out a long sigh, she dug out her pills and popped one into her mouth, washing it down with the dregs from the orange juice and another giant fistful of gummies. The bloody taste cut straight through the candy's sweetness, nearly making her gag, but it worked. The moment the pill slid down her throat, her body firmed back up, snapping the big, tough biker back into shape like someone had yanked his laces.

Lola closed her eyes in relief as her magic stabilized, cursing the Rider for making her waste a pill. She didn't know why the urban legend had it out for her, but she didn't have the resources for this. Until they found Victor, she was going to be as cautious as

53

possible and do her best to make each pill last. If she kept it low-key enough and conserved her energy, she might be able to eke another day out of the eleven she had left.

With that in mind, Lola restarted her bike and pulled into traffic, driving very slowly and very safely under the bridges toward downtown.

~~~

Back up on the Skyways, a night janitor with the name Marty stitched onto his maintenance uniform stood in the light of the burning car, watching nervously as the big man in the black motorcycle suit examined the dented side of the SUV parked down the street. He had no idea how the man could see anything through his black-tinted helmet, but he was staring at the wrecked door as if it was the most interesting thing in the world. He had to be on drugs, Marty concluded. Nothing else explained it.

"You *sure* you don't want me to call an ambulance?" he asked the man again, tilting his head at the wrecked car that was still burning in the middle of the road. "Looks like you had some pretty serious trouble."

The man in black shook his head.

"I'm gonna have to call security," Marty warned, keeping his distance. "Part of my employment contract. Nothing personal."

The man nodded but didn't turn his black-tinted visor in Marty's direction. He just walked over to the totaled car and reached under the flames to grab something.

Marty watched skeptically. Lord knew what the druggie thought he was doing. That car was a goner, and anything beneath it was bound to be worse. That thought was still going through his mind when the helmeted man lifted the smoking wreckage and pulled a fully intact black motorcycle out from underneath.

"Good Lord!" Marty cried, jumping back. That had *not* just happened!

The man in black stumbled as if someone had kicked him in the gut, and his head swung toward Marty. The moment the black visor was pointed at him, Marty felt something hard, cold, and sharp strike the back of his head.

The next thing he knew, he was face-down on the pavement. He groaned and tried to roll over only to find he couldn't. There was something heavy and freezing cold holding him down. He did manage to get his head up enough to see the motorcycle man bring his black fist down on the remains of what had once been a very nice Mustang. The wreckage shuddered when his fist landed, and then the car melted away.

Marty blinked, head swimming, but it didn't change what he'd seen. The wrecked car had *vanished*, just went away like water on a hot sidewalk. He was still trying to wrap his head around it when he felt a large, leather-clad arm slide under his waist and lift him up.

When poor old Marty opened his eyes again, it was nearly five a.m. He was lying on one of the fancy couches in the lobby of the office building he cleaned every night, and his head was killing him. Groaning, he sat up and touched the back of his scalp, trying to remember what the devil had happened. He knew there'd been an accident and a druggie in black, but after that, nothing. He was shifting his arms to push himself up when he noticed something lying on his chest.

When Marty glanced down to see what, his old eyes shot wide. There was a mountain of money stacked on top of him. His surprised jerk unsettled it, sending Marty scrambling to catch all the bills before they scattered all over the polished floor. Heart pounding, he scooped the money back into his lap. He was still getting it together when he caught sight of something yellow stuck to one of the twenties.

It was a sticky note from the secretary's desk, and written across it in large, blocky letters was one word.

Sorry.

Marty stared at the note for a good half minute, then he peeled the thing off and tossed it in the trash. Who cared what dirty business the man in black had been up to? What mattered was that he'd paid Marty for his trouble, and Marty was all about getting paid.

With that, all thoughts of the Black Rider vanished from his mind, leaving only giddy anticipation as he started counting his new wealth.

Chapter 4

11 pills

Lola made it all the way to Tristan's without seeing the Black Rider again. She looked over her shoulder the whole way, jumping every time she spotted a blue light of any kind, but it was never him.

That both relaxed and frustrated her. Lola still didn't know why the Rider had attacked, but considering the timing, she now suspected it had something to do with Victor's disappearance. Her master had made enemies of everyone else in the city, so why not an urban legend? She wanted to call Simon and ask his opinion, but the mage would be right in the middle of casting his tracking spell. Interrupting him would set them back far more than waiting a few hours until he was finished, so Lola did her best not to think about the Rider as she cruised down Tristan's block.

At least she didn't have to worry about getting cornered in an empty alley here. Tristan's home was smack in the middle of downtown, which meant he lived in tourist central. Every inch of this part of the Underground was lit with flashing signs and filled with gawking people. Squawking AR ads floated in the air hawking DFZ T-shirts, tours, and collectibles, all spookified for the season.

As with every holiday in the city of capitalism, businesses were squeezing Halloween for all it was worth. Bars selling overpriced, Halloween-themed versions of DFZ classics like the Deep Sink—a horrific concoction of corn liquor and engine lubricant with the seasonal addition of pumpkin spice—were everywhere, and the VR parlors had lines out the door for the new total-immersion, no-safeties edition of *Fenrir*. Why anyone would pay to watch from the ground as one of the screaming extras in a giant monster movie, Lola could not fathom, but the flashing signs promised it would be the fright of a lifetime, guaranteed to "Make you pee your pants, or your money back!"

Not that money-back guarantees meant anything in the DFZ. The famously free-wheeling city's laws could be counted on one hand: no killing, no slavery, no polluting the water, and no blood magic. None of those said anything about consumer protections, but you were generally pretty safe in the tourist areas, at least physically. Your bank account would suffer a mass murder, but injuring paying customers was bad for business, even if your business was 99% scam.

It wasn't all shysters and thieves, though. There were plenty of legitimate shops down here as well, like God of Noodles, a noodle restaurant run by the Spirit of Hand-Cut Noodles.

Not all spirits were living cities or faces of death. Now that magic had flooded the world again, smaller gods were rising in droves to claim their worshipers, and not just the traditional ones. Thanks to the addition of billions more humans since the last time the world had been flooded with magic eleven hundred years ago, there was now a magical embodiment for pretty much any concept you could think of. There was a spirit of dental floss, a spirit of the shock of pain you felt when you stubbed your toe, and, of course, a spirit for every different kind of noodle.

Lola stared longingly at God of Noodles as she zipped by on her motorcycle. She'd always wanted to eat the perfect incarnation of noodles as made by their representative spirit, but Victor never left her alone long enough to actually wait out the huge line that always crowded the door. Every time she'd tried, he'd invariably call just before her number came up, wasting her time *and* money since all orders had to be paid for in advance.

It was little things like that that ground her the most. Her master had known she was waiting in line because she'd told him, and then he'd ordered her to his side anyway because he was petty like that. If she hadn't been so short on pills, Lola would have parked her bike and gotten in line right now just so she could finally do something *she* wanted without Victor yanking her leash.

Alas, there was no time. Thanks to the Rider, she might already be too late to catch Tristan at home. Trying to find a fairy's barrow was pointless if they weren't in it. She'd come too far to turn around now, though, and she *really* needed a lead on that fairy to find Victor before one of his enemies found them, so Lola pulled off the busy street lit with orange paper lanterns painted to look like pumpkins into the cool, greenish fluorescents of Tristan's parking deck.

After everything that had happened, she half expected to find the Rider waiting for her. He wasn't, thank goodness, so Lola put him firmly out of her mind. Tristan wasn't a bad sort, as fairies went. He was still a fairy, though, and only idiots let themselves be distracted around the fair folk.

After looking to make sure there were no security cameras or other residents around, Lola pulled her bike into the deck's darkest corner and changed shape, melting her burly biker into something much smaller. Her beer gut, leather vest, and hairy arms vanished, replaced with a slender waist and delicate, doll-like limbs swathed in an oversized dress of frothy white lace. Her beard and impressive sideburns followed suit, replaced by a youthful, innocent girl's face dusted with freckles. Beautiful red-blond hair fell in long waves around her now gently sloping shoulders, but her limpid, cornflower-blue eyes were disgusted when Lola summoned a mirror to check herself.

The body was Victor's design. It was the first he'd taught her to take and the one he'd commanded her to appear in every day for the first five years she'd lived with him. Lola didn't know if he just

59

liked waifs or if he'd specifically chosen the weakest, most breakable-looking body possible to help keep her in her place, but she *hated* it. The only reason she'd put it on now was because it was her most stable form.

That almost made her hate the body more. She despised that her best shape was one Victor had forced on her. But she was about to enter a fairy barrow, which meant there was no room for pride.

Unlike the illusions human mages used to fill rich people's yards with ghouls and ghosts, fairy barrows were practically separate realities: tunnels dug into the barrier that separated humanity's plane of reality from everything beyond it. Barrows were how the fairies had first gotten in thousands of years ago, tunneling into Earth's reality like termites through tree bark.

Lola didn't know how deep Tristan's barrow ran, but she was smart enough to fear it. Like spiders and their parlors, fairies were most powerful inside their barrows. There were still protections you could invoke if you knew about them, like the rules of hospitality, and no fairy could lie.

Not that it seemed to matter. Every fairy Lola had had the displeasure of meeting was so good at half-truths they didn't need actual deception, and barrows only made it worse. Once you stepped into their home, a fairy controlled everything you perceived. Simon hadn't been wrong when he'd said coming here was dangerous, but Lola had been to Tristan's barrow several times, and while she wasn't naive enough to trust him, she was pretty sure she'd be able to get out again.

Holding that confidence like a candle, Lola vanished her mirror and started walking toward the elevator. Like everything involving fairies, finding a barrow was tricky. Accidentally stumbling into one was easy. Humans did it all the time, usually to their regret. To enter a barrow on purpose, though, you had to

60

know the lock the fairy used to hide their home from reality.

Riddles and rhyming couplets were popular, as were physical actions like bowing or turning widdershins. Tristan being, well, Tristan, his lock was that anyone who wanted to find his home had to imagine a dirty fantasy. Starring him.

Dirty fantasies weren't exactly Lola's forte. It wasn't that she didn't have those kind of urges—she was totally into sexy things, way more than anyone suspected from a changeling who was technically incapable of reproduction—she just had zero actual experience. Victor didn't like her getting attached to anyone other than him, and Lola was *never* going there. She had nursed an enormous crush on Simon when they were younger, but they both knew their master would never allow it, so she'd given up on that long ago. She *had* read some interesting books, though.

Mind churning, Lola stepped into the elevator that served the apartment building where Tristan hid his home. The scuffed walls and dull panel full of neatly lined-up buttons all looked perfectly normal, which meant she hadn't gotten his attention yet, so Lola closed the red-head's eyes and imagined the cover of an old-style Romance novel. She imagined the shirtless hero clutching the winsome heroine, who was also falling out of her clothes, against his broad chest. Once the scene was firmly in her mind, Lola replaced the shirtless rake with Tristan as she'd last seen him and the heroine with herself in her current body. She imagined the press of their chests: his hard, hers soft and yielding. Tristan would look down at her, his smug, cocksure smile widening as he bent down to press his lips against—

And that was as far as Lola was going. Face flaming, she opened her eyes and looked at the elevator panel for the button, which had better be there. Thankfully, it was: a bright-white circle twice the size of any of the other buttons that definitely hadn't been there when she'd entered.

Rolling her eyes at the ridiculousness of it all, Lola mashed the new button with her thumb and leaned back against the scuffed walls as the elevator began to trundle upward. When the bell dinged for the thirteenth floor in a building that was only supposed to have twelve, the elevator doors opened to reveal a pristine white hallway with sky-blue carpeting and no windows. The only door was all the way at the far end, more than twenty feet away.

That was a lot farther than it had been last time. But like everything fairies made, including herself, barrows were ever changing. Nothing looked like it was going to collapse on her, at least, so Lola stepped out of the elevator and started down the hall.

The blue carpet was soft as down under her feet, and the white walls were immaculate, as if they'd been painted fresh this morning, though she smelled no trace of paint. The hallway smelled more like the sea than anything else, fresh and cold and a little bit salty, which was a welcome change after the grimy, sour, slightly greasy air of the DFZ's tourist zone. The door at the end was as white as the walls, with no handle or knob. Lola was wondering if Tristan expected her to claw her way inside when her phone rang.

She went to grab it only to realize the floofy dress she'd conjured for her waif body didn't have pockets. Shaking her head in disgust, she whipped herself up some nice big ones and fished out her phone. The number came up as "Unknown Caller," but when she tapped the icon to accept, Tristan's insulted voice sounded through the speaker.

"A Romance novel cover? *Really?* I don't think I should accept a fantasy tame enough to be displayed on a supermarket shelf. Surely you can do better than that, Lola-cat."

"That's the best you're going to get," Lola said, trying her absolute best not to snap. She was here to ask him a favor, after all.

"Let me in, Tristan. Your new hallway is creepy."

"Let you in?" Tristan's voice was so cheery, she could practically hear his grin. "Big demands from a little changeling scratching at my door in the middle of the night. If you want to come in, you'd better make it worth my while." The voice on the phone grew deep and seductive. "Will you promise me a dream, Lola-belle?"

Lola frowned. She didn't like the way he'd asked, but the request wasn't actually unreasonable. She'd already fed him several times before, so the damage was done. Another dream wouldn't hurt.

"Fine," she said with a long sigh. "Just open the door."

The call clicked off, and the white door slid open to reveal an enormous loft-style apartment with a panoramic view of the Golden Gate Bridge.

Lola's eyes went wide at the sight. "You moved to San Francisco?"

"Hello to you, too," Tristan said right beside her.

She jumped and whirled to see him leaning against the doorframe not an inch away, looking down at her with a crooked, predatory smile.

On first glance, Tristan looked almost silly. Well over six feet tall and beanpole thin, he was dressed like a rock star in tight white leather pants and shiny white shoes with pointed toes. His belt was huge and covered with silver studs, and his white, floofy shirt with its big open V down the front looked like he'd stolen it from a Renaissance fair. Over all of that was a white leather jacket with a collar so high that it brushed the razor-sharp edges of his jaw.

Unlike most fairies who changed their features every week or so to keep up with the latest trends, Tristan had worn the same face for as long as she'd known him. A perfectly conventionally

63

handsome one, but there was something about his deep-set eyes and hollow cheeks that gave him an air of tragedy, as if he were a young soldier going off to a war he knew he'd never return from.

But all of this was just his glamour, his surface. Depending on which human emotion they preferred to eat, fairies made themselves up to dazzle, seduce, or terrify. Tristan's tragic pretty-boy aesthetic made his tastes obvious, but like all fairies, he kept his true form carefully hidden.

As a changeling, Lola could see through most fairy illusions if she tried hard enough, but she'd never caught so much as a hint of Tristan's true face, and she didn't want to. Annoying as he could be, she vastly preferred Tristan the ostentatious flirt to the predator she sometimes spotted looking out at her from behind his smiling, sea-blue eyes.

"Not that I'm complaining," Tristan said as he looked her up and down, "but I thought you said you were done with that body."

"It's been a rough night, and I wanted something stable," Lola replied nonchalantly, determined to retake control of the situation. "I'm here on business. Do you have a moment?"

"For you, Lola-lamb, I have hours," Tristan purred, shutting the door behind her with a wave of his hand. "Can I offer you some dinner?"

He nodded at the marble banquet table that had suddenly appeared under the apartment's expansive windows, its surface covered in platters of sushi as fresh and glistening as if the chef had placed them only seconds before.

"No thanks," Lola said, quickly looking away before the feast drew her in.

No one who knew anything would ever take food from a fairy. The more you interacted with a barrow, the deeper into the dream you fell, and the harder it became to escape. Tristan was the one who'd taught her that, but it never stopped him from offering.

He smiled at her rejection and strolled over to the table, snatching up a perfect piece of salmon nigiri and popping it into his mouth with a smug grin. Licking the stray grains of rice from his fingers, he walked over to the circle of red leather couches surrounding the penthouse's suspended glass fireplace. He plopped down on the biggest one and patted the cushion beside him invitingly. Lola ignored the offer, taking a seat on the cowhide footstool at the end instead.

She'd meant to get straight to business, but with the Golden Gate Bridge shining like a river of light through the windows, she couldn't help asking. "Are we *really* in San Francisco?"

"Of course," Tristan said, summoning a glass of amber whiskey to his hands with a flick of his long fingers. "Why else would I bother with the hallway?"

She'd known it. "So you just let me walk a low road with no warning?"

The fairy shrugged as if it were no big deal, but then, to him, it wasn't. Low roads were fairy highways through reality. They could get you anywhere in the world in a flash, taking you from, say, DFZ to San Francisco in ten steps. They could also get you lost for years if you didn't know you were in one.

"I'm sorry," he said, giving her a scathing look. "Who burst in on whom?"

"You could have put up a sign." Lola grumbled. "Or gotten a phone number so I could just call you instead of having to walk two thousand miles."

Tristan smiled benignly and leaned forward, dangling the whiskey glass between his hands. "Why are you here, Changeling?"

His voice was soft, but the threat didn't need to be loud. Tristan was still smiling, but his eyes were staring at her now with a predator's appraisal. Suddenly, Lola was very, very aware that

65

she was the least powerful thing in the room.

"Victor didn't send me," she said, dropping her eyes. "You always said to come to you if I had a problem. Well, I've got a big one, and I need your help."

It was a sign of just how bad things were that she was using the H-word. Obligation was a big deal in the fairy world. Asking for help was like asking to become a slave, but she and Tristan went way back, and her association with Victor protected her somewhat. Even the fairy queen would hesitate to touch what the blood mage had claimed.

Tristan set his drink down as he considered her request. "A boon, then," he said at last. "What are your terms?"

"Only that you do your best to help and that you tell no one what I'm about to tell you," Lola said.

"'Best to help' is a very open clause," Tristan warned, but his voice was intrigued. "You said you came here on your own. I'm guessing that means you would be the one indebted and not your master?"

Lola nodded, and Tristan's eyes flared instantly. "Done," he said, holding out his hand.

She eyed his slender fingers warily. "Shouldn't you tell me the price of the debt first?"

"Since you're not going to tell me what I'll be doing to earn it, I'm afraid the answer is no." His handsome face split into a dazzling grin. "Blind leading the blind, Lola-bear."

Lola clenched her hands in her lap. As hard as she'd worked to get in here, she was seriously considering bailing. A debt to a fairy was bad enough, but an open-ended debt with no terms was horrifying. She could end up serving Tristan forever.

"Lola?"

Something in Tristan's voice made her look up. When their eyes met, he smiled at her, his face uncharacteristically sincere.

"You have my word I will not take advantage. I pledge it on my honor."

Those were heavy words. Tristan took his honor deathly seriously. Even if he did screw her over, though, what would it matter? She only had eleven pills left. If they didn't find Victor in the next five and a half days, it wouldn't matter what Tristan did. She'd already be gone.

That thought gave Lola the final burst of courage she needed. Tristan's hand was warm when she took it, but as his fingers latched around hers, a chill rolled through her like the wind off an icy sea. It vanished as quickly as it had come, and Tristan dropped her hand with a disapproving look.

"You're missing quite a bit of gossamer, Lola-kitten. Why don't you start at the beginning?"

In Lola's mind, the trouble had started at Frank's. She didn't think Victor would like her blabbing about his business, though, so she began with the alarm. Tristan listened attentively as she described the state of Victor's workshop and her own assessment of the wreckage. When she mentioned the fairy magic, however, he held out his hand.

"Let me taste."

"Of course," she said, happy he'd agreed so quickly. "How would you like me to—"

Tristan's smirk grew positively evil as his eyes locked on her lips. "I can think of a way."

Her face must have been a sight, because Tristan burst out laughing. Cheeks burning, Lola dug into her new giant pockets, focusing her mind on what she wanted her gossamer to spin. When she drew her hand out again, she was holding a piece of candy wrapped in gold foil.

Tristan took the candy and unwrapped it with a disappointed huff before popping it into his mouth. Lola shivered as his gossamer wrapped around hers. Tristan's magic always reminded her of the sea: cold, endless, unrelenting. This was why she'd come here, though, so she gritted her teeth and bore it until he motioned for her to take her gossamer back.

Lola dissolved the candy she'd made, letting the magic flow out of him and back into her as Tristan settled thoughtfully into his couch.

"Well?" she asked as her gossamer resettled. "Is it someone you recognize?"

"Perhaps," he said, tapping the toe of his pointed shoe rapidly against the floor. "I can tell you it's not Alva nor any of her court."

"I already figured that much out myself," Lola said. "But if it's not one of them, who could it be? Alva controls the entire DFZ. Except for you and a few others who already had barrows here before she claimed the throne, no fairy can enter the city without the queen's say-so."

"Alva is not queen."

The words came out with such vehemence that Lola shrank back. Tristan's body hadn't changed that she could see, but he suddenly felt bigger. *Much* bigger, as if she was standing at the foot of a cliff. Then, as fast as it had come, the overwhelming presence left, and Tristan wiped a hand over his face.

"Sorry," he said, smile snapping back into place. "Old grudge."

Lola nodded. She'd seen this anger before. Twenty years ago, there had been a different fairy queen who ruled the DFZ. Lola had heard her called by several names, but Tristan called her Morgan. Apparently, she'd been queen since fairies had invented the title, leading her court through the starvation of the magical drought and the chaos that came after. Even among the eternally shifting fairies, it was assumed she'd rule forever. Then Alva had come out of nowhere and killed her, taking Morgan's title, powers, and throne.

The coup had rocked the fairy world. Some of Morgan's court went on like nothing had happened. Others fled, vanishing back into their own realm. A few, mostly Morgan's older, stronger champions like Tristan, balked entirely, refusing to swear fealty to Alva or even acknowledge her victory. Like any tyrant, Alva had retaliated, and the result was a lot of bad blood that was still shaking out two decades later.

Fairies had long lives and longer memories. Twenty years was all the time that Lola could remember. For Tristan, though, the wound was clearly still fresh, and Lola made a mental note to mention Alva only by her given name in the future.

"You still haven't told me how you lost your gossamer," Tristan said, pointedly turning the conversation.

Lola blew out a breath and told him briefly about her incident with the Black Rider. Just talking about the chase left her shaking. Even Tristan looked upset by the time she finished her story at his door.

"So you've caught the Black Rider's attention," he said quietly. "That's not good."

"Obviously not," Lola said crossly. "But do you think he had something to do with Victor's disappearance?"

"No," Tristan said, shaking his head. "He is very dangerous, though. You should stay away."

"That's what I was *trying* to do," Lola huffed. "But I don't have time to pussyfoot around a stalker. I've only got five days left before my pills run out."

Tristan was one of the few outsiders who knew about Lola's dependency. "How many pills does Victor usually give you at a time?"

"Thirty. He conjures them whenever I'm running low."

"With your blood or his?"

Lola held her breath. She'd told Tristan a lot, but she'd never told him about the blood.

"I can taste his magic on you," Tristan explained, his eyes staring into hers, intense but strangely unfocused, as though he were looking at something behind her rather than her face. "Five days isn't much time, so I was wondering if I could support you myself."

Lola froze. "Could you?"

Tristan shook his head, shattering her newborn hopes. "You're a strange little creature, Lola-button. If you were human, I could simply enthrall you. Likewise, if you were a pure changeling, I could take over your gossamer and keep you safe here."

"I thought changelings could only be commanded by the fairy who made them."

"Outside, yes," Tristan said with a grin. "But this is my barrow. All gossamer, even that of other fairies, is mine to command here. My house, my rules."

Lola leaned away from him. "*All* gossamer?"

Tristan's grin grew wicked. "Normally, yes. Alas, Victor's hold on you prevents any takeover. Trust me, sweeting. If I could control your gossamer, you wouldn't be wearing that dull grandma frock."

Lola clutched her lace dress with a blush, and Tristan basked in her discomfort for a moment before continuing.

"Unfortunately, Lola-cat, you're something altogether odd. A changeling held long, long past your time by a human spell woven so deep, it's become indistinguishable from your own magic. You eat human food rather than human desires, you dream like one of them, yet you can spin and regenerate gossamer like a fairy. You were able to walk right into my barrow tonight despite the fact that I had a strong barrier up because I was going to be busy."

He sighed dramatically, spreading his hands in defeat. "Frankly, my darling, I don't know what you are or how to keep

70

you that way, so I fear you are right. Our only hope is to find the blood mage."

Lola had known that from the beginning, but the fact that Tristan had even suggested there might be another option still made her feel crushed that it hadn't panned out. That said, something else Tristan had said had caught her attention.

"What were you going to be busy with tonight?"

"You're not the only one having a crisis," Tristan informed her gleefully. "Alva's in a tizzy. The DFZ is dreaming."

"Dreaming?" Lola repeated since the word often meant something different when a fairy said it.

Tristan nodded. "Someone's been working great magic over the city since nightfall. It's no big trick to send a dream to a human, but this is unprecedented. Every sleeper in the city—Underground and Skyways—is having the same dream tonight."

"About what?"

"I don't know," Tristan said. "Not being human, I don't dream." He eyed her eagerly. "Have you—"

"Nope," Lola said, shaking her head. "I haven't been to sleep yet tonight. Even if I had, I don't think I'd see it. Fairy magic doesn't like me."

"More like you don't like it," Tristan corrected. "My barriers work perfectly; you just ignore them."

Lola could only shrug at that, and Tristan turned to look out his window. "I'm most curious to see what they're dreaming about," he said. "Fairy magic of this scale hasn't been seen since before the Drought. Alva's claiming credit, of course. She has to, or else she'll look a fool. But anyone who knows her knows she doesn't have the power to pull off anything close to this."

Lola's stomach began to sink. She did not like where this was going. "Do you think this new fairy could be the one who broke into Victor's?"

71

"Who knows?" Tristan said with a shrug. "But I agree the timing is suspicious. And potentially dangerous." His voice dropped suddenly, and Lola caught a hint of real intensity. "Magic this large requires a true fae ruler."

Like Morgan had been. But the True Queen was dead by Alva's hand, so who did that leave?

"Tricky question," Tristan said when she asked. "In the olden days, there were dozens of fairy courts, but the Drought took a heavy toll. Of all the rulers that survived, there are only two I'd count as true monarchs. My queen was one. The other is a disgraced king we no longer speak of."

Lola whistled. "What did he do?"

"Threatened us all," Tristan said, leaning back into the cushions. "Everyone enjoys a good hunt now and again, but this king was reckless. He killed so many humans, the whole world began to notice us. It had to stop, so Morgan sealed the king and his entire court inside his barrow."

"She did that for humanity?" Lola whispered, stunned.

"She did that for us," Tristan said. "Humans are fine, fat prey, but their ability to move magic makes them dangerous in large numbers. Steal one child, and nothing much happens. Ride through the sky murdering entire villages to feast on their fear, and you get a *very* strong reaction even in the age before mass media."

Lola could see that. "So where is this banished king now?"

"I'm not sure," Tristan said. "Morgan shoved him way out beyond where we normally build our barrows. It's not impossible that he's escaped, but I don't believe it. Trust me, Lola-lamb. If the king were back, we'd know. He's not a subtle hunter."

"Well, if he's not the one sending the dreams, who is?" Lola asked impatiently.

Tristan gave her a haughty look. "If I knew that, do you think we'd be sitting here?"

She rubbed her hands over her face with a groan. So much for getting an ID on the fairy intruder. She just hoped Simon was having better luck with his material link, because her plan looked like a wash.

"You keep looking, then, I guess," she said, rising to her feet. "I'm going to check on Simon's progress. Call me if you find something."

Tristan looked at her in surprise. "Leaving so soon?"

"Why not?" she asked. "You can't tell me who broke into Victor's, so what else is there?"

"The matter of my payment, for one," Tristan said, scooting to the edge of the couch.

Lola winced. She'd hoped he'd forgotten about that. "What do you want?"

"I think I'll let you dangle for now," he said with a cruel smile. "We'll discuss proper reimbursement once I actually find this fairy and see how much work it'll be to bring them down. At the moment, though, there's still the matter of the dream you promised for letting you in. It's been a long night, and I'm hungry."

"Fine," Lola snapped, sitting back down. "But I'm not doing any more dirty thoughts starring you."

"Desire is delicious," Tristan said. "But it also grows tiresome. We live in the DFZ. The very air is soaked with yearning and ambition, and I'm sick of it." He held out his arms. "Give me a happy dream, Lola-dove. A pure heart's desire, and your tab will be paid."

Lola eyed him warily, but she got up in the end, shuffling over to the couch to take a seat beside him. Tristan's arms wrapped around her at once, surrounding her whole body in the cold, wild-ocean feel of his gossamer. The sudden closeness was overwhelming, and Lola went stiff.

"Shh," Tristan whispered into her hair. "I won't hurt you. All I want is a dream. Just close your eyes and think of what you want most in all the world."

Lola nodded and squeezed her eyes tight, but it took a while to steady her thoughts. Tristan's power was heavy around her, and she felt trapped both by his arms and by the memory of the first time he'd eaten her dreams when she was sixteen. That time, she'd been a payment, a boon to mark the end of some debt between Tristan and her master.

It had been her first time meeting a real fairy. She'd been so nervous she could hardly look at him, though Tristan had been nothing but kind. He'd even told her she didn't have to give him a dream if she didn't want to, but Lola had been so terrified of Victor back then that she wouldn't leave until he ate one, and eventually, he had.

If she'd known then that letting a fairy eat one of your dreams meant they could find you forever, no matter where you went or what shape you took, Lola would have taken Tristan's out. To this day, she still didn't know what debt she'd been payment for or why Victor had agreed, knowing it meant her powers as a changeling would be compromised against Tristan forever. She *did* know that Tristan had never dealt with Victor again after that. He'd always kept in touch with her, though.

That thought made Lola smile, and she finally relaxed a little, letting her mind drift off, lulled by the gentle rhythm of Tristan's sea-scented gossamer.

The dream came on slowly. She saw herself in a cozy house somewhere in the woods where it rained enough to make everything green. It was her house, a real one made of wood and stone, not gossamer, and Victor had no idea where she was.

In this house, she wore a face that wasn't stolen. It didn't come from an ad or a movie. It was her face, hers alone, and it was

74

smiling as she sat in her chair by the rainy window with her hands resting on the plump cat that was sleeping in her lap.

Her sister's silver thread was still there in the dream, shining like white fire on her wrist, but it didn't vanish into the air like it did in real life. It ran down her legs instead, snaking over the colorful rugs and around the corner into her house's cozy kitchen, where someone was making dinner. No, not just someone. It was her sister, no longer stolen by the fairies but home and safe. They were two sisters with their own faces, free to live however they liked with no Victor or fairies or monsters.

Peace fell over her, thick and heavy as a down comforter. Lola sank deeper into the overstuffed chair, staring out the window at the rain as it dripped through the trees. When she reached for the mug of tea sitting on the little table beside her, her fingers bumped into a cool, masculine hand.

Lola jumped in surprise and turned to see Tristan sitting in the chair beside hers. His face was profoundly calm as he caught her fingers and gripped them hard, raising her stolen mug to his lips with his free hand. She was about to tell him to go make his own tea when the dream dissolved.

Lola's eyes shot open. She was back on the couch next to Tristan. There was no cabin, no tea, no rain, no sister, no face of her own. For a moment, the loss was more than she could bear. She closed her eyes again, raising her hand to head off the tears. It was silly to cry for something that had never even been, but it had felt so *real.*

"I'm sorry," Tristan whispered.

Lola shook her head and tried to move away, but the fairy's arms were still locked around her.

"A moment more, please," he begged, his voice ragged. "I always forget how powerful your dreams are."

"How do you mean?" she asked, relaxing back into him.

75

"I can't describe it," Tristan murmured into her hair. "I don't know if it's because you're a mix of fairy and human magic, but your dreams are..." He trailed off, searching for the right word. "Vivid," he said at last. "I could feel the peace of that place all the way to my core."

The room fell silent, and then Tristan's arms dropped, setting her free.

"Thank you," he said as Lola stood up. "I haven't felt peaceful like that for a long, long time."

Neither had Lola. Never, really. That felt too personal to admit to a fairy, though, so she just nodded, straightening her rumpled dress.

Tristan raked a hand through his hair with a deep sigh. Then his wry smile returned.

"Go home, Lola-cat," he told her, rising to his feet. "I'll keep fighting the good fight. You go home and get some sleep."

Lola gave him an incredulous look. "Sleep? *Now?* Weren't you listening to *anything* I told you?"

"What's happening out there doesn't have any bearing on what's needed in here," he said, tapping the side of her head. "Fairies don't sleep unless they're at death's door, but I could feel your tiredness just now as if it were my own. Think of it as reconnaissance on the dream magic if you have to, but if you keep pushing yourself like this, you're going to fall apart no matter how many pills you take."

Lola sighed. Tristan was never so irritating as when he was right. When she finally nodded, he snapped his fingers, and a white card appeared in her hand.

"You can reach me at this number if you need me," he said as Lola jumped in surprise. "I'll contact you when I know something."

"Got it," Lola said, sliding the card into her gossamer. "Thank you, Tristan."

He tutted at her. "That's a dangerous thing to say to a fairy. Did I teach you nothing?"

"Good night, then," she said instead. "Or is it morning now?"

Tristan shrugged. "Sure you won't eat something before you go?"

He gestured again at the banquet table, which was now laid out with a mouthwatering assortment of pastries, biscuits, and a large platter of bacon. The food looked so good, Lola actually took a step toward it before catching herself.

"Nice try."

Tristan smiled and waved the door open for her. "Drive safely."

He didn't have to say what he meant by that. Lola ducked her head and scuttled away, getting back to the elevator as quickly as possible now that she knew the hallway was a low road. The elevator door opened the second she hit the button, but as she settled back against the scuffed paneling to catch her breath, the tiredness she'd been putting off hit her hard.

Head swimming, Lola dug out her phone to check the time, groaning when she saw it was nearly five in the morning. No wonder Tristan could feel her exhaustion. She'd been up for more than twenty hours straight. Add in the loss of her gossamer and feeding Tristan a dream and it was a miracle she wasn't dead on her feet.

Too tired to shed the redheaded body as she stumbled into the parking deck, Lola summoned another motorcycle, a sleek little Honda electric this time, and started for home. Even at this hour, the DFZ was hopping, but Tristan's place wasn't that far from her apartment, so at least she didn't have to deal with the traffic for long. Better still, she didn't see so much as a glimmer of the Black Rider.

By the time she pulled into the little garage that made up the bottom floor of her one-bedroom townhome in New Mexicantown, Lola was nearly asleep on her handlebars. She dissolved her bike with a yawn and dragged herself up the stairs to her living room.

Buster was waiting when she got in. He was the same plump cat she'd been petting in her dream, only this was the real version, and he was meowing loudly for his now very late dinner. Lola fed him dutifully while she munched on some dry cereal from her cabinet. When she'd made a good cushion, she grabbed the pill bottle out of her pocket and popped a red tab into her mouth, following it up with a long slug of water. She was just putting the glass on the drying rack when she realized what she'd done.

She swore so loudly she made Buster jump. The cat looked at her accusingly before going back to his dinner/breakfast, but Lola was too upset at her own stupidity to care. After twenty years of taking a pill every time she went out in the morning and every time she came home at night, popping one now had been pure habit. But done was done. The pill was down, blood and all, and it was too late to get it back.

Calling herself every name she could think of, Lola took her bottle out again and carefully tapped two more pills onto the counter. She got a piece of Tupperware from her cabinet next and put the pills inside, sealing the lid tight before putting the container into the fridge. That would be her emergency supply, Lola decided. If today's fiascos were any indication, keeping all her pills in one place no longer seemed like a smart move, especially if she was going to be so dumb about it.

Feeling slightly better, Lola cut the lights and shifted her clothes to a soft tank top and pajama shorts. She brushed her teeth, used the bathroom, and had another huge glass of water before dragging herself to bed, wondering idly if she would get to see what kind of dream a fairy could cast over an entire city.

She didn't even get to finish the thought. The second her head hit the pillow, Lola was out. And while she did dream, the images were entirely her own, full of woods and water and two laughing girls tied together by a silver thread that could never be broken.

Chapter 5

10 pills

Lola woke to the sound of her nightstand buzzing. She reached out groggily, groping until her fingers touched the slick, cool, madly vibrating shape of her phone.

The call picked up automatically, and Simon's voice spoke tentatively through the speaker. "Lola?"

"Yeah?" she replied, shoving the phone somewhere near-ish her face.

"I finished the tracking spell."

Lola sat bolt upright, instantly awake. "*And?*"

"I couldn't find him."

Disappointment hit her like a truck. "What happened?" she cried. "You said my pill could find him anywhere in the world!"

"It should have," Simon said, speaking very quickly now. "I don't know what went wrong. There's no reason my spell shouldn't have found him."

"What if he was in a barrow?" Lola asked. "Tristan couldn't give me a lead, but he did say there's some weird fairy mojo going on. Maybe—"

"That doesn't matter," Simon insisted. "Blood is the strongest material link there is. Victor could be in a barrow or dead or on another plane entirely, and that spell still should have pointed the way." He sighed so hard, Lola could almost hear him rubbing his forehead in frustration. "The only explanation I can think of is that Victor doesn't want to be found."

"Why would he hide from us?" she demanded. "He owns us!"

"It's the only thing that makes sense. The only power strong enough to block a blood material link would be the blood mage

80

that it came from."

"What about whoever took him?" Lola asked. "Anyone who could get the better of Victor has to be super strong, right? Maybe they're hiding him somewhere even blood can't reach."

"Maybe," Simon said, but Lola could tell he didn't believe it.

"We're not out of options yet," he said firmly. "Jamie's been on the phone all night, convincing Victor's enemies that nothing is wrong. It won't last forever, but she's bought us some time. I've been using it to explore other options since the spell failed, and I've found something I think you should see. Can you come to my place?"

Lola glanced at her clock and groaned. It was almost noon. "Sure," she said, hauling herself out of bed. "I didn't mean to sleep this late. Let me shower and grab some breakfast, and I'll be right over."

"Great. I'll see you soon."

Lola ended the call and tossed the phone onto her bed before heading to the bathroom. She showered quickly and wrapped herself in a towel. A real one, because gossamer didn't absorb water at all.

When she was dry, she stepped in front of the mirror and took stock. The gossamer she'd cut off from her Mustang was still missing, but the rest of her was looking reasonably together. That was good, since taking her usual morning pill wasn't an option. But while she really should have been conserving her energy, she wasn't willing to stay in the redheaded body.

She'd left it on last night because she'd been too tired to change. Now, though, Lola shoved the hated shape away. She darkened the paper-thin, porcelain skin and replaced the red-blond hair with thick black waves, strong and shiny. Leaning into her mirror, she redid her face completely, throwing away the striking doll features for the ambiguous beauty of her favorite

81

yogurt lady.

When she was finished, the woman in the mirror could have been anywhere in her late twenties or early thirties and any race from Latina to Filipina to mixed-blooded American Indian. Grinning at the familiar face, Lola pulled her thick black hair into a ponytail and walked into the living room to pick out her clothes for the day.

She had the world to choose from. Life as Victor's monster didn't leave much room for pleasure, but other than the specific bodies he demanded for jobs—like the leggy model he always made her put on whenever she visited Frank—her master didn't care what she wore. That left a lot to play around with, especially when you could create anything you wanted from a picture.

It was one of the few things she actually got to enjoy about being a changeling, so Lola had gone big. Every wall in her living room was covered with pictures of whatever fashions she was feeling at the moment. Advertisements, catalogs, fashion magazines, snapshots she'd taken covertly of people she'd seen on the street, it all went into her collage. She even had a stretch of wall dedicated entirely to faces, including the ad her yogurt lady had come from.

There was enough in here to redo her entire body from tip to toes. *That* would throw off the Black Rider if he came looking for her again. That said, supporting bodies she wasn't familiar with was hard on her magic, and it was broad daylight right now. The Rider had a lot of stories, but they all agreed he only hunted at night, so Lola decided to keep it simple for her gossamer's sake, going with a pair of vintage jeans and an oversized novelty Halloween sweatshirt decorated all over with happy cartoon candy corns.

A pair of bright red boots and big sunglasses finished off the look. Not that anyone who lived in the Underground actually

82

needed sunnies, but dark lenses freed her from the burden of eye contact, so Lola propped them on and walked over to say goodbye to her cat.

As usual, Buster was sleeping on the back of her couch. He looked up when Lola came over, butting his soft head against her hand. She gave him several hard pets, promising up and down that dinner would not be late tonight. When he was purring up a storm, she left him to his nap and went to the fridge to make sure her emergency stash was still there.

It was, of course. She checked her pill bottle next, but everything was right where she'd left it. Shaking her head, she tucked the worrisomely light-feeling bottle into her pocket, switched off the lights, and headed for the garage, checking her phone on the way to make sure the ever-shifting DFZ hadn't moved Simon's house since the last time she'd visited.

She'd already dissolved her bike from last night, so the garage was empty except for the huge spread of car reference photos she'd taped onto the walls. According to the latest DFZ map, Simon's house was still about fifteen minutes away, so Lola spun herself an Algonquin Corp electric two-door in neon blue. The color was flashier than was probably wise, but Lola felt the need for some brightness today, and the cheap little coupes were everywhere in the city. They were also the only cars small enough not to strain her diminished magic.

When her ride finished coming together, Lola spun herself a garage door opener and dropped into the driver's seat. The little car purred to life as the garage door rolled open, letting in the grayish glow that was as close to daylight as the Underground got. She'd just cleared her neighbor's trashcans and was about to start the three-point-turn needed to actually get her car pointed the right direction in the narrow alley when she saw the Black Rider.

He was sitting on his bike not ten feet away, watching her

apartment from the shadow of a parked truck. Lola stomped on the brakes when she saw him, jerking her car to a stop. For three deep breaths, they stared at each other. Then Lola hit the gas, turning her three-point-turn into a wall-scraping arc as she gunned her coupe down the alley. The Black Rider followed a second later, his bike making no sound at all as he tore after her.

Lola drove as fast as she could without crashing, cursing the charmingly narrow streets and quaint hairpin turns she usually loved about her neighborhood. She cursed the Rider, too, while she was at it. Who did he think he was, making her already-difficult life more dangerous? And how was he stalking her *now*? Not that much light got down here, but according to his own legends, the Black Rider should only be active at night.

Clearly, no one had told him that. The specter behind her looked plenty solid, his black helmet flashing beneath the always-on streetlights in her rearview mirror. Furious, Lola pushed her gossamer faster, drawing angry yells from her neighbors as she shot down the residential street.

The attention tore at her, as always, but Lola didn't let up. Unlike their chase last night, this was the Underground. There were no cops to worry about down here, and she knew all the roads, which made this her best opportunity to lose him.

But while the Black Rider's bike was better at handling the sharp turns than her tiny coupe, he didn't try to get up next to her window like he had last night. Instead, he stuck to her tail, following so close that Lola could look straight into his visor through her rearview mirror.

In a flash of inspiration, Lola slammed on her brakes. The coupe's tires squealed as she skidded to a stop, and then the whole car shuddered with a satisfactory *crunch* as the Black Rider slammed into her rear bumper. The back wheel of his bike flipped up, throwing the Rider over the top of her car. The low roof

84

dented above her head when he hit, and then he rolled down her windshield and across her hood to fall sprawling onto the street.

Lola sat glued to her seat, gossamer fluttering like a terrified bird. A few feet ahead, the Black Rider lay still on the asphalt. For an insane moment, Lola had the overwhelming urge to get out and see if he was okay. Then the Rider's body jerked, and he started pushing himself back up.

She stomped on the gas, forcing the Rider to curl into a ball as her car flew over his head. She left him in her dust, grinning at his shrinking figure in the mirror, but her triumph was short-lived. In her eagerness to put distance between them, Lola hadn't noticed the blind intersection ahead of her or the garbage truck that was coming the other way.

One second after she blew through the intersection, the garbage truck T-boned her. Her blue coupe vanished as her gossamer shattered, and for one horrible moment, Lola shattered too. She swore she could feel her body breaking into a billion droplets only to slam back together when she hit the ground.

There was no gossamer blanket to shield her this time. She hit the pavement hard, tumbling who knew how many times before rolling to a stop against the curb a dozen feet down the street. But while her outside had stopped moving, her insides were another story.

The crash would have been hard even when she was at her best. With everything Lola's gossamer had been through recently, it was almost her end. Her magic was wobbling like warm jelly, making her terrified that she was about to trickle down the storm drain. The only thing that still had solid shape was the silver thread around her wrist, so that was what Lola grabbed, clinging to her sister as she willed her body to stay together.

It did so by the barest fraction. She could feel her human shape twisting and warping as she crammed her pieces back together.

85

Utter and complete silence rang in her ears as Lola raised a hand to check her face, but the thing that came up wasn't a hand. It was a claw. A huge, monstrous, fur-covered—

Panic, raw and primal, shot through her at the sight. *No*, Lola commanded, squeezing her eyes tight. Not yet. Not here. Not now. Not *ever*.

But her body wasn't listening, and the men who'd hit her were getting out of their truck. If they saw her like this, it was over, so Lola made a decision.

Closing her eyes tight so she wouldn't have to see the claw that had been her hand, she dug into the mess of her gossamer and pulled out her pills. Like everything else, the orange plastic bottle had been crushed by the impact, but her pills were still inside, whole and unbroken.

She pried off the warped lid and shook one into her mouth, careful not to let it hit any of her teeth, which were now the size of golf tees. The pill hit her tongue like a splash of fresh blood. The magic her master had poured over her all those years ago surged in reply, crushing her back into shape so hard, it made her ears ring.

Lola didn't care. She nearly wept with relief as the monster's claws and teeth retracted. Her body was still a wreck from its tumble across the pavement, but even that pain felt sweet, because it was human. *She* was human again, and Lola hugged herself hard as the roar of the world came rushing back.

As always, her pills were her first concern. The plastic bottle had been crushed nearly flat, but it was still in one piece. Lola counted her pills twice to make sure they were all still there before cramming the broken lid back on and shoving the bottle deep into her gossamer. Satisfied that the most important matter was taken care of, she looked around for her car before remembering it was gone. All of her gossamer had shattered when she'd been hit, which meant…

Lola went still as the full brunt of what she'd done finally hit her. She'd vanished her car in broad daylight. Vanished it in the middle of the street without considering who was watching or what they might—

"What the hell?"

Lola stiffened as the disbelieving words crashed into her. Half a block away, two men were standing in front of the garbage truck she'd crashed into. The first was already gawking at her, his eyes jumping all over her body, which was leaking rainbow gossamer before Lola changed it to look like red blood. She'd just hoped to keep him from seeing what she really was, but the lie came with its own consequences, because now that she was bleeding profusely all over the pavement, the man went from gawking to running straight toward her.

"Call an ambulance!" he shouted to his partner. "She's bleeding bad!"

"Where's the car?" the driver shouted back, turning in a circle on the empty street. "I *know* I hit a blue car!"

"Forget the car!" the first man hollered as he dropped to his knees at Lola's side. "We gotta get her to a hospital!"

Any other time, Lola would have been touched by his concern. Right now, though, all she wanted was for the man to stop caring and go away. His scrutiny was already turning her barely reconstructed gossamer back to jelly as he searched her body for the wound that was leaking all that blood. A wound Lola didn't have because she wasn't actually human. To make things even worse, his partner was still looking for her car, and every second he didn't find it, Lola could feel his disbelief building.

This was really, *really* bad. The confusion of the accident had bought her some time, but the combination of disbelief and scrutiny was rapidly undoing the pill she'd just taken. If she didn't think of something fast, the human part of her would melt away completely, leaving nothing to hold the monster back.

But then, just as Lola's own panic started to eat at the tiny bit of control she'd managed to regain, the driver searching for her car stumbled as if he'd been hit over the head with an invisible barrel. Seconds later, the man trying to put pressure on the wound Lola didn't have grunted and slumped over. An invisible force caught him as he fell, laying him gently on the street at the Black Rider's feet.

Lola stared in terrified wonder. The Black Rider was practically on top of her, so close that she could see her own messed-up face reflected in his visor. The sight scared her more than the Rider did. No wonder the man had been so frantic. She looked horrifying, barely human at all.

She curled into a ball with a moan, covering her face to hide the ugly truth, which was why she didn't see the Black Rider reaching down to smack her on the head with his black-gloved palm. The blow landed with surprising gentleness, and then everything went black, dropping Lola into a deep, dreamless sleep.

~~~

After that, Lola didn't expect to wake up again. When she did, it was with a start, hands flying instinctively to her face, but there was no need. She was human and stable again, her gossamer settled back into the yogurt lady she'd put on this morning. Her outfit was pretty messed up, the clothes scrambled all over from how she'd come apart, but her body felt solid, and her pills were still in her pocket, which was what mattered.

Satisfied that the crisis was over, at least for the moment, Lola turned her attention to her surroundings.

She was in a living room. It was much smaller than hers and even more raggedly furnished. The couch she was lying on was an ugly, sea-foam-green monstrosity with squishy, worn cushions that bled yellow foam. The windows had heavy, dusty curtains pulled over them, but she could hear the sound of cars speeding by very close, as if there was a highway right on the other side of the wall.

They must have been near something industrial, because the room was scorching hot. There was a battered wooden door in the wall beside the couch and another metal one set at the end of the tiny hall beside a dark nook that might have been a kitchen. It was hard to tell with the overhead light off and the thick curtains blocking what little brightness the windows might have let in, leaving the room very dim. Though not dim enough to hide the figure in the corner.

The Black Rider was leaning against the far wall. Despite the suffocating heat, he was still wearing his full motorcycle suit, complete with leather gloves, black boots, and helmet. Lola shrank into the couch as she caught sight of herself reflected in his glossy black visor, but it wasn't nearly as bad this time. Obviously, being trapped in a hellishly hot room with a murderous urban legend was not ideal, but at least her face looked human again, which gave Lola the courage to ask.

"What do you want with me?"

The Black Rider didn't answer. He just stood there, watching her, completely silent. This went on for a creepily long time, but Lola figured if he meant to kill, eat, dismember, or whatever else his stories said he did to the people he caught, he would have done it already. There must be a reason he'd gone through so much trouble to bring her here alive, and Lola was determined to figure out what that was, if only to spare herself the disaster of another car chase.

"I'm not going to run," she said, holding her hands up in surrender. "I just want to know why you've been chasing me."

She paused, waiting for the Black Rider to respond, but he didn't say a word. He did, however, push off the wall and walk toward her. Lola stiffened as he approached, but the Black Rider didn't come all the way to the couch. Instead, he grabbed a folding chair that was lying on the threadbare carpet. He opened it with a shake and flipped it around, sitting down backward with his arms folded across the metal backrest and his inscrutable helmet still fixed on her.

Lola swallowed. She hadn't realized until he sat down just how *big* the Black Rider was. Even hunched over four feet away, his presence filled the small room. Lola could feel her panic rising again as the feeling of being trapped came rushing back. The surge was too much for her battered gossamer to handle. If she was going to stay together, she needed a moment away.

"I'm sorry," she said, staying very still. "Do you have a bathroom I could use?"

To her great surprise, the Black Rider nodded and pointed at the wooden door behind the couch. Moving slowly as she would to avoid provoking a wild animal, Lola rose from her seat and walked to the door he'd indicated, turning the cheap metal knob with a loud *click*.

The room on the other side was even darker than the living room. Lola reached out on instinct, her hand falling easily to the light switch. When the light flickered on, she saw that she was in a bedroom.

More accurately, it was a room with a bed. There was no frame or sheets, just a bare mattress lying on the floor in its original factory plastic, clearly never used. Aside from this, the room was completely empty, but at least that meant the bathroom was easy to find. It was directly to her left, door wide open.

Lola went inside, switching on the light as she did. After the weirdly empty bedroom, she was braced for something creepy, but the tiny bathroom was shockingly normal. There was soap in the shower and cheap towels on the rack above the toilet. The sink counter was scattered with the usual single-man arsenal of shaving cream, razors, a worn toothbrush, and floss.

It wasn't particularly clean, but it wasn't filthy, either. It was just a bathroom, like any other, save for one important difference. The mirror above the sink was missing, leaving ragged holes in the drywall where the screws had been ripped out.

Lola frowned, poking the damage with her fingers. Why would the Black Rider take down a mirror? Were mirrors his weakness?

It was possible, she supposed, but it didn't feel right. Humans ascribed all sorts of powers to mirrors, which meant pseudo-spirits like the Rider should have loved them. The more she thought about it, though, the more she wondered if her initial assumption about the Black Rider had been wrong. He was obviously magical, but so far as Lola knew, urban legends didn't have apartments. They were constructs given life by humanity's collective imagination, appearing and disappearing as their stories commanded. They didn't need toothbrushes or showers, and they certainly didn't have dirty laundry, which the Black Rider did, judging by the hamper in the corner. Of course, this was assuming this actually *was* the Black Rider's apartment and not the abandoned home of some poor man he'd taken as his prey.

Shivering, Lola forced that thought from her mind and focused on getting herself together. She used the restroom and washed the street grime off her skin in the sink. Then, focusing her magic, she wove a mirror of her own and set it on the counter to check her face. When she was confident nothing was out of place, she reached into her gossamer for her pills.

The bottle was more cracked than she remembered, but they were all still in there. Counting the two she'd left as backup in her fridge, she had nine left.

That was a terrifyingly low number, but seeing as she'd just taken one, Lola was hopeful she wouldn't need another until tomorrow, provided she didn't have any more disasters. That was a bold assumption given recent events, but Lola tried to stay optimistic as she tucked the cracked bottle back into her gossamer.

She checked her phone next. Like everything else, the screen had shattered when she'd hit the pavement, but the AR interface still seemed to be working. That would do for now, so Lola shoved it back into her gossamer and moved on to her clothes.

As she'd noticed earlier, they'd been warped by her collapse, with scraps of denim from her pants covering her shoulders and bits of red leather from her boots running across her sleeves. The whole thing was a mess, so Lola started over, recreating her outfit as best she could from memory.

The jeans weren't quite as stylish this time, and the happy candy corns on her sweatshirt weren't as adorably unique without the photo reference, but it got the job done. She didn't bother with the sunglasses or cute boots, opting for a pair of comfortable sneakers instead. You never knew when you were going to have to run.

In fresh clothes, with the horror of the crash no longer splattered across her body, Lola felt worlds better. She checked herself in her mirror one last time, briefly considering switching out her yogurt-lady face for something prettier. Beauty was a good defense against most things, but the Black Rider had already seen her monster peeking out after the crash. He'd know any beauty she put on now was just another mask, so Lola left her face the way it was. She vanished her mirror and took a deep breath. Then, wrapping what little gossamer she had left around her like a suit of armor, she marched out of the bathroom to face the enemy.

The Black Rider's chair was empty when she got back to the

living room. She stopped at once, looking around warily until she heard the soft sound of a cabinet shutting in the dark kitchen. The Black Rider came out a second later, carrying a bowl, an unopened half gallon of milk, and a brightly colored bag of off-brand sugar-frosted cereal. He set all of these, along with a spoon, down on the folding card table that was now deployed in front of the couch and returned to his chair in the center of the room, his helmet turning toward her expectantly as he sat down.

Lola looked at him, then at the breakfast setup, then back again. "Is that for me?"

The Black Rider nodded.

Biting her lip, Lola slid herself between the card table and the couch and sat down. This was all getting a little too weird. Being trapped in an apartment with the Black Rider was one thing, but Lola didn't know if her brain could handle him feeding her breakfast like she was a kid come over to watch cartoons.

But while part of her was worrying like mad over all the implications, the rest of her was fixated on the cereal. She hadn't had any food yet today, and she'd been pushing her gossamer hard. Victor always said that she ate sugar like normal fairies ate dreams. Lola didn't know if that was strictly true, but she wasn't about to turn a big bowlful down now.

Throwing caution to the wind, Lola poured herself a healthy helping of sugary flakes, soaked them in milk, and dug in. She ate two bowls in rapid succession while the Black Rider watched silently from his chair.

"Thanks," she said when she'd drained the milk from her second bowl. "For the food, and for saving me, and—"

Her voice dropped off. He had saved her, hadn't he? If he hadn't done… whatever he'd done to the men in the garbage truck, she'd be the monster right now. Of course, she wouldn't have been in that mess at all if he hadn't been waiting outside her apartment like a stalker.

"Why are you chasing me?" Lola asked crisply, crossing her arms over her chest.

The Black Rider unzipped the chest pocket of his motorcycle suit and pulled out a hand-sized memo pad and a golf pencil. Turning his chair around and scooting it closer to the card table, he plopped the tiny notebook down and began to write, leaning low over the page like a kid doing his homework. This put him closer to Lola than ever, and she backed away, squeezing herself deep into the squishy couch cushions, but he made no other moves. He just sat there writing, reading his words over to make sure they were right before turning the pad toward Lola.

Do you know where Victor is?

Lola froze, mind racing as she stared at the huge man across the flimsy table. If the Black Rider had something to do with Victor's disappearance, this could be a trap. If he didn't, it was *definitely* a trap to get her to give something away. Or maybe it was something else entirely? Victor did sell miracles. Maybe the Black Rider needed one, and this whole thing was just bad timing.

The silence stretched on and on as Lola scrambled to think of how to address the Rider's question without giving too much away. In the end, she settled for asking a question of her own.

"How do you know about Victor?"

The Black Rider turned the pad back around but hesitated before he wrote, tapping the little pencil against his helmet. Finally, he wrote a line and pushed the paper back toward her.

I work for him.

"You're lying," Lola said instantly. "I know everyone who works for Victor." She'd helped draw most of them in.

Instead of writing his response, the Black Rider reached into another pocket and drew out a cell phone. Not an AR-enabled smartphone like Lola's, but one of those cheap disposable flip units

94

with the big buttons. He tapped it a few times before holding it out, gesturing for her to take it.

Stomach sinking, Lola did as he wanted, pinching the phone gingerly between her fingers like she would a dead rat as she turned it around to see what she was dreading. There, glowing big and bright across the tiny screen, was Victor's thirteen-digit number, the one only those who belonged to him could remember, write, or dial. It was the same number she'd used to prove her own identity to Jamie, which meant...

"You're not an urban legend, are you?" Lola said, careful not to touch his leather-clad fingers as she handed the phone back.

The Black Rider shook his head.

That should have made her feel better. At least now she knew his actions weren't bound by all those horrible stories, but his silent head shake made Lola more uneasy than ever. An urban legend was terrifying, but at least it was something she understood. The man sitting across the table was now a complete enigma, and that made him more dangerous than anything.

"What are you?"

The Black Rider shook his head and pointed at the second sentence on his note pad, the one that said he worked for Victor.

"Right," Lola muttered, getting the hint. "And since I'm here, I'm guessing you already know what I am?"

The Black Rider nodded and wrote again on his pad.

I have to find Victor.

"That makes two of us, buddy," Lola said, digging the heels of her hands into her eye sockets as she tried to decide what to do next. She no longer doubted the Rider's word. Honestly, it had been stupid to assume she knew everyone who worked for her master. The only person who knew the whole of Victor's game was Victor.

"Okay," she said at last. "I believe you work for him, but I don't know where Victor is."

But you're working on finding him? the Rider wrote.

"I'm trying," Lola said. "You're sort of interrupting the process." She stopped. "Wait, if you work for Victor, why did you stalk me like that? Why didn't you just pass me a note or something?"

The Black Rider hesitated, tiny pencil gripped awkwardly between his big, gloved fingers.

I tried to, he wrote eventually. But you ran away.

"So why did you chase me? You scared me half to death!"

I wasn't trying to.

"What was I supposed to think?" she cried, suddenly furious. "You were waiting for me outside my house! Do you know what you look like?"

The Black Rider threw down his pencil and leaned back in his chair, arms crossed over his massive chest. The hot room grew cold as he did so, the temperature dropping to frosty in an instant, like someone had opened a freezer. The arctic blast shocked Lola out of her anger, and she slumped back into the ratty sofa, covering her face with her hands.

Eventually, the cold faded, and she looked up to see the Black Rider writing again. He pushed the notebook toward her when he'd finished. The words were smaller than the other lines he'd written, and Lola had to pick the pad up to read it.

I'm sorry I scared you. I would have contacted you a different way if I'd known how. Victor doesn't like the other parts of his business to know about me. I'm technically breaking my oaths right now just by talking to you, but I didn't know any other way to find him.

The next part had been crossed out so many times, Lola couldn't possibly read it. The text picked up again several lines below, the strokes firm and bold against the crinkled page.

I can't do this on my own. I need your help.

Lola glanced up. The Rider was sitting hunched in his chair. He was perfectly still with both hands on the table as if he was deliberately keeping them where she could see them. He was clearly trying not to scare her, but his posture looked tense, like a coiled spring. He was scared too, she realized with a start.

With that thought, Lola looked at the Rider again. He was still huge and scary and definitely dangerous, but he no longer looked like a monster. At least, no more of a monster than she was.

"All right," she said, putting the notepad back down on the table between them. "What do you know about Victor's disappearance?"

The Black Rider grabbed the notebook and started writing again. Lola scooted forward on the couch, lowering her head over his hand to read the words as they appeared.

Victor and I are connected. I felt him vanish right before I got the message from his security system. I can still feel our connection, so I know he's not dead, but I can't locate him. I usually know exactly where he is at all times, but not anymore. It's like he fell off the face of the Earth.

Lola bit her lip. When he'd first written that he and Victor were connected, she'd wanted to tell him they were all like that, but now she was glad she'd held her tongue. The kind of connection the Rider described seemed to be on a whole different level than the one Lola shared with their master. She'd only known something was wrong because of the alarm, which jumped her mind back to the second time she'd seen the Rider that day, when he'd blown past her coming out of Victor's neighborhood.

"You went to his house," she said, face splitting into a smile as the mystery came together. "That's why you were in University Heights that night! You were answering the alarm, too."

He nodded, and she scooted closer. "Did you find anything?"

Nothing, the Rider wrote. The workroom was destroyed, but nothing else was touched. I couldn't find any sign of the enemy or Victor's location, so I left.

"You didn't wait for anyone else to arrive?"

The Black Rider stiffened and pointed at the paragraph he'd written farther up, tapping the line that said *Victor doesn't like the other parts of his business to know about me.*

"Right," Lola muttered, scrubbing a hand through the yogurt lady's thick hair. "I guess we need to—"

She cut off with a jump as both of their phones went off at the same time.

Lola fished hers out of her pocket, turning on the AR since the screen was busted, to see a new message from Victor's security system. Just like last night, there was no explanation, only the highest-level emergency code. Across from her, the Black Rider was staring at his own phone, and Lola could see the exact same message reflected in his black visor.

And just like that, the Black Rider's position as an ally was cemented in Lola's mind. Neither Simon nor Jamie had gotten the alarm text, but the Rider had, which meant whatever the man in front of her was, Victor trusted him completely. *Owned* him completely, just as he owned Lola, which was all she needed to know.

"Come on," she said, hopping off the couch. "Let's go check it out. Maybe the villain has returned to the scene of the crime."

The Black Rider looked up so quickly she could almost feel his surprise. The hesitation lasted less than a second before he shot to his feet as well, marching toward the metal door that led outside.

The Rider's apartment turned out to be on the fifth floor of a walk-up building tucked underneath the highway. The moment he opened the door, the roar of the cars got so loud, Lola couldn't hear anything else. It was midafternoon, and the building was deserted. The Black Rider passed her on the stairs and beat her to the parking lot. As soon as he hit the ground, he snapped his fingers. The snap was surprisingly loud considering he was wearing thick driving gloves, and as soon as it finished, a black motorcycle appeared out of thin air.

Lola jumped with a squeak. It was as if the cycle had condensed out of the shadows under the stairs, warping the light around it as the Black Rider hopped on. From the way the frame was shaking, Lola knew the bike was running, but she couldn't hear a thing. The machine was silent as a ghost, its blue light flickering like a haunted candle.

The Black Rider settled onto the seat and motioned at her, but it took a few tries before Lola realized he was telling her to get on. Once she figured it out, Lola put her foot down. Working with the Rider was one thing, but riding on his freaky ghost cycle while everyone stared and took pictures was a bridge too far.

"No way," she said, sending out her gossamer. "I'm driving."

The Black Rider crossed his arms. If he had anything close to a human face behind that black visor, Lola was sure it was set in an exasperated scowl, but she didn't care. Her gossamer was already condensing into the blue coupe from that morning. She opened the driver's door as soon as it finished, fixing her eyes on the Rider as she pointed at the passenger side.

"Get in."

The Black Rider shook his head, but Lola held her ground. "You might be indestructible, but I'm not. There is no way I'm getting on that death trap with the way you drive, and I can't have you riding next to me, drawing attention. This is the simplest solution for both of us. Now get in. We're wasting time."

The Rider held out for a few more seconds. Then his silent motorcycle vanished as suddenly as it had appeared, dropping his boots neatly to the ground. He stomped over to the passenger door

99

and climbed inside, cramming his large body into the coupe's tiny interior.

"That helmet's going to draw attention in a car," Lola said as she dropped into the driver's seat. "I don't suppose it comes off?"

The Rider turned his helmet to give her a look so cutting, she felt it right through his visor.

"Didn't think so," she said, cranking the car with a sigh. That helmet really was going to be a problem. She thought about it for a moment then reached out and tapped the coupe's windows, tinting the glass as dark as it could go without actually being opaque.

"There," she said proudly when she'd finished. "That should keep out prying eyes. Now how do I get to the highway?"

The Black Rider pointed at the tiny street that dead-ended into the apartment building's parking lot. Lola nodded and tapped the gas, pulling them out toward the already worsening traffic.

Chapter 6
9 pills

Lola didn't bother talking to the Rider during the drive. She wasn't sure if whatever was behind that helmet was incapable of speech or if his muteness was a choice, but there was no way she could read his notes while battling rush-hour traffic. They drove the whole way in silence, pulling into the tiny driveway of Victor's false-front tiny house just as the setting sun was starting to blast right into Lola's eyes.

The Black Rider got out first, uncoiling like a spring the moment the car stopped moving. Lola got out more slowly, ears straining for a hint of whatever had triggered the alarm this time, but all she heard were the soft, domestic noises of people coming home to their families. Glancing nervously over her shoulder at the kids riding their bikes down Victor's street, several of whom had already stopped to gawk at the man in the motorcycle helmet, Lola stuck her hand behind her back and conjured a canvas car cover.

Grinning at her own cleverness, she threw the cover over the coupe. The moment the car was hidden from view, she took back her gossamer, leaving the cover standing like an empty tent. She'd be in trouble if anyone peeked underneath, but she no longer had magic to waste on cars she wasn't actively driving, and she had a feeling she was going to need all the power she could get.

The Black Rider was already striding through Victor's gate, his huge shape vanishing slightly too quickly behind the overgrown bushes on the other side. Patting her fake car one last time to make sure the empty cover wouldn't collapse if someone bumped into it, Lola followed suit, scuttling down the cement path into their master's secret world.

If she hadn't already believed the Rider worked for Victor, the fact that he was able to walk through the layers of wards and protections as easily as Lola did would have sealed the deal. He was already waiting in the emerald clearing when she came out, his black helmet tilted up as if he was searching the sky.

Lola stopped as well, ears straining. But other than the fact that it was sunny afternoon now instead of moonlit night, the impossibly beautiful valley didn't look any different than it had yesterday. She was about to suggest it was a false alarm when she noticed the Rider still hadn't moved.

"What's wrong?" she asked, falling into a defensive crouch. "Do you hear something?"

The Rider shook his helmet and started toward the house, clearing the big stone steps through the jade forest two at a time. Lola followed suit, lengthening her legs until she looked like an Olympic sprinter to match the Rider's pace up the familiar stairs. Here as well, though, everything looked normal—or at least as normal as Victor's tiger-infested jade forest ever looked—but the nightingales had stopped singing.

Lola shrank her legs back to normal and moved closer to the Rider. The nightingales were one of Victor's secret tells. They never sang for outsiders, so if they were quiet, something was here. Lola strained her ears in the silence, trying to hear what it was, but all she caught was the musical clacking of the forest.

She glanced nervously at the Rider, but he was still marching forward. Lola ran after him, keeping as close to his shadow as she dared as they left the forest and started down the path through the field of thorny roses toward Victor's castle-like house. The Rider stopped twenty feet from the giant front doors, which were still hanging open from where Lola had gone through yesterday. She was about to whisper-ask if he'd spotted anything when he swung

102

his arm forward.

The sudden motion made her jump. From Lola's perspective, it looked as if the Black Rider had just pitched an invisible softball underhanded. A second after his arm fully extended, though, the towering doors of Victor's workshop exploded like someone had thrown a car through them.

Lola ducked as chunks of wood flew everywhere, but none of it hit her. There was something invisible, some force between them and the explosion that bounced the shrapnel like a plastic dome. Good thing, too, because not five seconds later, a smoking glob of green slime smacked into the invisible shield right in front of them.

Lola jumped when it hit, arms coming up instinctively to protect her face even though she'd already seen the goo hit the invisible shield. She lowered them just in time to see something lumbering behind the destroyed doors, and her gossamer began to crawl.

It was a troll. The actual shape was hard to make out in the darkness of Victor's destroyed workshop, but there was nothing else she knew of that looked that hideous. Its scent must have been contained by the doors, because now that the Rider had blown them off, Lola could smell the telltale reek of bog and rotted meat so strongly, it made her gag.

The troll stepped through the destroyed doorway as she watched, lumbering out to face them now that its cover was blown. As it moved into the warm evening sunlight, Lola got her first good look at its mossy, knobbled hide. The thing looked like a pile of dirty rocks with a spider's face, giant tusks, and four arms tipped with curving black claws, one of which was wiping a line of seaweed-green goo from its mouth.

The horrific sight—and the smell it produced—made her step back. She'd never seen a troll in action before. They were ancient monsters brought over by the fairies from their own realm. Trolls and their smaller goblin cousins had been popular as guards back in the old days when everyone just accepted that monsters were real. Now that humanity had gone through the Enlightenment, times were tougher. Even in the DFZ where dragons blocking traffic were a regular complaint, people still expected the stuff they saw to make rational sense.

Trolls had never done that. Like Lola, they were made of gossamer and thus were subject to the tyranny of belief. Unlike her, though, they couldn't change their shape to meet expectations. A troll might be strong enough to derail a bullet train, but set it against a group of hikers who didn't believe trolls had ever existed, and it melted into something closer to a bullfrog.

That would have been a handy trick right now. Unfortunately, Lola very much believed in trolls, and this one was enormous. She hadn't realized just how big it was until it cleared the wreckage of the doorway and got outside where it could straighten up.

The stupid thing had to be twenty feet tall. It roared when it got free, spraying another jet of stinking green spittle across the rose beds. Lola ducked as the steaming goo splattered over whatever craziness the Black Rider was using to shield them. That turned out to be the right move, because as soon as the last glob of acidic phlegm landed, the barrier vanished, and the Rider attacked.

She didn't even see him move. One moment, he was standing in front of her; the next, he was standing on the troll's gnarled shoulder with his arm flying down as if he meant to karate chop it. Whatever hit the troll when the blow struck, though, it wasn't the Rider's hand. Lola could actually see the outline of the impact on the troll's knobby flesh. It was an enormous wedged shape like an invisible ax the size of a fridge.

A sickening *crack* echoed across the quiet gardens, and the troll screamed as the Rider's wedge chopped clean through its shoulder

104

joint, dropping its arm like a felled tree. Its black blood sprayed out in an arc, forcing Lola to jump back now that the barrier was gone. Like a true monster, though, the loss of its arm only slowed the troll for a moment. Not five seconds later, it was back on the attack, reaching up with its remaining three arms to crush the Rider like a bug.

He dodged the huge claws easily, running across the troll's cliff-like shoulders nimbly as a squirrel to take a crack at its armored neck. Lola watched him go with growing amazement. No wonder Victor kept the Rider secret. Anyone who could take a troll head-on was worth keeping in your pocket. She was wondering what horrible magic their master had done to get something as powerful as the Rider on his leash when she heard snickering behind her.

She tore her eyes off the fight and whirled around to see two goblins coming out of the jade forest. They were the color of cooked spinach, smooth and glossy as frogs. The taller of the two only came up to Lola's elbow, but the gleaming teeth they flashed were the size of steak knives. They snickered at her one last time before jumping for her throat.

In all her years as Victor's monster, Lola had never had to worry much about fighting. Frank and his stupid gun notwithstanding, her jobs mostly involved making people cry as she ripped their lives apart at Victor's behest. The nonemotional violence got assigned to other members of her master's circus, which meant Lola had little experience with actual combat. What she *was* good at, though, was improvising. One second, the goblins were leaping at her; the next, they were crushed under a delivery van filled with cement.

The whole garden shook as the van crashed into the flagstone path. Lola rocked on her feet, her body reeling from the effort of throwing so much gossamer at once. Below the van's crumpled door, she saw one of the goblin's long, five-jointed fingers give a final twitch, and then their gossamer melted, leaving the sour taste of Alva's magic hanging thick in the air.

Lola grimaced as she pulled her gossamer back, leaving only the dirt crater and the greasy spots where the goblins had died. So much for keeping the fairy queen out of this. She didn't know why Alva was attacking Victor's empty house, but the queen of the DFZ was clearly playing hardball, which meant they were in trouble.

Her worries were interrupted by a crash behind her. Jumping at the sound, Lola whirled again, drawing in her gossamer to create whatever she needed to create. By the time she actually made it all the way around, though, it was already too late.

Back by the blown-up doors, the troll was on its knees with the Black Rider standing on top of its lumpy head like a mountaineer. It was still alive, but four of its twelve spider-like eyes were punctured and weeping sticky fluid, and its bulging body was riddled with missing chunks from the Rider's invisible wedge. It tried one last time to grab him with its lone remaining arm, but the Black Rider was too fast. He jumped easily out of the way, grabbing the troll's yellow tusks as he swung down to stand on top of its protruding nose.

The troll gave an enraged roar, lashing out with its surfboard-sized green tongue to knock the attacker away. But the glistening, fleshy appendage didn't make it as far as the Rider's boots before he smacked his gloved palm down on the soft, squishy skin of the troll's forehead.

Lola didn't know what made the open palm different than his other attacks, but the troll froze the moment the Rider's hand made contact, going still as a mammoth frozen in ice. Even its eyes were stuck, locked helplessly on the Rider as he raised his other hand and brought his fist down on the top of the troll's massive head.

It was more like a tap than a punch, but as the Rider's fist made contact, a wave of staggering cold washed over the garden. The supernatural chill turned Lola's gossamer nearly solid, slowing her down until she could barely move. It hit the troll even harder, racing through its body until it looked flash-frozen, like a fish at the seafood counter.

The knobbly flesh cracked as it froze, splitting along the fault lines of its impossible-looking body until the whole thing fell apart. The Rider hopped down as it crumbled, landing neatly on the flagstone path in front of what was now a rapidly growing pile of frozen troll chunks. The bits started melting a few seconds later, dissolving into gossamer just like the goblins had. By the time Lola's magic warmed up enough for her to walk over, the corpse was completely melted, dissolving into the air to leave no sign it had ever existed save for the sour taste of Alva's meddling.

"You'd think a fairy queen would taste better," Lola said, making a disgusted face. "But at least we know what tripped the alarm this time. Those were definitely Alva's doing."

The Rider nodded as if this was old news, and Lola gaped at him. "Can you taste gossamer too?"

He wiggled his gloved hand in a "so-so" gesture she wasn't sure how to interpret.

"You must have some way of telling," she insisted. "You knew they were here way before I did." She glanced nervously into the dark workshop on the other side of the wrecked doors. "Are there any more?"

The Rider shook his head and turned away, marching back toward the stairs that led to the gate.

"Wait!" Lola cried, running after him. "We should look around to see if we can figure out what they were doing. Goblins are a dime a dozen, but trolls aren't cheap. If Alva sent one of hers here, it had to be for something important."

The Rider shook his head again and kept striding down the stairs. Frustrated, Lola lengthened her legs and caught up.

"What did you do to the troll?" she asked, determined to get some kind of answer. "You put your palm on my head the same way when you knocked me out after the accident. What kind of magic is that? Does it only work on gossamer?"

The Rider picked up the pace, taking the steps so fast, even Lola's new long legs had trouble keeping up. She tried a few more questions, but the Rider's hunched shoulders made it clear he wouldn't have answered even if he could speak, so Lola let it drop. She had enough on her plate already without piling the Rider's mysteries on top.

Finding the fairy queen's minions inside Victor's stronghold had several implications, none of them good. First, it meant that Victor's wards were degrading. Her master never let anything he used fall into disrepair. If his protections were starting to fail, it meant that wherever he was, he'd either given up on guarding his house or couldn't spare the magic.

Lola dismissed the former immediately. A fairyless barrow was too rare a prize for Victor to ever give it up, but she didn't like the option that left. The idea of her master not being able to do something as basic as support his own wards felt like a fundamental law of the universe had broken. But however Alva's minions had gotten in, the fairy queen now knew Victor was missing for certain. And if she knew, it wouldn't be long before all his other enemies did as well.

Lola dug her cracked phone out of her pocket. She needed to call Simon and warn him that the respite Jamie's calls had bought them was about to end. When she finally got her contact list to display on her broken phone's janky AR, though, the interface was crammed with missed call notifications, all from the same number.

She cursed so loudly the Rider looked over his shoulder in alarm. She'd completely forgotten she'd been on her way to Simon's when the Black Rider started chasing her. That had been shortly after noon. It was now four-thirty.

Cursing again, Lola put her phone to her ear and turned around, giving the Rider her back for what was likely to be a very unpleasant phone call.

Simon picked up before the first ring had even finished, his angry shout so loud, Lola had to jerk the phone away. *"Where have you been?"*

"Sorry, sorry, sorry!" Lola said in a rush. "I was on my way, but things got complicated."

"So complicated you couldn't call?" he yelled. "Do you have any idea how worried I've been? I thought you'd been snatched too!"

His voice was seething, but the fear behind Simon's anger made Lola smile. "Thanks for caring," she told him sincerely. "I should have called you earlier, but everything was so crazy, I completely forgot."

"What kind of crazy?"

"The bad kind," she said, lowering her voice even though the Rider already knew. "Alva sent a troll to the mansion."

"A troll?" Simon's voice grew grim. "Are you okay?"

"We're fine," Lola assured him. "But the queen definitely knows Victor's missing."

"It was only a matter of time," Simon said, then his tone grew sharp again. "But what did you mean by 'we'? Who's with you?"

Lola glanced at the Black Rider, who'd stopped his frantic walking and was now waiting quietly on the step just below hers. "It's too much to explain over the phone. We're headed to your place right now. I'll tell you the whole story when I get there."

"Just make sure you actually make it this time," Simon grumbled. "I don't think my heart can take another afternoon like this one."

Lola promised to go straight there and hung up, turning to face the Rider, who wasn't even trying to hide his eavesdropping.

"You heard the man," she said, shoving her broken phone back into her gossamer. "We're going to Simon's."

If the Black Rider had a problem with that, he didn't mention it. He just followed her placidly to the gate, waiting while she remade the car under the cover and then getting into the passenger seat without prompting. Lola gave him a funny look as she dropped into the driver's seat. She wasn't sure what had caused this flip in behavior, but the Rider clearly wasn't about to pull out his pad and fill her in.

She needed to focus on getting to Simon's, anyway. Now that Alva knew they were headless, all of Victor's enemies would be coming out of the woodwork. Information like that was way too valuable for the queen to keep to herself. She'd trade it to the whole city for favors, which meant they were about to be up to their necks in trouble.

Lola was confident in her ability to hide, but the Rider was very noticeable. If other people knew he worked for Victor, then just having him in her car made them a target. When she leaned forward to darken the protective window tinting even more, though, a flash of movement caught her eye.

Lola jumped in her seat. The Rider jumped as well, helmet turning to locate the threat, but Lola didn't know what to tell him. The flash was already gone, leaving her staring at the decoy house where Victor's thralls lived.

With no blood mage around to reinforce their slavery, several of the thralls had broken free. Only two were still watching TV on the couch, and their smiles were already looking strained. Lola was happy some good had come from Victor's disappearance, at least, but she couldn't shake the feeling that something was off. Other than the missing thralls, everything about the house looked exactly the same as the night before. For a split second there, though, Lola would've sworn she'd seen a boy standing on top of the roof.

She rolled down her window and breathed in through her mouth, but there was nothing to find. Just the usual autumn smell of rotting leaves and the ubiquitous, bloody tinge of Victor's magic. She was trying again when a finger tapped her on the shoulder.

Lola turned to see the Rider looking at her, his glossy helmet tilted forward in a way that reminded her of a worried dog.

"Sorry," she said, rolling up her window. "Thought I saw something."

She glanced out the windshield one last time, but all she saw was the house and the gray October sky already darkening toward night, reminding her of how much time they'd lost.

"Let's get out of here," she muttered, starting the car with a thought and turning around in her seat to back them out of Victor's tiny driveway.

As usual for the evenings, and pretty much every other time of day, traffic to Simon's was awful. The elevated highways were all jammed, as were the Underground grid streets. When the traffic did move, it crawled so slowly that Lola had plenty of time to read the fine print on all the *Fenrir* advertisements her damaged phone's AR kept tossing into her face. Some even came with a downloadable app that would play the whole movie for free on your car's windshield while you were sitting in traffic.

After thirty minutes of this, Lola almost wished the monster would show up and knock a few cars out of their way, but no dice. They were stuck good and proper, and there was nothing to do but wait it out.

Lola did so with far less grace than usual. Traffic when you're in a hurry is frustrating, but traffic when you're in a hurry and you have a silent, deadly man of unknown magical qualities brooding in your passenger seat was unbearable. She tried several times to start a conversation about what had happened at the mansion, but the Rider just stared out the window, his black boot tapping irritably on the floor mat.

For someone who never spoke, he was certainly good at letting her know he didn't want to talk. The cold silence was rapidly getting under her skin, so she conjured a radio for her car. Nothing too fancy. Complicated electronics were beyond her, but she could manage a box that picked up radio waves. She turned it on with a click, spinning the old-fashioned dial through the thousands of low-budget pirate channels that had taken over the DFZ's airwaves until she found one that didn't sound too crazy.

The news was the usual downer of war, economic collapse, and partisan politics. Dragons were fighting over territory in South America, there was a typhoon spirit causing massive flooding in China, and so forth. Lola listened with half an ear as she jockeyed for position at ten miles an hour. She was angling for a gap in front of an SUV full of screaming kids when the reporter said something that caught her full attention.

"...award winning producer Frank Grimes was found dead in his Windsor, Canada, home early this morning. In what Canadian police are calling a cartel-style execution, Grimes's headless body was discovered by his wife when—"

Lola's hand shot down to click off the radio. As the broadcaster's voice vanished, the silence in the car turned thick as frozen mud. Lola put both hands on the wheel and focused on staying in her lane, but her mind was racing. One by one, things she'd previously dismissed as unimportant were clicking into place: the message she'd seen Victor sending after saying he'd "take care" of Frank, her first sighting of the Black Rider when he'd blown past her on the bridge toward Windsor, the deadly way she'd seen the Rider move today.

"That was you, wasn't it?" she asked, glancing at him out of the corner of her eye. "You killed Frank."

The Rider was looking out the window. He was so still, Lola was certain he was ignoring her. But then, slowly, he nodded.

"Is that the work Victor makes you do for him?" she whispered, her throat tight. "All those people he 'takes care of,' that's you?"

The Black Rider nodded again, and Lola swallowed. It wasn't that she was surprised, exactly. Victor didn't keep useless tools, and what other purpose could someone like the Black Rider have? Of course he was Victor's weapon. That actually made Lola fear the Rider less, though, because they were the same.

"I'm sorry," she told him. "Sounds like you got the short end of the Victor stick."

The seat creaked as the Rider turned to look at her, and Lola smiled. "You'll get no judgment from me. You might have put the period on Frank's life, but I'm the one who ruined it. He didn't even know Victor existed until I slipped that first bottle of pills into his pocket. My hands are just as dirty as yours, so I'm sorry if I made you feel bad about it just now."

She turned to see if he was still upset and found the Rider staring straight at her. Lola wasn't sure what kind of expression he was wearing under that shiny black visor, but the silence in the car no longer felt like it was smothering her. She gave him what she hoped was a comforting smile and turned the radio back on, spinning the dial until she found some music this time: a mariachi battle of the bands sponsored by someone named Bob for his pigeon's birthday. That made no sense at all to Lola, but at least it cheered the drive as they crept slowly down the river of cars.

Simon's house was in an up-and-coming Underground neighborhood below the Financial District. Despite being walled in on all sides by cliff-like superscraper foundations, Simon and his neighbors kept it old-school classy with historically accurate reconstructions of old Detroit houses. The shops here had the best vegan food, hand-thrown pottery, and alternative bookstores in the DFZ, and Simon's business fit right in. According to his sign, he was a natural healer specializing in traditional medicines, but all his patients knew him as a soul surgeon.

That clever bit of marketing had been Victor's idea. With blood magic being one of the few things that was actually illegal in the DFZ, Simon couldn't just hang out a shingle like most mages. But even when he'd been under Victor's direct tutelage, Simon's magic had always focused on improving rather than breaking. Where Victor used his magic to invade and control the minds of his victims, Simon went in and removed things. Traumatic memories, flashbacks, intrusive thoughts: any baggage his patients no longer wanted to carry, Simon cut away.

They *had* to know it was blood magic. For the patients he helped, though, that didn't matter. They kept Simon's secret tight as a promise and kept his waiting list filled for months at a time, which was the only reason Victor tolerated his apprentice's "gross waste of talent."

The only thing their master hated more than Simon squandering his skills on healing people was the world's intolerance of blood magic. Victor couldn't stand that what he saw as humanity's "true" power was illegal. Even if he didn't approve of how Simon used it, having so many people singing his apprentice's praises gratified his ego, so he'd let Simon do as he pleased, provided he still made himself available whenever Victor needed another set of hands.

It was a surprisingly tolerant balance for their master, but Lola was glad they'd made it work as she parked her car on the street in front of Simon's home/clinic. Like before, the Rider was out the second they stopped moving. Lola briefly considered asking him to wait with the car, but she didn't know how long this was going to take, and the Rider had said he'd wanted to help. Simon was going to flip, but the way Lola saw it, they were all in the same rapidly sinking boat. Might as well bail together.

Motioning for the Rider to follow, Lola walked up the wheelchair ramp to the ornately carved front porch of Simon's three-story Gothic revival. The sign in the curtained window said the clinic was closed, but the door whipped open the second Lola's foot hit the multilingual welcome mat.

"Lola," Simon breathed, rushing out to hug her. "I thought you were dead!"

"When have I ever been dead?" she teased, hugging him back.

As usual after a big spell, Simon looked exhausted. He was dressed for work in a white lab coat tossed over the same black turtleneck he'd had on at Jamie's, making Lola wonder if he'd slept yet. But while he initially looked delighted that she'd made it safe and sound, his face fell into a murderous scowl when he saw who was standing behind her.

"What are you doing here?" he demanded, grabbing Lola and pulling her behind him.

As usual, the Rider didn't answer, so Lola did it for him.

"Chill out, Simon," she said, wiggling back out onto the porch. "He works for Victor too. He asked for help finding him, so I took him along. Figured we'd need all the hands we could get."

Simon still didn't look happy, and Lola couldn't blame him. She'd probably have hit the roof if Simon had brought an urban legend to her house with no warning. But while some initial shock was understandable, the way Simon kept glaring at the Rider felt off. His whole body was stiff as a board but not with fear.

He was angry, Lola realized at last. Furious, actually, which was why it had taken her so long to recognize the emotion. Simon

115

got pissed at the drop of a hat, but she hadn't seen him get really, really mad in a long time.

"Get out of here," he ordered, his voice as icy as the Rider's magic. "Victor told you to stay away from her."

"You knew about him?" Lola asked, surprised. Then the rest of what he'd said sank in. "Wait, Victor told the Rider to stay away from *me*?"

"Get out," Simon said again, ignoring her.

The Black Rider folded his arms over his chest, and the temperature on the porch began to drop. A thin layer of frost spread across the painted boards from the Rider's boots, and Lola's breaths turned into white puffs as they left her lips. When she felt Simon start pulling magic in from the air too, Lola decided she'd had enough.

"Excuse us a moment," she said as she grabbed Simon and shoved him into the house, slamming the door behind her.

"What is your problem?" she yelled when they were alone in his cozily decorated waiting room. "Since when do you enforce Victor's rules?"

"I do when they're set for good reasons," Simon snapped, removing his glasses to wipe away the frost the Rider's strange magic had covered them in. "Can't you see he's dangerous?"

"We're all dangerous!" Lola cried. "Victor wouldn't keep us around if we weren't! But dangerous isn't always a bad thing. I've seen the Rider fight, and I want that on my side, because unlike you, I've got something to lose if Victor doesn't come back!"

Simon winced, and Lola immediately felt terrible. "Sorry," she muttered, rubbing her face with a sigh. "It's been a stressful twenty-four hours."

"You're telling me," he said, giving her a weak smile. "But that's why this is so important. If you've seen the Rider fight, you know why Victor kept him on a tight leash. Without Victor, none of us

116

can predict or control what the Rider will do. He could destroy you."

"So could you," Lola reminded him, pointing at Simon's hands, which were still humming with the same bloody magic as their master's. "Blood magic is the only thing keeping me together. You could rip those safeties out at any time, but you don't see me telling you to go away."

"Because I would never hurt you."

"And I don't believe the Rider will, either," she said, giving him a smile. "Have a little faith in your fellow monsters, Simon. We're all on the same team."

Simon clearly didn't buy that for a second. He must have realized the fight was lost, though, because all he did was sigh.

"You're going to be the death of me," he muttered, opening the door for the Rider, who was standing just on the other side. "You can come in," he said with a disgusted look. "Just don't try any of that frozen nastiness in my house if you don't want to get fried by my wards."

The Rider nodded and stepped cautiously over the threshold. Simon closed the door the moment he was through, turning the deadbolt and resetting the three wards lovingly carved into the wood with a chisel, not blood. Once they were safely enveloped in his protective—and not nearly as bloody as Victor's—magic, Lola got back on track.

"You said you had something to show me?"

With a final baleful look at the Black Rider, Simon motioned for them to follow him upstairs. Lola did so at once, helping herself to a cookie from the plate Simon's receptionist left out for patients. It was dry and healthy-tasting, but a cookie was a cookie, and Lola had the feeling she was going to need all the fuel she could get as she hurried up the rickety old steps with the Rider following silently behind her.

117

Only the bottom floor of Simon's house was used for patients. The second floor held his bedroom, library, and kitchen, plus the guest room Lola used when she stayed over. The third-floor attic was his workshop where he did all his serious magic, usually under Victor's orders, and that was where he took them now.

Just like Victor's, the floor of Simon's workshop was covered in dozens of interlocking magical circles. Unlike the golden ones at the mansion, though, these were all still intact and looked to be in use. They were all glowing faintly red except for the center circle, which was blazing brilliant white. In the center was a silver plate covered in painstakingly written bloody spellwork and a picture in a metal frame.

Lola recognized the blood as soon as she saw it. It was Victor's, taken from her pill. She could actually feel it calling to her from inside the circle, promising to make her whole again, a human instead of a monster—which, unfortunately, meant the spell had already been popped. Even if she licked the plate clean, the blood wouldn't work as a pill anymore. Sighing at the loss, Lola walked around to check out the picture instead.

Surprisingly, it was a photo of her and Simon. As ever, Lola's age was impossible to tell, but she was wearing Victor's redheaded doll body, so it must have been a decade ago at least. Probably longer, given how young Simon looked.

In the picture, he was still a lanky teenager, his long limbs splayed awkwardly over the red boulder they were both sitting on. The background was nothing but blue desert sky, and they were both dressed for hot weather. Lola had her arms around Simon's shoulders, grinning openly at the camera while he smiled his usual "I'm too serious to have a good time" half-smirk. She was crouching to get a better look when Simon swooped in and snatched the photo away.

"I was trying to cast a locating spell on you when you called," he explained, carrying the picture over to the large desk in the corner of the attic. "It's a good thing you did. Turns out, changelings are impossible to pin down."

"That's why I earn the big bucks," Lola joked, pointing at the picture he was locking in a drawer. "That's from when Victor took us to the Grand Canyon, isn't it?"

Simon nodded, plopping down in his worn chair.

"What was that, twelve years ago?"

"Thirteen," he said. "I usually do that spell with a lock of hair, but since your hair's gossamer just like the rest of you, I couldn't just go grab some from your apartment, so I had to make do with Victor's blood and a happy memory."

Lola took a seat on his desk since there were no other chairs. "I wasn't aware you had any happy memories from your apprenticeship."

Simon flashed her one of his rare, shy smiles. "I have a few."

Lola smiled back and turned to check on the Rider, who was leaning against the wall on the opposite side of the room. That was pretty far away for someone who supposedly wanted to help, but it was probably a wise move given how pointedly Simon was ignoring him. Back on the porch, Lola didn't think it would have been much of a match, but they were in Simon's house now, and a mage in his home was almost as dangerous as a fairy in their barrow.

"How do you know him?" she whispered.

Simon didn't ask who she meant. "Victor had us work together on occasion."

Lola's eyes went wide. "You mean he made you…"

She couldn't even say it. Simon could be overbearing, but he was also the gentlest person Lola knew. There was a reason his patients trusted him to enter their minds and remove their traumatic memories. She couldn't imagine him doing the things the Rider did, and the thought that Victor had forced him made her feel sick.

"Victor made us all do things we'd rather not," Simon said at her horrified expression. "But that doesn't explain how you ended up with *him*."

He shot a pointed glare at the Rider's dark shape, and Lola sighed.

"I was pretty terrified at first," she admitted. "But once he showed me he was also getting the emergency messages from Victor's house, I knew I could trust him. At least when it comes to getting Victor back, which is the only thing I care about at the moment."

Simon gave her a worried look. "How many pills have you got left?"

"Not enough," Lola said. "That's the other reason I decided to bring him along. We're going to need all the muscle we can muster now that Alva knows Victor's gone."

"She's not the only one we have to worry about," Simon said grimly. "I just got a tip from one of my patients who works at Merlin Tower. The Paladins are on the move."

Lola threw her head back with a groan. "That's it, then. We're toast. Are they hunting the streets for us yet?"

"They were still negotiating with the DFZ last I heard," Simon said. "It won't be long, though. The Living City hates outside authorities of any kind, but she hates blood mages even more, and apparently, the surge of magic Victor made the night he vanished was her last straw."

"Guess even barrows can't block everything," Lola said with a sigh. "What are we going to do?"

"The only thing we can do," Simon replied. "Find Victor. He's our biggest gun. Without him, we're all prey."

Lola could only nod at that. "So what did you want to show

me?"

Simon waved his hand over his desk, and the mana-integrated glass top lit up with an AR display Lola could see too since she was sitting on it. She got up at once, keeping her fingers on the glass to maintain her contact as she leaned in to examine the display.

The air above Simon's desk was now filled with meticulously organized spreadsheets that appeared to form a calendar. Each day was divided into multiple color-coded segments full of abbreviations that made no sense, at least not to Lola.

"What am I looking at?"

"Victor's schedule," Simon said. "I asked Jamie to send it over. This is yesterday." He pointed at a glowing column covered in blocks floating in the middle of the screen. "And this is tomorrow."

He waved his hand to move the spreadsheets to the right, but Lola had already given up.

"Simon, you know I can't read Jamie's perfect secretary gobbledygook. Just tell me what it is, already."

The mage arched an eyebrow but obliged. "Victor delegates a lot, but his schedule is always full of things he has to see to himself. Shake-downs, soul-selling sessions, that sort of thing. Starting yesterday, though, Victor has nothing on his personal schedule after your meeting with Frank Grimes. No appointments, no pill making, nothing. Jamie still has all the things she handles for him, which is why the schedule isn't blank, but Victor's timeline is empty for the foreseeable future. It's like he—"

"Knew he was going to disappear," Lola finished.

Simon nodded grimly. "I suspected something was off when the finding spell failed, which was why I asked Jamie to send this over. It gets weirder, though. Watch."

He tapped the glass desktop to bring up a new display, this one full of numbers. Very, very *large* numbers.

"Holy Toledo," she whispered, her eyes going huge. "Is that...?"

121

"Victor's bank accounts," Simon said with a nod.

Lola whistled. She'd known her master was rich, but according to those numbers, her estimates had been off by a few powers of ten. "Just how much money does he have?"

"Not as much as he used to," Simon said, tapping the icon for the overview.

Up in the air, the glowing AR display switched to show a graph of Victor's balances over the last two years plotted out with the sort of obsessive attention to detail that was Jamie's hallmark. The line wobbled up and down in tiny undulations for the first half, then the numbers launched into a swan dive that was still going.

"What happened?"

"So far as I can tell, he made an investment," Simon said. "A bad one. Over the last thirteen months, Victor has sunk over half his fortune into *Fenrir*."

Lola gaped at him. "You mean the monster movie?"

Simon nodded. "He did it all through shell companies, of course, but as you can see, he's been dumping money into the thing nonstop, especially here in the DFZ."

"So you're saying all the constant advertising, the *Fenrir* promotional drinks and annoying AR ads, that was Victor?"

When Simon nodded again, Lola threw up her hands. "But *why*? Victor doesn't even like movies. And why would he dump money into promoting a film that's not even in theaters anymore? I just saw an ad on the way over here that would have let me watch the whole thing in my car for free."

"I don't know what he's trying to do," Simon said with a scowl, "but he's losing money hand over fist doing it."

Lola scowled at the graph floating above Simon's desk. The amount of money Victor had lost on *Fenrir* was so big, she was having trouble wrapping her head around it. According to Jamie's sheets, he'd been pushing the thing all over the world, paying to have the movie translated into over a hundred languages, even paying theater owners to screen it for free.

"It's like he wants every person on the planet to see it," she muttered.

"It makes no sense," Simon agreed, taking off his glasses to rub his eyes. "Victor always said that money was just another tool, but it's not like him to throw his tools away. It doesn't matter how many people watch *Fenrir* at this point. There's no way he'll make his money back when his costs are this high."

"Then money must not be what he's after," Lola said, thinking hard. "Have you watched the movie yet?"

Simon shook his head, so Lola pulled out her phone and typed *Fenrir* into the search bar. The very first link was for the official site. She tapped it and placed her phone on Simon's desk, letting his far superior augmented-reality projector grab her screen and throw it up in front of them.

"See?" she said when the movie's page came up, pointing at the embedded video that was the centerpiece of the whole design. "You can watch the full movie right here. There's not even any ads."

Simon's scowl deepened as he scrolled down the page with his finger, stopping at the bottom where the production credits were listed.

"Look at this."

Lola leaned in, squinting at the tiny glowing letters. "Brought to you by Grimes Films," she read, eyes flying wide. "As in Frank Grimes?"

"Has to be," Simon said. "Unless you think it's a coincidence?"

Lola snorted. "With Victor? Never."

She scrolled back up the page and poked her finger through the link that pulled up a list of everyone who'd worked on the

123

movie. It was a surprisingly short list for a full-length motion picture, but the really shocking thing was that Lola recognized every name on it.

"Everyone in the credits belongs to Victor," Simon said, speaking out loud what she'd just thought.

He grabbed his own phone before she could say anything, typing in name after name. Lola watched nervously over his shoulder, but she had a feeling she already knew what he would find. Frank wasn't the only client Victor had cut off recently. A lot of those people were no longer what their master referred to as "viable," and according to Simon's search, an uncomfortable number of them were either missing or dead.

Lola's hands began to shake as the list got longer. She'd gone to all those people and told them it was over. Like Frank, everyone had pitched a fit, but that always happened. It'd never occurred to her that they could be connected. Or that they'd end up like this.

Unbidden, her eyes flicked to the Rider leaning on the wall across the room. She was tempted to ask if this was his work but decided against it at the last minute. If Victor really was the reason all those people were gone, then her hands were just as dirty, and knowing which members of the production team Victor's Rider had "taken care of" wasn't nearly as important as knowing *why*.

"I think we need to watch that movie."

Simon nodded grimly and reached up to restart the video, which had already begun playing on mute in the background. Lola took a seat on the edge of his desk as he turned up the sound, filling the attic with mournful, swelling music as the film began to roll.

As it was precisely the sort of movie she hated most, Lola had taken great pains never to watch so much as a trailer for *Fenrir*. Like any modern person raised on the internet, she was familiar with the monster movie tropes, but Victor's movie didn't bother

124

with those. There was no room full of scientists discovering an anomaly or secret nuclear waste dumping gone awry. Instead, the film opened cold with Fenrir clawing its way out of the ground to begin rampaging through a city that was clearly supposed to be the DFZ.

That was it. There were no human characters or dialog other than screaming. Just a giant wolf doing horrific violence to a city. Every few minutes, something would appear to stop it—dragons, spirits, the military, mages—but none of them got more than thirty seconds of screen time before Fenrir smacked them down.

It was so weird. From the posters, Lola had expected a cheesy action-horror flick, but *Fenrir* was more like an art film. A very long, very depressing art film whose only focus seemed to be destruction porn.

At least that part was good. Unlike other monster movies, with their excessive green-screening and cheap digital effects, *Fenrir*'s destruction scenes were freakishly realistic. The level of detail put into the shattering glass when the giant wolf's howl broke all the windows was nothing short of sublime. It was also extremely boring.

For all the beautiful fires and dramatically toppling skyscrapers, there were only so many times you could watch a giant wolf wreck things before it got old. Lola felt a burst of excitement every time a new defender came on screen, hoping that maybe this time, something would be different, but it never was. Even the flight of dragons that came in to breathe fire on the wolf went down with barely a fight, which made no sense. Surely *someone* had to rise up and beat the monster in a monster movie? But Fenrir was the same from start to finish, stomping on building after building until the screen faded to black.

"Wait," Lola said as the credits began to roll. "That's it? *That's* the hit movie of the summer?"

"I don't know," Simon said, blinking as if he was coming out of a dream. "I thought it was pretty compelling."

"It was two hours of pointless destruction!" Lola argued. "I mean, the graphics were great, but there were no characters, no plot, nothing. It was just Fenrir wrecking things from start to finish. Can you even call that a movie?"

"You're right," Simon said, looking confused. "It *was* terrible. So why couldn't I stop watching?"

Lola had been wondering the same thing. If Victor hadn't been involved, she would have bailed after the first twenty minutes, but Simon had looked enthralled. Even the Rider had come over, reaching out a gloved hand to touch the desk so he could watch the augmented reality, too. Simon *must* have been super into the movie, because he jumped when he saw the Rider so close, shooing him back to his spot on the wall with a furious scowl.

"Maybe I found it interesting because it felt so familiar," he said once the Rider had been sent back to his corner. "The ads are inescapable. I swear, I dreamed about that stupid wolf last night."

Lola went still. "You dreamed about Fenrir?"

Simon nodded with a yawn. "I caught a bit of a nap before I called you. I hadn't even seen the movie yet, but that's the power of advertising. Gets into your head."

"I don't think that was just advertising," she said nervously.

Simon gave her a funny look. "What do you mean?"

Taking a deep breath, Lola launched into a truncated version of her visit to Tristan's, leaving out the part where he'd eaten her dream to focus on the unknown fairy sending dreams across all of the DFZ.

"And this started the night Victor vanished?" Simon said when she finished. "You're sure?"

"That's what Tristan said, and you know he can't lie." Lola leaned in closer. "Do you think your Fenrir dream could have been

126

a fairy sending?"

"I don't know," he said. "I've never had a fairy dream to compare, but it's all a little too lined up for my tastes." He turned back to the screen. "Maybe we should watch the movie again?"

"Please, no," Lola begged. "I realize it's our clue to finding Victor, but I can't sit through that again. It's depressing, and you know how I feel about monsters."

"Fair enough," Simon said, giving her a smile. "I'll watch it, but I'm going to call my mother first. She hasn't seen a new movie in twenty years. If she's dreaming about *Fenrir*, we'll know something's up."

"Ask Jamie, too," Lola said, getting off his desk with a stretch. "I'll call Tristan and let him know what the dream's about. Maybe then he'll be able to figure out who's behind it." She pulled out her cracked phone and checked the time. Thanks to the movie, it was nearly nine. "I should also go home and feed Buster."

Simon grabbed her sleeve as she started to step away, but he didn't even have to open his mouth. Lola already knew that stubborn expression. He was going to try to make her stay.

"Forget it," she said before he could speak. "I appreciate the sentiment, but I'm not going to spend what could be my last days cowering in your house."

"I'm trying to make sure you get those days," Simon pleaded. "This isn't just about tracking Victor anymore. The Paladins and Alva are both out there hunting us now."

"Who are they going to look for?" Lola challenged, shifting in a flash until her face was a spitting image of Simon's own. He glowered, and, point made, Lola changed back into her yogurt lady.

"I've only got nine pills left, Simon," she told him plainly. "I get what you're saying, but I don't have time to play this safe. Somewhere out there, a fairy's casting dreams of Victor's stupid movie all over the city. You said yourself that can't be coincidence, but I'm not going to find out anything locked inside your house."

"All right, all right," he said. "But do you have to take *him?*"

He tilted his head at the Rider, and Lola shrugged. "Why shouldn't I? He's been good help so far, and unlike some people, *he* doesn't keep trying to stop me."

Simon heaved a defeated sigh. "Touché," he muttered, rubbing his face. "But dammit, Lola. Don't you realize people worry about you when you run off?"

His concern was sweet, but it didn't change her mind.

"I've got to do this," she said, sticking out her arm to show him her left wrist. "You know what's at stake for me. Whatever happens, I have to keep trying. For her sake."

Simon sighed again, reaching out to take her hand. Unlike Victor, he'd never been able to see her sister's thread, but he'd heard Lola talk about her enough to know how important this was.

"I understand," he whispered, squeezing her fingers. "Just keep in touch this time, Tinkerbell, or you're going to give me an ulcer."

"Will do, Mr. Wizard."

He looked nonplussed as always at the old nickname, but he didn't try to stop her again.

Lola flashed him a grin and started for the stairs. The Black Rider followed a second later, stalking behind her like a big, mean, black cat. When they got back to her car, Lola hopped right in, but the Rider didn't follow. Instead, he grabbed the pad and golf pencil from his pocket and started writing.

I've had the dream too, the paper read when he held it out for her to see. *About the monster.*

Lola blinked in surprise. She still didn't know what the Black Rider was, but the idea of him having something as human as a dream struck her as odd.

"Had you seen the movie before?"

Not until tonight.

Lola bit her lip. "Okay," she said, putting the car into reverse. "Hop in. We're going to get some food, and then I'm going to call Tristan. I think we can all agree it's no longer a question of if Victor planned his disappearance but why and for how long." Her throat tightened as she felt how light the pill bottle was tucked inside her gossamer. "I just hope he hurries up."

The Black Rider got into the car and placed his pad on his knee, writing furiously before he held it up again.

Victor won't let you change. He's invested too much of his power in you. Abandoning you at this point would be wasteful, and Victor doesn't like waste.

"Thanks for the vote of confidence," Lola said, giving him a smile. "Buckle up, and let's go get some dinner."

The Rider nodded and slipped his pad back into his pocket as he reached for the seatbelt. Once he'd strapped in, Lola backed into the empty street, cruising past the chic, healthy restaurants of Simon's too-hip neighborhood toward something more fitting for a fairy hack-job who lived off cheap carbs.

Since the Rider didn't seem interested in food, Lola declared they were getting ice cream. There was a great drive-thru place just a mile away that she and Simon used to hit up on summer nights. She ordered herself a banana split with all the toppings, then drove a few blocks to an empty commuter parking lot where she could take her medicine and make her calls in peace.

She'd been hoping she could get by without one tonight since she'd *just* taken a pill during that debacle with the Rider outside her apartment. The stress of the last few days must have been wearing on her, though, because her gossamer was itching as if she hadn't taken a pill all day. Clearly, skipping wasn't going to be an option, so Lola fished a red pill out of her crushed container and tossed it into her mouth.

The bloody taste was almost a relief when it hit her tongue, crushing her gossamer into shape and reasserting control instantly. When she was stable again, Lola buried the awful flavor under a huge spoonful of butter pecan, plopping down on the hood of her car to eat her sundae and watch the Black Rider pace.

It was more interesting than she would have thought. Despite his size, the Rider moved with a quick, liquid grace that carried his weight like a weapon rather than a burden. She didn't understand how he wasn't sweating buckets with a helmet and all that leather—even this late in October, the underside of the Skyways got hot as an oven at night—but the Rider didn't seem to notice the temperature. He just paced back and forth, his head turned down toward his feet as if he was thinking.

Lola was polishing off the last dregs of her ice cream when he suddenly stopped.

"What?" she asked, instantly on full alert.

The Rider held up his hand, and Lola shut up, ears straining, but all she heard were the normal sounds of the city. The parking lot she'd chosen was tucked between a support beam and a spiral ramp that went up to the Skyways above. It was a safe, hidden place she'd used before, somewhere she could relax without worrying about human attention.

The streetlights painted everything bright orange, letting Lola see all the way to the corners of the lot. There was no sign of movement, not even a breeze, but the Rider was still frozen like a dog who'd caught a sound. Lola was about to conjure up a pad and pencil of her own to write her questions out when the Rider spun and grabbed her arm, yanking Lola to the ground.

"*Ow!*" she cried as she tumbled onto the pavement. He jumped on top of her a second later, covering her with his body.

"What the—"

The rest of her question was drowned out by the wave of fire as it engulfed her car.

Chapter 7

8 pills

Lola flattened against the pavement as the fire washed over them. The Black Rider was above her, his body a huge, black bulwark. Heat crackled in the air, but the fire did not touch them. The Rider's strange barrier was up again, holding back the flames.

It seemed to go on forever. Lola could feel the intense heat against the gossamer of her car. She almost called it back to spare herself the discomfort, but she didn't know who was watching, and the coupe *was* helping block the flames, so she let it be, cowering in the Rider's shadow until, at last, the fire vanished. When Lola lifted her head to see what was left, they were surrounded.

Three SWAT trucks with huge, blinding banks of floodlights on their roofs were parked in a triangle around her car. Armed men in black riot gear piled out as she watched, their uniforms stamped with *Toledo PD*. Lola was wondering what force of nature had convinced the DFZ to allow American police over her borders when she saw it.

There, standing at the apex of the ring of trucks, were three figures in what could only be described as modern full plate. They looked like Knights Templar but without the religious imagery. Their white surcoats were covered in crisp, embroidered spellwork swirling around a silver sword with a single drop of ruby-red blood dripping off its tip, the emblem of the Paladins.

"Servants of the wanted blood mage, Victor Conrath," announced the armored figure in the center. She sounded like a middle-aged woman, though it was impossible to say for certain with the shiny, spellworked plastic-and-steel helmet she was wearing over her face. "You are in violation of the Detroit Free Zone's anti-blood mage law. With the Living City's permission, we are here to take you into custody. Surrender peacefully, and you will be shown mercy."

Yeah, right. Paladins were zealots, an international organization of mages who'd dedicated their lives to a single purpose: the total eradication of blood magic. "Mercy" wasn't a word in their vocabulary.

But while Lola normally sympathized with anyone who hated blood mages, Victor's magic was the only thing holding her together at the moment, and she wasn't dying tonight.

"Let's make a break for it," she whispered to the Rider, who was still covering her on the ground. "On the count of three, I'll crash my car into the trucks behind us. Once I've made a gap, we'll—"

The Black Rider grabbed her before she could finish. His gloved hands felt like cold iron on her shoulders as he pushed Lola under her car, which was still uncomfortably warm from the fire. He held her there for a second, like he was making sure she would stay put, and then he vanished.

It happened so suddenly, it took Lola a second to realize the Rider hadn't actually disappeared. He'd moved. Very, very quickly.

By the time her eyes found him again, he was in the air above the Paladins, his black-gloved hand already out for the karate-chop move that had cut off the troll's arm. But the Paladins weren't dumb piles of gossamer. The woman in the middle was already turning to block him, a shield made of burning silver light appearing on her arm as she went. The Paladin to her left was also glowing, his spellworked armor flashing neon orange as he slammed another wave of flames at the Rider's chest.

The Black Rider dodged both. Moving like the ghost she'd always thought he was, he slipped around the Paladin's shield to

133

slam his strange, invisible force into her stomach. He turned his body as he went, letting the wave of fire slide right past him as he kicked the third Paladin, who hadn't done anything yet, into the SWAT team that was running over to help.

The armored man hit the cops like a bowling ball, knocking them to the pavement, but the victory was short-lived. The head Paladin was already back on her feet, the spellwork on her armor glowing like white phosphorus as she summoned a burning sword to match her shield.

"Abomination!" she cried, her voice gleeful in its hate as she swung her glowing sword at the Rider. "Burn with your master!"

Lola glowered in the darkness beneath her car. Seriously, did *everybody* know the Rider worked for Victor except her?

But while he'd opened strong, the Rider was rapidly being surrounded. The Paladin he'd thrown into the cops was back on his feet and drawing his own weapon, some kind of crazy-looking shotgun covered in spellwork that was already glowing a nauseating shade of green. Fire Guy had also repositioned and looked like he was preparing for another blast, twisting the spellworked rings on his wrist into a new configuration that presumably wouldn't hit his boss, who was swinging her sword at the Rider like a kid going at a piñata.

Even for someone as scary as the Rider, those odds didn't look good. If he went down, Lola didn't have a prayer, so she scrambled out from under her car, shouting a warning to the Rider as she did. She was spinning the coupe's wheels to run Fire Paladin over when the lady with the sword gave a whoop of triumph, and Lola looked up just in time to see the edge of her glowing shield slam into the Rider's head.

Slam into it and take it right off.

Lola screamed as the Rider's head flew sideways, his black helmet cracking on the pavement as it bounced away. Helpless, motionless, she stared at the Rider's headless body. In her mind, she could already see it happening. His knees would give out slowly, dropping him to the ground, where he would keel over like a felled tree, just like in the movies.

The shock of the Rider's sudden death was so unexpectedly overwhelming, it took Lola several seconds to realize he was not, in fact, dead. His headless body hadn't even fallen over. Quite the opposite, he was still going after the Paladin with the sword, using her surprise at suddenly fighting a headless opponent to smack his fist into her armored gut.

She flew backward with a grunt, landing hard on her back on the pavement. The headless Rider turned on her allies next, fists up to take them on, but they backed away in horror, and with good reason. Lola could see it, too, from where she was standing by her car. Where the Black Rider's head should have been, there was nothing. No blood, no neck, not even a wound. Just a black hole going down into the darkness of his motorcycle jacket.

The world started to tilt. For the first time in her life, Lola wondered if she was going to faint. The only reason she didn't was because the Rider was still fighting, landing a solid hit on Fire Paladin's shoulder. The Paladin with the gun finally did something and emptied his strange weapon into the Rider's back, but whatever the spellwork on the shotgun was supposed to do, it didn't work on the headless Rider. The nauseatingly green blasts rolled off his back like sparks off an anvil, doing nothing but illuminating the terror on Fire Paladin's face as the Rider knocked off his helmet and slammed him into the ground.

It was around this point that Lola began to think they might actually survive this. The Rider's helmet must have been entirely for show, because he seemed to actually fight better without it. No wonder the Paladins had come in with so much force. He was untouchable, throwing the SWAT cops that tried to dogpile him

135

off like insects. He was rounding on the sword lady, who'd just pushed back to her knees, when everything changed.

It started with Fire Paladin. He was still lying on the ground where the Rider had tossed him, screaming in pain as he popped his dislocated shoulder back into place. When both his arms were working again, he shouted something final-sounding and pointed his hands at the Rider, lighting up every bit of spellwork on his armor as he did. The orange glare was so bright, Lola was blinded for a moment, but nothing could hide the surge of unfamiliar magic rising in the air or the heat it brought with it. Lola's gossamer actually began to blacken as the Paladin shouted a battle cry and launched a wall of fire straight into the Rider.

There was so much even he couldn't dodge. The fire hit him full on, engulfing his body in a swirling tornado of orange-and-yellow flame. He hunkered at once, curling his headless body into a ball. But while everything else Fire Paladin threw at him had washed over the Rider like waves over a rock, this was too much. The Rider held out for nearly thirty seconds, but eventually his leather motorcycle suit was consumed. The darkness that formed his body went with it, blowing away like ash in the wind. When the flames finally stopped, there was nothing left of the Rider but a scorch mark on the pavement.

The humans cheered at the empty place where he'd been, but Lola couldn't even move. It just didn't seem possible. The Rider had survived her throwing a car at him. He'd fought a troll and won single-handedly. He'd just gone toe-to-toe with three Paladins and *lost his head* without slowing down. There was no way he could actually be dead. It couldn't be true, but she didn't feel a hint of his cold gossamer anymore, not even when one of the SWAT team ran over and grabbed the Rider's helmet, turning it over to show the rest of his team that it was empty inside.

"A monster to the end," the female Paladin proclaimed when

they brought the empty helmet over to show her. "One to go."

Her smooth faceplate turned toward Lola as she finished, and the changeling stepped back.

"What is she?" asked the Paladin with the gun who had been giving medical attention to Fire Paladin, who seemed to have passed out. "She looks human, but something feels off."

"Who cares?" replied their leader, hefting her glowing sword. "She's drenched in blood magic. I can see the stain from here." She lifted her visor to show Lola her scarred face, her thin mouth curving in a zealot's grin. "Let's see what Conrath made you."

Lola's eyes went huge. She ran for her car, not even caring what anyone saw or thought as she started to merge her gossamer into the car's. If she could just get into her vehicle and ram the trucks out of the way like she'd planned instead of watching the Rider like an idiot, maybe she could still get away. She'd barely touched her fingers to the scorched car door, though, when the Paladin's magic landed on her like a meat cleaver.

As with everything Victor did, the spell that held Lola together was a work of complex mastery. Despite what she'd said to Simon earlier, it wasn't something just any mage could undo. It was treacherous and filled with snares, traps that would turn the attacker's own magic against them. But the Paladin must have known more about blood magic than her zealotry suggested, because she picked it apart, blasting through Victor's safeguards to begin ripping up the strings that held Lola's human mask in place.

Lola tried to fight back. It didn't matter that all the humans were staring. Nothing would keep her together if Victor's spell was destroyed, so she hit the Paladin with everything she had, which, unfortunately, turned out not to be much.

With half her gossamer still missing and so many eyes turning the little she had left to jelly, the best she could manage was to paw weakly at the woman, hitting her with blobs of gossamer that were supposed to be cement bricks but landed more like wet snow. She was losing control over even that when her pill bottle slid out of her melting gossamer and hit the ground, rolling across the uneven pavement to tap against the Paladin's boot.

"What's this?" the woman asked, pausing her assault on Lola's underpinnings to pick up the cracked orange bottle.

"Looks like drugs, ma'am," said one of the SWAT officers.

The Paladin frowned and ripped open the cracked bottle, dumping the pills out into her metal-gloved hand. Lola watched them hungrily, but while she could smell the precious scent of her master's blood from here, Victor was no fool. All the pills he made, including hers, were spelled to look like common painkillers to anyone who didn't already know what they were. It must have been good enough to trick the Paladin, because she shrugged and turned her hand, dropping the red tabs onto the pavement.

Time stood still as Lola watched her pills—her precious, precious pills—fall to the ground. They scattered as they hit the asphalt, bouncing off in all directions. That was the last thing she saw before she exploded.

Her gossamer surged with a will of its own, filling Lola with a roar that could not possibly have come from a human throat. Even the Paladin stepped back, her scarred face going pale with fear.

Lola didn't care. She was lost in rage. Rage at this woman for carelessly throwing away the pills that were her only hope. Rage for the Rider, who'd died trying to protect her. Rage for her sister, who was going to be lost forever because of this. Rage at herself for not stopping it. So much rage, even the pain of her melting gossamer couldn't touch it. The magic ran away from her like melting sugar, leaving Lola's hands looking more like claws as they came up to encircle the Paladin's throat.

Something hit her in the side, and Lola glanced down to see Gun Paladin standing with his hands out. He'd thrown a spell at her, she realized. Whatever it was, though, it hadn't worked. The creature she'd become smirked down at him, showing the Paladin the enormous wall of her sharp, sharp teeth. Those tricks wouldn't fly with her. She was the changeling, and it was time someone showed these humans what it really meant to hunt monsters.

The creature gurgled with delight at the idea, but inside, the small core that was still Lola was screaming in panic. The change had never come on this fast before. No, no, *no*, she couldn't let this happen! Not after so long, and certainly not because of something like this. She'd never even seen these mages before!

She *had* to get herself back together, for her sister's sake if nothing else. But for all her determination, Lola didn't see a way out. The monster had already grown so huge that the Paladins were far below her now. She could hear them screaming at their men to open fire, feel the *plink* of cops' bullets sliding harmlessly through her gossamer, but she couldn't see. Her vision was already fading, the world sliding back into the monster's black and white.

That scared Lola more than anything, but the monster didn't need to see. It could smell the humans' fear, and it threw its head back with a hunter's roar. Lola cried out, too, a small, despairing sound as she tried one last, desperate attempt to pull the monster back, but it was no use. The damage to Victor's spell combined with her weakened gossamer had already pushed her over the edge. She could feel her mind slipping faster and faster, her human voice vanishing beneath the enormous wall of the monster's teeth.

But as the last of the color left her vision, the monster spotted something that made them both pause. The Paladins and their men had pulled back to the cover of the SWAT trucks, but there was a third party standing on top of Lola's car, which was somehow still together despite everything.

It looked like a child. A boy of not more than twelve dressed like a prince in rich russet silks and curled-toe boots with golden bells on the tips. The same boy she'd thought she'd seen on the roof of Victor's decoy house that afternoon.

Even to the monster's terrible eyes, his tanned skin and thick blond hair made him look like he was made of gold. He hopped off the car as Lola watched, strolling straight through the police's line of fire. The officers didn't seem to see him at all, but the monster shuffled back, whimpering in fear as the boy moved closer.

"It's all right," he called, grinning at the beast as if Lola's monster was a show dog who'd done him proud. "Come down here."

Lola gaped in wonder. The boy's voice was clear and beautiful as a trumpet call. Just the sound of it made her desperate to obey, except she couldn't. She was the monster now, and the monster listened to no one.

The idea that she couldn't do what the beautiful boy wanted made her want to weep, but then something extraordinary happened. The monster leaned down. It shuffled forward and fell to one knee, its claws digging three-foot trenches in the asphalt as it lowered its huge, shaggy head until its beady eyes were level with the boy's own.

"There's a good girl," he said, smiling so beautifully, it made what was left of Lola clench. "You did exactly what you're supposed to, but it's not time for that yet."

He held out his hand, his little fist a tiny gold speck below the creature's enormous black nose, and opened his fingers. Deep inside the monster, Lola gasped. There, resting on the boy's palm like a blood drop, was one of her pills. The creature keened when it smelled the blood and tried to turn its huge head away, but the boy grabbed hold of one of its teeth.

"None of that," he scolded in his ringing voice. Then, moving faster than Lola could follow through the monster's beady eyes, he yanked its mouth open and slammed the pill inside.

Lola and the monster howled as Victor's spell broke over them. Just like the first time they'd changed, blood poured down in a cascade. So much blood, far more than could have fit in one little pill, but that didn't stop it from crushing the monster like a fist until only Lola was left.

She dropped onto the pavement with enough force to send her gossamer spilling in all directions. When she tried to pull it back, all she got was blood. It coated her from head to toe, soaking her hair, her skin, her clothes. It was in her hair, in her eyes, in her mouth, and everywhere it touched, her master's voice followed.

Bound to me in blood and service.

The words of the spell fell on her like burning hammers, pounding her back into shape. When they faded at last, Lola cracked her eyes open to see that the blood was gone. The monster was gone too, leaving her lying on the cratered pavement in her yogurt-lady body with the Paladins—the two that could still stand, anyway—looming over her.

"What the hell was that?"

"Blood magic," the woman in charge replied, turning Lola's face with the flat of her burning sword. "Look at her. I've never seen a mage so stained."

Gun Paladin gave her a skeptical look. "Are you sure that's what it was? I've never seen a spell, blood magic or otherwise, that could change a body like that."

"Who knows what these monsters are capable of?" the head Paladin said, sliding her sword over Lola's panting throat. "But she's definitely one of Conrath's. I can smell his stench from here."

She bared her teeth one last time, and then she flicked her hand, vanishing her glowing sword as she turned to the ring of cops surrounding them. "Put her in cuffs and take her back to base. We'll question her after we find Conrath's apprentice."

Fear for Simon hit her like a punch, but Lola didn't dare move.

141

The other Paladin was still staring at her suspiciously, but he did as he was told, yelling for the cops to bring the warded cuffs. They were booking a blood mage.

Lola almost sighed in relief when one of the SWAT team ran forward with the spellworked handcuffs they used for criminal mages. Being shackled sucked, but the moment the head Paladin decreed her a blood mage, all the people under her command had started looking at Lola as a human monster rather than a *monster* monster. The force of their belief worked with the pill the strange boy had shoved into her mouth, adding extra weight to the pressure that kept Lola's jumping gossamer in place. Between the two, Lola managed to stay almost totally human as the policemen slapped the restraints on her and tossed her limp body into the back of their truck.

~~~

On the other side of the city, in a cheap apartment tucked directly under the highway, a man in a black leather motorcycle suit materialized on the plastic-covered mattress in his bedroom. He appeared in an instant, his body forming out of the air like condensing water, at least up until his neck. At the top of the spine where his head should have been, there was nothing. His collar just cut off in empty blackness, as if his riding suit was nothing but a shell filled with shadows.

For several long minutes, the headless man lay still as death. Then, like a shock had gone through him, he bolted off the mattress. Moving in frantic, angry jerks, he lurched toward his closet and yanked the cheap doors open to reveal a shelf full of identical black motorcycle helmets with mirrored visors.

He grabbed one at random, his jerky movements like silent curses as he tucked the helmet under his arm. Then, rising to his full impressive height, the headless man reached up to push aside one of the panels of his drop ceiling, revealing a hidden metal container the size of a hatbox.

In marked contrast to his earlier violence, he handled the box with extreme gentleness, plucking it gently as a flower from its hiding spot. When he had it safely in his hands, the headless man carried the box and the helmet into the bathroom.

Five minutes later, the Black Rider burst out of his apartment. He looked exactly as he always did: shiny black helmet, black leather riding suit covering every inch of flesh, his black boots falling silent as snowflakes as he raced down the cement stairs. Behind him, his apartment door slammed shut on its own, the deadbolt clicking into place as if an invisible hand had turned it from the inside.

His motorcycle was waiting for him by the time he got to the bottom of the stairs, its engine revved and purring silently, but it wasn't alone. Sitting on the bike with his small body leaned forward so he could rest his elbows on the handlebars was a lovely blond boy.

The Black Rider froze when he saw him, his gloved hands coming up for a fight. But the strange boy just laughed and held up a cheap flip-style cell phone, its tiny screen glowing with an incoming call from a thirteen-digit number.

For a long, silent moment, the Rider didn't move. Then he reached out a shaking hand and took the phone gently between his black-gloved fingers, holding it up to his helmet as a deep, educated voice spoke from the tinny speaker.

"Hello, my champion."

The Rider went stiff as a statue. Then he fell to one knee, helmet bent low in obedience. This only made the beautiful boy laugh harder. He rolled on the seat of the Rider's bike, his hooting voice bouncing like a trumpet off the highway bridge above.

And all around them, completely unaware, the sleeping city dreamed.

Chapter 8
7 pills

Being arrested wasn't the worst experience of Lola's life, but it was up there. She was forced to lie facedown on the floor of the SWAT truck while six cops stared at her like hawks watching a wounded rabbit. If they hadn't been convinced she was a blood mage who could take over their minds and move them like puppets, their scrutiny would have melted Lola on the spot. But in a strange twist, all that intense hatred actually helped Lola stay together, because at least blood mages were human. She actually felt more in control of her gossamer after an hour of being stared at than when they'd cuffed her, which was a huge relief. Though after what had happened in the parking lot, Lola wasn't sure she'd ever be truly "back together" ever again.

Just the memory was enough to make her twitch, causing the humans to tighten their fingers on their guns. She'd had breakdowns before but never anything close to that fast, or that *big*. Her memories of the incident were chaotic, but Lola was sure her monster must have been twenty feet tall by the end, which was crazy. Even with all her gossamer intact, she'd never been able to take a form that big. If that strange boy hadn't appeared with her pill, who knew how bad things might have gotten?

Happy as she was for the assist, though, the boy represented a whole other bag of problems. Given her reaction to his voice, Lola was certain he was a fairy, but why would a random fairy help her like that? She hadn't gotten a taste of his gossamer, but she was pretty sure she'd never met him before. He hadn't looked shocked at the sight of her monster, though, and he'd known exactly how to use her pills. Those were supposed to be a secret to everyone except Victor's closest people and a few special exceptions like Tristan, so how had this random fairy known to grab a pill off the ground and shove it into her mouth?

She fretted over it for the whole drive, which turned out to be a long one. Lola couldn't see where they were going from the back of the SWAT truck, but they had to be well outside the DFZ by this point. Where outside the city, though, she couldn't begin to guess. The brightly lit warehouse they dragged her into when they finally stopped could have been anywhere.

At least the guards let her walk on her own this time. The SWAT team formed a circle around her, marching Lola through a pair of security doors and down a long hall that was clearly part of a prison facility. The cell they stopped at was a windowless cement box with spellwork-covered walls clearly designed to hold mages.

Not actually being a mage, Lola didn't care about that. She was far more upset about the inch-thick wall of bulletproof glass. Steel bars she could have shifted through no problem, but those tiny air holes would have been a challenge even at her best, which she most definitely was not. Add in the cameras bolted to every wall, and Lola's hopes for wiggling out of this trap were sinking lower by the second.

At least the SWAT team didn't stick around. The second she was in the cell, the cops started marching down the hall so fast, they were practically running. Lola didn't blame them. She might not actually be the blood mage they thought she was, but if she'd seen the thing she'd turned into back in the parking lot, she'd have run away too.

Once they were out of sight, Lola shrank her wrists a fraction to give herself some room inside the tight handcuffs and walked over to test the glass. Sure enough, it was thick as a brick. The air holes were way up high too. She'd have to drastically stretch her shape to reach them, which was a no-go due to the cameras. If her

146

gossamer hadn't been in such sorry shape, she might have risked it, but now that Lola no longer had six cops browbeating her with their belief that she was an evil—but human!—blood mage, her magic was jerking all over the place.

Pulling her magic in tight in a vain effort to keep herself together, Lola slid down the glass and closed her eyes to focus on the car she'd left in the parking lot. Leaving so much of her gossamer behind had been a calculated risk. The missing chunk made her weaker, but unlike this body, her car was still in the DFZ. If she could just switch her consciousness over, she could cut this form free and flit right back to where the Paladin had dropped her pills.

There was no reason it shouldn't have worked. All of her was made from the same gossamer, which meant any body she took was just a conceit. A real fairy could have done it, but Lola wasn't one of those. She wasn't even a properly functioning changeling anymore. Even with the taste of Victor's pill still coating her tongue, Lola could already feel the monster lurking just under her skin. If she stretched her magic too far, the control Victor's blood had given her would snap, and she'd be lost again.

She had to do something, though, so Lola gave it a try, clenching her fists as she struggled to imagine the car as her body and this body as dust. She could still feel the coupe clearly somewhere to the north, but the moment she tried to reach out, she knew it wouldn't work. She was just too fragile. Her gossamer was already as soft as paraffin wax, and her mind wasn't doing much better. Every time she went to push, she saw the monster waiting to eat her, and her magic fell apart.

Lola slammed her fists down on the white-painted cement floor. On her wrist beneath the handcuffs, her sister's silver thread began to lash in reply, jerking so hard that it cut through her softening gossamer. Lola clutched her bound hands to her chest at

147

once, looking nervously at the camera despite the fact that no human but Victor had ever been able to see it.

"Shh," she whispered, bending down to kiss the jerking thread as she smoothed her gossamer back over it. "It's all right. I'll get us out of here somehow."

As ever, she had no idea if her sister could hear her, but Lola said the words with as much confidence as she could muster, because she needed to hear them, too. No matter how tired and weak she felt right now, if it was for her sister, she could endure. Lola had already survived more for her sister's sake than she ever could have managed on her own. This was no different. She could do it. She just had to—

"If you're going to lie to yourself, you should at least make it believable."

Lola jumped so high, she lost her balance and crashed onto the cold cement floor. She scrambled back to her knees a second later, whipping around to see a small figure standing on the other side of the glass wall.

It was the boy from before, the fairy. He still looked golden and perfect in the harsh prison lights, and his voice was still the loveliest thing she'd ever heard. But there was something unsettling about the way he was grinning down at her, like a cat playing with a mouse.

"Who are you?" Lola demanded, folding the wrist with her sister's thread against her chest. "Why are you following me?"

"Me? Follow *you?*" He laughed, a beautiful, cruel sound. "Don't be ridiculous. I wouldn't lift a finger for a changeling. I'm only here because of her."

He pointed at the wrist Lola was jealously guarding, and the silver thread gave its strongest jerk yet, ripping through the protective layer of gossamer Lola had just pressed over it to shine like a flame in the harsh fluorescents.

"There's my lovely!" the fairy said, his face splitting into a dazzling smile before turning to a scowl as his golden eyes went back to Lola. "You upset my treasure. She doesn't like it when you panic."

Lola felt as if the floor had fallen out from under her. She didn't even feel her jumping gossamer anymore. The whole world had shrunk to the smiling boy standing on the other side of the glass.

"You're the fairy who stole my sister."

The boy looked insulted. "There are fairies and there are *fairies*," he said, turning up his nose. "As for your 'sister,' what a curious notion. You, related to a human?" The fairy scoffed. "I'm closer to you than she is, considering *I* made you."

"Give her back!" Lola cried, banging her bound fists against the glass. There was a whirr as the security cameras in the hallway turned toward the noise, but Lola didn't care. She had her purpose, clean and bold and right in front of her, and she threw herself at it with everything she had left.

"Give me back my sister!"

"No," the fairy said, the little bells on his turned-up shoes jingling gracefully as he began to pace in front of her prison cell. "Firstly, you never had her to begin with, so how could I give her back? Second, even if I did agree to your ridiculous demand, what would you do with her? You can't possibly think you could make her happier than I do. I'm a being of enormous power. You're a changeling who can't even keep herself out of a human jail."

"This isn't my fault!" Lola cried. "Victor's the one that everybody hates! I'd be fine if he hadn't decided to screw everyone over and vanish with my pills!"

The fairy wagged a finger at her. "Uh-uh-uh, there you go, lying again. You could have avoided all of this by staying safely at home like a good little monster, but no. You had to go mucking

149

about with things you shouldn't, and now I have to clean up the mess."

He smirked at her as he finished, but Lola just stared. "How do you know all this?"

"That's a very rude question to ask the benevolent soul who's come all this way to get you out of that cell."

Lola blinked at him. That couldn't be true, but fairies couldn't lie.

"You don't have to look so surprised," he huffed, crossing his slender arms over his chest. "Do you think I put you back into that form just so the humans would have an easier time locking you away? And here Victor said you were smart."

Hope soared inside her. "You know Victor?"

"How could I not?" the fairy said, reaching straight through the glass to tweak her nose. "He's been dumping his blood into you for years."

His brief touch burned like a cinder, but Lola ignored it. "Do you know where he is?"

"He's where he always is," the fairy said, giving her a sharp-toothed smile. "Exactly where he wants to be. You're the one who's out of place, but I'm here to fix that. For a price, of course."

Of course. Fairies never did anything without payment, but Lola wasn't convinced. "How are you going to do it? This is a prison. There are cameras everywhere."

"I can do anything I want when it comes to you," the fairy replied smugly. "You're *my* changeling, never forget. All I have to do is—"

He snapped his fingers, and Lola suddenly found herself on the other side of the glass. It happened so quickly, she barely had time to feel the floor under her feet before he snapped again and sent her back.

"See?" he told her with a grin. "Easy-peasy."

150

Lola stumbled against the glass wall, clenching her gossamer out of habit, but there was no need. Despite being jerked like a fish on a line, her magic felt no better or worse than when they'd thrown her in here. She didn't even feel any nudges from the humans that had to be watching her through the cameras. No guards came through the doors, either, even though the boy was standing right outside her cell, which meant they still must not be able to see him. Had he made her invisible too? If so, then maybe he really *could* get her out.

"Okay," Lola whispered, straightening back up with a steadying breath. "What's your price? And *don't* say my sister. I'll die in this cell before I let her go."

"As if I'd waste my breath asking for something that's not even yours to give," the fairy said. Then his face curled back into that mocking smile. "But I'm nothing if not open to suggestion. Tell me, little changeling, what are you willing to trade for your freedom?"

That was a good question. Lola didn't exactly have much to work with at the moment, but she did have one card left.

"A dream," she offered, pressing her face against the glass. "I'll feed you a dream."

That was normally enough to make fairies salivate, but the boy just rolled his golden eyes. "What would *I* do with a changeling dream? Haven't you been paying attention? You're a copy, and a far degraded one at that. I have the original: my own beautiful girl who gives me all the dreams I want. You're insulting both of us if you think you can match her. Try again."

Lola hit the glass with a snarl. How dare he talk about her sister like she was nothing but a trough for him to feed off? She was tempted to tell him to shove his offer, but her anger had brought the monster near the surface again, reminding Lola that this was no time to pick fights she couldn't win. If she didn't get out of here and back to her pills, this arrogant brat would keep her sister forever. There was nothing Lola wouldn't give to prevent that. No pride she wouldn't swallow as she bowed her head.

"What do you want from me?"

The fairy tapped his pointed chin, making a great deal of thinking it over. "A promise," he said at last. "I'll get you out of this cage, but in return, you must promise that the next time you see me, you will claim me as your guest."

Lola gave him a suspicious look. "That's it?"

"You want me to add more?"

"No," she said quickly, but her mind was racing. This *had* to be a trap, but what kind and to what purpose, Lola had no idea. She couldn't stay locked up in here, though. It hadn't even been two hours, but her jumpy gossamer was already itching like crazy. If she didn't get her pills back soon, she might as well have just stayed the monster.

"All right," she said with a sinking feeling. "I promise."

The fairy smiled and snapped his fingers. The sound of it was still echoing in her ears when Lola found herself standing next to him on the other side of the glass. Just as before, there'd been no sense of movement. She'd simply been one place, then another.

"Don't even think about going back on your word," he warned, looking up at her. "Unlike lying humans, you're made of gossamer. You break that promise, your own magic—which is to say *my* magic—will make you regret it."

"I know how my gossamer works," she snapped, stepping away from him.

"At least you weren't stupid enough to thank me," the fairy said, giving her a wink. "See you soon."

He was already starting to disappear when Lola cried, "Wait!"

The fairy reemerged with a scowl, and Lola fell to her knees. "Please," she said, swallowing her anger in the name of something

152

much dearer. "Before you go, can you at least tell me my sister's name?"

The fairy turned up his nose. "The changeling presumes she is worthy of such a gift?"

"You're the one who made me like this," Lola reminded him. "You took my sister. *You* made me a monster. The least you can do is tell me her name!"

She was yelling by the end. She'd intended to flatter and beg since she'd yet to meet the fairy who didn't love a good suck-up, but twenty years of suppressed anger was boiling up inside her. She would have killed him in that moment if she could have, but the fairy just smiled and grabbed her face.

"You forget yourself," he whispered, his touch burning like hot iron. "It was the blood mage who made you a monster at your invitation. *I* made you beautiful."

The "beautiful" was still echoing in her ears when the fairy vanished. There was no puff of smoke, no dissolving gossamer. He simply was no longer there, leaving Lola gasping on the floor of the prison hallway as the alarms began to blare.

She forced herself to her feet at the sound, cursing the fairy as she charged down the hall. She stopped directly beneath the first camera she saw, taking advantage of the blind spot to ditch the spellworked handcuffs. She shed her yogurt-lady body as well, puffing up her misbehaving gossamer until she'd taken the form of the largest of the SWAT team members.

It wasn't a perfect copy since they'd kept their helmets on in her presence, but the nice thing about uniforms was that they still worked even when you only got them mostly right. She didn't feel any whacks of disbelief when she ran under the cameras, so it must have been good enough, but something still felt off. Every light in the prison was flashing angry red now, the alarms blaring like banshees, but Lola didn't see anyone running toward her cell.

That made no sense. The prison they'd walked her in through hadn't been *that* big. She should definitely have seen a guard by now, but the hall in front of her was empty.

Maybe they were afraid of sending people in because they still thought she was a blood mage. That didn't seem right, but Lola was too desperate to look her good fortune in the mouth. She marched her stolen SWAT body straight down the hall like a man on a mission, grateful the emergency gave her an excuse to keep her helmet on as she approached the checkpoint at the end of the hall.

The steel door was locked when she reached it, but the pair of guards who'd been sitting in chairs on the other side when she'd been brought in were gone. She didn't see anyone sitting in the security office on the other side of the bulletproof windows, either. It was impossible to get a full view from out in the hall, but the desks that watched the cameras all appeared to be unmanned.

Lola had no idea what miracle had sucked the guards away, but she thanked her lucky stars for it. Firming up her guard costume, Lola took the keycard off his belt and tapped it confidently against the sensor panel beside the door.

Having only seen the card in glimpses in a dark truck while her face was pressed into the ground, Lola's copy was less than perfect. But while even the most basic security systems could handle human mages these days, she'd yet to find one that could deal with a changeling. It didn't matter that the keycard was just a figment of her imagination. All she had to do was believe it would work and her gossamer took care of the rest, turning the red light to green as the heavy security door opened with a *click*.

She ran through in a rush, hoping to fool anyone watching on the other side into believing she was just another panicked officer responding to the alarm, but it was a wasted display. The guard office really was empty, as was the hallway on the other side that led to the parking garage where she'd been brought in. That struck Lola as very suspicious, so she slowed her pace, creeping down the hallway with her back pressed against the cinder block wall.

She heard the ruckus long before she saw it. Directly ahead of her, past the big steel doors that led to the warehouse where the SWAT trucks were parked, dozens of people were shouting at the top of their lungs. There were crashes, too, as if someone was driving a truck into a wall repeatedly.

It sounded like a riot, but it wasn't until she peeked through the garage door's metal-hatched window that Lola understood. The reason there'd been no guards to stop her from escaping was because the alarms hadn't been for her. They were for the Black Rider, who was in the garage directly ahead of her, fighting every cop in the building.

Lola wouldn't have believed it if it hadn't so clearly been so. The Rider looked exactly as he had before he'd lost his head. He even moved the same, his leather-clad body sliding between the riot-geared officers like water before he sent them all flying with a shove of his invisible power. He was still hugely outnumbered, but these were normal policemen, not Paladins. The Rider tossed them around like plastic action figures, his invisible shield full of caught bullets from their useless guns.

Lola watched in awe. If she'd tried a stunt like that, she would have melted after the first shot, but the Rider must really have been something different. Maybe he really *was* an urban legend, because the more the guards shouted about the Black Rider being real, the stronger he seemed to become, throwing whole SWAT trucks with his invisible power as he cut a path toward the door where Lola was hiding.

She had it open before he got there, keeping her guard costume just long enough to get one more swipe out of his keycard before ditching the disguise so the Rider wouldn't attack her by accident. He froze when she came out, just stopped in his tracks with a guard dangling in the air above him. Then he tossed the man into the wall and ran straight at her.

She ran toward him as well, her yogurt-lady face bursting into a smile as she realized what had happened. He'd come for her! Whether he'd done it out of caring or because he still needed her help to find Victor, Lola didn't care. No one had ever come to her rescue before! She was always expected to fend for herself, but the Rider was charging straight at her, sweeping a squad of men out of the way with a wave of his hand as he ran to her side.

"I thought you were dead!" she cried, throwing her arms around him.

The Rider stumbled when she grabbed him. As ever, though, he recovered in an instant, snapping his fingers to summon his black bike out of the shadows just as he'd done before.

"Get on."

Lola jumped at the deep voice. "You can *talk?!*"

The Rider's answer to that was to snatch her off the ground and place her on his motorcycle. He jumped on right after. The bike dipped sharply from his weight, forcing Lola to grab onto his leather jacket.

"What is going on?" she yelled.

"I tripped the alarm," he explained as he started his bike. "The Paladins will be here any minute, which means we need to go."

The words were quick and no-nonsense, but they still left her speechless. The Rider's voice was just so rich, as deep and warm as fresh caramel, nothing at all like the cold aura he projected. She was still lost in the contrast when the Rider launched his bike forward.

As ever, the black motorcycle made no sound at all as he raced them out of the garage and through the destroyed front gates of the Toledo PD Special Response compound. Lola could barely

156

even feel it moving as the Rider picked up speed, shooting them down the municipal side road onto a state highway already buzzing with early morning traffic.

As the prison faded into the dark behind them, Lola relaxed onto the bike's hard seat, moving closer to the wall of the Rider's back as he wove between the cars.

"We need to get back to the DFZ!" she yelled over the wind.

"Can't," he replied, his deep voice cutting through the wind like a stone. "The city's turned against us. She's the one who told the Paladins where we were. If we go back, they'll come after us again."

Lola shook her head against his back. "The Paladin dumped my pills out in the parking lot. I have to go back for them, and we have to help Simon! They were going for him next."

"Simon's fine," the Rider said. "I already messaged to check on him. He's safe in his house, hidden behind his wards."

That was a relief. Simon's home was almost as well warded as Victor's. Lola didn't know if that would stop a spirit like the DFZ, but the Paladins wouldn't be able to get the jump on him, at least.

But while she no longer had to worry about Simon, Lola herself was another story. She wasn't sure what time it was—her phone was gone, probably dropped back in the parking lot with her pills—but it couldn't be that long until morning. Even if her gossamer had been acting normal, she'd need a pill shortly after sunrise no matter what. As she was now, Lola could feel the monster growing under her skin again, pulling her gossamer tight, like a balloon about to burst.

"I need my medicine."

The Rider's body sighed against hers, and then he leaned to the side, taking them across three lanes toward the turnoff for Highway 75 to the DFZ.

~~~

It took them an hour to drive from the outskirts of south Toledo, Ohio, to the DFZ. It would have taken Lola twice as long by herself, but the Rider wasn't bothered by things like morning traffic. His bike threaded through the cars like a darting fish. Soon, the sky ahead of them was bright with the gleaming, cliff-like spires of the Skyway's famous superscrapers. It really had been a miraculously fast journey, but for Lola, it still wasn't fast enough.

It couldn't have been more than six hours since the fairy had forced the pill into the monster's mouth, but Lola's gossamer already felt close to its limit, and not in the usual way. Normally when she was late for a pill, her magic felt slidy and loose, like melting ice cream. This time, though, Lola felt tight and full to the brim, like she was being squeezed to death by her own gossamer.

It was a new and terrifying feeling. The Paladin who'd ripped into Victor's spell must have broken something serious, because they hadn't even cleared the Toledo suburbs when Lola got the prickly feeling that meant she was growing fur. The helmet she'd conjured to hide herself from the drivers the Rider blew past started to warp as her mouth filled up with teeth. Even the streetlights grew dimmer, their flashing orange turning gray in the monster's terrible vision.

She huddled in the Rider's shadow as they raced down the highway, terrified that someone would look out their car window and see her. In her current state, all it would take was one puzzled look to push her gossamer over the edge. The Rider must have done something special, though, because none of the early-morning commuters so much as glanced their direction. It wasn't until she noticed she couldn't feel the wind anymore that Lola realized the Rider had wrapped them in a bubble, using his invisible power to make them invisible, too, as he shot north along

158

the shore of Lake Erie toward the bright lights of the DFZ.

That was the only reason she made it. By the time they crossed the border, Lola couldn't have passed for human at a monster-costume convention. Traffic got thicker as they entered the city, forcing the Rider to slow down if he didn't want cars crashing into his invisible barrier. Eager as Lola was to get back to her dropped pills before something happened to them, she knew she wasn't going to make it to the parking lot at this rate, so she told the Rider to head for her apartment instead since it was closer.

At least, that was what she attempted to tell him. It was hard to get words past her giant teeth. The Rider must have understood enough, though, because he turned them at once, racing down the ramp into the Undercity.

For once, Lola was glad he'd stalked her. It meant she didn't have to give him directions as he wove through the cozy alleys that had attracted her to the New Mexicantown neighborhood and came to a stop in front of her garage. She rolled off his bike like a pile of fur pillows, keeping low behind her neighbor's trashcans to hide her horrible appearance as she grabbed the metal garage door and wrenched it out of her way.

She vanished her helmet the moment she was inside, which turned out to be a mistake. As warped as the helmet had gotten, its presence had helped to reinforce Lola's belief in her own humanity. Once it was gone, there was nothing to hide the horror of her jagged teeth, and her change started to speed up.

With a pitiful keening she couldn't believe was coming from her own throat, Lola threw herself up the garage stairs toward her living room door. Her paws had grown too big to use the knob, so she ripped it open, her claws shredding the heavy wood like paper.

Crawling over the splinters, Lola shambled into her living room, wincing as the low keening sound got louder. She sounded like a dying animal, but she couldn't make the noise stop, so Lola tried not to worry about it, focusing all her energy on getting to the kitchen.

Her massive paws took the handle clean off the fridge the first time she reached for it. She heard Buster run for cover at the crash, but her eyes were so bad now that she couldn't see him. She could barely make out the fridge light when she finally got the door open. When she reached inside, though, she moved her unfamiliar paw too hard, breaking straight through the glass shelf she'd been reaching for and sending its contents scattering across the kitchen floor.

The monster began making frantic noises as she pawed through the mess. She had to find her pills. Had to. But her beady little eyes couldn't make out the plastic container among the broken pickle jars and leftover takeout boxes. She was starting to panic for real when she felt something large, solid, and man-shaped press into her back. An arm reached over her shoulder next, taking something out of the fridge and placing it in her hand.

Lola nearly cried in gratitude when her claws closed around the hard plastic container that held her pills. Then she nearly cried in frustration when the lid refused to come off. It was one of those little cup containers, the kind with the screw-on top, but her claws were too long and curved to get a good grip. She was still fumbling with it when the Rider snatched the container back. She heard the pills rattle as he opened the lid, and then she felt the cool, tiny, bloody touch as the two tabs landed in her padded paw.

She really did start crying then. Big, monstrous tears of thankfulness and shame as she opened her mouth and threw both pills down her gaping maw. The Rider helped her do it, covering her jagged teeth with his gloves to keep the pills inside her mouth long enough for her to swallow. She heard the faucet going next, and then something cool and smooth was shoved into her hand. A glass. He'd gotten her a glass of water.

160

Sobbing in thanks, the monster brought the glass to her teeth and tipped it back, not caring if she spilled. She'd never taken two pills at once before, and the taste of blood was overwhelming. It spread through her like a stain, and then the monster's body snapped like a whip as the spell began to work.

Lola fell backward, landing on the floor with enough force to shake the building. The pain was beautiful, cleansing. It washed away the horror she'd become, all the ugly, shameful things she didn't want to be. She could already feel her claws retracting, the jagged teeth shrinking back into her jaw. Her body collapsed back into its normal proportions, and the fur and scales disappeared, leaving only smooth, human skin behind.

When it was over, she was lying sprawled on her kitchen floor. The chill told her she was naked, but Lola couldn't bring herself to care. She was exhausted, wrung out. All she wanted to do was sleep for a century.

She'd closed her eyes to do just that when she felt something smooth and warm against her new skin. Leather, she thought dimly. Arms slid under her, lifting her gently off the floor and carrying her to a soft, flat surface that smelled like cat. Her couch, Lola realized as a blanket landed on top of her. The Black Rider had laid her on her couch.

Lola went still as her exhausted brain finally caught up with what that meant. The Rider had seen her. The real her.

A sob burst out before she could stop it. She heard the Rider jump at the sound, but Lola just rolled over, pulling the blanket over her head.

It was pointless, of course. There was no hiding anymore. The Rider knew what she was now. Knew she was a monster, and not a beautiful, deadly, useful one like him. She was an abomination. A huge, ugly, clumsy, out-of-control menace.

Another sob ripped out of her. Lola buried her face in the

couch cushions, fighting to hold it in, but the cries came hiccupping out no matter what she did. Each one hit her tender gossamer like a punch, reminding her of what was at stake. She couldn't let herself go to pieces now. Even after two pills, she still felt like she was barely holding on. If she put any more stress on her magic, it'd all fall apart again, and she didn't have any more pills stashed in her apartment. She *had* to keep it together, but even the feel of her sister's thread jerking on her wrist couldn't stop the sobbing. She was still trying when something heavy landed on her shoulder.

Lola froze, not moving for a full five seconds before she realized the weight was the Rider's hand. He didn't speak, didn't make a sound. If not for the pressure of his gloved fingers, she wouldn't have known he was there at all.

For several moments, the pressure just sat there on her shoulder. Then, hesitantly, the Rider's hand slid down her arm and vanished. It landed again on her shoulder a second later, then brushed down again before returning to her shoulder to repeat the motion.

Lola blinked in confusion. The Rider was *petting* her, stroking her through the thick blanket as if she was a skittish cat. She normally would have found that insulting, but she was so desperate for any comfort right now that the motion felt soothing. She leaned into it a second later, the sobs subsiding as her body relaxed into the couch.

It didn't solve any of her problems, but the calm, heavy pressure of the Rider's hand sliding down her arm was just unexpected enough to knock Lola out of her downward spiral. As the panic receded, exhaustion rose to take its place, making her gossamer feel heavy as lead as she sank deeper into the cushions.

She felt the couch creak as the Rider sat down on the edge next to her, but the petting didn't stop. Lola wasn't sure if that was weird or sweet, but she threw herself into it all the same, her exhausted body going boneless under the Rider's warm, firm pressure until it lulled her into a deep, dreamless sleep.

~~~

She woke several hours later to a throbbing pain in her head. Lola groaned and rolled over, reaching up to mash her fingers into her forehead. The pressure relieved the pain a little, and she decided to risk opening her eyes.

The first thing she saw was the blanket, still over her head. That was good, because she was still naked. Curious, Lola glanced at her hand, eyebrows rising when she saw that her skin was porcelain pale. A quick glance at the red hair spilling over her shoulders confirmed it, and she cursed under her breath.

It was a sign of just how bad things had gotten if she'd ended up in Victor's doll body, though Lola was hard-pressed to imagine how it could have been worse. She'd never needed two pills before. Never reverted to the monster twice in twenty-four hours, either. Her gossamer still didn't feel right, either, making her worry that she'd really broken something this time.

If that was true, she was done for. Assuming she could find all the pills the Paladin had dumped out in the parking lot, she only had five left. That was barely enough for a single day if she had to take a double dose every time. But while her gossamer still had that weird, itchy, overfull feeling, her current body seemed stable aside from the headache. It definitely wasn't safe to dawdle too long in the DFZ now, so Lola decided to suck it up and get moving.

The first step was clothes. She closed her eyes and focused, imagining herself in a long T-shirt and sweat pants. Big, thick, ugly ones.

163

The thought that the Rider had seen her naked while she was the redhead made Lola want to bury her head in the sand. It was a stupid reaction. All of her bodies were made up, so it didn't matter what the Rider thought of any of them, but Lola still didn't want him thinking *this* was the form she'd chosen.

If she'd had the strength, she would have turned herself into literally anything besides Victor's doe-eyed doll. She seriously considered changing into a dog just so she could avoid what was sure to be an awkward conversation. But a dog on a motorcycle would have drawn even more attention than the redhead. She was already dressed in any case, so Lola kicked the blanket off and sat up to face the world.

The first thing she saw was her trashed living room. The front door was completely gone, clawed to pieces. Her carpet, the nice, new, soft carpet she'd put in just last year, was ripped to shreds where the monster had walked across it, and her fridge door was completely off its hinges. The shelf she'd broken was fixed, though, and someone had cleaned all the spilled food off the floor.

There was only one person it could have been. It took Lola a surprisingly long time to find him, though, because the Black Rider was squatting in her kitchen, his helmet shoved inside the cabinets as if he was looking for something. Whatever it was, he must have found it, because he stood up a few seconds later. Lola was pushing herself up for a better look when he turned and walked back into the living room, carrying what appeared to be a bowl balanced delicately between his black gloves.

He put the bowl down on the coffee table in front of her, and Lola leaned forward to see that it was oatmeal. Her own instant vanilla oatmeal, complete with spoon. She looked up at the Rider, but he'd already walked off toward her bedroom. He returned a moment later with the rolling chair from her computer desk, pushing it over to make himself a seat on the other side of the table.

The whole thing gave Lola an intense feeling of *déjà vu*. She almost expected him to get out his pad and start writing, but he didn't. He just sat there, his visor a blank, reflective mask as he waited for her to eat.

Never one to waste food, Lola grabbed the bowl and dug in. Her gossamer was still tender, so she ate slowly, letting the steam from the oatmeal ease her headache. By the time she'd cleaned the bowl, she felt much better.

"Thank you," she said as she set the empty bowl aside. "For the food and for coming to get me. You saved my life."

The Rider shrugged, and Lola frowned. Had he decided to stop talking again?

"Any sign of the Paladins?" she asked when the silence had gone on too long.

The chair creaked as the Rider shook his head. "No. We've been here long enough for an ambush, but I haven't seen a thing. My guess is the DFZ didn't like them bringing a bunch of heavily armed American cops into her Free Zone and revoked their access."

Lola closed her eyes. There it was again, that supernaturally rich, deep voice. She could almost taste the magic in it, but it didn't feel menacing. Lola leaned closer, watching her reflection in the rider's glossy helmet. *What are you?* she wanted to ask. *Why didn't you talk before?*

If he'd spoken to her in that voice from the beginning, she probably wouldn't have run. In fact, if he hadn't been acting just like he always did, Lola would have suspected this talking man wasn't the Rider at all. The warm, alluring voice was just too disconnected from the big, scary monster who killed with a flick of his hands.

"How are you here?" she asked. "I saw you turn to ash."

The Rider shrugged again, and Lola sighed. Clearly, this new chattiness didn't apply to conversations about himself. As curious as she was, though, Lola didn't push.

She owed the Rider big-time now, and not because of the prison break. Anyone who could face her monster—*touch* her monster—and not run screaming deserved his secrets. Unfortunately, she was going to have to ask his help again. She'd pulled it back this time thanks to her reserve pill stash, but those were gone now. All the pills she had left were scattered across a parking lot under the Financial District, and Lola didn't have the gossamer to change her body right now, much less to make a car.

"We need to keep looking for Victor," she said, pushing up from the couch to carry her bowl back to the kitchen. "I have a lead on a fairy who might know where he is."

And a taste of his gossamer, she thought, remembering the burning bite of the fairy's magic. If she got that to Tristan, he should be able to tell her the fairy's name, maybe even take her straight to him. Unfortunately, the card he'd given her with his number had been lost with her phone and everything else. She'd just have to go to his barrow and hope he was there, *after* she got her pills.

"We have to go back to that parking lot," she said as she put her bowl in the sink. "Once I get my pills and collect the gossamer I left in my car, I'll go to Tristan and get an ID on the fairy. If we can find him, I'm sure we'll find Victor. Does that sound good to you?"

The Rider nodded and stood up. He walked over to her ruined door and stopped, visor turned toward her expectantly.

Lola got the hint. "Let me feed Buster," she said, opening the cabinet where she kept the cat food.

Normally, the sound of the can opener would have brought her big chonk running, but he didn't come today. Lola didn't know

166

if that was because the Rider was here or if he was still traumatized from seeing her monster. She *really* hoped it was the Rider, because the thought of her kitty being afraid of her almost sent Lola back over the edge. She caught herself before it went too far, but the fact that she was still so unstable was terrifying.

She didn't have much longer, Lola realized. Even if she got her pills back, it was obvious that her gossamer was falling apart. Her sister's thread was jerking on her arm all the time now, reminding her of what was at stake. She had to focus on getting as much done in the next twenty-four hours as possible, because that might be all she had left.

Setting the cat bowl down with shaking hands, Lola made a mental note to ask Simon to look after Buster. He was allergic himself, but he'd make sure her cat found a good home with someone who wouldn't terrify him. That thought threatened to dissolve her again, so Lola forced it out of her head as she followed the Rider down the stairs into her garage.

His bike was ready and waiting by the time they reached the bottom of the stairs. The Rider hopped on, motioning for her to follow. Lola did so slowly, concentrating hard until she'd formed her misbehaving gossamer into a black helmet of her own.

Technically, it wouldn't keep her any safer than her bare head since gossamer was gossamer, but she'd learned from the Rider the value of hiding one's face. She definitely didn't want Victor's redhead showing up on any of the Black Rider's urban legend fan sites, so she slipped the helmet onto her head. When she was completely covered, she sat down on the bike and spun herself a garage door remote to let them out.

The garage door had a hard time going up with the gap her monster had bent in the bottom, but it rose enough for the Rider to slip under. Lola closed it behind them with a click before dissolving the remote. The Rider was kind enough to hop off and bend the metal door back into shape so Buster couldn't just run out. Lola thanked him in a whisper as he got back on his bike, hands shaking nervously as she wrapped them around his chest.

Even though she knew there was nothing inside his leather suit, Lola hadn't exactly touched a lot of people in her life. Not in a good way, at least. So far, though, every time the Rider had touched her, something good had happened, like when he'd petted away her panic or when he'd shoved her out of the way of the Paladin's fireball. That should have made her comfortable, but weirdly, Lola felt more nervous than ever, especially when she realized she still didn't know his name.

"Um," she said as he started down the alley. "Is there anything you'd like me to call you? Something besides Black Rider?"

He accelerated down the street as she spoke, covering her words in a rush of wind. Lola didn't even know if the Rider had heard her. She'd decided to just forget about the whole thing when he suddenly replied.

"Valente," he said, his rich voice rumbling through his chest into hers. "My mother named me Valente."

"Valente," Lola repeated with a smile. "Nice to meet you."

The Rider nodded, but he didn't say anything else as they whipped down the road, shooting through the maze of the Underground toward the parking lot, where, hopefully, her pills would still be lying on the ground.

Chapter 9
5 pills

Despite the Rider's perfectly good theory about the city revoking her deal with the Paladins, Lola kept a gossamer grenade ready to throw as they pulled into the parking lot where they'd been attacked last night. It was still empty this morning despite it being nearly nine a.m., probably because it looked like a war zone. The asphalt was scorched black, and there were hundreds of bullets lodged in the cement face of the support pillar that ran alongside it, but the real candle on the cake was Lola's car.

The two-door coupe lay in the middle of the scorched parking lot like a defeated tank. Its electric-blue paint job was bubbled and blackened from the fire, and its windows were completely shot out. If it had been a real car, it would have been irrecoverable. Because it was gossamer, though, the only real damage was a bit of stiffness from being left out on its own for so many hours.

It was going to take some finessing to get all of that hardened magic back inside, so Lola let the car be for the moment and got straight to the more important work of locating her pills. She found the spot where she'd turned into the monster easily by the gouges her claws had left in the pavement, but when she vanished her helmet to get a better look at the ground, all she saw were spent bullet casings.

"No, no, no," she whispered, rolling the shells frantically with her hands in the hopes of catching a glimpse of red. "They *have* to be here!"

She heard the crunch of the Rider's boots as he came closer, but Lola waved at him to stop. Victor's pills were delicate. She couldn't risk him stepping on one. Even when she pressed her

169

nose against the ashy pavement, she didn't catch so much as a whiff of blood. But just as she was starting to panic in earnest, she heard a familiar voice speak above her.

"You know, the best way to find a needle is to burn the haystack."

Lola jumped with a squawk, scrambling backward to see Tristan standing over her with an amused look on his handsome face. As usual, he was ridiculously dressed in a slim-cut white suit and pointed white-leather wingtip shoes. His hair was long and blowing in the wind, and for some reason, he was wearing a gold-caged rapier dangling from his belt. Lola didn't know if the sword was real or just part of his outfit, but it didn't bode well.

"What are you doing here?"

"Looking for you," the fairy said, glancing at her car. "That's not normally a problem since the dream you fed me acts as a pointer, but when I followed it this morning, I found the larger portion of your gossamer in ruins and *you* nowhere to be seen. What have you been doing?"

"Unless you're here to help, that's none of your business," Lola replied, pressing her face against the pavement to search under her car.

"Looking for these?" Tristan asked, holding up a small plastic baggie with red pills glinting like drops of blood inside.

"You found them!" Lola cried, leaping for the bag. Tristan let her grab it, but Lola's soaring elation came crashing back down once her trembling fingers counted the pills inside.

"Three?" she squeaked, suddenly frantic again. "There's only *three*? That can't be right! Where are the rest?"

"That was all I could find," Tristan said apologetically, taking a seat on the hood of her destroyed car. "And you're lucky I got those. The scavengers were all over this place by the time I arrived. If I hadn't come looking for you when I did, they'd have

170

junked your gossamer car for parts, and you'd be in even worse shape than you already are."

Lola didn't feel lucky. Three pills wouldn't get her past tomorrow even at the usual rate. The way she'd been popping them since Victor had vanished, it might not be enough to see her until sundown.

"Don't look so sad, Lola-cat," Tristan said, giving her a smile. "We're not beaten yet! Though I would feel better about our chances if you'd actually followed my advice."

His sea-blue eyes slid to the Rider standing behind her, but Lola shook her head.

"It's okay. He's a friend."

The fairy snorted. "I *highly* doubt that."

Lola stood up with a glare. "He saved my life."

"Is that so?" Tristan said, hopping off the hood of her car. "Would you excuse us a moment?"

Lola didn't realize that last part was directed at the Rider until Tristan's sea-salt gossamer washed over her. The next thing she knew, the trashed parking lot was gone. So were the Rider and his bike, leaving Lola standing next to her shiny, fully-repaired coupe on an empty stretch of highway by the sea. Stone cliffs rose like a wall at her back while the ocean stretched out to the horizon in front of her, sparkling and blue-black beneath the light of a full moon. The taste of the warm, salty air felt so real on her tongue, Lola had to remind herself several times that it was only gossamer as she turned to Tristan.

"Where is this?"

"Southern coast of California," Tristan replied, leaning against the guardrail that separated them from the fall to the rocky shore below. "I cleaned your car."

He smiled as if he expected a thank you, but Lola just crossed her arms.

171

"What are you doing?"

"I could ask you the same thing," he said, tapping his fingers against the ornate handle of his sword. "I specifically recall telling you to keep away from the Rider, and yet here you are, riding double with him."

"And I'm telling you it's okay," Lola insisted. "The Rider works for Victor too."

"That's a large part of why I warned you to stay away from him."

Lola gaped at him. "You knew he was working for Victor the whole time?" Seriously, did *everyone* know except her? "Why didn't you tell me?"

"Because I didn't want you falling into his clutches," Tristan said. "He's not safe."

"Why do you think I'm with him?" Lola snapped. "If the burned car didn't tip you off, I need some danger on my side right now."

Tristan shook his head. "The fact that you think he's on your side is the most dangerous thing of all. He belongs to Victor."

"So do I."

"There are differences of degree in all things," Tristan warned, giving her a hard look. "What will it take to convince you to stay away from him?"

"A lot," Lola said. "He's saved a whole pig's worth of my bacon in the last twenty-four hours."

"How chivalrous of him," Tristan said, his scornful voice twisting the word into an insult. "But the thing you call the Black Rider belongs to Victor in ways you can't imagine, and he's especially dangerous to fairies. He was built to be a weapon, and whatever he might have done to make you think otherwise, a weapon's all he can ever be."

She gave him a baleful look, and the fairy sighed. "Haven't you wondered why Victor worked so hard to keep the two of you separated for all these years?"

Lola rolled her eyes. She didn't want to play this game, but Tristan didn't normally talk about these things, and she *was* curious. "Okay, why?"

Tristan leaned closer. "It's because your dear Rider eats dreams."

"He's a fairy?" Lola asked, surprised.

"I would never call him such. He shares a few of our characteristics but none of our control." The fairy flashed her a knowing smile. "That's why your master feared to let his Rider near you. Changeling dreams are very delicious, and Victor didn't want his Rider developing a taste for what he couldn't have."

Lola looked away with a sigh. Of *course* Victor had done it because he didn't want his weapon being compromised. Clearly, all this turning-into-a-monster business was making her insane, because for a second there, she'd almost thought Victor had ordered the Rider to stay away out of concern for *her*.

"Don't give him your dreams, Lola," Tristan warned.

"Why not?" she asked, genuinely curious. She'd never fed anyone except Tristan.

"Because he won't be nearly as nice with them as I am," he replied. "And because your dreams belong only to me."

Any other time, Lola would have put that down to Tristan's eternal flirting, but he didn't look flirtatious now. His blue eyes were sharp and hungry, staring down at her like a hawk with a cornered mouse, and suddenly, Lola felt very, very small.

The feeling lasted only a second, and it was Tristan himself who broke the spell. As suddenly as he'd shifted, he popped back to his old smiling self. "We'll have to pick this up later, Lola-lamb," he said, glancing up at the sky. "Your *friend* is growing impatient."

Before Lola could ask what he meant by that, the warm sea

night began to warp around them. The moonlit sky caved in, the stars stretching out as if the whole thing was just a projection and someone was pushing on the back of the screen. It was nauseating to watch and more than a little terrifying, but Tristan just shook his head and moved his hand in a sweeping motion.

The lonely highway vanished as quickly as it had appeared. Tristan's gossamer melted like sugar, leaving behind only a faint, sea-salt tang on Lola's tongue as the wrecked parking lot burst back into view. As it faded, Tristan sat back down on the hood of her still-gleaming car, the only thing left of the illusion he'd woven. Now, though, instead of the sea, the Rider stood in front of them with his arms crossed over his chest and the ground at his feet covered in a thick layer of frost.

"Temper, temper, *Herr Ritter*," Tristan scolded, moving his sword to rest across his knees. "Nothing wrong with a private chat between old friends."

The Rider stepped forward, and Lola felt a pressure land on her shoulders. She gasped at the weight of it. The stuff felt almost like gossamer but thicker and numbingly cold.

But while she instantly started shivering, Tristan grew very still. He didn't stiffen when the Rider's power landed, didn't flinch. He just… stopped. And then, in a voice that was even colder than the invisible weight lying against Lola's skin, he said, "You will remove this filth from me, or I will remove it for you."

As he spoke, something in Tristan changed. Lola couldn't say what it was, exactly. Nothing looked different. He was still flamboyantly ridiculous with his snatched suit, gleaming sword, and perfectly tousled hair. But while all of the pieces were the same, the whole they formed was now completely different. This Tristan looked like a drawn blade. He hadn't moved from his relaxed seat on the coupe's hood, but all the casualness was gone from his posture as he drummed his fingers on the hilt of his sword, which Lola was now certain was not for show.

Any other day, that would have been her cue to run or at least conjure up some cover. Right now, though, Lola simply didn't have the time.

"Knock it off," she snapped, using her changeling knack of ignoring other people's magic to slide through the freezing pressure as she walked over to put herself between them. "I've only got three pills left, and I'm not wasting them on whatever this is, so can we please focus?"

To her surprise, Tristan acquiesced at once, his friendly mask snapping back into place as quickly as it had fallen. "Lola-kitten jumps to your rescue," he said, blowing the Rider a kiss before leaning back to grin at Lola. "Should I be jealous?"

"Only if you enjoy being delusional," Lola said, reaching into her pocket to pull out another of her foil-wrapped, gossamer-tasting candies. "I found the fairy who's been sending dreams all over the DFZ. He also claims that he's the one who made me, *and* he's working with Victor. I need you to taste his gossamer and tell me who he is."

"No need," Tristan said, hopping to his feet. "If even half of what you just said is true, we won't be able to take him by ourselves, and speaking his name will do nothing but attract his attention."

Lola couldn't believe what she was hearing. "But you promised," she said, fist clenching around the gossamer she'd made. "You *promised* me you'd help!"

"I *am* helping," Tristan said, his face growing serious. "You're in a lot more trouble than you realize, Lola-lark. I didn't come looking for you this early because I enjoy morning walks. I'm here because a matter has come to my attention that can no longer be ignored. Alva wants to see you."

Lola frowned. "What does the fairy queen want with me?"

175

"The *pretender to the throne,*" Tristan corrected sharply, "is having trouble adjusting to the magical changes going on in her territory. She might be weak, but Alva isn't stupid. She knows something big is happening, and she's invited you to her court to discuss it."

Lola scoffed. "Invited? She can't actually expect me to just forget she sent a troll to trash Victor's house and join her for coffee."

"She sent a *troll* to Victor's house?" Tristan repeated, incredibly intrigued. "How did you defeat it?"

The Rider twitched at the question. It was just a tiny motion, but Lola got the hint.

"Even when he's not home, Victor's secrets keep themselves," she said, lifting her chin. "Alva learned that the hard way."

"That certainly explains her urgency," Tristan said, looking delighted by the idea. "But loath as I am to defend anything of hers, I believe this invitation is Alva's way of being polite. Under the doctrine of hospitality that is an integral part of all barrow magic, she can't harm a guest she invites into her home. Of course, this also means you won't be able to harm her."

"Not planning on it," Lola said. "Not planning on going at all, actually."

Tristan shook his head. "On the contrary, I think you should."

"I don't have time for fairy politics."

"Maybe not," he said. "But if you don't answer her summons, she'll hunt you in earnest. Better to take the hospitality now than risk being taken prisoner and having no protections at all. Also, while you and I might not be able to stop this fairy you're so concerned about, Alva is another matter."

Lola sighed. "She's *not* going to help me."

"But she will absolutely help herself," Tristan argued. "You think Alva likes having a fairy that strong running rampant in her

176

territory? She's gnawing herself to pieces over this, which is exactly the position you want her in. All you have to do is offer up your knowledge of this stranger in exchange for Victor's safe return, and you'll have her whole court on your side."

He didn't make a bad point, but... "I've only got three pills left!" Lola cried. "I can't be wasting hours trying to trick someone who hates Victor into helping me find him."

"I'd argue this is the *best* use of your time," Tristan said gently. "Unless you think you can find Victor by yourself with the three pills you have left."

Lola dragged her hands through the doll body's red hair. Parleying with a fairy still felt like a stupid gamble, but so did driving around the city, chasing a fairy that could appear and disappear on a whim. That math changed quickly, though, if they could get the queen on their side. Even Tristan didn't deny that Alva was powerful, and she had a lot of fairies under her thumb. If Lola could convince her that they had a common enemy, it would put a lot of useful cards in their hand. Victor would hate it, too, which perversely made Lola want to do it more than any of Tristan's logic. There was just one problem.

"Other than the laws of hospitality," she said slowly, "how do I know this isn't a trap?"

"Oh, it's definitely a trap," Tristan said, giving her a dashing smile. "But traps are no worry when you have a proper escort."

He placed one hand on his sword while gallantly offering her the other. It was such a charming display, Lola was actually touched for a moment before her common sense kicked back in.

"What's the price?"

"How marvelously shrewd of you," Tristan said. "Fortunately, today's price is very cheap. All I ask in return for my protection is that you claim me as your guard."

"That's it?" Lola said, instantly wary. "Your price for coming with me is that you get to come with me?"

"The barrow Alva is currently infesting belongs to the true queen," Tristan explained. "Unfortunately, I have been unable to enter it since my lady vanished. When I heard Alva was looking for you, it seemed a bit of a golden opportunity. I get into the queen's barrow by Alva's own invitation, *and* I get to deny her plans for you."

"Two birds with one stone."

Tristan beamed at her. "Exactly."

Lola sighed. She still didn't want to do this, especially now that she knew Tristan's queen was involved. Morgan was the only one he'd ever shown true loyalty toward, but for the first time since she'd met him, Tristan had messed up. He'd told her what he wanted before he got it.

"I'll be your ticket into Alva's barrow on one condition," Lola said. "You have to tell me the name of the fairy who stole my sister."

"It won't do you any good," Tristan warned. "But very well. I promise I'll tell you the fairy's name *after* we go to Alva's."

"Now," Lola countered.

"And risk you running off on me?" Tristan shook his head. "I'll give you yours once I get mine, though it would be kinder not to tell you at all. This isn't a bear you should be poking, remember?"

"Fine," Lola said. "But I'm bringing my own guard." She looked over her shoulder at the Rider, who was still standing in his circle of frost. "Would you come with me?"

The Rider nodded instantly. Tristan, on the other hand, began to scowl. "I would recommend against it," he said. "Alva might be little more than a hobgoblin with delusions of grandeur, but she's still a fairy in a queen's lair. Are you sure you want to put a weapon like the Rider into her hands?"

Lola shrugged. "He'd be protected by hospitality, too, right?"

"Hospitality only means Alva can't kill or physically harm you," Tristan reminded her. "That leaves a great deal of room for creativity."

"I'm going."

The Rider's deep voice broke through the argument like a gong. For a moment, Tristan's face was shocked, and then his scowl returned, deeper than ever. "If you can talk, I *strongly* suggest you don't go."

"I don't care," he said, black visor fixed on Tristan. "I don't trust you."

"I'm sure I'll get over it," Tristan said, turning back to Lola. "Last chance not to make a terrible mistake."

"Let's just get this over with," Lola said, patting the bag of pills in the pocket of her sweatpants. "I have a fairy and a blood mage to find and not a lot of time to do it."

Tristan waved his hand, and a candy-red classic Lamborghini screeched into the parking lot. The car spun around the scorched pavement in a donut before sliding to a stop beside Lola's refurbished coupe, its doors going up with a pneumatic hiss. Lola rolled her eyes at the ridiculous display and placed a hand on her own car, finally letting the gossamer flow back into her, since Tristan had so clearly volunteered to drive.

Normally, reclaiming her magic felt good, like sticking a lost piece back into place. This time, though, the car's return only increased the strange, uncomfortably overfull feeling Lola had been struggling with all morning. She ignored the sensation, settling her gossamer with a shake as she walked around to the Lamborghini's passenger-side door.

Tristan was already in the driver's seat. He patted the bucket seat beside his invitingly, but Lola couldn't bear the idea of the tall Rider folding himself into the antique supercar's tiny rear seat, so she climbed into the back instead. Tristan gave her a sullen look

179

but refrained from comment as the Rider gingerly got in, sinking into the smooth leather passenger seat like a boulder.

"So," Tristan said as his gossamer car began to drive itself away. "Tell me how you managed to drop your pills all over a commuter parking lot."

"I'd rather not," Lola said, pointedly not looking at the scratched-up section of pavement where she'd turned into the monster. "But I did find out what the fairy's making the DFZ dream about. It's *Fenrir*."

"The monster movie?" Tristan pursed his lips. "Interesting choice."

"It gets weirder," Lola said before telling him what they'd learned at Simon's.

Tristan seemed not at all surprised to hear that Victor's disappearance had been planned, but he looked as puzzled as the rest of them when he heard how much of his fortune—in both money and people—the blood mage had poured into the movie.

"I wonder what he's after," Tristan said, tapping his fingers on the leather-wrapped steering wheel that didn't even seem to be connected to what the gossamer car was actually doing. "With the notable exception of yourself, human magic and fairy gossamer aren't terribly compatible. We're like a magician and his audience: the moment people know the trick, the whole thing falls apart."

"They're clearly doing something together," Lola insisted. "The boy fairy practically said that much to my face." She narrowed her eyes at Tristan. "Are you *sure* you can't tell me his name?"

"Trust me, Lola-love. If this visit doesn't clear things up, I'll take you back to my barrow and tell you all my postulations. How does that sound?"

"Like you're brushing me off," she said, flopping back against the tiny bench that passed for the Lamborghini's rear seat. "And while you play fairy politics, I'm going to pop."

"Nonsense," Tristan said, turning around. "Listen to your own story. You know Victor is alive and up to something with that fairy, right? Well, if that's true, then you're safe as safe can be. The blood mage has invested twenty years of effort into keeping your monster managed. He's not going to risk losing all of that over something as easily remedied as a few pills."

That was the same reasoning the Rider had given her, and though Lola absolutely believed her master would throw her under the bus the moment it suited him, it soothed her a little. The strange fairy hadn't let her die in the parking lot, after all, nor had he left her to the Paladins. That was a lot of effort for someone they intended to let die, so Lola tried to take heart, wrapping her hand around her sister's wildly jerking thread as Tristan's candy-red car drove them up onto the Skyways.

~~~

As befitted the self-styled queen of the DFZ, Alva's barrow was in Lakeview, the single most expensive neighborhood of the entire city. Unlike everywhere else on the Skyways, it wasn't a towering superscraper or a cluster of super-tall buildings like the one Jamie lived in. This was even more luxurious: a five-block stretch of landscaped parkland overlooking the water with lots big enough to build an actual house on.

Lola had lived in the DFZ her entire life, and the idea of a freestanding house on the Skyways still blew her mind. Even Victor's clients weren't rich enough to live here, so she'd only been by a few times, mostly to sightsee. Tristan's classic Lamborghini fit right in, though. The candy-red car didn't even draw a second glance from the incredibly stylish people walking their purebred dogs down the tree-lined streets. People who were themselves likely only employees of the mega-rich who actually lived here.

181

"Does every house have its own helicopter pad?" Lola asked, wedging her face into the triangle of the sports car's minuscule rear window.

"Some have two," Tristan replied. "And the street itself converts into a landing strip for private jets, though you do have to book ahead so people have time to move their cars."

Lola whistled, trying to look every direction at once as Tristan's summoned car drove them through a black iron gate onto a flagstone driveway through the biggest—and only—front yard Lola had ever seen on the Skyways.

It was so huge, it had its own flock of peacocks. Lola didn't know if the birds were gossamer or real, but just having the space to hold them in a city where the majority of the residents lived in apartments under bridges was an insulting level of luxury. The grounds were meticulously manicured and covered with the tallest bushes that would grow in the climate, since large trees didn't have the root-room to grow up here on the bridges, which meant gossamer trees were out as well. Even fairy queens had to wrangle with disbelief, and people in this neighborhood were absolutely judging the heck out of every plant choice.

Probably because the show-off yard took up the majority of the lot's space, the house itself was smaller than Lola expected. It was only three stories, but it was built in that pretentious boxy plantation style with a fantastic view of the lake. Very stereotypical rich person, but stereotypes were what fairies thrived on, and now that Tristan's car had pulled up to the front steps, Lola could smell Alva's gossamer like rotten fruit on the wind.

"Stay close," Tristan ordered as they got out. "And let me do the talking."

Lola had no argument with that. She was too busy trying not to gag as Tristan led them up the brick stairs to the mansion's ostentatious portico. The gossamer was thick as syrup now that they were standing on the threshold. But though it tasted strongly of Alva, the magic clearly did not belong to her.

It was such a weird disconnect, Lola couldn't actually put her finger on what was wrong. Finally, she decided that the gossamer felt slack, like a sail when the wind has gone out of it. The magic was still there, still potent, but while Alva was clearly the one holding the rope, it was obvious she didn't have full control.

Tristan must have thought so, too, because his face grew more disgusted by the second. By the time they were standing in front of the brass-plated front door, he looked like he was going to kill something.

"Are you okay?" Lola whispered.

"I will be once I'm out of here," Tristan whispered back, knocking on the door with the hilt of his sword.

The door opened immediately, swinging on its own to let them into a white marble entry hall. Tristan strode in at once. Lola followed more timidly with the Rider keeping close behind, his reflective helmet turning constantly like he was trying to look at everything at once.

Now that they were inside, Lola saw that the mansion's impeccable upkeep was only skin-deep. The estate's face was all perfectly kept gardens and flawless masonry, but the inside was dusty from neglect. There was no furniture, no fixtures, no sign that anyone had been in here in years. Tristan glared at the decay as if it was a personal insult as he drew his sword.

The rapier slid out of its sheath with a beautiful metallic ring. It sang again as Tristan swung it casually, cutting the air with a musical sound. Then, with a flick of his wrist, Tristan brought the slender blade up to nick his palm. Lola gasped as red blood welled from the wound, even though she knew it was only gossamer. For his part, Tristan looked affronted as he held out his hand to let the blood drip onto the dusty white stone.

"Really?" He sneered at the empty room. "Blood? *That's* your entry price? Couldn't you at least try to be creative?"

"You would have preferred something dearer?"

Lola jumped. The scratchy voice seemed to speak out of nowhere. As its words faded, the dusty room vanished, revealing the barrow Tristan's blood had paid to enter.

It was a field. A huge, open meadow like the grasslands of the Great Plains, only instead of grass, this land was carpeted in flowers. Every kind of bloom Lola had ever heard of and several she didn't recognize at all were growing in absurd profusion, the blossoms pushing over each other like they were fighting for position. But unlike the plants in the epic yard outside, which had looked almost too perfect, these flowers were clearly past their prime. They were still blooming, still lovely, but brown spots marred the petals' edges, and some stalks had fallen over entirely, their blossoms shriveled like deflated balloons.

It was still a jaw-droppingly impressive sight. Lola was turning in a circle, trying to take it all in, when she realized they were no longer alone.

A beautiful man stood in the flowers just in front of Tristan. His face looked human, but he was clearly a fairy. If the impossible, otherworldly beauty wasn't enough of a tip-off, the fact that his skin was the color of pine bark and his suit was made from still-growing evergreen fronds clinched it.

"Welcome to the queen's barrow," the fairy said in the same scratchy voice from before, the words rubbing against each other like branches as he swept into a graceful, if shallow, bow. He straightened again immediately, his pine-green eyes flicking from Tristan to the Rider.

"I'm sorry," he said, his voice completely unapologetic. "The queen's invitation was for the changeling only. You two will have to wait outside."

"Nice try, Juniper," Tristan said, wrapping his arm around Lola's shoulders. "But the lovely changeling requested an escort, so I"—he paused, throwing the Rider a weary look—"*we* are here as her guests. I'm afraid Alva will have to accept all of us if she wants to talk."

"You are in no position to make demands, fallen knight!" the fairy called Juniper snarled, his mouth opening to show a forest of spiny black teeth. "You should be grateful the queen permits your presence at all."

"Those are the terms," Tristan said, vanishing the last drops of his blood from his sword before sheathing it again. "Does Alva want to see the girl or not?"

The fairy glowered, but then, to Lola's surprise on a lot of levels, he pulled a sleek modern cell phone out of his needles. He turned his back to them and raised the phone to his ear, saying something low to the person on the other end. There was a short, tense conversation, and then the fairy shoved the phone back into his branches and turned again to face them.

"The Fairy Queen of Detroit is eager to meet the changeling who commands Morgan's White Knight and the blood mage's Black Rider," he said haughtily. "To see such power brought so low is a rare treat indeed. You will attend her in the throne room."

If Tristan was insulted by the fairy's words, he didn't let it show. He just strolled off into the flowers, one hand in his pocket, the other tapping his sheathed sword against his shoulder. Lola and the Rider followed a moment later, leaving Juniper glaring at their backs as they walked across the field to a little set of stone steps that descended a gentle slope.

Despite the fact that they didn't seem to be going much of anywhere, the smell of Alva's magic grew exponentially thicker with each step Lola took. The stairs under their feet were a white stone far finer than marble. White jade, maybe, or something entirely fanciful that only existed here. Whatever it was, it was beautifully carved with intricate patterns of twirling leaves and spreading blossoms.

The patterns wove up and down the steps without break, flowing down the little hill in a mesmerizing cascade. It was so interesting, Lola stopped to get a closer look several times. Whenever her feet stopped moving, though, Tristan's hand landed on her arm to pull her forward again.

"Stop looking at them," he whispered, eyes pointedly ahead. "The pattern delights in distraction."

Lola nodded and turned her face up instead, fixing her eyes on the bright, cloudless sky, which, she suddenly realized, had no sun.

The stairs ended in another field exactly like the first, except the flowers here were even thicker. So thick, in fact, that Lola wasn't sure how they were going to get through without a machete. As her foot left the last slick white stone step, though, the scenery suddenly changed again.

Lola froze, eyes darting as she tried to look in every direction at once. The patterned stairs were still behind her, only now, the steps went up into an aspen forest. Beautiful white-barked trees spread out as far as Lola could see in all directions, their golden leaves rustling in the soft breeze.

As she stared at the quaking branches, Lola became aware of a strange tingling in her gossamer. It was very slight, but once Lola noticed it, the sensation spread quickly, seeping through her like oil through cloth. It rushed through her magic, picking up speed as it replaced the hum of her own gossamer with Alva's sour scent. Then, as quickly as it had started, the tingling was washed away by a wave of cold that tasted like the sea, and Lola looked up to see Tristan standing over her with his hands on her shoulders.

"Thank you," she murmured.

"Don't thank me yet," Tristan warned, resuming his walk

down the leaf-littered path between the aspens. "The hard part's still to come. I just hope your boy can handle it."

Lola glanced over her shoulder at the Rider, who had just finished stepping off the white stair and was calmly turning his helmet to take in the trees as if forests miraculously sprang up around him every day. He didn't seem to be having trouble, but Lola was still nervous as she hurried to catch up with Tristan.

She'd nearly made it when the forest suddenly opened up. As with everything in this place, there was no warning. One second, they were walking through miles of aspen grove; the next, they were standing in a wide, grassy clearing with sunlight beating down on them.

It came on so quickly, Lola was blinded by the sudden brightness. Even so, she was immediately aware of two things. First, Tristan's cold-sea gossamer had fallen over her again, covering her from head to toes like a cloak. Second, the fairy queen was standing right in front of them, and she had the biggest teeth Lola had ever seen.

Chapter 10
3 pills

Lola jerked backward with a gasp. For a horrible moment, she was standing in front of something inhuman and huge with a gaping mouth packed full of enormous, gleaming white teeth as sharp as swords. Then the creature vanished, replaced by a petite brunette with a crown of roses on her head and a face like a movie star.

To say a fairy was beautiful was to state the obvious, but Lola couldn't help it. Alva was just so... pretty. Even prettier than Jamie with her shining chestnut hair and her eyes the color of red tea. Her skin was flawless and pale, her body covered in a fall of scarlet roses that looked like they'd go tumbling off and leave her exposed if she made one wrong move. But Alva seemed incapable of anything so unseemly as a mistake as she stepped forward to inspect her guests.

The throne room, as it turned out, wasn't a room at all. It was a clearing ringed in by the aspen forest on all sides with a small, crystal-clear creek dividing it in two. Grass—greener, softer, and thicker than anything seen outside of dreams—covered the sloping ground. There were other fairies here as well, Alva's court, but they were little more than shadows in the forest behind their queen, or maybe she just outshone them. Watching Alva stepping as gracefully as a falling leaf over the flowing stream, Lola couldn't help thinking she was glad that Morgan was dead. If this stunning beauty was only a shadow, seeing the true queen might have undone her completely.

"You are a rude guest, changeling," Alva said, her voice as lovely and rich as her rose perfume. "My invitation didn't include a plus one, much less a plus two."

The apology almost left Lola's lips before she caught herself. Now that the shock of first seeing her was fading, Lola could feel Alva's sour gossamer shoving beauty at her like soft, wet snow. It was pure fairy manipulation at its most heavy-handed. But knowing the hooks were there didn't mean they weren't effective, as evidenced by the sting of rejection Lola felt when the fairy queen's eyes left her to fall on Tristan.

"I never thought to see you here, knight," she said, the corners of her perfect red mouth turning up in a smile. "Changed your mind about my offer?"

"How could I when it was not yours to offer in the first place?" Tristan replied, his voice bored. He wasn't even looking at Alva. His eyes were roving over the forest behind her, their blue color sharp as sea ice. "My life and blade are forever sworn to the true queen."

Alva scowled, and for a moment, her beauty flickered. Then it was back with a vengeance, and she gave Tristan a shrug. "Your loss, masterless knight. If you want to continue your half existence, cut off from the power of my court, wasting your potential pining for a fairy I defeated and ate long ago, that's your business. Fortunately, the little changeling brought me someone much more exciting."

The queen's eyes fell on Valente next, and Lola felt him go still as Alva's face lit up in its most beautiful smile yet.

"The famous Black Rider," Alva said, all but purring in delight. "If I'd known you'd be the one to bring him to me, Changeling, I would have invited you ages ago." She held out her hand, crooking her red-nailed fingers. "Come here, darling, and let me have a better look at you."

Lola scowled. Suddenly, the fairy queen didn't look so pretty anymore. She was about to tell Alva they weren't here to flirt

189

when the Black Rider marched forward. Lola gaped in amazement as Valente walked past her and Tristan, his black boots soundless on the pillow-soft grass as he crossed the clearing to fall to his knees at the queen's feet.

"There's a good boy," Alva said, leaning down to peer into the Rider's helmet.

Lola went stiff. She'd already noticed the queen's beauty went up and down depending on how much of her attention you were getting. When Alva turned her full focus to the Rider, though, her illusion skewed completely. She didn't revert to the big-toothed monster, but something about her was definitely off, like when Lola tried to copy a photo-manipulated model. From one angle, she looked fantastic. From the rest, she just looked *wrong*.

But while Lola had shaken free of the queen's appeal, the Rider was spellbound. He knelt perfectly still at Alva's feet, his chest rising in deep, even breaths, almost as if he were asleep.

"What's happening?" Lola whispered.

"He's enthralled," Tristan replied, his voice oddly distracted. When Lola turned to glare at him, she saw the fairy wasn't even paying attention. He was still staring off into the forest, his sharp brows furrowed like he was searching for something.

"Tristan!"

"What?" he said, stopping his search to give her a pointed look. "I told you not to bring him."

"You didn't tell me he could be enthralled!" Lola hissed.

"I thought it was obvious," Tristan said, turning back to the forest. "He's still partially human, after all."

Lola scoffed. This was the Black Rider they were talking about. The man who came back from the dead and walked around without a head. How could *that* be human? Then she remembered Valente standing outside her car after Simon's telling her he'd also dreamed about *Fenrir*, and her gossamer began to sink.

190

"It only makes sense," Tristan continued, turning on his heel to scan the forest behind them. "You don't respond predictably to any magic, and I'm completely out of her reach, so Alva focused her efforts on the easier target. Cleverest thing I've seen her do, actually."

"What about hospitality?" Lola asked, watching with growing dread as Alva began petting the Rider's helmet. "I thought he was protected so long as I claimed him as my guest."

"Protected from harm, yes," Tristan said. "But she's not exactly hurting him, is she?"

Few men would call having the full attention of a gorgeous woman harm, but Lola wasn't stupid enough to think Alva was doing this for the Rider's benefit.

"We have to save him."

"Why?" Tristan asked, looking at her again. "Aren't you curious?"

"About what?"

The fairy smiled. "What's under that black mask."

Lola looked away with a scowl. She didn't need his taunting. She'd already seen what was under the Rider's helmet, but it looked like Tristan was right. The fairy queen had stopped her petting and was now whispering over the Rider's head, imploring him to remove his mask and show everyone his lovely face.

It was working, too. Though he was clearly trying to fight it, Valente's gloved hands were rising inexorably toward his head, and Lola felt a stab of anger. She'd almost been looking forward to Alva's disappointment when the helmet came off to reveal the nothing Lola knew was underneath, but seeing how clearly Valente didn't want to do it changed her mind.

His headlessness was his secret to keep. Alva had no right to force him to expose himself in front of all these strangers, but it was too late. The Rider's hands were already grasping his helmet,

191

and Lola braced for the shock of seeing his headless body again. It never came, though, because as the Rider's helmet came off, Lola caught sight of *hair*. Dark-brown hair cut short over what could only be a *head*.

The helmet was completely off before Lola finally accepted what she was seeing. The headless Rider was no longer headless. Where last night, there'd been nothing but a black hole going down into his coat, he now had a perfectly normal crop of dark, normal hair that brushed over normal ears to a normal neck that fit perfectly onto his broad, normal shoulders. His back was to her, so Lola couldn't see his face, but the fairy queen could, and her eyes flew wide in surprise.

"So it is you," she whispered, her velvety voice turning sharp as broken glass. "I'd heard you were defeated, but I never imagined..." She trailed off as she brushed her fingers over the Rider's cheek. "What has that awful man done to you?"

Valente didn't answer, but he moved away from her hand, causing Lola's hopes to rise. He was still enthralled, but the queen's hold must not have been a hundred percent. Alva scowled at his resistance, but then her lips curved up as though she'd just had a *marvelous* idea.

"I suppose it matters not," she said, her voice suddenly singsongy as she stepped away from the Rider. "You were great once, but your violent kind always dies before their time. How much of your power did the blood mage leave, I wonder?" Her eyes flicked back to Lola. "Shall we see?"

Lola had no idea what Alva was talking about, but Valente must have, because he began to shake.

"No."

The word came out of him like a scrape, and Lola bit her lip. She supposed it made sense that the Rider's sudden ability to speak came with a head, but it wasn't doing him any good. As beautiful as his new voice was, it held no sway over Alva.

"Don't be selfish," the fairy queen scolded. "You barge in here uninvited and demand hospitality. I believe I'm owed a little entertainment for my trouble. Now turn around and let the changeling see your face."

"No," the Rider said again, louder this time. Around his knees, tendrils of frost were spreading over the soft grass. They grew as Lola watched, creeping out until the ice brushed the fairy queen's bare feet.

Alva scooted back with a scowl. Then she leaned down, her lovely face sharpening until Lola could almost see her teeth again as she yelled in the Rider's face. *Show her!*

His whole body flinched at the command. Terrified of what was coming, Lola turned to Tristan, but the fairy was standing with his arms crossed over his chest, watching the drama unfold with a cold, bemused expression. Since he clearly wasn't going to be any help, Lola turned back to tell the queen to stop this or she was leaving, but the words vanished from her throat.

The Rider had turned around. His head was down and his fists were clenched, still clearly trying to fight. But even though his eyes were locked on the ground, Lola could see his face was... human?

She blinked in surprise. Given how hard he'd tried to prevent this and what he'd done to the mirror in his apartment, Lola had been expecting horrors, but the Rider's face was nothing of the sort. She would even go so far as to say he was handsome with his high cheekbones, full mouth, and prominent, sharp nose. His eyebrows were as dark and thick as his hair, and his skin was a warm brown, albeit a bit pasty from never seeing the sun.

He certainly wasn't beautiful like the fairies, but he had a rugged, human attractiveness that Lola found perfectly adequate. She was wondering what all the fuss was about when Valente finally raised his eyes.

Lola jerked back. The Rider's eyes were the same glowing, ghostly blue as the lights on his motorcycle. Looking at them made her feel cold and exposed, like she was standing at the edge of a pit that had no bottom. The Rider must have seen her flinch, because he opened his mouth to say something, but that only made Lola jump again. Behind his normal, human lips, the Rider had *fangs*. Not fangs like a movie vampire, fangs like a jaguar. Big, sharp white teeth meant for ripping out throats.

It was alarming to be sure, but after the initial shock had faded, Lola started getting angry. This was what the Rider was hiding? After what he'd seen her turn into, *this* was what he'd fought tooth and nail not to show her? Some freaky eyes and big teeth?

It was almost insulting. Even now, Valente was staring at her in wonder, like he was amazed she hadn't run screaming, and Lola clenched her fists. She couldn't believe she was wasting her *extremely limited* time on this.

"If you're done playing with my escort, can we get this over with?" Lola demanded, crossing her arms over her chest as she glared at the fairy queen. "Some of us have schedules to keep."

The haughty look fell off Alva's lovely face. "You're immune to him?"

"Lola's immune to most things," Tristan said before Lola could ask what the queen was talking about. "A fact you'd know if you'd bothered to do any research on your enemies before inviting them to your home."

Alva hissed at him, but Lola didn't bother listening to what was undoubtedly a quippy comeback. Her attention was completely on Valente, who was still on his knees, staring at Lola with those ghostly eyes like he'd never seen her before. She gave him a "hurry up" gesture, but he didn't move. He just knelt there, still as a statue, and then his eyes slid shut, cutting off that strange, blue light as his whole body began to vibrate like an overcranked

194

engine.

"Uh oh," Tristan said, breaking into a smile. "Better hurry it up, Alva. Your toy grows as tired of your company as we do."

The queen looked down in alarm at the quaking Rider, then she lifted her chin with a haughty jerk. As she moved, the enthrallment melted, and Valente slumped forward, landing on his hands in the icy grass.

The stillness lasted only a second before the Rider shot to his feet. Moving like dark water, he slammed his helmet back onto his head with one hand while swinging the other like an ax straight at Alva. In the barrow's shimmering light, Lola could actually see the glistening edge of his strange, invisible power as it sliced toward Alva's neck. But then, when the attack was less than an inch from her, the Rider suddenly stopped cold.

"Silly boy," Alva taunted, walking around the Rider, who was still frozen in midswing. "Even your blasphemous powers can't breach hospitality." She reached out to hook her delicate fingers under his leather collar. "Back you go!"

She flicked her wrist, throwing the Rider across the clearing. He landed in a crouch at Lola's feet, his gloved hands already up to attack again. But though she could feel his ghostly blue eyes burning even with his helmet back on, the Rider didn't make another try for the queen. He retreated instead, rising to his feet to take up position beside Lola.

Tristan snickered at the sight. "That was careless of you, Alva," he chided. "I'm surprised you've survived this long, making such dangerous enemies with so little thought."

The fairy queen tossed her glossy hair over her shoulder. "This is my barrow," she said haughtily. "Nothing can harm me here, and I never leave. I can make all the enemies I like."

"That's where you're wrong," said Lola, who'd had enough of this. "Maybe you haven't figured it out, *Alva*, but there's a fairy in

195

the DFZ who's way stronger than you are. Someone who doesn't have to rely on trolls to do his dirty work."

"What do you know of strength?" Alva sneered. "A troll can still become a fairy if it's ruthless enough, but a changeling is just a spell made to trick humans. Even goblins have souls, but you're only a lump of gossamer some fairy was willing to waste securing a human toy. Why, you're no better than the enchantment I use to clean up after my animals."

The woods tittered as the hidden fairies laughed at this, but Lola refused to give them the satisfaction of a reaction.

"My servants were merely confirming the blood mage's death," Alva went on. "It seems your master finally bit off more than he could chew. It happens to all uppity humans eventually, but his reckless ambition set off a chain of events that now threatens my court's feeding grounds. I only invited you here because someone's been sending dreams over *my* city." Alva's tongue shot out of her mouth, tasting the air like a snake. "Someone who tastes very much like you."

Lola went still, clenching the fist below her sister's jerking thread.

"I thought if I brought you into my barrow, I'd be able to follow his magic to the source," Alva said as she walked toward her. "Now that you're in front of me, though, all I can taste is the reek of that man's blood." She stopped directly in front of Lola, licking her red lips. "Maybe if I take a bite?"

Lola flinched away with a grimace. But before she could tell this fairy that would happen only over her dead body, another voice spoke from her lips. A voice that wasn't hers.

"If the human's blood is all you can taste, you're even more of a sham than I thought."

Alva jumped back like she'd been burned. Lola jumped as well. Or, rather, she tried to. Something huge was holding her in place, as if a mountain had fallen on top of her. The weird, too-full feeling in her gossamer boiled up as it landed, but Lola couldn't shift to give it more space. All she could do was stand there as the air around her flickered and congealed, twisting her gossamer all kinds of directions until she thought she was going to turn inside out.

That was better than turning into the monster, but it was still terrifying. It felt like her body was being warped into a tube. But then, just when she was sure she'd never be the same, Lola's gossamer snapped back into place hard enough to make her stumble, and a small, lovely boy stepped out of her shadow.

"Who are you?" the fairy queen demanded, her voice rising in panic.

"I'm her guest," the fairy said, looking up at Lola. "Aren't I?"

The moment he said it, the promise Lola had made in the cell began to burn like molten metal in her throat.

"That's right," she choked out. "My guest."

The boy nodded and turned his grin on Alva. "I do so love the hospitality of a gracious host."

The fairy queen bared her teeth. *How did you get in here?*

"You invited me," he said, leaning against Lola, who still couldn't move.

"I did no such thing," Alva spat. "Nor will I ever tender hospitality to a *stowaway* such as—"

"Stowaway?" The boy laughed in that beautiful, clear, trumpeting voice of his. "If anything, I'm the only legitimate guest here. You invited *my* changeling made of *my* gossamer. All I had to do was step through, and here I am."

Lola's eyes went wide as he finished. Of course. Changelings were spells, constructions made from the gossamer of the fairy that created them. Just as Lola had moved into the black car she'd used to distract the Skyway police, so could this fairy move through her.

That thought made her feel sick and violated, but when Lola looked around for help, she found that her "guards" had both stepped back. Tristan was watching the new fairy with a strange look on his face, his body very still, almost as if he were holding his breath. The Rider, on the other hand, was standing like a dog at the end of his chain. He clearly wanted to go to her, but something was holding him back. Lola stared at him pleadingly, but Valente didn't move a muscle, not even when the fairy boy grabbed her hand and started dragging her toward Alva.

"Why the surprised face, fairy queen?" he asked, his lovely face gleeful as he stalked forward. "Still haven't figured out who I am?"

"You dare," Alva whispered, but she was the one backing up.

"You should know," he taunted, moving closer still. "You vanquished Queen Morgan, didn't you? So go ahead. Search her memories and find my name."

Alva took another step backward, her alabaster skin turning a sickly gray. She looked over her shoulder for help, but the forest of aspen was empty. The other fairies had vanished. Her court had abandoned her.

"Let me give you a hint," the boy dragging Lola whispered when he'd backed Alva all the way to the tree line. "When you were a newly hatched hobgoblin scavenging the leavings of other, stronger fairies for your first meal, I had already ruled for centuries beyond counting."

Alva lowered her eyes with a whimper, which was when Lola realized the boy's head was now higher than the queen's. She wasn't sure when he'd grown, but over the course of their walk, he'd gone from barely tall enough to reach the shoulder of Lola's redheaded body to towering over Alva. There was no other change. He didn't look any older or stronger. Just bigger, looming over the clearing like a giant as his voice filled the air.

"I have warred and made peace with the queen whose throne you presume to claim more times than you have drawn breath," he said, the booming words echoing through the aspen trees. "I have ridden through the midnight sky with creatures you have only known in stories. Slain dragons and skinned their young for sport. I have given my favorites greater treasures than you can imagine in return for the smallest favors. Not because they deserved them, but because my wealth was so vast that I never felt the loss."

His voice grew louder with each syllable, and Lola found herself sinking to the ground. It felt like her gossamer was being pulled down a drain, only this time, she wasn't the only one that changed.

All around them, Alva's barrow was transforming. The slender aspen trees hardened and darkened until they looked like stone pillars. The bright sky lost its brilliance, curving and clouding until it was a sky no longer but the ceiling of a vast cave hung with stalactites the size of redwoods.

The carpet of green grass vanished, replaced by a great field of black stone broken up by gold veins that ran like rivers and huge outcroppings of jewels so lovely, Lola's heart ached for them. Even the babbling brook was replaced by a flow of molten lava. And at the center of this new creation, the fairy boy towered over Alva like a lion over a mouse, his beautiful face cut in half by a huge, sharp-toothed smile.

"I have eaten more kings than you could ever hope to meet!" he boomed triumphantly. "Ridden at the head of the Wild Hunt as ruler of a kingdom so vast, even I did not know its limits! My names run through a thousand tales, yet still only a fraction have ever been spoken. But I believe you can guess one now, pretender to the crown of Morgan." His giant smile widened farther still. "Speak it, little fairy. Speak it or die."

Alva began to weep at his feet as her human form melted

away, revealing a round, bulbous shape with a black shell and an absurdly large mouth full of teeth. Lola gaped in wonder at the change. Before, a single glimpse of Alva's true form had been enough to terrify her. Now, cowering in the other fairy's shadow, she looked pathetic and small, a sharp-toothed tick caught out in the sun when her log is turned over. Even her voice had shrunk to a squeak when she did as the fairy commanded, bowing low at the child's feet as she whispered his name.

"Alberich, the Underground King."

As the name echoed through the endless cavern, everything vanished. In the blink of an eye, they were back in the aspen clearing. Alva's human shape was back as well, lying panting at the feet of the fairy boy, who was back to his normal height.

"Quite right," the boy said, gazing down at her in disgust. "Though you'd have known it without all the drama if you were Morgan's true successor."

"I—" Alva gasped, fingers clawing into the grass. "I *am* the fairy queen! I ate her! Her crown is mine!"

"You? Eat Morgan?" The boy scoffed at the very idea. "You may have gotten a bite or two. Enough to control this barrow, though not enough to leave it. Enough to fool the idiots who wanted her gone but not to command her knight."

He glanced at Tristan as he said that last part. The fairy stood straighter in reply, his hand going to his sword as he said, "Morgan is, was, and always will be the true queen."

"Precisely," Alberich agreed, reaching down to tweak the nose of the terrified fairy at his feet. "You can't just kill a queen, you know. To surpass her, you would have had to *become* her. You would have had to eat her head and take all that was her into yourself, but you didn't do that, did you? I can't feel Morgan's head in this barrow at all." He stood back up with a sigh, putting his hands on his hips as if all of this was too much. "You don't even

200

know where it is, do you?"

"Only a... matter of... time," Alva gasped.

"It is you who is running out of time, parasite," the king replied, turning his back on her. "Go and gather your court, or what's left of it. They might be cowards, but you're going to need them when the world changes."

"You think you can frighten me?" Alva snarled, though the effect was undermined by the warble in her voice. "The world is always changing, fairy king! You were the one who could not change with it!"

"This time is different," Alberich promised as he dragged Lola back to Tristan and the Rider. "Please know that the only reason I'm not killing you is because I don't want to take that pleasure from Morgan. Enjoy your remaining time, little parasite, and when the true queen returns, tell her her husband says hello."

Alva shot to her feet, eyes shining with malice. But before she could even promise retribution, the aspen clearing vanished, leaving them standing in the driveway of the huge, empty house.

"Well," Alberich said, finally letting go of Lola to clap his hands. "That was fun!"

Lola fell to the pavement when he released her. She lay there, stunned, for a moment, trying to think of what to say. If anything *could* be said in the face of such utter defeat. It turned out not to matter, though. Before any words came together in her mind, her gossamer, which the king had been mashing around like clay, suddenly boiled out of control.

She doubled over, screaming in pain and panic as the monster ripped out of her body. Just like last night, the change was instant. The monster roared through her like a fist through paper, shredding her gossamer into greasy fur and curving claws, dripping fangs and great, hulking limbs. It all happened so quickly, her mind couldn't even keep up with how fast she was falling into the abyss. But as the monster began to roar, a firm voice spoke through the chaos.

"Open your mouth."

The command was like an arrow to her chest. The monster obeyed instinctively, opening its great jaw. For a moment, Lola tasted the deep, underground heat of Alberich's burning gossamer as his small hand slid between the monster's teeth. Once he dropped the pill onto her pointed tongue, though, all she knew was blood.

The familiar noose of her master's magic made her want to cry. As fast as the monster had exploded out of her, Lola shrank back down, collapsing into her human body as Victor's blood wrenched her gossamer back into place. When she opened her eyes again, she saw the familiar, capable hands of her yogurt lady resting inside the craters her monster's paws had left behind.

"There we are," Alberich's voice drifted over her head. "Good as new."

Something light landed in the dirt beside her, and Lola looked to see the clear plastic baggie Tristan had gathered her pills in. The bag that was supposed to have three pills but now held only two.

Two pills.

Her vision started to go blurry. Lola scrubbed the wetness away furiously. Not because she was ashamed of the tears, but because she was afraid a breakdown would trigger the monster again, and she was no longer sure she had enough pills to bring herself back.

"Why?" she whispered when she could speak again.

"Why what?" Alberich said.

"*Why did you do this to me?*" she screamed, head snapping up as she bared her small, flat teeth at the fairy. "You knew I only had three pills left! Why did you wreck my gossamer? Was it just to make a show? To scare Alva at my expense?"

"Technically, it was at my own expense," Alberich reminded her. "You're my creation."

"I don't belong to you," Lola snarled, clutching the bag with her last two pills to her chest as her silver thread thrashed wildly. "I don't belong to anyone! I'm my own person!"

Even as she said them, Lola knew the words weren't true. She'd never been a person, human or fairy. She was just a glob of magic whose time was running out.

"I never had a chance, did I?" she whispered, wiping her face again as she looked at Tristan. "You knew we weren't going to get Alva's help. You lied to me."

Tristan had the good grace to look abashed. "It wasn't technically a lie," he said, as if that made things any better. "There was always a chance it would work, and I truly never did mean you harm, changeling. I simply couldn't miss an opportunity to look for my queen. My oaths—"

"Screw your oaths," Lola said sourly. "You said you'd help me and you didn't. Neither of you."

Her eyes landed on the Rider next, but it was impossible to tell what he was thinking behind that visor. She was about to turn her back on all of them when Alberich grabbed her hand.

"Don't be mad at them," he chided. "What could they have done? I'm the Underground King! Morgan was the only one who could ever stand against me, and she's gone. As for what happened just now, I don't see why you're so upset. Yes, you're running low on pills, but they were never more than a stopgap, and a poor-taste one at that. It's not as if you were ever *really* human."

Something broke in Lola when he said that. There was nothing new, nothing she didn't already know. But hearing him tell her she'd never be real in that mocking, crowing voice was more than she could take.

For a dark moment, Lola thought it might be worth turning

into a monster forever if she got to wipe that smug look off the fairy's face. The only thing that stopped her was her sister. The silver thread was yanking on her arm, twitching so fast it cut right through her gossamer to dance in Alberich's face. The fairy grinned when he saw it, reaching out a finger to pluck the delicate filament like a harp string.

"Stop!" Lola cried, jerking her arm back. "Don't touch her!"

Alberich looked her straight in the eyes and snapped his fingers. The moment the sound hit her, Lola's gossamer froze. Just like before, she was stuck in the air, trapped like a statue as the Underground King reached out to grab her sister's silver thread.

Fresh tears welled up in Lola's eyes. She'd never wanted to do violence to another person like she wanted to do to Alberich in this moment, but she couldn't even blink. His grip on her gossamer was stronger than Victor's had ever been, making her feel more helpless than she'd ever felt in her entire life.

"Amazing," the fairy king said, reaching up to collect one of the tears that rolled down her cheek. "I can actually feel your despair in my gossamer." He frowned. "I can't say I enjoy the sensation. How do you go on like that?"

Lola pulled the gossamer tears back in. This fairy deserved nothing, not even her sadness. When she didn't answer, Alberich rolled his eyes and released her.

"Try not to have another of your incidents," he scolded as Lola fell onto the driveway. "You've only got two pills left, so you'll need to be extra careful if you're going to make it to tomorrow night."

Lola didn't want to give him the satisfaction of asking, but she had to know. "What happens tomorrow night?"

Alberich blinked at her in disbelief before turning to the Rider. "You didn't tell her?"

The Rider didn't answer, so the fairy said it for him.

204

"That's when Victor comes back."

The world tilted as he spoke, causing her to fall back to the ground she'd been trying to get up from. The Rider stepped in to help her, but Lola slapped his hand away, gossamer thrumming in her ears.

"You knew?"

"Of course he knew," Alberich said, hopping up to clap the much taller Rider on the shoulder. "I was there when Victor told him. He knew this was coming just like Tristan knew I was the one behind the dreams."

Lola had already suspected that, but it didn't make the words hurt any less. "Is it true?" she asked Tristan.

The knight scowled, clearly trying to think of a way around his inability to lie. "Not at the beginning," he answered eventually.

"But later," Lola said, fists clenching. "This morning?"

He nodded, and Lola looked away, staring at the ground, the trees, anywhere she wasn't being betrayed.

This is your own fault, you know, the memory of Victor whispered in her ear. *How many times did I warn you not to trust? This is why you'll never get away, my monster. You're just too stupid to take good advice.*

"Shut up," Lola whispered, turning on her heel to start marching down the driveway.

"Where are you going?" Alberich called after her.

"Away from all of you," Lola yelled, picking up the pace. She still had twenty-four hours before the monster ate her or Victor returned to put his boot back on her neck. Whichever it ended up being, she didn't intend to waste her last day with people who treated her like a tool.

She was stomping down Alva's driveway when Alberich's dainty, curled-toed shoes appeared on the paving stones in front of her. Lola swerved to go around him, but the fairy grabbed her by

205

the wrist and, like a fly caught in honey, Lola stopped.

"Here," he said, pushing something into her hand. "You'll need these."

The paralysis vanished the moment he released her, and Lola looked down to see that she was holding a pair of tickets. Concert tickets for a special Halloween stadium show happening tomorrow at seven.

"Victor is coming back for the Spooktacular Stravaganza?" she asked, too exhausted to even be surprised.

"Don't be late," Alberich said, his pretty face smiling.

Lola didn't say another word. She just kept walking, throwing out her hands to make herself a ride.

Her gossamer was so watery, it took her two tries, but eventually, Lola formed a small scooter. The bike was neon yellow, the complete opposite of the Rider's, and its little engine roared like a lion when Lola grabbed the handlebars, shooting her off through Alva's open gates toward nowhere in particular.

~~~

"I hope that was worth it, Alberich," Tristan said as Lola drove away. "You just cost me a decade of building that girl's trust."

"The key, knight, is to stop thinking of her as a girl," Alberich said, stretching his arms over his head as he walked back over to join them. "And we shall all benefit from this afternoon's labors." His golden eyes darted up to Tristan's. "Word of friendly advice: don't be in town tomorrow."

"Why should I be?" Tristan snapped. Now that his progress with Lola was crushed, there was no point in doing anything until things calmed down. There was no point in keeping up this face anymore, either. Tristan relaxed his gossamer with a sigh, letting his true form show a little more clearly.

206

"I don't suppose you'll tell me what the blood mage is planning?"

"Of course not," Alberich said. "But I can promise you'll thank us for it once you stop being angry."

"That's hardly comforting."

"Buck up, Sir Knight," the Underground King said, slapping Tristan on the shoulder. "At least now you know that your queen lives!"

"I always knew she was alive," Tristan said. "I just had to make sure her head wasn't still hidden in the barrow."

And it wasn't. He'd searched the whole place while Alva played her games with the Rider, and he hadn't felt a trace of his queen, which was both good and bad. Not feeling her meant Alva couldn't prey on her while she was weak, but he now had no idea where her head was, and he was running out of time. If Alberich was running free again, Morgan's power must be almost gone.

He was thinking of a sly way to ask the Underground King how he'd escaped his prison when Tristan felt the hateful pressure of the Black Rider's power. He looked up just in time to see the blue flash of his taillights as the Rider's motorcycle shot silently down the driveway after Lola.

"Where does he think he's going?" Alberich asked. "There's no way she'll take him back."

"Who knows what goes on in that cursed head of his?" Tristan replied with a grimace. "I'm just glad to be rid of him. He's an abomination. I don't understand why you're working with him."

"One uses the tools one has," the king replied with a shrug. "And from what I've heard, you worked with him first."

"For a greater end," Tristan insisted. And a greater reward, though that had yet to be delivered. Looking at Alberich, Tristan was starting to wonder if it ever would be.

"We're all working toward a greater end, knight," the king

assured him. "You'll see when everything comes together."

"Assuming the changeling plays along," Tristan said. "You must need her for your plan, or you wouldn't have told her about Victor's return. But while the blood mage did his best to crush it, Lola has a rebellious streak. Your little stunt just now might have been the final straw."

"She'll come," the king said smugly. "Because if she doesn't, she'll die. Even if she does decide to spite me, I have her darling 'sister.'" He smiled. "Mark me, knight, she'll do as she's told, and then everything will happen exactly as the blood mage has arranged."

"Why do you put so much trust in him?" Tristan asked, genuinely curious. "He's human. Since when does the Underground King obey a mortal?"

"I obey no one!" Alberich snarled, his voice rising like an earthquake before falling just as quickly. "We're merely using each other, an arrangement of mutual benefit."

Tristan shook his head and grabbed the door to his car, shifting the gossamer inside to transform the driver's seat into a tunnel back to his barrow. Before he could get in, though, Alberich grabbed his arm.

"The Hunt draws nigh, knight of Morgan. Will you ride with us, or will you be ridden over?"

"I ride for my queen alone," Tristan said, yanking his arm away. "Take care you do not expose yourself overmuch, Alberich. However 'mutual' you might think this is, the blood mage eats his own in the end."

He vanished after that, slipping down the low road without another word.

When the king was alone in front of the barrow that had once been his wife's, Alberich reached out to pluck a twisting silver thread from the empty air. "Morgan's noble knight forgets, my treasure," he whispered to the frantically weaving strand. "The young ones always forget. It is *I* who eat."

As though in answer, the thread gave a sharp jerk, nearly yanking out of the king's hands before he caught it. Smiling indulgently, Alberich let the thread pull him away, his small body vanishing like a mirage beneath the noon sun.

Chapter 11

2 pills

Lola drove until the sun set. She was too angry to go anywhere in particular, so she just drove. Skyways, Undercity, downtown, under downtown, but no matter how fast she went, the hurt and anger followed, sapping the joy out of everything until she was ready to scream.

The tickets Alberich had given her were still in her back pocket. Lola had nearly thrown them away a dozen times, but she'd never quite managed it. Part of her wanted to say screw it and drive off into the Yukon. She wasn't even afraid of dying anymore, especially since it now seemed that doing so would wreck Victor's precious plans. But every time she imagined sticking it to her master and going out on her own terms, Lola would see her sister's thread shining on her wrist, and all her ambitions crumbled away.

By the time she'd accepted that she couldn't do it, it was full dark, and her stomach was empty. She hadn't eaten anything but pills since the Rider had made her oatmeal in her apartment.

Lola pushed the memory away with a scowl. She was done with that. Right now, she had to get some food and figure out her next step. If she wasn't going to run, that left facing Victor's return tomorrow, which wasn't something she wanted to go into unprepared. So much had happened in the last twenty-four hours, though, Lola didn't even know where to start. There was simply too much new information to hold in her head. She needed someone to talk through everything with, but there was no one left that she trusted.

As she came to a wobbly stop at the bottom of a seven-way

intersection, Lola realized that wasn't quite true. There was still one. One last person who knew her secrets and hadn't betrayed her. With that, Lola stopped driving aimlessly and started looking for a phone.

Pay phones were artifacts of ancient history, but this was the DFZ. You could buy *anything* here. Soon enough, Lola found a vending machine selling prepackaged single-use burner phones. And since the only people who used burner phones typically didn't want to leave a transaction trail, it still accepted cash.

Forming her wobbly gossamer into just enough bills to buy the cheapest model, Lola fed them one by one into the machine and punched in the number. When her selected package *thunked* into the slot, she pulled her gossamer back out through the cash box and ripped the plastic wrapper off her new phone with her teeth.

According to the packaging, the phone had just enough juice for one ten-minute call. When the tiny screen flashed Ready, Lola walked across the street to a quiet gap under the bridges and dialed the number she still had memorized after all these years.

As ever, Simon picked up on the second ring. "Who is this?"

"Have you had dinner yet?"

"Lola," he breathed, his voice thick with relief. "Thank God. Where are you? Did the Paladins catch you?"

Lola didn't feel like talking about any of that now, so she answered his questions with one of her own. "Can you meet me at Peaches in twenty minutes?"

"The diner?" Simon sounded incredulous. "Why don't you come to my house?"

"Because I'm hungry," Lola said. "And I'm not in the mood to chew through one of your healthy kale salads."

It was a sign of how worried he was that Simon didn't even take offense at that. "I'll meet you wherever you want," he promised. "Who should I look for?"

211

"Don't worry," Lola said. "You won't be able to miss me."

She could almost hear him shaking his head. "I'll see you soon, then."

"See you."

The burner phone made a popping sound when she ended the call. Holding the now-smoking phone away from her with a wince, Lola tossed it into the trashcan on the corner and jogged across the busy street, back to her bike. She started the engine with a roar and took off down the road, weaving through six lanes of traffic toward the river.

And back by the vending machines, unseen, a black motorcycle pulled silently out of the shadows to take off after her.

~~~

"When you said I couldn't miss you, this wasn't what I had in mind," Simon said as he slid into the booth across from her.

Peaches was your typical Underground diner. The food was unremarkable, but the atmosphere was cozy and the prices were right. More importantly, it wasn't the sort of place anyone would think to look for a fairy changeling and a mage. Lola wasn't taking any chances, though, which was why she was wearing a face she'd never worn before today: that of Simon's sweet, elderly mother.

"Good to see you, too," Lola said, sipping her sugary coffee.

Simon winced. "Do you know how weird it is to hear your voice from my mom?"

"If you were seen out with a stranger, anyone could guess it was me," Lola said. "But who's going to question a good son taking his mother out for dinner?"

He shook his head and leaned forward, resting his elbows on the plastic-covered table. "Lola, why don't you tell me what's going on? What happened with the Paladins? I heard they attacked you."

212

"I ditched them," Lola said, which was technically true.

"Where's the Rider?" Simon asked next. "Did you finally kick him to the curb?"

"Something like that," she said, watching him carefully over her coffee mug. "Have you heard from Victor?"

"Of course not." Simon gave her an odd look. "Have you?"

Lola shook her head and smiled into her coffee. Simon had always been a terrible liar. If he'd been in contact with their master, she was sure it would have shown, but he'd seemed genuinely surprised by her question. Surprised and worried, which fit Simon to a T, and suddenly, Lola was so relieved she almost cried. She hadn't realized how braced she'd been for Simon to betray her as well until he hadn't.

He must have seen it on her face, because Simon reached out to grab her hands. "Lola, what's wrong?"

She did cry a little then, because he was looking at her like he actually cared, and all at once, Lola realized Simon had *always* cared about her. From the first night she'd met him, when she'd been seven and barely able to hold her shape together and he'd been eleven and looking like he'd just woken up from a coma, because he *had,* even then, Simon had cared. That caring showed on his face now clearer than ever, and Lola felt like a traitor for having doubted him.

She squeezed his hands back hard. Then, like a dam bursting, she told him everything. She told him about the fight with the Paladins, about discovering the Rider had no head, and how she'd turned into the monster before Alberich turned her back. She told him about Alberich revealing he was the fairy who'd taken her sister, how the Rider had busted her out of jail and taken her back to her apartment when she'd almost changed again. She told him about Tristan and the disastrous trip to Alva's, and how Alberich had revealed himself as the Underground King.

Lola broke down again at that part, both from the memory of the betrayal and her embarrassment at being burned by the Rider and Tristan even after Simon had warned her. To his credit, Simon didn't offer a single I-told-you-so. He didn't interrupt her at all except to ask the occasional question when she started going too fast.

In the end, the only thing Lola didn't tell him was the Black Rider's real name. She felt stupid for keeping his secret, stupid for still feeling indebted to the man who'd only kept her alive because Victor wasn't done using her. She justified it by telling herself that Valente's name was unimportant and Simon wouldn't care anyway, but the truth was that Lola couldn't shake the feeling that the faith the Rider had shown when he'd given it to her had been real. The only real thing they'd had between them.

Their food had arrived by the time she finished talking. Simon took several minutes to think everything over while Lola ate her pancakes. She was using the last bite to mop the dregs of blueberry syrup off her plate when he asked, "Are you going to the concert?"

"I have to," Lola said. "I've only got two pills left."

Simon looked down at the table, drumming his fingers on the edge of his untouched tofu scramble. Lola couldn't see his face, but she didn't have to. She knew that pose. Simon was trying to think up something clever, some way out of Victor's trap. He always tried, and he always failed, but that never stopped him from trying again.

"It's okay, Simon," she said, reaching out to touch his hand. "Even if you did think of something, I couldn't take the risk. If I die, my sister's lost. That's not the sort of thing I can gamble with."

"Fine," he said. "But I'm going with you."

Lola nodded. "There are two tickets."

"No need," Simon said, pulling out his phone to start making notes. "I'm going over to the venue tonight so I can ward and comb the place. Maybe we can find out what Victor is planning in advance of his grand return."

"You want me to come with you?"

He shook his head. "I think you should stay as far away as you can until the last second. I'll call you if I find anything."

"Okay, but I don't have a phone anymore."

Without missing a beat, Simon stopped taking notes and handed her his phone.

"Are you sure?" Lola asked. "What about your patients?"

"I'm taking the next three days off, and that's my private phone. I have another one for work." He moved her syrup-stained plate aside and placed the phone on the table in front of her. "Take it. I won't be able to concentrate if you don't."

More touched than she could say, Lola picked up the phone and slid it into her pocket. "Thank you."

Simon waved her words away. "Don't mention it. We watch each other's backs, remember?"

Lola did remember. She and Simon had always stuck together like glue. At first, she'd thought he stayed so close because he didn't want to be alone. Much later, she realized he'd been trying to protect her.

She hadn't known it at the time, but the first time Lola met Simon, he'd just come back from the dead. Literally. Two weeks before Victor had brought him to the mansion, he'd been in a car wreck. The accident had killed his older brother, and Simon had gone to the hospital in critical condition. His heart had stopped on the operating table, and it had taken the trauma team twenty minutes to get it going again. After that, he'd been in a coma, completely unresponsive, until Victor had shown up.

He'd sold Simon's family a miracle that night, and their son had been the price. For the next ten years, even though he had family living just over the border in Michigan, Simon had lived with Victor as his apprentice. During that time, Victor had taught him how to do blood magic, trusting that the boy would fall in love with its power just as he had, but Simon never did. He'd learned because he'd be punished if he didn't, but he'd never done the things Victor had.

That hadn't stopped their master from trying to make him. He'd punished Simon for his disobedience harder than he'd ever punished Lola, keeping him in isolation for years to break him of his "misguided empathy." During that time, Lola had been the only one other than Victor that was allowed to see him. They'd been all each other had, two frightened souls in a world where Victor was god and king combined.

She'd cried for weeks when Victor had finally accepted that Simon was never going to be what he wanted and sent him back to his family. She'd just started doing Victor's work in earnest then: setting up his victims, delivering his pills, watching people break. Simon had been her rock more than ever through those dirty beginnings, and losing him had felt like losing a limb.

But even though he'd left the mansion, Simon had never left her. He was bossy and overbearing, and sometimes he drove her insane, but right now, sitting across the table from the one person in her life that hadn't betrayed her, Lola realized that Simon was the closest thing she had in this world to a family. He was her brother and her friend and her anchor, and she would never forgive herself if she died without telling him.

"I love you," she said suddenly, looking up to catch his eyes. "I'm sorry, I should have said it sooner. Thanked you sooner. You've always been there for me, and I wanted to say how much it meant, just in case."

Simon looked away, but he didn't let go of her hand. "I love you, too, Lola," he said softly. "Other than my family, you're the only good thing in my life."

216

Lola smiled. "Remember when Victor would disappear for days and not leave us any food?"

Simon laughed softly. "I had to go into the forest and steal peaches off the enchanted trees so we didn't starve. The tigers nearly ate me."

Lola laughed too, then she went quiet. "Those were the good times," she whispered. "When he wasn't there."

Simon nodded slowly, bringing his other hand up so that he was cupping her fingers between his palms. "Do you remember the clear nights when Victor would take us up to the roof?"

Lola did. Those nights had terrified her. Sometimes, when an experiment wasn't going his way or when one of his two charges had failed him especially badly, Victor would float them all up to the top of his tallest tower. There were no stairs up there, no way to get down except a hundred-foot drop. The view might have been spectacular, but all Lola remembered was the tower's steep ledge and how cold and slippery the golden roof had felt under her feet.

"I thought I'd die every time," she said, shivering at the memory. "The only thing that kept me from having a panic attack was remembering he wouldn't let us fall because we'd be too much trouble to replace."

That had been Victor's favorite line in dangerous situations: "Take care not to injure yourself, you're too much trouble to replace." As they'd grown older, he'd said it less and less, though Lola wasn't sure if this was because she and Simon were better able to handle themselves or if the trouble to replace them was no longer so great.

"Do you remember how he used to rant?" Simon asked, shaking his head. "It was always the worst on the roof. He used to stand there, going on and on about how humanity had thrown away its greatest gift out of fear. I remember one night in particular, he pushed me right up to the edge and told me that I was everything that was wrong with mankind, the 'epitome of our lost potential.'"

Lola frowned. "I don't remember him saying that."

"I think you were more worried about the fall," Simon said, staring hard at their joined hands. "I didn't mind the drop. I hated Victor. I hated his magic, hated being near him, hated his damn lessons and how I could never learn them fast enough. He used to tell me every day that I'd never see my family again if I didn't do what he wanted, that my soul was stained anyway, and I might as well do the blood magic since it was all I was good for anymore."

His fingers tightened around her hand, his short nails biting into her skin as his voice dropped to a whisper. "The only thing that kept me on that tower was you."

"Simon," Lola said, shaking their joined hands. "Simon, look at me."

"I can't."

Lola felt a twinge of fear. "Why not?"

"Because it's too embarrassing to say this stuff to my mother," he muttered, releasing her hand to rub his face.

Lola slumped down in the booth. "You should be the one to run. You don't need his pills. You could leave the DFZ tonight. Just run away and start a new clinic somewhere he can't find you."

"I can't do that," Simon said, raising his eyes to hers at last. "I won't abandon you."

Lola shook her head hard. "I can never get free. Victor owns me. Even when he vanishes, I'm still his, but you're different." She dug her nails into the red-checkered tablecloth. "Don't you dare stay for me, Simon. Don't make me the millstone that drowns you. Forget the concert. You've still got a full day before Victor returns. You can make it."

Simon shook his head. "I've stuck it out for this long. No way

218

am I leaving you to face him alone now, especially since we don't know what condition he'll be in when he comes back. Whatever airs he puts on, Victor's still human. He isn't actually the devil."

Lola went still. Frank had said something very similar the night he'd died. Hearing it again now sent a shiver through her gossamer, but Simon was still talking.

"Humans make mistakes," he said, clenching his fists on the table. "Sooner or later, Victor will, too. When he does, we're running, Lola. The both of us, together, and we're never looking back."

When he said it like that, it actually sounded possible. For a moment, Lola let herself imagine her and Simon driving off into the sunset with no pills and no Victor on their heels. But the dream had barely formed in her head when her gossamer started to itch.

Even though she'd just had one this afternoon, she could already feel the urge to take a pill coming on again, mocking Simon's promise. Escape from Victor? Lola couldn't live without the bastard even when he left of his own accord. She glanced at Simon again, but the hope in his eyes was like a lead weight on her chest, and she looked away again immediately.

"Thanks for meeting me for dinner," she said quietly. "I'd better get going."

Simon reached over the table, grabbing her fingers. "Come home with me," he said, staring at her with an intensity that made Lola pause.

"I can't," she said at last. She'd already made up her mind about this before she called him. Alva wasn't likely to forgive today's humiliation, and there were still the Paladins to worry about. Any of those would be a headache for a human, but Lola was a changeling: a ghost with an ever-changing face who was immune to fairy charm and most mage barriers. She could evade their enemies, but Simon couldn't, and Lola was determined not to bring any more trouble to his door. Also, this was very possibly her last night alive. If Simon really was intent on going ahead of her to the concert, he'd be working there until morning, and Lola wasn't about to spend her final hours waiting by herself in his house.

"I'll see you tomorrow," she said, slipping her fingers out of his grasp. "Where should I meet you?"

Simon's hand closed slowly over the empty spot where hers had been, and then he dropped his arm with a heavy sigh. "I'll call you," he said at last. "Keep your phone on, and take care of yourself, okay?"

"You too," she said, leaning down to kiss him on the head.

She gave his shoulders one last squeeze and walked out of the diner, careful to keep her gait to the slow, stately pace of the old woman she was pretending to be. Once she was safely hidden behind the dumpsters at the back of the restaurant, Lola let Simon's mother fall away as she shifted back into her yogurt lady.

She shook her arms with a relieved breath as the change finished. Keeping the shape of Simon's mother had been a lot harder than she'd expected, what with all the emotional strain and the lingering effects from her breakdown at Alva's. To make things worse, her gossamer was still itching like crazy. She wasn't in any immediate danger, but she'd need a pill in the next hour for sure.

Heaving a long sigh, Lola stepped away from the dumpsters and trudged back to her bike. Forget going along with Victor's plan. She wasn't even going to make it to the seven o'clock deadline at this rate.

That kind of thinking only made her gossamer worse, so Lola forced herself to perk up as she stepped into the narrow alley where she'd hidden her scooter. She'd only gotten about three feet in when she spotted a motorcycle parked in the dark beside her yellow bike, its running engine perfectly silent.

Lola's eyes went wide when she saw it. She turned to run next, whirling on her heels and charging back up the alley... straight into the leather wall of the Rider's chest.

~~~

When the waitress came to clear Lola's plates, Simon asked for the check and another cup of coffee. As the waitress left, the woman who'd been sitting alone in a booth on the diner's opposite end stood up and sauntered over, sliding into the seat Lola had just vacated.

The waitress did a double take when she returned with the coffee. Simon didn't blame her. Jamie was beautiful enough to stop most people in their tracks. Too bad it was all on the surface.

"That was a touching little display," Jamie said, nails tapping on the table like little knives. "You know she meant that 'I love you' in a sibling sort of way, right? She'll never *really* love you, not like you want her to. Fairies aren't capable of those kinds of emotions."

"She's a changeling, not a fairy," Simon said, taking a sip of his coffee. "And since you're hardly an expert on magic or relationships, I suggest you keep your advice to yourself."

Jamie rolled her eyes. "This isn't some teen drama, Simon. You're playing with a nuclear weapon. This is your last chance not to make the worst decision of your life."

Simon glared at her over the lip of his mug. "And strangely, my answer is exactly the same as it was when we had this conversation an hour ago: no. I won't sell out Lola, and I'm done with Victor."

"Come on," she said with a laugh. "You of all people should

221

know no one's ever 'done' with Victor."

"I am," he said. "I know how the old man works, and I know how to beat his Rider. He can't just crush me into obedience like he does everyone else."

"Don't be stupid," Jamie warned, her lovely face going serious. "You lucked out tonight because the changeling had already decided to go to the concert without any further urging from you. Don't waste that. We're standing on the cusp of everything our master's been planning for decades. If you play your cards right, you could still be the man standing at his right hand. You'd have to be crazy to throw that away for a girl who isn't even your species. Or even really a girl."

Simon set down his cup with a heavy clink. "I've made my decision."

As his words finished, every person in the diner stopped what they were doing and turned to look at Jamie. The customers, the staff, even the cooks back in the kitchen. They didn't do anything but stare, but the pressure of so many people watching in intense silence was enough to make anyone nervous, even someone as used to blood magic as Jamie. She shrank back into the booth, her lavender eyes flicking nervously to Simon, who just took another sip of his coffee before letting the magic go.

All at once, the people in the diner resumed their business as if nothing had happened. The waitress brought out a diner combo, people chatted and ate their food, the cooks slung hash. All was just as it had been, but the weight of what had almost happened now hung over Simon's table like a knife.

"Are you crazy, doing something like that in public?" Jamie hissed, pulling herself back up in her booth. "If you're trying to threaten me—"

"It wasn't a threat," Simon said, setting his half-empty mug on the table and pulling out his wallet. "It was a demonstration.

222

Victor knew what I was capable of at twenty, but I'm not the apprentice he abused anymore. I'm done being one of his monsters, and I'm done watching him make Lola suffer. I'm *done,* Jamie, and when Victor comes back, I'll tell him so myself."

"He'll kill you."

Jamie said this with the same certainty someone else would use to claim that gravity pulls you down, but Simon just chuckled. "I've already been dead once," he reminded her, dropping a pile of cash on the check. "He'll have to do better than that."

"Have it your way," she said, throwing up her hands. "I tried being reasonable. Really, I did. I didn't want to have to do this."

"What are you going to do?" Simon taunted. "Victor might be the world's greatest blood mage, but you're about as magical as that coffee cup."

Jamie just smiled and reached into her purse. She pulled a piece of paper out of one of the zipped inner pockets and held it out to him. Simon glanced at the paper skeptically. He knew he should just walk away, but the paper seemed to be pulling him toward it...

He recognized the compulsion for what it was a second too late. Already, he was taking the paper from Jamie's fingers. It was a business card, blindingly white, with one line of text written across its center in Victor's neat handwriting.

No one escapes me, Simon.

Simon's blood turned to ice. The words vanished as he read them, the black letters fading only to be replaced by others written in blood-red. He tried to look away, tried to close his eyes, but the compulsion Victor had implanted into his mind over years gripped him tight. He could no more stop reading than he could have stopped seeing, and as he read, the spell formed in his mind, coiling in his magic like a viper.

Had things been different, had Simon been someone else, this was where he could have possibly saved himself. He could have thrown the half-finished spell at Jamie or forced the other diners to come knock him over, anything to get his eyes off the horrid words. But Victor had trained his apprentice well. Even knowing what was coming, Simon couldn't stop reading until he reached the end, when the red words on the white card swam together to create a new sentence.

See you soon.

The last thing Simon saw was Jamie waving goodbye before the blood magic prison he'd just woven around his own mind snapped shut, locking him back into the coma he'd never really left.

~~~

Lola jumped away from the Rider with a shriek, shoving him with her palms in a vain attempt to knock him away. It was a stupid thing to do. The man had taken a car to the face without missing a step. Her little push didn't even make him wobble, but Lola didn't put her hands down as she backed away.

"What are you doing here?"

"I need to talk to you," Valente said, holding up his hands in surrender. "Please."

Lola blinked in astonishment. She hadn't expected an answer, especially not one with "please" at the end. But her bewilderment lasted only a second before righteous anger overwhelmed it.

"Why should I talk to *you?*" she snapped, glaring at her own reflection in his sleek black visor. "Do you have somewhere else Victor needs me to go? Dinner with the fairy king, perhaps?"

"Just hear me out," the Rider begged, his deep voice full of some strong emotion. If Lola hadn't known better, she'd have called it desperation.

224

"No thanks," Lola said, stomping back to her scooter. "I only do the blind-trust-for-man-who-saves-my-life thing once, and that bridge is burned."

The Rider was in front of her in an instant, grabbing the handlebars of her light electric cycle before she could get a leg over the seat. "I'll answer any question you want. I'll tell you everything I know. Just don't leave."

She shook her head, twitching her gossamer in preparation to dissolve her bike right out of his grip.

"*Please*, Lola!"

She glared at him hard, weighing the whole thing out in her mind, not that there was much to consider. The Rider was owned by Victor. He'd said so himself and then shown her just how much by his actions. She had no reason to trust him to do anything except hand her over to their master, but there was something in the frantic way his hands had locked onto her handlebars that called to her, and Lola decided to try a test.

"Ask me to my face," she said, crossing her arms over her chest. "Take off your helmet."

The Rider's body went rigid, and Lola smiled. He wouldn't do it. But then, just as she went again to dissolve her bike out of his grip, the Rider released her handlebars. His hands shot up to his helmet, gripping the black, glossy plastic as he lifted it off.

Lola stared in amazement as the Rider's face came into view. He'd actually done it, though he was clearly not happy about it. His glowing eyes were locked on the ground, illuminating his face in the dark alley with their eerie blue light. Other than that, though, Lola was again struck by just how *normal* the Rider looked. With his lips pressed tight to hide his fangs, he looked like any other handsome twenty-something who hit the gym on the regular. Give him some sunglasses to hide the eyes, and Lola could have passed him on the street with little more than an appreciative glance.

"Why do you wear it?" she asked, pointing at his helmet. "You look much less scary like this."

"I'll tell you if you promise not to run," Valente said, lifting those crazy glowing eyes to hers.

Lola frowned. "Anything I want? No lies?"

"Anything I can tell you, I will," he promised. "Just don't go."

It was clearly a trap, but the Rider looked so terrified by the idea of her leaving that Lola hesitated. And the more she hesitated, the more she realized it probably wasn't a trap. She was being forced back to Victor tomorrow anyway. It made no sense for her master to waste time on a convoluted snare like this, especially since he didn't even want his Rider near her in the first place. If it wasn't a trap, though, that meant Valente really did want to talk to her.

Lola mulled that over for a moment before deciding why not? It wasn't like he could betray her again now that all trust was gone, and having the Rider around would be a good defense if she ran into trouble. Plus, his promise of answers had caught Lola's curiosity. She was reasonably sure she could tell if he was lying so long as the helmet was off. The man clearly had no poker face at all.

"Okay," she said, letting go of her bike. "I'll stay with you on three conditions. First, until I go to the concert tomorrow, you'll escort me anywhere I want to go. Second, you answer every question I ask truthfully and completely, and if you can't answer, you have to tell me why. Third, the helmet stays off whenever you talk to me."

That last demand brought a look of sheer panic to the Rider's face. "I can't have the mask off in public."

"Then take me somewhere where you can," Lola said with a shrug. "Oh, and you're buying me all the food I want until Victor returns. Four conditions."

Valente took a deep breath. "And you won't run?"

"Not unless you give me reason to."

The Rider nodded. "Done."

Lola stuck out her hand to shake on it, but the Rider just stared at her fingers as if she'd offered him something inexplicable. Finally, he took it, his leather-gloved hand squeezing hers gently. Once the deal was sealed, Lola dissolved her bike and spun herself a big, glossy helmet to hide her face from the attention being with the Rider always risked.

"First order of business," she announced, shortening the yogurt lady's long hair so her helmet would fit better. "It's pill time, so we're getting secondsies."

Valente nodded and slipped his own helmet back into place. "Where to?"

"God of Noodles," Lola said at once. Because if she had a chauffeur and free eats, she was getting the *best*.

The Rider nodded and motioned for her to get on. Lola climbed onto the silent black bike, wrapping her arms gingerly around Valente's chest when he took his place in front of her. The moment she was secure, the bike shot forward, its black wheels moving soundlessly over the pavement as the Rider turned them out into the night.

~~~

Thirty minutes later, Lola was sitting on an overpass with her legs dangling over the neon-lit city below, eating the best noodles she'd ever conceived of out of a paper takeout box.

"So *gooooood*," she moaned as she shoved another chopstick full of thick, chewy, hand-torn noodles drenched in chili oil and black vinegar into her mouth. "I mean, I knew it would be since it's

227

made by a literal god, but *still*." She closed her eyes in bliss as the numbing spiciness spread through her gossamer. "It's unfair how delicious that is. Totally worth the effort."

It had taken a bit of finagling. As always, the line for God of Noodles had been two blocks out the door. Lola had taken one look at it and told the Rider to circle around. The moment he was gone, she'd transformed herself into one of the dishwashers, walked in the back, and snitched a takeout order right off the counter.

She'd left a pile of the Rider's cash to make up for it, but the theft had still been beneath her. The only reason she'd done it was time. If she hadn't had three hours to wait in that line before, she definitely didn't tonight, and like hell was she dying before she'd tasted noodles made by their representative spirit.

"Are you *sure* you don't want some?" she asked, turning to look at the Rider, who was sitting nervously on his bike between her and the traffic flying by on the highway behind them. "Seems a shame to pass on the best noodles in existence now that you've got a mouth."

The Rider shook his head. He didn't talk unless he had to, she'd noticed. Chewing her way through another thick, red-oil-drenched noodle, Lola wondered if that was because he wasn't used to talking or if something else was going on. It definitely couldn't be his voice. Even now, when she knew better, there was something about the Rider's deep, rich voice that made her feel relaxed and trusting, like a cat's purr.

When she had a good noodly cushion in her stomach, Lola reached into her pocket and brought out the little baggie with her two remaining pills. Careful as a jeweler, she grabbed one with her fingers. Then, bracing, she popped it into her mouth, chasing it immediately with another chopstick-full of noodles.

The explosion of garlic and numbing spice couldn't drown the

228

bloody taste out completely, but it was close. Once the pill was down, the itchy, overfull feeling faded as her gossamer settled, and Lola breathed a sigh of relief.

Staring glumly at her last pill, Lola closed her fist around the baggie and sent it back into her gossamer. One pill didn't seem like enough to get her all the way to tomorrow evening, but there was nothing she could do. Walking around with her gossamer in the red was just asking for the monster to come out. Better to take her pills early and play it safe, she'd decided. At least if they were in her, she couldn't lose them, and if she ran out before she got to the concert tomorrow… well, she'd ruin Victor's plan, which wasn't a bad consolation prize.

"We should get moving," Valente said. "Alva's goblins are getting close."

"How can you tell?" Lola asked, sweeping the spicy dregs out of the bottom of the takeout box into her mouth with the last noodle.

"I have feelers out."

Lola gave him a funny look as she dropped her trash into a dumpster way down on the street below. "What does that mean?"

"I can't really explain. It's just something I can do."

"Why didn't you feel the ones in Victor's mansion?" she asked as she climbed onto his bike. When the Rider didn't answer, she made like she was getting back off.

"Because I didn't have my head on then," he said quickly. "It makes my powers stronger."

Lola smiled smugly and settled back onto the bike. "So it's something you can take on and off?"

"Yes," Valente bit out, clearly uncomfortable.

"If it makes you more powerful, why don't you wear it all the time?"

"Because I hate it," he spat.

She was about to ask him why when the Rider came back with

229

a question of his own.

"Where next?"

Lola thought long and hard as she put on her helmet. "Somewhere I can see the stars."

The Rider nodded and kicked his bike into motion, merging them deep into the speeding highway traffic so that the noise and wind would make talking impossible. Arching an eyebrow at the dodge, Lola used the time to pick her next questions with care.

They drove north, away from the city into the bump where Michigan butted up against Lake Huron. The highway grew darker and emptier the farther they got from the DFZ. Valente's silent bike raced through the night, picking up speed as the traffic fell off until Lola felt like she was flying.

It took an hour to clear the suburbs that ringed the DFZ like moss around a seep. Eventually, though, they entered the dark quiet of the countryside. Above them, the moon was nowhere to be seen. Instead, the sky was filled with glittering stars shining bright and clear now that they'd left the city's light and smog behind. The farther they went, the more stars Lola saw. When Valente finally stopped them at a point that jutted out into the dark lake, Lola swore she could see the whole Milky Way spread across the sky like a river of light.

"Amazing," she said, vanishing her helmet for a better look. "I've never seen this many stars before."

The Rider didn't say anything, but she could tell by the jaunty way he got off his bike that he was pleased by her reaction. His motorcycle dissolved as he left it, the blue light winking out like a snuffed candle, plunging them into the dark. Lola spun her gossamer without thinking, and a kerosene lantern appeared in her hand, already lit.

Valente flinched at the light, but he didn't say anything as they walked away from the road down the short path to the pier at the point's end. When they got there, Valente took a seat on the wooden bench at the dock's end. Lola sat down as well, placing the lantern between them as she whipped herself up a coat to shield against the cold night wind. Technically, it was no different from the rest of her gossamer, but seeing the fluffy pink jacket made her feel warmer, which was good enough.

"Remember the rules," she told the Rider, pointing at his helmet. "Hats off."

Valente stiffened, but he obeyed, taking off his helmet and setting it carefully on the boards at his feet.

"Okay," Lola said, turning around on the bench until she was facing him. "First question: what are you?"

"I'm human," Valente answered. "Or at least I used to be. Now I'm a mix of fairy and human."

He kept his eyes down as he spoke. The warm light from the kerosene flame softened their eerie glow, but every time he opened his mouth, Lola caught a glimpse of his fangs.

"How did it happen?"

He paused, biting his lip with his sharp teeth. This was clearly costing him dearly, and Lola sighed. "If you hate talking so much, why did you agree to my terms?"

"I had to keep you from leaving," Valente said, running his gloved hand nervously through his dark hair.

Lola snorted. "You're the guy who melts trolls. Surely you could have kept me by force."

"I could," the Rider admitted. "But I didn't want to. I just wanted to talk to you."

"Why?" she pressed.

Valente lifted his eyes a fraction. "Because you're the only person I've ever met besides Victor who can handle my face."

"What's wrong with your face?" Lola said, bending over to get a better look. "You look fine to me. The teeth are a bit alarming,

231

but otherwise..."

She trailed off with a shrug, and Valente stared at her in wonder. "You really don't react to it."

"How do people normally react?"

This question obviously made Valente very uncomfortable, so Lola tried another approach. "You said you don't wear your head even though it makes you more powerful because you hate it. Why?"

"Because it's not mine."

Lola's eyes went wide. Suddenly, everything made way more sense. "That's a fairy head, isn't it?"

Valente nodded, and her jaw fell open.

"How did you end up with a fairy's head?"

The dock went silent as Valente looked away. When he finally answered, it was only one word.

"Victor."

Lola sighed. Should have known. "How did it happen?"

"When I was a teenager, a man came to my family's door," Valente said, still not looking at her. "He was the most beautiful man we'd ever seen. Being around him was like being in a cloud. We said yes to everything he said."

Lola nodded. "Fairy enthrallment."

"It was more than that," Valente insisted. "He had a power that made anyone who looked at him fall madly in love. He used this to gather slaves. He had a place out in the desert. He made us fight."

Lola swallowed. The Rider's voice grew harder with every word. His fangs were clearly showing now, and his eyes were glowing with fury.

"I hated him," Valente whispered. "For years and years, I hated that fairy, but only while he was away. Whenever I saw his face, I'd fall in love with him all over again. I thought I'd be his slave forever, but then Victor came to his door."

"And?" Lola asked.

"And I'm forbidden to speak of what happened next," Valente said, clearly relieved. "But I can tell you that the fairy died."

"And you ended up with his head," Lola finished. *And with a blood mage as your new master*, she added bitterly to herself.

Valente placed his gloved hands over his face. "It's a kind of hell, wearing the head of the thing you hated most in the world. It still works, too. Everyone who sees my face falls under the fairy's spell, only I can't control the magic like he did. Before I learned to keep my face hidden, I had to kill people to free them from the enthrallment."

Lola hissed as she realized what that meant. "*That's* why Alva had you look at me! She couldn't do anything herself because of hospitality, so she was going to use your head to enthrall me and make me do her bidding that way!"

"But it didn't work," Valente said quickly.

"Of course not," Lola scoffed. "I'm a changeling."

"And that's why I had to talk to you, no matter what," he said eagerly. "It's been years since I could talk to anyone besides Victor."

"Fate worse than death," Lola said, looking up at the stars again. "I guess this explains why you took down your mirror."

"That, and there's the part where I can still enthrall the human part of myself," Valente said in a bitter voice. "You don't know what it's like, falling in love with your own reflection." He touched his gloved fingers to his throat. "Even my voice is his. I can barely remember what my own voice sounded like anymore."

Lola sighed. When she'd agreed to go with the Rider, she'd steeled herself against feeling any pity for him. Now, though, that steel was going brittle. He just sounded so lost and lonely, and it didn't help that he kept looking at her like she was the most amazing thing he'd ever seen.

233

"I'm sorry," he said suddenly. "I should have told you Victor contacted me. I would have done it if I could, but he ordered me to tell you nothing, and I can't disobey."

As he spoke, Lola remembered Tristan's warning, how there was a difference in degree between her bond to Victor and the Rider's. Valente really did look torn up, though, and Lola sighed.

"I understand," she said, leaning back against the bench. "I mean, I'm not happy, but I understand you had to do it."

"I should have tried harder," Valente whispered, staring at the lantern. "You said you trusted me. No one's trusted me since I was a kid, and the first person who does, I betray."

His voice was rich with sorrow as he said this, and Lola realized that before the fairy and Victor took it away, trust must have been something Valente took very seriously.

"Well, for what it's worth, I forgive you," Lola said. "I know what it's like to be stuck between a Victor and a hard place, but were you at least telling me the truth when you asked me to help you back at your apartment?"

Valente nodded rapidly. "I didn't know anything about Victor's return until I woke up after the fight with the Paladins. That was also the first time I saw Alberich. He was the one who put Victor in contact with me."

There was no way Lola could know if that was true or not, but she'd already come this far, so she decided to believe him. He certainly looked earnest, and while that was the same false premise that had gotten her in trouble this morning, Lola was already tired of mistrusting everyone. It was like treading water all the time, and she simply didn't have the energy.

"Can you tell me what Victor has planned for tomorrow?"

"I don't know," Valente said. "All Victor told me was that he was coming back and that I needed to guard you against his enemies until he did."

"Is that what you're doing now?" Lola asked.

"Yes," Valente confessed, "but I mostly just wanted to talk to you."

Lola closed her eyes. She should have known Victor's hand was still on her leash. She wondered if the Rider would chase her if she turned into a porpoise and jumped into the lake. The only reason she didn't give it a go was because it wouldn't matter. She'd already decided to go back, and it would be cruel to force the Rider to do the job he so clearly hated when he was just as much a victim of Victor as she was.

"You said he contacted you after you woke up from the fight with the Paladins," she said, changing the subject. "What do you mean by 'woke up'? I saw you turn to ash."

"So long as my head's safe, my body is expendable," Valente told her matter-of-factly. "Even if I'm completely destroyed, if my head is still intact, I'll wake up somewhere near it within the hour."

"You could have told me that before," Lola snapped. "I thought you were dead!"

A shy smile spread over Valente's face at her upset, and Lola rolled her eyes. "What other fairy things can you do? Do you have a barrow?"

"No," he said. "I can't cast illusions or make things like you can, either, but I can reach out with gossamer."

To prove it, he tossed a big rock off the shore behind them into the water. It was the same invisible pressure Lola had seen him use countless times. Now that she knew what it was, though, her jaw fell open.

All of the Rider's mysterious barriers, the invisible force that followed his hands when he chopped things, it had all been done using *raw* gossamer. Unless it was locked into a shape, like a car, gossamer was soft as jelly. What the Rider was doing was the

235

equivalent of cutting things in half using a pudding cup. Lola couldn't even comprehend the level of control it must take to hone raw gossamer into a cutting edge, but it put her in mind of another inexplicable thing she'd seen the Rider do.

"What about when you dissolved that troll?" she asked. "How did you do that?"

Valente shifted uncomfortably. "My gossamer's different because of… how I was made. I can change other fairies' gossamer when I touch it if I want. That's how I dissolved the troll. I invaded his gossamer and melted it."

"That's crazy," Lola said, shoving a hand through her hair. No wonder Tristan had called him a weapon. If the Rider could melt gossamer at will, there wasn't a fairy in the world who was safe around him. That was probably how he'd knocked her out after the crash in the alley, Lola realized belatedly. He'd just put his hand on her head and turned her gossamer off like a light.

"No wonder Victor keeps such good track of you," she said, her mind racing with sudden possibilities. "If you can melt gossamer, could you hold it together?"

"No," Valente said sadly. "I can control if I melt it and by how much, but that's all I can do."

"Drat," Lola muttered. "Can you lie?"

"Yes, but it's hard, and I can only do it in writing."

Because he had the fairy's voice.

"I see like a fairy, too," Valente added, turning his glowing eyes on her.

"What does that mean?" she asked, because Tristan had never mentioned seeing things differently.

"I see the world like before, but I can also see through glamour," he explained. "It's like looking through a double image, the projection and the truth underneath."

Lola shrank into the bench. If Valente could see through

236

glamour, that meant he could see through *her*. Did he see the blood? The monster?

Part of her wanted to ask, but a far larger part wanted to bury the information and pretend it had never been. Without her glamour, Lola couldn't even pretend to be human. She watched Valente warily, but he was still just looking at her, his glowing eyes shining in the lantern light, and Lola slowly sat back up.

He wasn't running, she reasoned, so she couldn't look *that* bad. He'd already seen her at her worst, anyway, though if he really could see through glamour, he must have known what she was from the start. That made the fact that he'd chased her at the beginning even crazier, but Lola also found it comforting. Aside from Victor and the fairies, who were used to monsters, everyone who saw her real face ran screaming. Even Simon had fled from her the first time, but not Valente.

He'd never been afraid of her, she realized. He'd ridden with her monster all the way to her apartment and touched her fangs without hesitation to help her take her pill. That didn't make up for what had happened at Alva's, but it still counted for a lot. Far more than Lola was comfortable with, actually, and she quickly moved to other things.

"What do you do for food?" she asked, keeping her voice casual. "Can you eat normal stuff like I do?"

Valente shook his head. "Dreams only."

Tristan had told her as much, but it was good to hear it confirmed. Eating dreams was probably what made the Rider so powerful, actually. She could coast by on carbs, but real fairy magic needed real sustenance.

"Do you go hunting?"

That was what other fairies did, enthralling humans and feeding off their dreams before sending them away only a little worse for wear. Since he couldn't control his enthrallment, Lola

237

imagined Valente would have a harder time. When he didn't answer her at once, though, she started to get nervous. He was still the Black Rider, after all. Maybe he only ate nightmares.

"I don't hunt," Valente said at last. "Victor feeds me."

Her stomach twisted. She could barely stomach Victor's blood. The idea of living off the sick man's *dreams* was enough to make her want to throw up her noodles. She was still choking the feeling down when Lola realized the more immediate implications of Valente's confession.

"Wait, if Victor feeds you, when's the last time you ate?"

"Five days ago," he said, looking carefully at the ground.

Tristan could go that long without a dream, but Tristan was old and powerful. He was also a full fairy. "How often do you usually eat?"

Valente rubbed the back of his neck. "Every two days, more or less."

"Jeez," Lola breathed. "Aren't you hungry?"

"Yes," he said. "But there's nothing I can do about it. It's not like I can just go up to a human and take a dream without enthralling them, and if I show them my face, they get stuck on me for life." He let out a long breath. "I'll just have to wait it out. I've gone eight days without eating before. I can make it."

That didn't make Lola feel better. "You've never eaten anyone's dreams but Victor's?"

"No," Valente said, frustration creeping into his deep voice. "Can we stop talking about this?"

Lola frowned. As someone who'd also been starved by Victor, she felt deep sympathy for the Rider. More than that, though, Lola couldn't get over the idea that not only had Valente lost food when he'd gained his fairy head, he'd been limited to Victor's sick mind. She had no idea what their master dreamed about, but Lola got the feeling that living off his dreams was the fairy equivalent of living

238

off rancid meat—possible but not healthy and incredibly disgusting—and she felt compelled to do something about it.

It wasn't Valente's fault this had happened to him, after all. He was Victor's monster just like she was. He'd faced her real form and helped her when she needed it. Lola wasn't going to leave him in the lurch now, especially since the thing he needed was one of the few she still had to give.

"Would you like one of my dreams?"

Valente stared as if she'd just offered him her firstborn.

"There's no reason to go hungry," Lola went on. "And I have it on good authority that my dreams are delicious."

Valente's mouth started to move, but it was several more seconds before he actually got any words out. "You'd just *give* me a changeling dream?"

Lola shrugged. "It's not like I'm using them."

He looked away, his glowing eyes unfocused. He was clearly debating himself hard over the issue, but his hunger seemed to be winning. Already, Lola could see his teeth getting longer.

"You're sure?" he asked.

"Wouldn't have offered if I wasn't," Lola said, though the teeth were making her nervous. "You don't have to bite me or anything, do you?"

Valente shook his head, pressing his lips tight to hide his fangs. "Just touch you," he said, his voice shaking as he looked at her again. "You're really going to give me a dream?"

"Oh, for goodness' sake." Lola moved the lamp and scooted over on the bench until she was sitting right beside him. Valente tensed when she grabbed his hand, but he didn't try to stop her as she removed his glove. His hands were big and warm, not surprising since he always wore full leather, but as their skin made contact for the first time, Lola felt the unmistakable bite of frost.

All fairies had their own flavor of magic. Valente's tasted like a midwinter night, icy and clear. The cold pricked her skin, but the feeling wasn't unpleasant. It was actually kind of cozy to touch something so cold when she was all bundled up in her fuzzy jacket, and Lola took a moment to breathe out a long puff of frost before leaning in to rest her forehead against Valente's chest.

He almost jumped off the bench when her weight settled into him, and Lola bit back a laugh. "Just relax," she told him, squeezing his bare hand. "What kind of dream would you like?"

"I don't..." His words trailed off. "A good one," he said at last, his voice longing.

Lola nodded, closing her eyes. The Rider's tense breaths were harder to match than Tristan's, but she managed eventually. It helped that she was exhausted, and soon enough, she started to drift off. After a few minutes, the Rider shifted beneath her, and she felt his arm land lightly on her shoulders, his fingers petting her hesitantly, just as they had back at her apartment.

Now as then, the gentle pressure was soothing, and Lola melted against him, easing into the dream. She focused on good thoughts as she went: funny movies, pretty days, delicious milkshakes, anything happy that would give the Rider something to live on besides Victor's bloody obsessions.

But feeding a dream to Valente wasn't the same as feeding one to Tristan. When she'd done this before, it'd always been like drifting out to sea, but there was no drifting with the Rider. The moment the dream began to form, Lola felt his freezing gossamer tighten around her like a fist. It wasn't painful, but she was certainly stuck. She was about to open her eyes and ask what he was doing when Valente's gossamer yanked her hard, dragging Lola into the dark.

Chapter 12

1 pill

She was on a beach.

The water was crystal blue and calm as a bathtub, lapping gently against a huge expanse of white sand. In the distance, short, steep mountains rose over the thick tropical greenery that lined the white crescent coast. Below the trees, modest beach houses faced the surf, their windows flung open to let out lacy curtains that danced in the warm, salty breeze. Music drifted from somewhere behind her, horns and drums playing a happy, dancing beat. In front of her, the beach was speckled with families, the little children squealing as they ran from the tiny waves.

One such family was right in front of her. A handsome, older Hispanic man, his dark hair streaked with silver, was pulling picnic baskets out of the back of an old pickup. Next to him, a woman with a face wrinkled from years of smiling was lifting two small children out of the truck's cab, speaking Spanish to them in a singsong voice.

Another man came over to help unload as she watched. He was much younger than the first, but their bodies were similar, father and son. The young man was shirtless, already in his swimming trunks, his tanned skin warm and glowing in the bright summer sun. From this angle, all Lola could see was his back, but he was laughing and talking with the woman in a warm voice that called to Lola like a siren.

The children took off for the water the moment their feet hit the sand. The older couple followed more slowly with the picnic baskets and blankets, but the young man stayed put. He leaned on the pickup's side, watching the family as they made their way toward the sea with one bare foot propped on the truck's metal bumper, the other digging into the warm, rutted sand of the beach road. He looked so relaxed and carefree, Lola felt a stab of envy. But then, almost as if he could feel her staring, the man turned around, and Lola's breath caught.

His eyes were warm and brown, his smile showing flat, human teeth, but even so, it was Valente. He grinned when he saw her and pushed off the truck to jog over. Lola backed away instinctively, but she'd barely made it a step before her back hit the ribbed bark of a palm tree. She jumped away in surprise, and Valente laughed at her, the sound coming naturally. Then he stepped up and started speaking to her in Spanish.

Like most residents of the Americas, Lola spoke a little, but Valente was going way too fast for her to follow, and she was too caught up in the sound to string together the words she did catch. The voice he spoke to her with now was completely different than the Rider's. It was still deep, still warm, but the depths were measurable. Human, she realized. It was his human voice.

When he saw she didn't understand what he was saying, Valente grabbed her hand and started pulling her toward the beach. He swept his other arm out as they walked, waving his hand across the blue sea, the distant mountains, and the little houses that lined the coast. He looked back at her each time, and though Lola still couldn't understand what he was saying, the meaning was clear. *See?* his movements beckoned. *Isn't it beautiful?*

Lola could only nod in agreement. She'd never been anywhere so lovely. The afternoon air was warm and seasoned with the sea and the smell of good cooking. The sun was strong overhead, but the shade of the swaying palm trees blocked the glare. The ocean rolled off to the horizon, endless and sparkling blue, and as Valente wrapped a long, warm arm around her shoulder and started guiding her out onto the beach where the family, *his* family, was setting up their towels, Lola felt something clench deep in her chest.

The feeling was so unfamiliar, it took her several seconds to recognize it. Homesickness. She was feeling nostalgia, warmth, the loss of a happier time. For someone who'd never had a safe home or many happy times, the sensation was overwhelming, and to her horror, tears began to roll down Lola's cheeks.

Valente stopped at once. Lola tried to look away so she wouldn't ruin the happy dream, but he caught her and turned her face to his. He reached up, wiping her tears away with his broad thumbs, and Lola began to shake. His hands were just so warm, so *human*. There was no threat here, no looming death, no blood, no Victor. Nothing but sea and beautiful coast and the promise of dancing when evening came.

He'd just brushed the last of the wetness away when a voice called Valente's name. They both looked up to see the old woman waving at them, holding up a large plastic jug beaded with condensation. The liquid inside was a cloudy, pale yellow dotted with floating limes so bright green that Lola could already taste their sour bite. Valente yelled back, his smile returning in a flash.

His hand slid down to grab Lola's as he started again for the beach. She stumbled at the sudden motion, and Valente caught her. But when Lola was back on her feet, Valente didn't let her go. Instead, his arms snaked around her waist, pressing her body into his.

Even though she was still dressed in the fuzzy pink jacket she'd been wearing on the pier, Lola could feel the heat of Valente's sun-warmed body like they were touching skin to skin. He felt hard and strong against her, his face grinning down with such open, happy tenderness that Lola was struck dumb. And then, without warning, Valente leaned in, closing the difference between their heights to press his smiling mouth to hers.

She jumped at the sudden contact. Valente tasted of sweet limes and sea air, his lips warm and firm against her own. She could feel his smile against her skin, and then his arms tightened around her as he deepened the kiss, his tongue sliding into her mouth, filling her with warmth.

Lola had been kissed before. Just once, by Simon, back when they were awkward teens. But that had been a chaste, terrified thing, a tiny scrap snapped up in Victor's looming shadow. This was warmth and freedom and sunlight, making her knees go weak. Valente chuckled above her, the laughter rumbling through his chest and into hers. Then his arms lifted, pulling her up his tall body until her shoes were dangling in the sand.

Fully supported, Lola forgot about her weak knees. She forgot about standing, forgot about monsters. Her body went limp, melting into his as she let it all go. Her arms rose to wrap around his neck, fingers brushing against his hair as she tentatively met his tongue with her own.

And then, like a pulled plug, the dream vanished.

Lola's eyes shot open. The beach was gone. There was no smell of sea and limes, no warm summer breeze. Just the freezing wind off the black lake and the deep, cold, midwinter darkness of Valente's gossamer as he jerked away from her so fast, she nearly fell.

"Sorry, sorry!" he said, scrambling off the bench. "I didn't know—I wouldn't—I mean, it was never like that before!"

He stopped and looked away, his whole body reeling as he turned to face the lake. Even with his back to her, though, Lola swore she saw him blushing in the eerie blue glow of his eyes. His movements were exaggerated as he put more distance between them, his balance wavering almost like he was drunk. Lola felt a little drunk herself. Even though the dream was gone, the feel of it was still inside her, making her gossamer hum.

She'd never had a dream like that, a fairy dream that wasn't her own. Lola didn't know if that was because Valente was part human or because her gossamer was acting up again, but it had made her feel alive. Powerful, like she was the one who'd eaten the dream instead of him.

"Did it work?" she asked.

Valente jumped at her voice. He looked back over his shoulder, his eyes glowing brighter than ever with something very close to wonder. "Yes," he said softly. "It worked."

Lola smiled, relieved. Given how good she felt, she'd been half worried she'd messed up and pulled energy out rather than putting it in. Valente did look better, though. Even in the dim light of her camp lantern, his color was clearly improved. He was standing straighter, and the skin around his eyes no longer looked pinched. He was still looking at her, too, his glowing eyes fixed on her face. No, not her face, Lola realized with a flush. Her lips.

With that, the heat from the kiss came back in a rush, burning so hot that Lola could almost feel Valente's arms around her again. She put her hands over her face and turned away, but the heat didn't fade.

Lola had the feeling it wouldn't for a long, long time. Even the memory of the kiss was overwhelming, and not just because she'd never been touched like that before. It was everything: the warmth, the place, the sudden tenderness of his lips on hers. It had been so natural, so free. For the first time she could remember, maybe the first time ever, Lola hadn't felt like a monster hiding behind a mask. When Valente had dropped that smiling kiss to her mouth, she'd felt human. She'd felt like *Lola*.

She was still basking in the wonder of it when she heard the Rider move. Slowly, cautiously, and leaving a great deal of room, Valente sat back down on the bench beside her.

"Thank you for the dream," he said quietly, hands clutched on

245

his knees. "I'm sorry about what happened. It just felt so real, and I…" His deep voice faded to nothing. "I'm sorry. I shouldn't have done that. If you want me to go, I will."

Lola tilted her head at him. Valente was almost three feet away, sitting so close to the end of the bench that half his body was off it. His head was down, his expression appropriately apologetic, but his glowing eyes were full of loss.

As she saw it, the unfairness of both their lives hit Lola like a smack of disbelief. Victor wasn't even here right now, so how could he still make all of them so miserable? She, Simon, and the Rider were like three little tragedies, and Lola just couldn't see *why*. Why did it have to be like this? What did it take to get free?

She scooted closer to Valente. His eyes were glowing bright from his feeding, throwing his face into sharp relief. Even so, Lola could see the warm, smiling boy from the dream hovering under the cold image of the Rider like a ghost. It was like how Valente had described his vision, with the illusion overlying the truth, but where Lola's illusion was the human and her truth the monster, Valente was reversed.

Her hand was moving before she'd finished the thought. She reached out across the space between them and brushed her fingers over the stubble on his cheek. Valente closed his eyes at the touch, shutting off the ghostly light. This made him look even more human, and Lola stood up, walking slowly until she was standing right in front of him.

Valente stayed perfectly still, his eyes closed tight. He even seemed to be holding his breath as she looked him over. Seeing him like this, in the soft light of her lantern, Lola couldn't see the fairy head anymore. His face was just Valente's, and it was a good face. This close, Lola could even see the lines caused by the natural smile she remembered from the dream. Lines that clearly hadn't been used in a long, long time.

With that, the wave of homesickness for that place she'd never been came rolling back, only this time, the overwhelming loss of the happy kiss came with it. It hit Lola so hard that her whole body slumped. Suddenly, the idea that she would never be kissed that way again, that her life going on as it always had—lonely, terrified, and completely owned by Victor—was the best outcome she could hope for, felt completely unbearable.

Unbidden, her eyes dropped to Valente's lips. They looked just like she remembered. Would they feel the same?

Just the thought was enough to bring the old fear surging back. Before the Rider's new orders to watch over her, they weren't even supposed to be in contact. Giving him a dream was bad enough, but at least she could justify that to Victor as keeping his monster fed. A kiss was something else entirely.

She hadn't looked at Simon for weeks after Victor had come down on them. She couldn't imagine what he'd do if she kissed Valente like she wanted. The Rider must have known this, too. Even a dream kiss had been enough to send him running. But he'd been upset because he'd kissed her without permission, which was totally different than saying he didn't want to kiss her at all...

Lola bit her lip. This was dangerous territory. She should pull back now, before she did something their master wouldn't forgive. But even as the familiar warnings clanged in her mind, a new voice, tiny and belligerent, whispered in the dark.

Victor isn't here.

Her body began to shake. That was right. Even if her master returned tomorrow, he wasn't here yet. Victor had already claimed the whole of her life before this point. Was she really going to give him this, too?

Lola clenched her hands to fists. Then, before she could lose her nerve, she bent down. Her whole body was jumping, but for once, it had nothing to do with her gossamer. It was her heart, the

247

little organ she always made for every body even though she didn't technically need it, that was beating like a frantic bird as she closed her eyes and stepped forward to press her trembling lips against the Rider's.

The kiss was nothing like the one on the beach. That had been warm and laughing, full of sun and sea. Now, it was the freezing taste of Valente's gossamer that flooded through her, but Lola held her ground, pushing back with her own magic as her fingers found his shoulders.

As the initial shock of their touch faded, Lola felt the warmth of Valente's skin begin to bleed through the chill of his magic. The hardness of his lips was softening, too, his body relaxing a fraction as he adjusted to her touch. And then, without warning, Valente began to kiss her back.

He was the hesitant one this time. His lips pressed into hers as gently as two feathers, the soft, short fall of his hair brushing against her knuckles as he tilted his head to angle it to hers. Lola barely dared to breathe the entire time. Fear of Victor's anger was like a hand around her throat, but with every second it didn't choke her, Lola felt a little braver. Brave enough to dart her tongue between the Rider's lips when he opened them, brushing one of his fangs in the process.

Valente jerked away so fast, she lost her balance. Just like in the dream, he caught her at once, but he still held her away from him, keeping her at arm's length as he clamped his lips firmly over his long, sharp teeth.

"Stop," he said, the command barely louder than the wind.

Lola had barely scraped together the courage to start. Stopping was the last thing on her mind. "Victor—"

"Victor would hate all of this," Valente said, letting her go to rub his hands over his face. "That's not the point. It's not like the dream. I'm not—" He cut off with a frustrated breath, dropping his hands to show her his face again. "I'm not human."

The idea that he could dismiss their master so casually and yet be hung up on something so meaningless baffled Lola completely. "So?" she said. "Neither am I."

"It's different. *You* don't have fangs."

Lola gaped at him. Valente was one of the few people who'd seen her transformed, and he was worried she'd judge *him*?

Her expression must have been a sight, because Valente's scowl grew darker. He tried to move away then, but Lola caught him, holding onto his shoulders with her hands.

"It's not different," she said. "And my fangs are way worse than yours."

Valente closed his eyes as her hands pressed him back onto the bench. Lola took the chance to lean down, resting her forehead against the crown of his head.

"Don't you get tired of being his monster all the time?" she whispered into his hair. "What if..." She swallowed. "What if we tried being human? Just for one night?"

The danger of those words went through her like a sword. A kiss was one thing, but what she was suggesting was a whole other level. Lola could actually feel Victor's bloody, burning breath begin to smolder at the mention of such disobedience, and from the way Valente flinched, she knew he felt it too. The reaction was so swift, so absolute, Lola was about to tell him to forget it when Valente's hands grabbed her arms.

Lola froze as he gently moved her until her face was directly above his. When he had her where he wanted her, his hands slid up to cup her cheeks, his gloved fingers pressing so lightly, she could only feel them in brushes. But there was nothing light or gentle about the way he looked at her. His eerie, glowing eyes were staring at her with such longing, such long-held, secret hope, that Lola began to tremble. And as she shook against his gloved palms, the Rider rose up and kissed her.

Again, the kiss was different, neither the sweet, hot kiss from the beach nor the stumbling, hesitant kiss from before. This kiss was like a valve blowing, a frantic release of everything that had been crushed and buried under the Rider's silence, but what surprised Lola even more was her own reaction. Valente had barely moved before she was kissing him back just as hard. Even his icy magic couldn't touch the fire flaring up inside her, a burning that, for once, had nothing to do with gossamer and everything to do with the fact that she was here and alive in a place where, at least for tonight, Victor couldn't reach. For this one perfect moment, Lola was as close to free as she'd ever been, and she wasn't going to waste it being timid.

Valente must have felt it, too, because he grabbed her as if his life depended on it. His arms wrapped around her like a vise, trapping her against him as he kissed her until they were both breathless. But when Lola's shaking fingers finally made it to the zipper of his leather jacket, Valente broke the kiss.

"Not here," he whispered, his deep voice panting into her mouth. "Come on."

He lifted her off him and set her on the ground. He grabbed his helmet in one hand and took Lola's with the other, pulling her down the dark path back to the road. Lola barely had time to vanish the camp lantern before Valente lifted her onto his motorcycle as it emerged from the shadows. The moment she was on, he slammed his helmet back onto his head and sat down in front of her. Then, pulling Lola's arms tight around his chest, he gunned his silent bike and shot into the night, flying down the dark, empty road faster than she'd known he could go.

They didn't drive for long. Lola had barely settled into her seat before they pulled off the highway into the cracked parking lot of a tiny country motel. The lights were on in the front office, but

Valente didn't head there. Instead, he drove his silent cycle around to the back of the long line of rooms.

He grabbed her the moment they stopped, lifting her into his arms. The bike vanished beneath them, poofing silently into the shadows as Valente carried her toward the last door in the line. The room was closed with an old-style electronic lock. She was about to offer to make a keycard when she felt the icy pressure of Valente's gossamer squeeze around the cracks to open the deadbolt from the other side.

"Nice trick," Lola said as he carried her inside.

Valente didn't answer. He just kicked the door shut behind him, his icy gossamer turning the deadbolt back with a sharp *crack* as he set her down on the bed.

Lola landed with a gasp on the threadbare blanket, the springs creaking beneath her. Valente ripped off his helmet, tossing it away with a violence that startled her. His gloves went next, though these were merely dropped on the floor as he walked around to the side of the bed. Lola crawled over to the edge of the mattress to try and pull him down to join her, but Valente's arms cut her off, holding her in place a few inches away as he dropped to his knees on the carpet.

"Tell me to stop," he said, his blue-glowing eyes the only light in the room as he stared at her. "If you don't want this, tell me to stop."

His face was calm as he spoke, his deep voice smooth, but his hands were shaking where they rested on her arms. His magic was thick in the air around them, chilling the small, stuffy room until Lola could see her breath. It pressed down on her like a caress, and Lola closed her eyes, lowering her head until her lips brushed his forehead.

Valente took a hissing breath and leaned into her, his hands sliding down to her waist. Beneath the frozen bite of his magic, his

251

fingers were warm as they pushed under her fuzzy jacket, his long arms reaching up to peel it off of her. When he dropped it to the floor, Lola dissolved it to gossamer. But when she tried to help him by doing the same to her T-shirt, Valente shook his head.

"Let me do it," he whispered, arching up to kiss her neck as his hands slid under the smooth cotton.

Now it was Lola's turn to hiss. Her whole body went rigid as Valente's hands brushed over her stomach, but the shock was as much surprise as pleasure. Lola tried not to make a habit of longing for things she couldn't have, but in the few times she'd imagined what it would be like to be touched, she'd always worried it wouldn't be what she hoped. After all, her body was a construct, a doll formed out of gossamer. But as Valente's ragged breath landed on her skin, the cold of his magic giving way to the heat of his fingers as he peeled off her shirt and bra, Lola didn't feel like a fairy spell. She felt human. Warm, soft, deliciously *human*, and the gasp she let out as Valente's hands slid down her body was as real as anything she'd ever done.

He took off her shoes next, his deft fingers unknotting the laces of her sneakers in seconds. Cupping her feet, he pulled her shoes off gently, then her socks. When he reached up to undo the button of her pants, though, Lola tensed.

"Um," she said, crossing her arms over her naked chest. "I can do requests if you like. I mean, I've never done this before, but I can change anything you don't—"

"No."

The word came out of Valente like a shot, and Lola flinched. He leaned in at once, pressing a soft kiss to her collarbone. "No," he whispered again, the word puffing against her skin. "I like you just the way you are."

"'Just the way I am' changes, you know," Lola said with a smile. "I don't even know what I'm supposed to look like, so it's not an insult if you want something different."

"No," Valente said again, sitting back on his heels to give her a deadly serious look. "The glamour changes. You don't. The you I see is the same, always."

Lola stared at him in wonder. "What do I look like?"

The question was out of her mouth before she could stop it. She closed her eyes with a wince, cursing herself for an idiot. If Valente could look through gossamer, Lola already knew what he saw. Beneath her glamour mask, there was nothing but monsters and blood. Everything that was good about her was stolen from others: her face, her body, even her bravery was drawn from her sister. Before she could take the stupid question back, though, Valente answered.

"Sunlight."

His whisper was so close that Lola jumped, her eyes snapping open to see his glowing gaze inches from her own.

"You look like sunlight shining from far away," he said solemnly.

"You're lying," Lola said, her voice thin. "The blood—"

"I can't speak lies," Valente reminded her, moving one arm up to splay his large hand across her stomach. "The blood's there too, but it's not you." A smile spread across his face as his palm pressed into her skin. It wasn't as big or as warm as the smiles he'd given her in the dream, but it was the largest by far she'd seen on him in the real world, and it made Lola's heart stutter.

"You're beautiful," he whispered. "The first time I saw you, you took me completely by surprise. When my head's off, the fairy vision is all I can see. You nearly blinded me. I was unprepared. I think I still am." He ducked his head, pressing his lips against the skin between her breasts. When he spoke again, his words vibrated through her. "You are the most beautiful thing I've ever seen."

Lola stared at him, dumbfounded, but Valente just pulled her forward until her naked body was pressed tight against his. He didn't say anything else, but he didn't need to. He'd already said more than enough. As his bare hands swept over her back, his fingers touching her with hesitant wonder, Lola felt beautiful, *actually* beautiful, for the first time in her life.

She took a shaking breath and leaned down. Valente met her lips halfway, and his grip on her back tightened as his mouth closed over hers. The kiss was as wild as the one back by the lake, only now there was no thought of Victor in Lola's mind. Just as she had in the dream, Lola let it go. She forgot about pills, about monsters and death. Just for this moment, this place, this person, she let go of fear and shame and let the kiss take over.

Valente had her pants off in seconds. Her underwear followed shortly after, but while she was now completely naked, Valente had yet to remove anything but his helmet and gloves. This was unacceptable. The leather was soft against her skin, but Lola wanted to touch him as he was touching her. *Needed* to touch him, but when she reached for his jacket, Valente grabbed her wrists.

"There's nothing under there that you want to see," he said, gently pushing her hands away. "Just let me touch you. Let me…"

His voice trailed off as he kissed her, but Lola pushed back. "There's nothing you can show me that will make me stop."

"It's not—" Valente looked away suddenly, his whole body rising as he took a ragged breath. "I don't look like that."

The words were so quiet, Lola almost didn't hear, but she understood him. The happy man on the beach with his beautiful tan skin and warm looks didn't exist. Valente hadn't said how old he was when the fairy had taken him, but Lola got the feeling he'd been pretty young. The smiling man she'd seen in the dream was what Valente could have been, the future that had been stolen. But as much as she felt for his loss, Lola refused to be held back by it.

"I'm not going to judge you by a dream," she promised. "I'm not going to judge you at all. You saw what I look like, and we're still here. Let me do the same for you." She eased down and planted a soft kiss on his neck. "Let me want you back."

Valente took another deep breath, and then, slowly, he nodded.

Before he could change his mind, Lola reached out and grabbed the flap of his leather riding suit. She pulled, popping the snaps like firecrackers. The zipper went next, revealing the black T-shirt he wore beneath. With Valente's help, Lola pushed the leather off his shoulders, but as his arms came into view, Lola's hands stopped.

Valente's skin was riddled with scars. They crisscrossed his wrists, forearms, and up his biceps until the shirt's short sleeves hid them. Some were huge and jagged, as if his flesh had been ripped away with an ax. Others were small as razor cuts. All of them blended together to form a pale network over his skin. She was just reaching up to touch one when Valente shoved the leather back onto his shoulders.

"Don't," Lola said, catching his arms. "I mean, you don't have to. I was just surprised."

He gave her a disbelieving look, but before he could say anything, Lola slid off the bed to join him on the carpet. Facing him on her knees, she pushed the leather aside again and grabbed the hem of his shirt, tugging it up gently. A few seconds later, Valente gave in, removing his arms from the leather sleeves to help her pull the soft black cloth over his head.

Even though she'd braced for the worst, the sight of Valente's chest made Lola wince. The skin here was even more scarred than his arms, but what really startled her was the variety. There were shallow cuts and deep gouges, burns and scrapes, even the marks of what looked like shrapnel across his ribs. Strange, long scars she couldn't identify curled over his shoulders to continue down his back, and the base of his neck was ringed with dark, uneven marks, almost as if he'd been hanged.

"Did Victor…"

"No," Valente said. "No wound has stayed on me since I got the head. Those are from before."

Lola nodded. Before Victor, so back when he was with the fairy who'd enthralled him and his family. The one who'd made them fight. Instantly, her mind went back to the old couple she'd seen in the dream, and Lola's chest began to tighten.

"I'm sorry," she said quietly. "Sorry this happened to you, to your family. But I'm still happy you're here with me tonight." At his disbelieving expression, Lola gave him a small smile. "It was a happy dream for me, too."

Valente stared at her for what felt like hours. Then he reached down, encircling her with his arms. Lola jumped a little at the sudden contact. She could feel the dents and indentations of his scars clearly against her skin. The tingle of his icy magic nibbled at her, sucking away her warmth, but that only made her hug him harder. As her arms tightened, Valente stood up, taking her with him.

It happened so fast, Lola was afraid she'd hurt him, but there was no pain in Valente's face when he bent down to deposit her on the bed again. She was still trying to get her legs under her when he sat down as well. He pulled off his motorcycle boots, dropping them on the floor with a heavy thunk. His socks went next, then the rest of his motorcycle suit. When he was naked beside her, Valente took a deep breath and turned, fixing her with his glowing look.

"You can still tell me to stop."

"You're the only one talking about stopping," Lola said, holding out her arms.

Valente leaped into them. He took her down to the mattress, covering her body with his as he kissed her like he was starving. After a moment of shock, Lola responded in kind, dragging her fingers over his scars, which ran all down his legs as well. As always, his skin was a mix of warmth and cold gossamer, and there was so much of it now. For a moment, Lola thought the chill would freeze her, but even as she worried, the midwinter touch began to fade, leaving only the heat of his body.

The air grew colder as he began to warm, and when Valente's mouth finally left her lips to kiss her neck, Lola looked up to see tendrils of frost curling across the bed. The ice grew before her eyes, freezing the sheets, the blankets, the cheap wooden headboard, even the air itself.

But though it now looked like the Arctic all around them, Lola wasn't cold. Neither was Valente, not anymore. He was nothing but heat and need as he pushed inside.

Lola caught her breath. Of all the books she'd read, none of them had ever adequately described the fullness, the incredible connection. She could actually feel Valente's magic inside her, sense his gossamer as if it was an extension of her own. Valente must have felt it too, because he stopped with a gasp, his lips breaking from hers as he gritted his sharp teeth. For a moment, he hung there, his whole body pulled tight. Then, with a desperate moan, he began to move, pressing kisses to every bit of her he could touch.

Lola was just as frantic. She kissed him wildly, her hands scrambling to clutch his arms, his back, his short hair. With every touch, Lola fought to memorize this feeling so she could keep it forever. Part of her realized it was silly to cling so hard to something that passed so quickly, but Lola felt like a starving child who'd somehow wheedled her way into a banquet, and she was determined to keep every single scrap as she pulled Valente tighter.

It was such a small thing, a night spent between two people, but for Lola, it was so, so much more, because it was hers. This pleasure, Valente's warmth, the marvelous feeling building inside her, they were all hers. Hers and Valente's, and Victor couldn't touch them.

That thought was like a miracle, and it gave Lola the courage to do something else she'd never dared to do before. She thrust her master away. She locked Victor out of her mind and clung to what was hers, and as she did, she had the strangest sensation of flying even as Valente's warmth pinned her to the bed.

When the explosion finally hit, Lola threw herself into it wholeheartedly. The sudden pleasure came with a force that made her gossamer tingle and curl. Had Valente not been holding her down, she would have rolled into a ball. But he kept her pinned, pressing kiss after kiss to her neck and face as the shudders went through her, his hands dropping to grab her hips so hard it almost hurt.

His magic was thick in the air. Lola could feel the freezing pulse of it against her skin, but Valente's body was warm and wonderful as he thrust one last time before his rhythm broke. His whole body went rigid, seizing so tight, Lola didn't see how he could breathe, and then he collapsed on top of her.

Lola grunted as his weight landed. Valente rolled off at once, taking her with him so that they were lying on their sides, face to face. For a moment, they just stared at each other as they fought to catch their breath. Valente's eyes were open and glowing in the dark, but the expression in them was such a mixture of wonder, happiness, relief, and worry that Lola didn't know where to begin.

"Did I hurt you?" he whispered at last.

Lola's face broke into a wide smile. "Whatever the opposite of hurt is, that's what you did."

Valente laughed, and she jumped at the sound. Even though his voice was still the Rider's deep, smooth baritone, his laugh was so like the one from the dream that the wave of homesickness struck again. She shut her eyes against the pang, and the bed shifted as Valente moved closer, kissing her eyelids very, very gently.

She sank into his touch. They were lying so close together, pressed face to face with their legs tangled. Valente's warmth was still bleeding into her, and for the first time since Victor had disappeared, Lola's gossamer was completely still.

The lack of movement coupled with the safe contentment of Valente's arms made her sleepy. She struggled to keep her eyes open, desperate to stay awake and enjoy this rare moment of peace, but she was so relaxed, so warm, that she kept drifting off. She'd just shaken herself awake again when Valente rolled her over, tucking her into the crook of his body.

"Sleep," he whispered into her hair. "I won't let you go. Sleep, Lola."

Lola let herself fall limp. She'd never known her name could be spoken so tenderly. She wanted to hear him say it again, but before she could think of how to ask, she was asleep.

And that night, for the first time, Lola dreamed of Fenrir.

~~~

The fire comes first. It rolls over the city in waves, sucking up the air, sucking her down.

The monster comes next: a giant mass of black fur and dripping, jagged fangs that only barely resembles a wolf. It wades through the fire, shaking the world with its steps.

Boom. Boom.

The little girl feels them. She cowers on the broken highway,

259

head bent low as she hides from the monster between the husks of burning cars. She is seven again, barely human, and her body is covered in blood. It coats her skin like paint, warm and sticky as it drips down to join the puddle forming around her bare feet.

The smell of it makes her ill. For a moment, the girl feels that she will vomit. Just before she does, a pressure on her wrist distracts her. It's only a little motion, but the girl cries out as if she's been hit. Her sister! Her sister must not see this. Must not—

When she looks down, though, the little girl sees that she is wrong. It is *not* her sister tugging on their thread but a man's long-fingered hand, his neatly-trimmed nails tucked between the shining cord and her thin wrist.

"Hello, my monster."

The girl's eyes go wide. At her feet, the puddle of blood begins to ripple in time with her thudding heart. How is he here? He can't be here. This is her dream.

"Haven't you figured it out yet?" her master asks, pulling up on the thread to lift her out of the blood. "There is nothing of yours that is not also mine."

The girl jerks on the silver line like a hooked fish. No, no, no, she is free! Even if it's only for one night, he can't—

"Can't what?" he asks, grabbing her by her chin. "Haven't you realized what you've done? You fed my Rider a dream, knowing he was beholden to me." Her master shakes his head with a tsking sound. "When will you learn that stupidity and kindness go hand in hand?"

The girl squeezes her eyes shut. He's right. This is a dream. Her dream. She has the power here. She can make him go awa—

"Nonsense. You've never had any power over me. I own you, all of you. Every pain and every pleasure, every moment of your life, even those you spend befouling my Rider, they're all mine."

"No," the girl says, baring her little teeth, which aren't so little

260

anymore. "You're gone! You left us!"

Her master gives her a pitying look. "Stupid child. Even when I throw you away, you're still mine."

The blood on her body hums with the truth of his words, and the little girl slumps in defeat.

"Why are you here?" she whispers, because there must be a reason. Her master would never come just to see her.

"For the end of the story," Victor says, setting her back down in the blood. "The hero must defeat the monster."

The girl nods. That makes sense. Someone has to stop Fenrir, and who better than her master?

"That's right," Victor whispers, stroking her bloody hair. "You know better than anyone that I never lose. Tomorrow, you'll see that for certain. We're going to change the world, you and I."

"We?" the girl says, her voice confused. He's never included her like this before.

"Yes," her master says gravely. "Everything I've done, all these years of plots and maneuvers, it's all been for this. One great blow to set the world right." His face breaks into a proud smile. "I'm going to be the hero who saves humanity."

"And what am I?" the girl asks excitedly.

Victor looks surprised by her question, his hand stilling on her hair. "Stupid girl," he says, gazing down at her in pity. "You're the monster."

The girl is still reeling when the hand on her head pushes down, slamming her face into the blood-soaked pavement. Rather than breaking her nose on the asphalt, though, she sinks into the puddle like the pool of blood is a bottomless ocean. The booming sound of the monster's destruction vanishes instantly, replaced by red darkness growing darker. And as the blood swallows her, she clutches her sister's thread and screams. And screams. And screams.

The blood eats the sound as it drags her down.

~~~

Lola woke to the feeling of something icy and heavy covering her mouth. Her throat was on fire, her entire body pumping as if she'd just been running for her life. A sound was vibrating in her ears, a frantic, terrified, high-pitched wail. It was so horrible, she didn't realize the noise was coming from her until another voice shouted over it.

"Lola!"

Her name was a deep cry in her ear, and Lola jerked, eyes flying wide. Valente's face was right in front of hers, his hand pressed to her mouth. His other arm was wrapped around her body, holding her still. He was naked, as was she, both of them sitting in the middle of the creaking bed in the tiny motel room. From the gap in the blackout curtains, a thin splinter of sunlight shone through, lighting up the ugly orange carpet until it gleamed like fire.

The scream died in her throat, and the room fell silent except for the occasional sound of a car on the highway outside, but Valente didn't release his grip. "Lola," he said again, his deep voice measured. "It was only a dream."

Lola stared at him in confusion. It wasn't a dream. Victor knew. Victor *always* knew, and he was coming today. Coming to kill the monster. Coming to kill *her*.

At the thought, her gossamer began to surge. The calm of last night was gone as if it had never been, leaving her magic pitching like a ship in a hurricane as she lurched for her pills.

Valente let her go as Lola scrambled off the bed. For some reason, everything she touched was cold and wet. Her brain told her that was wrong, but Lola didn't have time to stop and see why.

262

She just lunged for her castoff pants, flopping onto the carpet in the process.

She found them at the end of the bed where Valente had dropped them. Miraculously, they still held their shape. Lola dissolved them at once, letting the plastic baggie fall into her hand. She ripped it open, tipping the contents into her hand. One red pill rolled out, landing like a drop of blood on her skin.

One pill left.

Lola sank onto the carpet, staring at the little red tab even as her gossamer raged. Above her, the bed creaked as Valente got up. She heard him go into the bathroom, and then the rush of the faucet. A few seconds later, a glass of water was thrust into her line of sight.

Lola took it wordlessly, but her eyes never left the pill. She put it off for as long as she could. Only when her hand started changing shape did she finally slap her palm against her lips. The little pill tumbled into her mouth, and Lola fought the urge to gag as the heavy taste of blood exploded over her tongue. For a moment, she was back in the dream, the blood eating everything as it poured down her throat. Only when she'd choked down the entire glass of water Valente pressed into her hand did the terrifying feeling of drowning ease, leaving only her fear behind.

Chapter 13

0 pills

While Valente went to the front office to pay for the room they'd commandeered, Lola stepped into the bathroom to reform her clothes. Such a simple shaping should have been reflex, but she was still shaking so badly from the dream that her gossamer kept falling apart. Finally, she managed to spin a simple sweatshirt and a pair of leggings. But even after she was sure the clothes would stick, the shaking didn't go away.

It wasn't fair. The aftertaste of the pill hadn't even left her mouth yet, and her gossamer was still pounding, bucking against the walls of Victor's spell like a mad animal. It wasn't painful, exactly, but it had never done this before. There was no longer anything she could do about it, though. The plastic baggie was empty. There were no pills left.

She scrubbed her hands through her yogurt lady's thick hair, her fingers stopping when they reached the place where Victor's hand had pushed her down. For a moment, Lola hung there, frozen, then started moving double time, yanking the black mess back into a ponytail and fixing it with a band of gossamer.

Now that the dream had had a while to fade, Lola was no longer quite as convinced it was really from Victor. He'd never entered her dreams before, and that didn't seem like the sort of tool he would have left unused. More likely, it was just her own version of the Fenrir dream that had been plaguing the DFZ for days now. Not that they were in the DFZ at the moment, but Valente had had the dream before, so it made sense that she could have picked it up from him, especially since their magic had been touching all night.

264

Lola blushed scarlet and glanced back into the bedroom. The flimsy mattress had been pushed partway off the box spring by their... activities, and that wasn't the only casualty. The carpet, walls, and headboard were all damp from where Valente had iced the room. Only the center of the bed, where they'd been lying, was dry and warm.

She smiled and took a deep breath, savoring the lingering, midwinter chill on the air. Sleeping with the Black Rider certainly hadn't been her plan, but Lola refused to regret it. Whatever happened from here, last night had been something good. Something no one could take away from them. Not even Victor, whatever he claimed.

Just thinking about his words in the dream made her start shaking again, so Lola distracted herself by washing her face. She was just drying off on the motel's paper-thin towel when she heard the door open.

She peeked out to see the Black Rider entering the room with a brown paper bag. "Breakfast," he said at Lola's inquisitive look.

She held out her hands, and he tossed her the bag, removing his helmet as she tore into it. Inside, she found a handful of gooey, grocery-store muffins and a stack of cheap Danishes, the sort with the factory fruit filling and plastic white icing. In short, her favorite.

"Thank you!" she cried, plunking down on the bed as she shoved a muffin into her mouth. "Where did you get these?"

"Complimentary breakfast," Valente replied as he sat down next to her, his weight making the cheap mattress sag. "Or maybe I had to pay for them? I don't know. I just threw the clerk double the room rate, and he didn't say anything when I walked out with the food."

The dip he was making in the mattress caused Lola to list toward him. Too busy eating to fight gravity, Lola flopped over,

265

leaning into Valente as she took a huge bite of cherry cheese Danish.

"See?" she said with her mouth full. "The scary helmet has its advantages."

"A few," Valente admitted, his arm coming up to wrap softly around her shoulders.

Even after what had happened last night, he still touched her hesitantly, as if he couldn't believe he was doing it. It was endearing, but it also made Lola wary. Now that their stolen night was over, she was back to being a changeling who, at best, was going to be shoved back into slavery today. Now wasn't the time to be forming attachments, but Valente didn't seem to see it that way. He'd already dropped his head to rest on hers, his cheek pressed against her hair.

Lola decided to focus on her Danish. "What did you dream about last night?"

"Fenrir again."

Lola let out a huff of relief. She *had* picked up his dream. "What do you see?"

"Fire mostly," Valente said. "And the monster, of course. It's pretty terrifying when it's happening, but I've had worse." His head turned, and she felt his lips land on her hair. "Of course, after your dream, they're all going to seem bad. You've spoiled me."

Lola grinned at the touch. She knew this was a dead-end road, but the affection was just so *nice.* When he started to move lower, though, she forced herself to break away.

"Come on," she said, standing up. "The morning's almost gone, and it's a long drive back to the DFZ."

Valente's whole body slumped at the loss of her. But he soldiered on and stood up, shoving his helmet back onto his head.

The day was bright and cold when they stepped out of the room that had been their sanctuary. It was finally Halloween, and

266

now that it wasn't pitch black, Lola saw that even the motel was decorated with paper cutouts of pumpkins and witch hats. Valente's bike was already ready and waiting in the parking lot. Lola spun herself a helmet and got on, wrapping her arms around Valente's waist as he settled into position.

"Where to?" he asked.

"My place," Lola answered. "Please."

Valente nodded and pulled them out into the sparse traffic of the rural highway. It was a lovely fall day for a ride through the country, and Lola was determined to enjoy it. Who knew the next time she'd get to stare at something that wasn't the underside of Victor's boot? If it was going to be seen, it had to be now, so she stared as hard as she could, clutching her sister's yanking thread as they shot along the sunlit lake toward the DFZ.

~~~

They reached her wrecked apartment shortly before noon. Lola then spent the next hour trying to coax Buster into his cat carrier. She eventually managed to lure him inside with hot dogs, and then, meowing cat crate in lap, she had Valente take her to a vet she didn't normally go to.

Her own phone was still missing, so Lola used the phone Simon had loaned her to pay for a month's worth of boarding. When the perky lady behind the counter asked where she was going, Lola said business trip. When she went to pet Buster goodbye, though, he cowered against the back of the crate. After that, Lola left the vet's office as fast as her legs would carry her.

"What happened?" Valente asked when she got back to the corner where he was waiting on his bike.

Lola just shook her head. Later, she was sure she'd find it hilarious that the rejection that had stung most had been her cat's.

267

Right now, though, Lola was an inch away from the sort of breakdown that could be her last. Valente didn't say anything, just held out his hand. When she took it, he pulled her in to his body.

The embrace lasted only a few seconds, but it helped to push the tears back. When she was in control again, Lola stepped away. "What time is it?"

"Almost two," Valente said.

Lola nodded. The concert Alberich had given her the tickets for didn't start until seven, but she meant to get there well in advance. She also needed to check in with Simon. She pulled out the phone he'd given her back at the diner and hit the number for his business line, pacing the sidewalk as it rang.

And rang.

And rang.

Lola hung up with a scowl and tried again, dialing by hand this time, but the result was the same. The call wasn't even going to voicemail. After her third unsuccessful attempt, Lola pocketed the phone with a deepening feeling of dread.

"Simon isn't picking up."

"He's probably working," Valente said. "You did say he was going ahead to check the venue."

"But he always picks up by the second ring," Lola insisted. "We should go check his house."

"I wouldn't do that."

"Why not?" she demanded, giving him a resentful look. "I know you don't like Simon, but—"

"I like him fine. He just doesn't like me," Valente corrected. "And that's not why I don't think you should go. Simon cares about your safety very much. If he's not answering your calls, that means he's either in hiding or in trouble. Either way, you going to his house will do nothing except give whoever he's up against more leverage."

Lola clenched her fists. "But—"

"If I were in Simon's position, I'd want you to stick to the plan and go to the concert since that's where Victor is going to be."

"Like he'd help," Lola grumbled. Victor didn't help. He extorted.

"He's still the most powerful blood mage alive," Valente reminded her. "I don't like him any more than you do, but if something did take out Simon, we're going to need Victor to get him back."

Lola started to pace, tapping Simon's phone rapidly against her fingers. It wasn't that she didn't understand what Valente was saying, but it felt wrong to just keep going when she didn't even know where Simon was. She squeezed the phone to bring up the AR, but the interface was just as clean now as when Simon had handed it to her. There were no missed calls, no messages, nothing. It was as if he'd dropped off the face of the earth.

"Something is *definitely* wrong."

"Maybe," the Rider said. "But you can't fix it when you're falling apart."

Lola rubbed her hands over her face. She *hated* this, all of it, but he was right. She couldn't help Simon right now. She'd barely been able to say goodbye to her cat without disaster. Whatever she was going to do, she needed her pills to do it, which left only one option.

"Let's get to the concert," she said, conjuring her helmet as she hopped onto his bike.

Valente nodded and rolled them out, turning down the tangled streets toward the ramp to Rentfree.

~~~

The old Gamekeeper's stadium had changed a lot in the last

five years. It used to be a blood-sport arena at the bottom of Rentfree, the cheapest, deepest, and sketchiest place in the DFZ. It was built around the giant pit the Spirit of the DFZ used to store her buildings before she moved or demolished them. Because the structures here changed every day, the DFZ didn't charge rent for living in them: hence the name Rentfree.

But all that free housing and complete untraceability of an address that moved daily had spawned a predictably horrific crime problem. It got so bad at one point that there used to be armored trucks taking tourists on safari through *"the DFZ's most dangerous neighborhood!"* These days, though, Rentfree was a tourist hotspot of a totally different sort thanks to the reconstructed stadium, which was now used for concerts, sporting events, and festivals, all free and open to the public. There was a museum of Old Detroit history and antiques right next to it that was also free, something unheard of in the city of capitalism.

Lola hadn't realized the Spirit of the DFZ knew the word "free" until she'd seen the museum with her own eyes. Even more surprising, it was *really* nice: a beautiful, open, well-curated space that looked like something you'd see in a city with way more than four laws. What miracle had brought such a thing to the DFZ, Lola didn't know, but the new stadium and the museum had really revitalized the otherwise terrible neighborhood. It was still down at the bottom of Rentfree's pit, though, which meant they had to walk.

"I'm *really* glad we came early now," Lola said as they climbed down the rickety, metal cage-enclosed stairwell. "It's going to take us an hour just to get down there."

"At least we don't have to worry about disguises," Valente said.

That was a definite plus. Normally, Lola would have just tossed some gossamer over them and called it good, but her magic was being so fussy right now that she could barely hold her own

270

clothes together. Fortunately, it was Halloween, the one night a year when Valente could walk into a crowded stadium and *not* cause a panic.

Between the recent craze for urban-legend-spotting and motorcycle gear plus helmet being a super low-bar costume, the streets were full of Black Riders. They'd already passed five on the walk down into Rentfree, two of whom had complimented Valente on his "perfect" outfit. Lola ended up being the one who stood out in her street clothes, so she'd stepped into a novelty photobooth to make herself a black dress and a witch hat.

It was a pathetic display compared to previous years. Halloween was usually Lola's time to shine, but low effort was the best she could manage with her gossamer being such a jumpy mess. Also, the witch hat's wide brim kept anyone from getting too good a look at her face, a critical feature since she was now having trouble keeping even her yogurt lady's features from sliding.

"Do *not* melt," she whispered, slapping her cheeks gently as they climbed down, down, down into the bowels of the city. "Keep it together."

The tickets the fairy king had given her said the gates didn't open until five, but this was the DFZ. There was *always* a way to buy in, and sure enough, the automated ticket kiosk had an option to get in early for twenty bucks. That seemed against the point of a concert that was supposedly "free and open to the public," but being a spirit birthed from the idea of a city where nothing was free but trouble, the DFZ could never stray too far from her roots.

If things hadn't been so dire, Lola would have refused to pay on principle. They were dire, though, so she kept her head down, hiding behind the brim of her witch hat as the Rider slipped the bot two twenties to let them in.

They weren't the only ones who'd paid. The stadium's lower

271

level was already thronged with people. Having a ticket got you in the door, but seating was first come, first served, and it seemed everyone had arrived early to get a good spot.

Since crowds and gossamer didn't usually get along, Lola had never been to one of Rentfree's seasonal events, but she knew they were a huge deal. Every major holiday, the city put on a show to build community and reinforce her position as the living god of the DFZ. Sort of like a church service, but with internationally popular musical groups, state-of-the-art illusion magic, and an extreme focus on local pride.

This being Halloween, everything at tonight's event was horror-themed. There were smoking drinks, risqué costumes, candy apples so covered in sugar they were barely recognizable as fruit, all the good stuff. Posters for *Fenrir* were, of course, everywhere, fueling Lola's growing sense of dread.

One of the VR parlors on the stadium's second level was even having a pre-concert *Fenrir* viewing party where you could get eaten by the monster with a bunch of other people in an interactive VR experience. It looked absolutely horrifying, but there was a line out the door, so what did Lola know? People obviously saw something in that slog of a movie that she didn't.

"I've been thinking about that," Valente said when she mentioned it to him. "Remember when we watched the movie back at Simon's, how you hated it, but he couldn't seem to tear his eyes away?"

"Yeah," Lola said. "But he's always been more into horror stuff than me."

"I don't think that's it," Valente said, shaking his head. "I'm not a fan of monster movies, either, but I also couldn't look away until the end. It certainly wasn't because the movie was good. Other than the special effects, I thought it was terrible, and you looked bored out of your mind."

"Guilty," Lola said, holding up her hand.

"That's what I'm talking about," he continued. "I think the movie *was* boring, and the only reason Simon and I liked it was because there was a bit of fairy enthrallment in the video."

Lola stopped midstep. "That's it!" she cried, grabbing his arm. "*That's* how he got everyone to watch his dumb movie so many times! They were enthralled!"

"Not by much," Valente said. "It'd have to be a tiny amount to keep people from noticing and breaking the whole thing with their disbelief. Normally, I'd say it was impossible for a fairy to do such subtle magic through a camera, but Alberich is very powerful."

"No, it makes total sense," Lola agreed, her thoughts spinning. "The only question left, as ever, is *why* did they need everyone to watch?"

They both looked up at the huge, augmented-reality advertisement of Fenrir roaring through the support beams that held up the stadium's third tier. He really was an ugly bastard. Lola normally liked every sort of dog, but she saw nothing cute about the snarling wolf with its dripping fangs and blood-red eyes.

Staring at it reminded Lola of what Victor had said in the dream. Now that she was really looking at him, Lola could admit Fenrir did look a little bit like her monster, but he was way too big. The wolf in the movie was big enough to knock over buildings. Even at her worst, Lola had never been anywhere near that size. Even if she could have reached those heights, turning into a monster in front of tons of people would do nothing but melt her into goo. It *had* to be something else, something she wasn't seeing yet.

"What is it, do you think?" she whispered, putting a hand over her sister's thread, which still hadn't stopped jerking. "What did he mean?"

273

"Are you talking to me?" Valente asked.

Lola shook her head and pushed her sister's thread deeper into her twitching gossamer under the guise of checking the watch she'd just materialized onto her wrist.

"We've got a good bit of time before the concert starts. We should spend it looking for Simon."

"Already working on it," Valente said.

Before Lola could ask what he meant, she felt the freezing brush of his magic slide over her gossamer, making her jump.

"What was that?" she asked with a shiver.

"Remember how I said I could send out feelers?" Valente replied. "I've had them out searching for Simon since we arrived."

"And?" Lola asked automatically, even though she already knew the answer. "You haven't found him."

The Rider shook his head. "That doesn't mean he's not here, though. If he's in trouble, he'll be hidden, so we should keep searching."

Lola nodded, clinging to hope. "How far can your feelers reach?" she asked as they pushed their way through the crowded promenade.

"Without my head, about five miles," Valente answered, placing a hand on her shoulder so they wouldn't get separated. "With my head, I haven't found the limit yet."

"How accurate are you?"

"Accurate enough. It was the first thing Victor taught me once he realized I couldn't spin illusions."

Lola frowned. "Was that how you kept finding me?"

"Sometimes. You're really hard to track."

"That's why I get paid the big bucks," Lola said, but her heart wasn't in it. The crowd was getting so thick now that searching was becoming impossible. Simon could be right next to her and she wouldn't even know. She was about to suggest they get somewhere higher when Valente spoke again.

"I can always find you now, though," he said, his voice warming until Lola could hear his smile through the helmet. "Ever since last night, it's like there's a compass in my mind that points only to you."

"That's the dream," Lola said. "Fairies can always find you once they've eaten your dream."

"I don't think it was just the dream."

There was a richness in his voice that made Lola blush. "Come on," she muttered, pulling him toward the stairs. "Let's get searching."

Valente nodded and moved in front of her, breaking a path through the ever-thickening crowd.

~~~

They looked for hours, walking in meticulous circles around the giant stadium as they searched for illusions, fairy magic, hidden doors, anything that might provide some clue. They uncovered a few pranks and several scams but nothing related to Victor's return or Simon's disappearance. Lola's heart jumped every time she saw a dark-skinned man with Simon's wiry build, but it was never him. She'd hoped maybe he'd call as the time grew closer, but her phone stayed silent, and he never answered his no matter how many times she tried.

By the time people started moving toward their seats for the show, they hadn't found a single thing. No Simon, no blood magic, not even a taste of a fairy. Even Valente's feelers came back empty-handed. It really did look like a perfectly normal concert in the DFZ, but Lola knew, *knew* that something dreadful was coming.

"Let's go take a look from the top again," Valente said. "Maybe there's something we missed."

There hadn't been anything the last two times they'd checked, but Lola didn't have a better idea, so she let him lead the way up to the nosebleed section. They were walking down the tunnel that led into the stands when Lola's phone rang.

She grabbed it at once, scrambling to get the thing out of her pocket. Her whole body jumped when she saw Simon's number on the screen, but when she slammed it to her ear, the voice on the other end wasn't his familiar baritone. It was bright and brassy as trumpets, the words almost laughing.

"Hello, changeling!"

The phone slipped a bit as Lola's fingers went limp.

"Not who you were expecting, I know," Alberich said. "But—"

"Where's Simon?" Lola yelled into the phone.

"No need to shout," the fairy said irritably. "I'm right behind you."

Lola turned almost before the Rider did. Sure enough, Alberich was standing directly behind them with Simon's work phone pressed against his delicate, pointed ear. He raised his eyebrows at them and threw the smartphone over his shoulder. It clattered across the cement floor, sliding through the metal grate to fall several stories to the rapidly filling seats below.

"I'm so happy you came," the fairy said, his boyish face splitting into a menacing, sharp-toothed grin. "It saves so much trouble when you're obedient, and you brought Victor's Rider with you! How thoughtful."

"I didn't do it for you," Lola snarled, body shaking, and not because of her gossamer for once. This was rage, pure and simple. A clean, deadly hate that sharpened her words to points.

"What did you do with Simon?"

"Nothing," Alberich said. "Victor is dealing with him. Seems your mage defied his master. That's bad business, you know."

And just like that, Lola's fury plunged into freezing dread.

276

"Victor?" she whispered. "Victor's here?"

"Not yet."

That should have made Lola feel better, but the dread only got worse. Before she could demand answers, though, the fairy king turned on his heel, beckoning over his shoulder.

"Follow me."

Valente's hand landed on Lola's shoulder, but she shook her head. The time for running was over. They'd walked into this trap with eyes wide open. Time to see where it went.

In the stadium behind them, tens of thousands of people began to cheer as the announcers started warming up the crowd. The roar of their voices shook the cement, covering the dull thud of Lola's heavy footsteps as she followed the Underground King down the ramp to a door that hadn't been there the first time they'd passed.

The stair Alberich led them into should have been impossible. They were high in the top-level bleachers above seven floors of shops and restaurants, but the fairy king took them straight down in a spiral, cutting through the levels without window or door. When they emerged at last, it was into a network of windowless cement tunnels lit with white fluorescents. Lola could still hear the crowd roaring through the walls, but it sounded much farther away now.

"Where are we?"

"The tunnels that run under the arena," Alberich said delightedly, skipping ahead. "In another few hundred feet, we'll be directly under the stage!"

Lola was about to ask what was so important about that when she felt Valente's leather glove brush her wide-brimmed witch hat.

"Get rid of that."

"Why?" Lola whispered.

The Black Rider tilted his helmet toward Alberich. "Because I don't want to risk dissolving anything of yours if it comes to that."

Lola nodded and did as he asked, concentrating hard to switch her floppy witch hat and poofy black dress for a much more compact combo of a tank top and leggings. Alberich didn't seem to notice the change in her appearance, or if he did, he didn't care. He'd already reached his destination: a nondescript stretch of gray-painted cement that was presumably below the stage.

"Here we are," he said, spinning around to grin at them. "Almost time!"

"Time for what?" Lola demanded with as much bravado as she could muster. "Victor's grand entrance?"

"No, no, that comes later," Alberich said, waving his hand dismissively. "Say, have you seen Fenrir?"

Lola grew wary. "The movie?"

"No, the wolf that eats the gods and begins Ragnarok. Oh, wait," Alberich gave her a pitying look, "that was before your time."

Lola glared at him.

"Good production, wasn't it?" Alberich went on, pulling a little golden dagger out of his belt and tossing it casually into the air. "Beautifully shot, fantastic effects, but the *monster*..." He stopped playing with his knife long enough to press his slender fingers to his lips for a chef's kiss. "Surpassingly gorgeous! Plot was nonexistent, but that wasn't my fault. We were limited by our audience. Humans do best with broad, simple stories."

Lola had already had her suspicions, but hearing him blurt it out like that caught her off guard. "You made that movie?"

"Of course," Alberich said, balancing the knife by its point on his finger. "Surely you didn't think *human* illusions could be anywhere near that breathtaking. We filmed the whole thing in my barrow. Built a whole fake city out of gossamer, complete with a million screaming extras we could actually kill! A bit over the

278

top, perhaps, but there was just no other way to get that depth of realism."

He looked at Lola like he expected her to clap, but all she could say was, "*Why?*"

"We had to make sure everybody saw," he explained. "First rule of good marketing: people have to know the product. We *needed* the world to watch our play, to ingrain every detail of destruction and chaos into their brains so they'd be primed for what's about to happen."

Lola knew she was putting her foot in the bear trap by asking, but, "What's about to happen?"

The fairy king flashed her a sharp-toothed grin. "You are."

His hand flicked as he spoke, launching his little golden dagger straight through her chest.

Lola had been stabbed before. And shot. And strangled. They were all hazards of being Victor's monster, but none of those had hurt like this did. Alberich's knife blasted through her gossamer like a cannonball, but the real damage was Victor's spell. The knife nicked the bloody, burning breath he'd blown into her as it passed, ripping a hole in the magic that held Lola together.

She dropped to her knees as it burst, bright-red blood bubbling out of her mouth. The muted roar of the crowd overhead blended with the pounding in her ears as the world began to spin. Blood was pouring down her front, pooling around her on the smooth cement floor just like it had in the dream.

Lola's chest began to heave. She knew that blood. She'd recognize it even if she'd never seen it before, because she knew the smell. It was the same coppery, gagging scent she'd smelled in her hospital room the first day she'd changed, the scent of her pills. It was Victor's blood, twenty years of it. She was watching his magic, the thing that kept her human, pour out onto the floor, and with each new pulse of blood, Lola's gossamer began to surge.

279

Above her, the fairy king watched with his predator's grin. He opened his mouth when he saw her looking, but the inevitable gloat never came, because that was when the Black Rider attacked.

Their connection from the night before must still have been lingering, because Lola felt Valente move before she saw him. He launched over her, his invisible gossamer flying at the fairy king's head. Alberich didn't even try to dodge, and Lola almost smiled. The Underground King's pride would be his undoing if he thought he could take the Rider's attack head-on without consequence. But then, just before Valente's freezing gossamer reached its target, the Rider stopped.

Lola's first thought was that Alberich had frozen him like he'd done to her back at Alva's, but that wasn't right. Valente was still moving. His blow had even landed, just not on Alberich. Instead of hitting the fairy king, the Rider's fist had landed on a blade. A wide, heavy, ancient sword, its surface covered in rust, that was suddenly floating in front of Alberich's face.

"Now, now," Alberich said, his brassy voice mocking as he peered around the blade hanging in thin air in front of him. "That's no way to treat a man in his home."

Lola was trying to figure out what he meant when something inside her seized. It was as if a hand had reached into her gut, and as it pulled, the long, featureless hallway began to change. The fluorescent lights vanished, replaced by a golden glow that came from a thousand yellow crystals. The cement floor became rocky and uneven, sprouting outcroppings of black stone and towering stalagmites. The narrow walls vanished, giving way to an endless cavern crisscrossed by golden veins and creeks of lava, the same endless cavern that had overwritten Alva's barrow just yesterday.

As the illusion of the cave replaced reality, a figure began to appear between the Rider and Alberich. The sword remained where it was, stopping Valente's fist an inch from the fairy king's face, but it was no longer floating in nothing. Now, the rusted blade was gripped by a hand wrapped in stained cloth.

The hand led to an armored arm, the chain mail links smudged with the same brown rust that covered the sword. After the arm came the body: a great, towering mountain of a man that made even the Rider look small. He was dressed like a crusader in chain mail and leather, with a pointed metal helmet that covered his entire face. His surcoat and jerkin were stained beyond recognition by the same brown mess that covered the rest of him, and it was only then that Lola realized he wasn't covered in rust.

It was blood. Ancient, dried blood turned brown by time, and the man standing between Valente and the fairy king was covered in it.

For a breathless moment, the four of them stood in tableaux. Then the bloody man swung wide, forcing Valente to jump away before the stained sword took off his head. The Rider landed several feet behind Lola but rushed back to her immediately, planting his body in front of hers. The bloody swordsman didn't attack again, though. He just lowered his weapon and straightened to attention beside Alberich, who was laughing uproariously.

"Stand down, you idiot," he cackled, doubling over as he laughed at the Rider. "We're on the same side, remember? Even if we weren't, you can't possibly hope to win." He patted the bloody giant's arm. "Don't you know who this is?"

Valente did not answer, and he did not move.

"All fairy monarchs may claim one knight," Alberich continued. "One champion to bind in eternal loyalty and empower above all others. This one is mine. Say hello, Orlando."

The bloody knight said nothing. He just stood there, breathing in long, rattling gasps with his enormous sword resting on his shoulder.

"He doesn't talk much," the Underground King said with a

shrug. "That might be because I destroyed his tongue a few centuries ago, but I can't remember. After so long, the years all just," he turned his hands in a lazy circle, "roll together. Unlike Morgan, though, I never saw much point in chatty knights. The oath that gives them strength forces them to be obedient whether they like it or not. After that, well, the conversation gets a bit dull."

He patted the giant man again, and the bloody knight made a sound behind his helmet like an angry rattlesnake.

"I know, I know, you're hungry," Alberich said, giving his knight an indulgent look, like a master with a favorite dog. "You haven't killed in many a century. But fret not, my champion! We'll ride again before the sun rises. All we need is for this one to finish dying, and you will have all the feasting you could desire."

He turned to grin at Lola, who was still kneeling in her pool of blood. The crimson gushing out of her chest hadn't slowed yet. Lola didn't understand how so much blood could fit inside the gossamer she had left, but the end had to be near. Her ears were ringing like fire alarms now, her mind unfocused and woozy, so much so that she didn't see the Rider move until he grabbed her.

She cried out at the touch, but Valente didn't stop. He scooped her into his arms and ran, moving with a speed that felt impossible, but there was nowhere to go. Alberich's cave stretched out in all directions, infinitely deep, infinitely wide, and as fast as the Rider was, Orlando was faster.

Lying in the Rider's arms, Lola saw the bloody knight's hand close around Valente's shoulder before he did. Before she could shout a warning, though, the monster threw them backward. The Rider's invisible magic caught them a second before they hit the ground, but it didn't matter. Orlando was already there, the rattlesnake buzz of his rage rattling in Lola's ears as he appeared right on top of them, his sword already falling.

Valente shifted Lola under his arm and caught the blade one-handed. Dangling under his elbow, Lola forced her head up. The motion caused a jolt of pain sharp enough to make her vision flicker, but if the Rider was going to die defending her, the least she could do was watch.

But though Orlando's blow had sent Valente to his knees, the sword did not pass through the Rider's gloved hand. It stopped, the notched edge biting into the leather of his palm. Then Valente's freezing magic swelled as his fingers closed around the bloody blade.

Cold washed over Lola like melt off a glacier. Frost raced across the cave floor at the same time, climbing up Orlando's legs as the knight tried to wrench his sword out of the Rider's grasp, but Valente did not let go. He crouched on the stone, his body like iron as his magic rose around them, the freezing, midwinter cold taking on an edge Lola recognized. It was the same thing he'd done when he'd dissolved the troll, but bigger. Much, *much* bigger, falling like an avalanche to smash Alberich's knight full in the face.

For one full second, the cave went dark as a midwinter night. Lola blinked in the blackness, watching eagerly for what she already knew she'd see. Valente had dissolved an entire troll without breaking a sweat, and he hadn't even had his head on then. There was no way even Alberich's knight could stand against the full force of the Rider's magic. When the light finally returned, though, Lola's eyes flew wide.

Orlando was still there, exactly as he'd been before. There was no dissolving, no freezing into chunks. He didn't even seem upset.

Valente must have been as shocked as she was, because his grip on the knight's sword slipped, and Orlando's blow slammed down. Valente rolled them out of the way in time, just barely, but they both got peppered with shrapnel as the knight's blade crashed into the stone where they'd just been. The rocks went right through Lola's jelly-soft gossamer, but the Rider was bleeding when he

283

came up, his blood human and red as it oozed from the cuts beneath his leather sleeves.

Lola went still. The whole time she'd been with him, she'd never seen him bleed. Even when he'd been fighting three Paladins at once, even when he'd *died*, his body had been like his motorcycle: a construct, a shadow.

It had to be because he was wearing his head. Fairies' heads were their strength and their weakness, the source of their magic and the only way they could be truly killed. The Rider's head had clearly given him enormous power, but now she was seeing the price, and that made her more afraid than anything.

"Stop," she pleaded as Valente scooped her into his arms to dodge the knight's next swing. "It's not worth it. I'm already—"

She stopped with a gasp as they jerked to a halt. For a moment, Lola thought Valente had listened, then she realized he was still straining with all his might. *She* was the one who'd stopped, her body frozen in the air as though she'd been set in cement.

"You really don't learn, do you?"

Lola winced at Alberich's brassy voice, or at least she tried to. Every part of her gossamer was frozen stiff. She couldn't even move her mouth to tell Valente to leave her, though she didn't think it mattered. The Rider was holding her like a grudge, his bleeding body angled toward the Underground King, who was strolling toward them as if he were out for a walk.

"I mean, A for effort and all that," he said, spinning his bloody dagger casually in his fingers. "But take a look around. That's my changeling, and this is my domain!"

He threw out his arms to take in the enormous cavern, and then he pointed at the Rider. Valente stumbled when the king's finger landed on him, and then he fell to his knees.

"Now you're starting to get it," the king said, strolling over to pat Valente on the helmet. "All gossamer belongs to me in this place, even your nasty business. If you weren't part human, I'd have had you dancing like a puppet from blow one."

He patted the Rider's head again, and Lola began to panic inside her frozen prison. This whole time, she'd thought the giant cave was an illusion, like the seaside highway Tristan had made. From the way Alberich was talking, though, it sounded as if this place was his barrow, but that just couldn't be so. The Underground King might be powerful, and Alva was certainly weak, but he couldn't build a barrow willy-nilly inside another monarch's territory. He just *couldn't*.

"There it is again," Alberich said, his golden eyes lighting up in wonder. "Incredible! I can actually feel your disbelief." He skipped over to her, ignoring the Rider entirely as he bent low over the stuck Lola.

"Stupid little changeling," he said with a grin. "Didn't I tell you before? I made you from my own gossamer, the same gossamer as my barrow. Wherever you are, there I may build my kingdom."

Lola tried to tell him she wasn't his land grab, but she still couldn't move her mouth. She couldn't even blink her eyes until Alberich crooked his little finger.

Just as it had outside of Alva's, Lola's gossamer obeyed, her body moving of its own accord to kneel beside the Rider at the king's feet.

"There's a good pet," Alberich said, turning away. "Now come. A duel is no place for little girls."

Still unable to speak, Lola stood and followed, her body jerking like a puppet. Valente was set free a moment later. He immediately tried to go after her, but Orlando's sword got there first, forcing him back. His next attempt ended the same way, Orlando keeping him neatly pinned as the fairy king led Lola back to the bloody pool where he'd first stabbed her.

"Kneel," he ordered, pointing at the blood.

285

Her legs buckled before the word was out of his mouth. The blood seemed to rise to meet her, lapping at her knees as they landed in the warm, red pool. When she was down, Alberich released his hold on her, and Lola doubled over, landing on her elbows in the blood.

The whole world turned red as she fell. Across the cavern, she could dimly see Valente still fighting to get to her, but he couldn't get past Orlando. Alberich's knight didn't even try to dodge the Rider's blows. He only attacked, his huge sword coming down on Valente like a butcher's ax.

Valente blocked each strike with fistfuls of invisible gossamer, pushing the bloody knight around like a bull, but he couldn't break free. No matter how far away he shoved the giant, Orlando always seemed to be right in front of him, his sword aimed unfailingly at the Rider's vulnerable head.

"Good show, isn't it?" Alberich said, sitting on Lola's back as he watched the fight. "It's been ages since I've seen a proper duel, but I'm afraid they won't have time to finish." He smiled down at her and cupped his hands around his pointed ears. "Listen."

Lola had zero intention of doing anything he said. Even if she'd wanted to pay attention, she was too busy trying to stay alive. But as she lay gasping in the red puddle, she heard it: a distant pounding, like a crash of thunder that never stopped. It wasn't until Alberich hopped off her, though, that Lola realized the thuds were hoofbeats.

"They're coming," Alberich said, his face shining with excitement. "All Hunts start with a duel. Blood calls to blood, and my riders heed it." The fairy licked his lips, his too-long tongue sliding over his face as his eyes locked on Valente again. "I'll feed that stolen head of his to whichever one of my riders gets here first. His cursed power will be a great addition to my court, while his human blood will make a fine offering to mark the Wild

Hunt's return."

Lola shook her head, her bloody lips moving soundlessly.

Alberich lifted his eyebrows and leaned closer. "Sorry, what was that?"

"The Rider... won't lose..." Lola wheezed, the words little more than air. "Victor..."

"Isn't here," Alberich said with a greedy smile. "But the Rider attacked us first, remember? If he dies because of his own stupidity, I don't see how the blood mage can blame *me*. Anyway, it's just a bit of fun. Something to help pass the time until we move on to the next act. But that curtain doesn't rise until you die, little changeling."

He prodded Lola's still-bleeding chest, poking his fingers into her ribs like he was trying to push the blood out faster. She cried out at the invasion, clenching her teeth, which were already getting bigger. Her limbs started warping next, the monster's claws pushing out through her nails, but that was nothing compared to her gossamer.

The magic that formed Lola's body was boiling beneath her skin, rising up in painful pulses. With each one, the blood falling from her chest spilled faster. She curled into a ball around the wound, trying desperately to keep it in, to keep from losing herself. But she'd barely dropped her head to her knees before Alberich's hand landed in her hair to wrench her head back up.

"Why are you being so selfish?" he scolded, his face so close that Lola could feel his sharp teeth against her gossamer. "You're the only one who can end this. Look."

The fairy wrenched her head around. Across the cavern, Valente was still fighting. There was a long crack across the front of his visor, and blood was dripping from his fists. He was still faster than a shadow, but Lola could see the desperation in his movements now, jumping out of the way of the bigger knight's sword as if the next blow might be his last.

"That's the price of using your head." Alberich tutted. "I give him two more minutes before Orlando turns him into Rider-mince, but it doesn't have to be that way." He wrenched Lola's face back toward his. "You're going to die tonight no matter what, but if you get it over with quickly, you'll give us something better to do than torture the poor little abomination. Think, changeling: you can save his life. All you have to do is stop being stubborn and—"

His voice cut off abruptly. It happened so suddenly that for a moment, Lola thought she'd actually gone and died. She dismissed the idea a second later. Whatever death was like, she was sure it wouldn't hurt this much. Besides, she could still feel the blood pouring out of her, as well as something else. A cold breeze that smelled like the wild northern sea.

"Let her go, Underground King."

Lola blinked. Between the blood and her worsening eyesight, she didn't see him at once, but eventually a man in a white suit slowly came into focus. He was standing in front of her with his sword—no longer a flashy rapier, but an old-fashioned Welsh longsword as long as her leg—resting against Alberich's neck.

The king scowled at the mirror-bright blade pressing into his throat, and when he spoke, his voice was no longer loud trumpets or cajoling sweetness. It was fury: the heavy, grinding anger of the deep places of the Earth.

"You dare too much, knight of Morgan."

"The changeling is mine," Tristan said calmly, his sword still as stone. "Bought and paid for. Even a king cannot break a bargain struck in good faith."

Lola had no idea what Tristan was talking about, and she definitely didn't like this business about buying and selling, but she wasn't in any position to complain. She reached out for Tristan

288

with her hand, which was now more like a bloody paw. Before she could even touch the pristine white cloth of his suit, though, Alberich grabbed Tristan's blade.

The monster's eyes had always been terrible, but no amount of poor vision could account for what Lola saw next. Alberich's hand was no longer a boy's delicate grip, nor even recognizably human. The thing that grabbed Tristan's graceful sword could only be described as an articulated claw. The stone scraped as the king stood, the boy's shape falling off him like a shed skin.

"I have forgiven you much for love of your queen," the new creature said in a deep, grinding voice. "But the Hunt *will* ride, knight, and you cannot stop it!"

"I do not seek to stop the Wild Hunt," Tristan said, his voice amazingly calm, considering how much smaller he now was than the thing towering above him. "I ask only for what is mine by right and claim."

The Underground King rumbled, a deep, horrible sound that Lola didn't even recognize as laughter until she heard the mockery in his voice. "You really are a white knight, aren't you?" he said, the goading words cracking like flint. "But whatever claim you might think you have over *my* changeling, you can't stop this. Look at the blood."

Lola could hardly see anything at this point, but she knew it was bad when she heard Tristan's intake of breath.

Alberich's grinding laughter grew worse. "Oh, yes. You know what that means."

When Tristan didn't answer, Lola pushed herself up, scrabbling and slipping on her claws until she was facing the wild-sea smell of Tristan's magic. "What does it mean?" she whispered around her fangs. "What's going to happen to—"

She never got to finish, because at that moment, the last of the blood Victor had spent twenty years pouring into her came flooding out.

Her gossamer exploded as it left. Black fur surged down her limbs. Her already-distorted mouth changed completely, her jaw filling with so many teeth, she thought it would crack. The last of her bloody vision vanished like a lost signal, plunging her into the dark.

Every other time she'd changed, Lola had had time to know it, to fear it. Even the night she'd changed in front of the Paladins, she'd had a chance to fight. This time, though, the monster roared out of her like someone was pushing it. Even the bloody reek of Victor's magic was consumed in the rush, but just before it vanished, Lola heard a voice. A man's hateful, familiar voice, whispering from deep inside her.

"Bound to me in blood and service."

It was so close, she could feel his breath on the memory of her skin. Feel his fingers sliding through the ghost of her hair to squeeze down on the place that had once been the crown of her skull as the silver thread on her wrist began to lash.

"Your life for mine, your power to me, now and ever after."

The moment the spell finished, the beast ate Lola whole. It took less than a bite, one split fraction of a second for the life that Lola had claimed as her own to snuff out like a candle, leaving only dark.

And somewhere in the distance, a monster roared.

Chapter 14
Breakdown

The opening act had just taken the stage when the floor of the arena began to shake. Up in the stands, fifty thousand concertgoers gasped in excitement as a deep roar vibrated up the stadium's metal supports. What an amazingly terrifying sound, they all agreed. The city had really outdone herself this year. This was going to be the best Spooktacular Stravaganza ever!

But the DFZ was not excited. Deep in the heart of her power, the Living City was calling her priests in panic. Something was digging its way out of the ground below the Gameskeeper's old arena. Something that must be stopped.

Using the magic given to her by the people of her city, the Spirit of the DFZ piled her ground deeper, adding layers of steel and cement between her citizens and what was coming. The crowd cheered wildly as her efforts lifted the arena several feet higher. On live broadcasts all over the world, announcers bemoaned the fact that their viewers couldn't be there to feel the shaking in person.

Up on the stage, the band played on, unsure what was happening but determined not to miss their part in what was rapidly becoming the best show the DFZ had ever put on. They kept hammering at their guitars all the way until the stage broke in half.

The drummer was killed instantly. The rest of the band ran screaming as the whole stage splintered, sending lights and scaffolding toppling off the sides as something emerged from below. A smoke machine that was supposed to be pumping out black fog in time to the music fell off the back and exploded,

291

spewing billows of kerosene smoke around the giant, car-sized claws that were digging their way out of the wreckage.

The crowd went wild. They'd all seen the movie or at least the advertising. They knew that black paw. It was Fenrir! This must be the secret movie tie-in event everyone had been speculating about!

The dark stands lit up as phones flew out of people's pockets. On all the live feeds, hosts went wild that they were here to witness what was clearly going to be a once-in-a-lifetime event. *The monster looks so real!* they cried. *Is everybody watching this?*

Everybody *was* watching, holding their breath as the monster roared again, a hollow, mournful sound. The stadium shook as the giant paw was followed by a giant arm, black and hairy and bending as no natural appendage should as the monster began pulling itself out of the ground.

People screamed and clapped as it rose through the wreckage of the stage. It was so big! So *real!* They could actually smell the monster's hot, fetid breath blasting into their faces through the hole. Just how much illusion magic was the city rolling?

Speculation was running rampant when the monster's head finally emerged from the ground. It didn't look quite like the movie at first. Didn't look like much of anything except fur and teeth. As more and more people turned to stare at it, though, the monster's face shifted until it looked *exactly* like the one from the movie: a world-ending wolf with dripping fangs and eyes that glowed blood-red. The whole stadium cheered when they saw it, whooping and whistling as Fenrir turned its giant head and lunged at the floor seats, eating the entire front row in a single bloody bite.

The crowd stopped cheering. Silence fell over the arena, broken only by the terrible crunching of bones in the monster's teeth. Up in the stands, a collective breath sucked in as the whole crowd came to the same conclusion all at once: that didn't look like special effects. It looked like people had *died*.

The monster's second paw was out of the hole now, bashing the last of the ruined stage away as it started hauling its huge body out of the ground. Down in the bloodbath that had been the floor seating, screams filled the air as people started fleeing for the exits, trampling each other in their panic. The monster snapped at them as they ran, shaking the ground as it lurched forward to gobble up whole families. And as more and more victims screamed and died, a new understanding began to spread through the audience like a stain.

This wasn't a show. The monster wasn't an illusion. Fenrir was *real*. It was *here*. And it was coming for them.

The panic that followed that realization drowned out even the monster's roar. All over the arena, all over the city, all over the planet in the houses of the millions watching online, humanity screamed at the new monster that was suddenly among them. Fenrir roared back in reply, its black-furred body doubling in size as all of that belief—that sudden, crystal-clear understanding that *this* was the movie monster come to life—crashed into it. Like any good monster, it ate the power whole, feasting on their fear until its head brushed the top of the seven-story arena.

That might have been as big as it could get on the beliefs of only fifty thousand, but news of the monster's appearance was racing around the world. People who didn't even know there was a concert tonight were getting alerts. Completely unrelated media streams were being interrupted by emergency broadcasts telling the world that Fenrir had appeared in the DFZ. Every second, more and more and more people tuned in to watch the disaster unfold, and as their belief in the story of Fenrir's birth joined the others, the monster got bigger.

And bigger.

And bigger.

By the time the DFZ was ready to fight, the monster's head was tall enough to be seen over the top of the Rentfree pit. But this was no movie set, no cardboard city. This was the Detroit Free Zone, the Living City, and she fought back with the tenacity she was famous for, raising buildings from the ground like spears to skewer the invader who dared attack her home.

The monster roared and staggered as the ever-moving buildings of Rentfree slammed into it. Its steaming blood splattered across the streets, the hot drops big enough to flatten the screaming, fleeing crowds. But though its body was stuck full of steel bars and broken glass, it did not go down. It couldn't, because this was in the movie, too.

The people already knew what was coming. Even those who were only now finding out what had happened at the concert had seen the movie, or at least knew its plot. Everybody did. Fenrir's unbeatability was so cliché it had become a meme. Even those who loved and believed in the DFZ knew that the monster beat the spirit in the film, and that knowledge was the city's undoing.

She was stronger than the monster, bigger and older, a greater god. In this specific instant, though, that didn't matter. Like all spirits birthed by human magic, she was only as strong as the concept that created her, and even a city of millions couldn't stand when the whole world already believed she was doomed to fail.

The DFZ didn't know that. As befit the City of Second Chances, she gave it everything she had. She threw buildings, buried the monster in the ground, wrapped it in highways. She stabbed it with a thousand lampposts, bled rivers of its stinking blood down the storm drains, electrocuted it with her entire grid.

But no matter how hard she fought, the monster did not die. Too many people knew its story. Too many believed it would always get back up, and so it always did, rising from each bloody crater that should have been its grave bigger and stronger than before.

By the time the DFZ realized she was only hurting her own people by attacking, the monster was the size of a skyscraper. Its head was tall enough to look through the penthouse windows as it started taking bites out of the buildings. Its giant paws crushed the Skyway bridges like rotten logs, leaving a path of destruction wherever it went.

In rage and despair, the city called out to her allies, the dragons she had sheltered for two decades, but they couldn't hurt the monster, either. Even the great Conrad Heartstriker, whose wings darkened the sky, couldn't pierce the monster's black hide. Not because he was weak or Fenrir was strong, but because that was how it had gone in the movie.

The story was entrenched now. Whether in person or through the power of global mass media, every human eye on the planet was locked on the monster. Over the feed of its destruction, newscasters told the tale of Fenrir in every language. As they spoke, the legend of the monster—how it had never been defeated, how it was the end of the world—grew stronger and stronger, digging itself into humanity's collective consciousness until it was the only story anyone cared about.

And the more they all believed, the bigger the monster grew.

~~~

Down in the crater left by Fenrir's emergence, the Black Rider removed his broken helmet and let it fall to the bloody floor. It landed with a *crack*, rocking back and forth on the uneven stone. Above him, Alberich's knight raised his bloody sword, but Valente didn't even look. He was too busy staring through the hole the monster had torn through the Underground King's barrow into the real world, frantically searching for the glimmer.

It had always been there before. He focused on the fairy's sight, ignoring the glamour of black fur and bloody claws for the truth that lay beneath. She *had* to be in there, his gleam of light. But no matter how hard he stared, he saw nothing. No light, no Lola, just darkness and fear. He kept searching anyway, looking so desperately for some sign that it wasn't true, that she wasn't gone, he didn't even notice Orlando's blade until it landed in his shoulder.

The blow sent him to his knees. Valente rolled on instinct, coming up ready to attack, but his hands fell back to his sides a second later. What was the point? There was no one to protect anymore. The compass that had pointed to Lola without fail since last night was spinning uselessly in his mind, telling him she was gone. She was gone, and he had failed her.

"Hold."

Alberich's voice was distant, but Orlando stopped at once, falling to one knee as his king strolled over. Valente lifted his head as he approached. Alberich was old enough that it was hard to tell his glamour from his truth, but the thing standing beside Orlando wasn't trying to hide anymore. He was the Underground King in all his terrible glory, a monster born of dark places and grisly old tales whose golden crown was drenched in sacrificial blood.

"Isn't it marvelous?" he asked, his ringing voice deafening despite the hole the monster's birth had punched through the top of his barrow. "It's really happening just like the blood mage said! Can't you taste their fear?"

The king's giant golden eyes closed in bliss as Fenrir's roar shook the ground above them, and then his huge clawed hand reached down to grab his knight's bloody shoulder.

"Rally my huntsmen," he ordered. "The Wild Hunt rides!"

Orlando nodded and walked away, vanishing between one step

296

and the next. A moment later, the cavern began to rumble as if an army were riding full tilt across it. The shaking made Valente stumble, leaving him dizzy and reeling as horns sounded through the cavern, their cries like ghostly screams. He was still trying to shake the terror the sound sent through the still-human parts of him when a hand grabbed his shoulder, wrenching him around with startling strength until he was staring into Tristan's extremely angry face.

"Where is your master?"

Valente started to say he didn't know, but he couldn't get the words out, because they were no longer true. Unbidden, his eyes moved to the pool of blood Lola had left behind. He'd been avoiding it, as though not looking could somehow deny her loss. Now, though, the cursed oaths he'd sworn forced him to break away from Tristan and walk straight toward it, falling to one knee at the pool's bloody edge.

The impact of his landing sent ripples across the crimson puddle. Then the blood began to move all on its own, pulling together to form a perfect circle on the irregular stone. Tristan hissed at the sight, but Valente couldn't even look back to see the knight's reaction. His eyes were locked on the thick red liquid as the shallow pool grew as smooth as glass. A dark shadow appeared at its center, as though something was rising from depths that did not exist. Then the blood parted, and Victor emerged.

The blood did not touch him as he left it. Not a drop stained his dark-gray suit or his crisp white shirt. His eyes were closed, and they stayed that way until he was standing on the blood's surface, his leather shoes resting on the liquid as if it was solid ground.

"Hello, my champion," he said as his eyes opened at last. "Right on time."

As always, his voice filled Valente's head, pushing out

everything that wasn't slavish obedience. It was similar to the fairy's enthrallment but even worse. At least back then he'd been lost in a haze of love while it was happening, but with Victor there was no such kindness. Valente knew *exactly* what he was doing. He just couldn't stop himself as he spun around and planted his body between his master and the furious fairy marching toward him.

"Blood mage!"

Victor cast Tristan a bored glance. "Yes, knight?"

Tristan thrust out his sword, whipping the mirror-bright blade up until its point was a hair's width from Valente's throat.

"You broke faith with me, human," Tristan growled, his normally ironclad glamour flickering to reveal something cold and white and predatory. "Two more years in your service, and then the changeling was mine! I held up my end of the bargain. I taught your abomination what you asked, and now you break our pact!"

Across the cavern, Alberich squawked. "*You* were the one who taught him the knighthood oaths?" he cried, flitting back to his guise as a small boy as he suddenly poked his head out from behind Victor's back. "Tsk, tsk, sir knight! Morgan will be very angry with you."

Tristan ignored the fairy king completely. "You swore to me," he whispered, his cold sea eyes boring into Victor. "The changeling's dreams forever if I made the Rider yours. That was our deal!"

"I did promise," Victor said, smiling behind his Rider. "I lied."

A cold sea wind began to howl through the cavern. "You lied?"

"Humans have that prerogative," Victor informed him. "But once you've gotten over your tantrum, I think you'll agree this is a much better use. You only wanted her as a trough, a bucket of dreams to keep you fed while you searched for your lost queen, whom—I might point out—you're *still* no closer to finding than you were when she vanished twenty years ago."

"Do not speak her name with your oath-breaking tongue," the knight snarled, his sword flicking closer until the point was cutting through the leather of Valente's collar. "Bring the changeling back, or I will kill you both where you stand."

"There is no coming back from this," Victor said, turning his head up toward the gaping hole in the barrow's roof. "Do you not see what I have done?"

"You brought a monster into the world," Tristan spat, his eyes flicking to Alberich, who was back in front of his Hunt. "Two of them. I had my suspicions when I tasted the bit of magic Lola brought to me, but I didn't want to believe you would be stupid enough to break the seal my queen put on the Underground King."

"Don't give him *all* the credit," Alberich called over his shoulder. "That seal started cracking the moment Morgan fell. I would have gotten out on my own in a century or so. All Victor did was speed things up. A boon for which he has been well compensated."

"Why did you do it?" Tristan demanded, ignoring the boy. "You knew my queen's mind. She sealed Alberich in his barrow because he would not stop hunting. You have doomed your entire race by setting him free, and for what? A monster?"

As if on cue, Fenrir roared above them, shaking the ground. Alberich raised his hands to the sound, his face breaking into a beatific smile.

"How can you even ask that question?" he whispered, his voice suddenly as huge as his cavern again as he appeared again in front of Tristan. "Your queen forgot what she was. All of you have! Too long you've hidden in shadows, lapping up the dregs of whatever dreams the humans see fit to drop. But our true sustenance—our true power—has always been *fear*."

"You will get us all killed!" Tristan snarled, baring his sharpening teeth. "There are too many of them for such recklessness and too few of us."

"So what?" the fairy king said. "The Hunt is always dangerous. That's what makes it fun."

He patted the knight on the cheek and vanished, reappearing in front of his knight, who was holding the reins of a screaming horse made of fire and clouds. Behind him was the Hunt, a whole host of ancient fairies in horrifying masks mounted on beasts made of nightmares. Alberich greeted them with a whoop and hopped onto his steed, the bloody crown reappearing on his head.

"We are done with hiding!" he cried, his huge voice ringing through the cavern like a trumpet call. "Morgan's reign of cowardice is over! No longer will we let the rabbits dictate how we shall feed! *The Hunt rides again!*"

The host behind him roared in reply, their teeth shining like knives in the light of the burning buildings overhead. Alberich closed his eyes at the sound, and his glamour fell away for the last time, revealing the full horror of the monster underneath. When the change finished, he took a golden sword from the myriad of weapons on his now-gigantic belt and tossed it into the blood at Victor's feet. As it splashed down, he extended his clawed hand to Tristan.

"Last chance, Knight of Morgan. Join my host! Ride with us to our true glory, or be ridden over with the rest of this world."

Tristan bared his too-white teeth. "I will *never* ride with you."

"Then you are dust beneath our hooves," Alberich said, withdrawing his hand to grip his reins. "To the feast!"

The Wild Hunt roared in reply as they lurched into motion, their thundering horses leaving the ground like a black tornado to swirl up into the chaos above. They were gone in an instant, leaving nothing but the empty barrow, the blood mage, and the two knights.

"I hope his 'compensation' was worth it," Tristan sneered,

glaring at Victor, who still hadn't stopped smiling. "You betrayed your entire species!"

"I betrayed nothing," Victor replied, smiling up at the sundered roof. "It is good for us to be hunted. After all, without wolves, humanity would never have invented knives."

Tristan shook his head. "You are mad."

"I am right," Victor said, turning back to the knight. "We have lived in safety for too long, and it has made us weak. We spend our magic lifting up false gods while our true power is reviled." He pointed at the blood beneath his feet. "They call it 'blood magic,' but blood is the only way man has ever changed anything. Like all great revolutions, this one will be bloody, but when it is over, we will emerge stronger, and even you will thank me."

"This is my queen's domain," Tristan whispered, gripping his sword with both hands. "I will not let you destroy it."

"Your queen is gone," the blood mage said. "But I would not rob you of your chance to die for her." He turned to Valente. "Do not let him interfere."

The words were barely out of his mouth when Tristan lunged, his hands stacked on the hilt of his sword to drive the shining blade through Valente and into his master. But the Black Rider's magic was already wrapped around the knight's weapon, turning the strike to the side as Victor walked away.

"You're a fool if you do this!" Tristan yelled, wrenching his sword out of Valente's hold. "Your abomination might buy you time, but you know I'll kill him eventually. Do you really want to lose both your weapons today?"

"My Rider knows his place," Victor replied, reaching down to pick up the gleaming, golden sword the fairy king had left for him. When he had it in his hand, he set the tip down in the pool of blood, filling the empty barrow with the metallic, coppery scent of his magic as he began to rise.

301

Tristan lunged after him, running on the air as if it was solid ground. The Rider's magic grabbed him before he'd taken two steps, slamming him back to the barrow's stone floor. He snarled as he landed, cursing in a language Valente didn't know as he turned to slice his sword through the Rider's arm.

Valente would have let him. If his choices had been his own, he would have helped Tristan take Victor's hateful head. But even if his master hadn't just specifically ordered it, he was bound to protect him. The oaths he'd sworn on his knees that day filled Valente like black, choking smoke, forcing him to move faster and faster as Tristan began attacking in earnest, driving the Rider across the cavern.

And above them, uncaring, the blood mage rose, his face shining as bright as the golden sword clutched in his fist as the blood lifted him through the hole the monster had left in the ceiling.

Chapter 15

Lola woke to the overwhelming smell of flowers. This was a surprise, and not because of the flowers. Lola was pretty sure she'd just died, but her body felt surprisingly normal. She was back in her favorite yogurt lady, still wearing the tank top and leggings she'd put on for the fight with Alberich. But while the simple outfit had been a struggle before, her gossamer now felt calm as a glassy pond.

It was such a novel sensation, she lay still for several seconds, just enjoying it. Eventually, though, curiosity overwhelmed comfort, and Lola opened her eyes.

She was lying in a small, windowless room that was absolutely filled with flowers. There were lilies and roses, violets and chrysanthemums, orchids and daisies and other blossoms Lola couldn't even name. Even the low ceiling was covered in bright-orange trumpet vines. It was so chaotic and beautiful, Lola didn't even notice the woman sitting in the middle of it all until she turned her head.

Now that she'd seen her, Lola didn't know how she'd looked at anything else. The woman was more beautiful than the flowers, more beautiful than any sight Lola had ever seen. Her alabaster face was a Renaissance painter's ideal, and her eyes were the color of spring leaves. Her golden hair was like a river of sunlit honey, and it flowed in dazzling abundance, falling from her head in a cascade to bury every other part of her body, even her hands.

"Welcome, changeling."

Lola's eyes went wide with wonder. Even the woman's voice was as sweet as water in the desert. She truly was too beautiful to be real, making Lola wonder.

"Am I dead?"

"Of course not," the beautiful woman assured her.

"But I felt myself die," Lola insisted.

The woman gave her a skeptical look, which struck Lola as fair. Anyone lively enough to argue that they were dead kind of undermined their own point. She knew what she'd felt, though, and the beautiful lady sighed.

"You can't be dead because you were never truly 'alive' to begin with," she explained. "You're a conjuration, a creation of pure gossamer. Think of yourself like that car you made to distract the police when you were running from poor Valente. It could drive itself, but you wouldn't call it alive. Not the way you mean the word, anyway."

She finished with a pitying smile, but Lola was too shocked to be insulted. "How did you know about the car?"

"You're the first guest I've had in twenty years," the woman said with a shrug. "Naturally, I took the liberty of looking through your memories. I'd apologize for the intrusion, but I'm not sorry in the slightest. I can't see a thing of what's going on in the outside world from in here, and it is a queen's first duty to be informed."

She smiled beatifically as she finished, and Lola shrank back into the wall of flowers. "I know who you are," she whispered, eyes huge. "You're Morgan, the fairy queen."

"Well," the woman said with a bitter laugh, "what's left of her."

She turned as she spoke, and the fall of her lovely hair shifted to show Lola that the golden waves weren't hiding her body as she'd initially assumed. The queen had no body at all. She was just a head sitting like a drop of dew on the top of a large spider lily.

"Not my best look, I'll admit," the queen's head said as Lola tried not to gag. "But one does what one must to survive. And speaking of surviving, let's talk about your 'death.'"

She turned to face the corner behind the patch of marigolds

304

where her guest was lying. A few shaky moments later, Lola followed suit, turning around on the flowers to see an old, chunky, CRT television sitting on top of a sunflower the size of her head.

"Was that always there?"

"It was and it wasn't," the queen replied unhelpfully. "Now, pay attention."

The screen flicked on as she spoke, showing a familiar scene of fire and destruction.

"I've seen that," Lola said. "It's the stupid *Fenrir* movie."

"No, it's not," the queen said sadly. "This is a live feed of what your monster is seeing right now. The two of you are still connected, because you were never actually 'two.' Like a fairy and her head, only part of you is here. The rest of you is still out there, which is how we're able to watch."

Lola stared silently, transfixed by the horror on the screen. The queen claimed it was what her monster was seeing, but the picture on the screen was *exactly* like the movie, right down to the camera's point of view. Through it, Lola could see Fenrir destroying things as if she was watching from the ground. The giant black wolf looked just like it did in the movie, but if the queen was right about it being Lola's monster, then that was all wrong. She hadn't spent much time looking in the mirror during her transformations, but Lola was pretty certain her monster's face was flat, not pointed like the wolf's, and she definitely didn't remember having a tail.

"What is going on?" she demanded, pointing at the screen. "Why do I look like that? How did I get that big? And why hasn't the DFZ murdered me yet?"

"I'm pretty sure she tried," the fairy queen said. "She just couldn't, because, right now, you're the most powerful thing in the world."

Lola blinked. "Excuse me?"

"It's the only explanation that makes sense," Morgan said. "Right now, you're being stared at by billions of horrified people. All that attention should have melted your gossamer to nothing, but you've never been one to melt away, have you? As a changeling, you should have vanished like the morning dew the moment the stolen child's parents suspected something was amiss, but you didn't."

"Because Victor saved me."

"Victor bound you," the queen corrected. "He helped hold you together through a critical juncture, but you're not made from blood. Your magic, fairy magic, is all about belief. As I said before: you are a construction, a spell. Spells are tools made for a purpose, but Alberich and the parents you were made to fool had already abandoned you, which was why you were disintegrating. To maintain your existence, Victor had to give you a new purpose, and it was *that*, not the blood, that ultimately allowed you to keep existing."

It was on the tip of her tongue to say the queen was wrong. Victor had only saved her to make a slave. He'd never given her anything so noble as a purpose. Before she could get the words out, though, Lola felt a familiar tugging on her wrist.

She looked down, eyes going wide. There, looped around her wrist just like always, was her sister's silver thread. It was jerking wilder than ever, dancing across her skin so violently, Lola was amazed she hadn't felt it before. She sure felt it now, though, and as she watched the beloved thread dance, she realized the queen was right. Victor *had* given her a purpose.

"I had to protect my sister."

Morgan's head nodded proudly on top of its flower. "Gossamer doesn't just rely on the belief of others. To keep you together, Victor had to give *you* something to believe in. Then, as usual, he made it all about himself, telling you it was his pills that kept you

306

from turning back into the monster, when really, it was your need to protect your sister."

"That *is* untrue," Lola insisted. "I really do need my pills."

The queen flashed her a coy smile. "Do you? Or did you only *think* you needed them, and your own belief made it so?"

Lola opened her mouth then closed it again. She'd been navigating the belief-based rules of her magic too long not to understand what the queen was saying, but the idea that she hadn't actually needed her pills when she'd gone through so much hell over them was more than Lola could deal with. If she could just believe her monster away, why hadn't she done it any of the times she'd been about to die?

"Because you were terrified," the queen said, answering her silent question. "And that gave it power." She smiled. "No one believed in the monster more than you."

Lola rubbed her temples with a groan. "Okay," she said, changing the subject. "You said I was the most powerful thing in the world. How is that possible when I'm just a hijacked fairy spell?"

The queen made a move that would have been a shrug if she'd had shoulders. "You don't need more than that to be powerful. Just look at spirits. They're nothing but globs of magic that humans have shoved into concepts. If people stopped thinking of the DFZ as a magical place where anything is possible, the Living City would cease to be alive. Even the famous Empty Wind is nothing but a manifestation of humanity's collective fear of being forgotten. Since the return of magic, spirits have gotten so powerful that humans have started referring to them as gods, but they're still just ideas. Concepts that have gained sentience. Control the concept and you control the god."

By the time the queen finished, Lola's jaw was halfway to the floor. "*That's* why Victor made the movie!" she cried, turning back to the TV, where Fenrir was batting dragons out of the sky. "He made a story about an undefeatable monster, and then he made the monster real."

The queen nodded. "I'm pretty sure he tried the same trick with the Black Rider first, but it didn't work. As you already observed, Valente is subject to none of his legend's restrictions despite the entire city knowing his story. That's because, in his heart, he's still human. Unlike spirits, who are just free-floating magic before they fall into their roles, a human soul is a definite thing. Even for someone like the Rider, whose humanity has been compromised with gossamer, it takes an *enormous* amount of magic to transmute a mortal soul into an immortal one. Far more than a few scary stories could account for. Good thing, too, or we'd have every rock star, viral streamer, and sports hero becoming a spirit, and then the world really would be doomed."

She chuckled at her own joke, but Lola's hands clenched into fists in her lap.

"Is that why Victor used me?" she whispered. "Because I'm not human?"

"You were an easy choice for a lot of reasons," the queen said. "Most important of which, I think, was that you already believed you were a monster. Victor didn't have to make up any special stories for you. All he had to do was remove the spell you saw as the only thing holding you together, and *pop,* off you went."

She turned back to the screen, her lovely face glowing in the light of the burning city. "Humanity did the rest. Your monster was the spark, but the moment they named you Fenrir, you belonged to them. That thing isn't even made of gossamer anymore. It's just a big sack of human fear lumbering around without a head."

The monster did seem to be rampaging mindlessly. It went after anything that came into its sphere, attacking dragons, helicopters, and billboards with the exact same ferocity. Its giant feet crushed everything regardless of whether it was actually in its way or not. It walked right through a strip mall where she and Simon used to get Chinese food as Lola watched, making her insides wrench.

"How do I stop it?"

Morgan frowned. "Tricky question."

"It can't be *that* tricky," Lola insisted, pointing at the screen. "I'm clearly still attached to it, and you just said I was the most powerful thing in the world."

"That's the tricky part I was alluding to," the queen said, giving Lola an annoyed look. "The blood mage and my husband poured all their efforts into teaching the world Fenrir was a monster that *could not be defeated.* Not by spirits, not by dragons, not by the military. You were designed to be an unstoppable force, and that's exactly what you've become. Now do you see the problem?"

"There has to be a way," Lola said stubbornly.

"There's always a way," the queen agreed. "No plan is perfect, and we've already found a chink in theirs."

"What?"

"You," she said, looking Lola over with a smile. "I'm certain Victor never intended your consciousness to survive the transformation, yet here you are. I'd be tempted to call it a miracle, but it's really just more of the same. Just as it's done for two decades now, your link to your sister kept you tethered."

Lola began to shake. All these years, she'd thought she was the anchor, but her sister had been holding on just as tightly. Even when the monster had eaten her whole, the silver thread had never broken.

"Thank you," she whispered, leaning down to kiss the dancing thread. "You never let me go. Even when I couldn't get to you, you kept us safe." She kissed it again, eyes full of tears. "*Thank you.*"

"It is a strong connection," Morgan said. "But don't underplay your own part in this, changeling. Alberich only spun that thread so he could pull the baby back to his barrow after his minions made the swap. It was your love, your belief in your family connection, that turned it into something more."

Lola closed her hand over the thread with a smile. "She always was my greatest treasure."

The fairy queen laughed at that, and Lola shot her a dirty look.

"I'm not laughing at you," Morgan said quickly. "I just wish I could see Victor's face when he finds out. The old blood bag was always *so* convinced of his own brilliance. I bet he didn't see this coming when he decided to use sisterhood as his binding mechanism."

That seemed too pointed an opinion to be gleaned from someone else's memories. "You knew Victor?"

"Of course," the queen said, her lovely voice growing bitter. "He's the one who cut off my head."

Lola's mouth fell open. "*Victor* cut off your head?" she cried. When the queen nodded, she added, "*How?*"

"A series of betrayals that *will* be avenged," Morgan promised darkly. "He was the lover of a member of my court at the time. He actually asked me for a changeling first. Said he wanted to do some experiments. Naturally, I told him no. Swapping gossamer for human children is good fun, but it draws too much attention to merit the risk. Changelings are one of the few magics that can be cast from inside a barrow, though, which was why Alberich made so many. They were his only source of food after I locked him and his court away."

"Why *did* you lock him up?" Lola asked. "Isn't he your husband?"

"And my enemy just as often," the queen said. "He is a powerful king, make no mistake, but he has no subtlety. He still

310

behaves as if we are a mighty host, but the drought killed more of us than he has bothered to count. He refuses to understand that humanity has gotten sharper while we have gotten weaker. It used to be only priests and the educated who could pierce gossamer. Now the whole world questions what they see."

She shook her golden head. "It's not a time for Hunts anymore. When we woke from the ravages of the drought, the other surviving monarchs and I agreed it was best for all of us to remain hidden while we rebuilt our power. Only Alberich refused, so I locked him away. I never dreamed that the blood mage would discover one of his changelings and contact him or that Alberich would be so desperate to ride again that he'd listen." The queen sighed wistfully. "He always was a beautiful idiot."

That wasn't how Lola would have described the Underground King. But fairies had weird tastes, especially old ones. She was just glad Morgan didn't seem the sort to spare someone out of sentimentality, but there was still part of this she didn't understand.

"I can see why Alberich did it," she said. "If his goal is to feast on fear, bringing Fenrir into the world makes perfect sense, but why would Victor do it? The DFZ's lack of law enforcement is the only reason he's been able to live as a blood mage for so long without getting caught. He needs this city, so why is he destroying it?" She shook her head. "There *has* to be another angle. Something else he's after that only Fenrir could get him."

"I'm sure I don't know," the queen said. "I've been stuck in here for twenty years. The only window I have is your memories, and you seem to have spent the last two decades thinking of him as a god."

"You try standing up to the only thing keeping you from dying," Lola snapped. "Of course I was terrified of Victor. He had a noose around my neck!"

"But that's not the case anymore, is it?" Morgan said. "Even if you don't believe me that it was your sister, not his pills, that was your true savior, his spell is gone. Alberich had to bleed it all out of you to push you over the final edge, and yet here you stand."

Lola blinked at her. That was right. The thing she'd feared her entire life had happened, and she was still here. She didn't even feel as if she'd lost anything. Quite the opposite—her gossamer felt steadier than ever before, as if it was Victor's blood that had been making her unstable and not the other way around.

"He really was lying the whole time."

"Mm-hmm," the queen said, but Lola barely heard her over the rush of her own thoughts.

"He doesn't control me anymore," she said, whirling back to the screen. "I don't have to do what he says. I can stop him!"

"But are you sure that's what you want?" Morgan asked, her eyes shining dangerously. "The blood mage has created something very powerful, and he doesn't expect you. You just said he must have another angle, some greater purpose than mere destruction. You could let him complete his vision and then come up from behind to take it for yourself."

That was a very fairy way to think, but Lola couldn't shake her head fast enough.

"No way. I've spent my whole life watching Victor destroy things. I could never do anything before, but now…" She stared at Fenrir roaring on the screen, and her hands clenched to fists. "If that really is my monster, then I'm going to do everything I can to make sure it rampages through *him*. I'm going to smash his power once and for all, and then I'm going to set all of us free."

"That, I can get behind," the queen said with a smile. "If you want to escape, I can tell you the way."

Lola eyed her suspiciously. "If you knew how to get out this whole time, why didn't you do it earlier?"

"It's hard to go anywhere when you're nothing but a head," Morgan said matter-of-factly. "It's simply impossible for me to break through the walls in my current state, but things are different now that you're here."

"Where *is* here?" Lola asked, looking around at the room full of flowers, which now seemed smaller than ever, almost like the inside of a coffin.

"I'm not entirely sure," the queen confessed. "I know it must be somewhere the blood mage controls utterly, or my knight would have rescued me already. My guess is we're in the place Victor buries the things he never wants to see again. That would also explain how you got here. We both died soaked in his bloody magic, so it makes sense that we'd both wash out at the same dead end."

Lola grimaced at the grisly description. "So how do we escape?"

"It's very simple," Morgan assured her. "Especially for you. Changelings are famously impossible to pin down, *and* you're tied to the unbeatable Fenrir. Why, I bet you could get out of here any time you wanted!"

Lola smiled and nodded, waiting for the queen to elaborate. But Morgan's head just sat on her piled hair, watching expectantly, and Lola sighed.

"What's the price?"

"It's quite fair," the queen promised. "I'll tell you how to leave this place, but in return, you have to take me with you."

That *did* sound fair, especially since Lola had already been planning to take Morgan anyway. The enemy of my enemy always made useful allies, and there were few enemies who engendered as much hatred as Victor.

"Deal," Lola said, spinning a tote bag out of her gossamer, which felt strong enough to make a fleet of cars now that Victor's blood wasn't holding it back. When she turned to collect the

313

queen, though, she hesitated.

"So, um… Do I just pick you up?"

"Yes, please," Morgan said. "Hair first, if you don't mind."

Lola did mind. The fairy queen had about fifty pounds of hair. She had to change her tote bag into a backpack to fit it all, but eventually, she got all the golden tresses shoved inside. This made a nice cushion for the queen's head, which Lola picked up last.

"Careful!" Morgan cried as Lola lifted her off the spider lily. "I'm more delicate than I look."

She wasn't kidding. The queen's head felt like a soap bubble in Lola's fingers. Just getting her into the backpack was nerve-racking, but soon Lola had her nestled like an egg down in the swirls of her hair. She had to zip the backpack closed so the queen's head wouldn't roll out if she had to bend over, but she left a two-inch gap at the top so Morgan wouldn't be left completely in the dark.

"How did a fairy queen end up in this state?" Lola asked when everything was finally settled. "From the way Alberich and Tristan talk, I thought you monarchs were crazy powerful."

"It was a very effective betrayal," Morgan replied testily. "And I *am* powerful. Do you know anyone else who could survive this long as nothing but a head?"

"Fair point," Lola said, sliding the backpack onto her shoulders. "So, how do we get out?"

"It's very simple," the queen assured her, her voice muffled only slightly from being inside the backpack. "You walk through the wall."

Lola scowled. "It can't be that easy."

"It's not," Morgan said. "'Walk through the wall' is sound advice for escaping any prison, but how applicable it is depends on the wall in question, and these are quite strong. Far stronger than I could break in my present state, but you're the monster here, so go

314

ahead. Smash us free!"

Lola didn't like Morgan calling her a monster any more than when Victor said it. It was hard to argue given the scene of destruction that was still playing on the TV, though, so she sucked it up and got to work, shoving her way through the thick flowers until her fingers hit something that felt like steel.

She gave the wall a few knocks with her knuckles and stepped back. Despite what the fairy queen had just said, smashing wasn't really Lola's specialty. She was more of a maker, so that was what she went with, spinning her gossamer into a wrecking ball already swinging on its steel cable straight at the wall.

Her new gossamer must have been even sturdier than she'd realized, because her wrecking ball worked *way* better than intended. It went through the steel wall like a knockout punch through tissue, sending flowers flying through a giant sucking hole that yanked Lola off her feet.

She fell through it with a yelp. The world was suddenly spinning too fast to see. For several horrifying moments, Lola worried that she'd just launched them into space. Then the spinning stopped as she landed face first on something fuzzy and soft. When she scrambled to her feet, Lola saw she was standing in the middle of an elaborately decorated parlor.

It looked like something out of an edgy interior designer's catalog shoot. There was a thick carpet—the soft thing she'd landed on—chairs, tables, and couches, all in a sleek modern style. The whole place was lit by an enormous abstract chandelier dangling from the high domed ceiling. There was even a fireplace with a big, cheery fire crackling inside. It would have been lovely, save for one critical flaw: it was all bloodred.

Everything—the furniture, the walls, the floor—was the same intense crimson color. Even the fire looked like dancing splashes of thick red liquid. But the most alarming part was the pictures.

315

The crimson walls were tiled in a grid of hand-sized photographs of people's faces. They were the same crimson as everything else, as if someone had printed out a black-and-white photo using only red ink. Each one had a thin, red frame with a red string dangling from the bottom corner, as if the photos were built to pop open when pulled.

Even for Lola, who'd thought she'd already seen the worst of Victor's dark magic, it was super creepy. *Especially* when she spotted Simon's photo glowering at her from the bottom of the line. She was tiptoeing across the soft red carpet to get a better look when the queen's head gasped inside her backpack.

Lola spun around, hands flying up to fight before she dropped them in wonder. Behind them, sitting like a trophy on an intricately worked crimson display table, was a blood-red safe. Not a huge one for storing guns in. This was a little safe similar to the kind you saw in nice hotel rooms, only its front was entirely blown out. Looking through the jagged hole, Lola could see the flower prison they'd just escaped. Even the TV was there, still playing the feed of Fenrir's destruction, but it was all in miniature, like a room in a dollhouse.

"This is *so* weird," Lola said, reaching in to brush her finger against the now-tiny flowers.

"It's not weird at all," Morgan said, sounding impressed despite herself. "It's *brilliant*. I finally understand why my knight never found me. We're inside the blood mage's death!"

That sounded so awful, Lola actually jumped. "The *what*?"

"His death," she repeated. "His vessel within the Sea of Magic."

When this failed to elicit a response, the fairy queen blew out a frustrated breath. "You *do* know what the Sea of Magic is, don't you?"

"No, because I'm not a mage," Lola huffed. "I'm not even human, and neither are you, so how do *you* know all this stuff?"

"Because this is how the world works!" Morgan cried. Then she took a calming breath.

"It's very simple," she explained, speaking slowly and sweetly like an announcer on a children's show. "You know how all humans can push magic around, right? And how mages are just humans that get to control how, where, and how much they push?"

"Uh huh," Lola said.

"Well, the Sea of Magic is where all that pushing actually happens. It's a separate world where only magic exists that's layered on top of the material plane we're all familiar with. When Earth's magic vanished during the thousand-year Drought, *this* is where it disappeared from. The sea literally dried up. Now that the magic's back, though, it's full and sloshing again."

"Okay," Lola said slowly, looking around the red-decorated room, which definitely didn't look like any sea she'd ever seen, magical or otherwise. "But if we're in this magical ocean or whatever, how are we also in the blood mages' death?"

"I didn't mean a specific death for all blood mages," the queen snapped. "We're inside Victor Conrath's own *personal* death."

"Still not understanding."

Morgan's head shifted inside the backpack like she was shaking it. "Everything that has magic has a place in the Sea," she said, her sweetly explaining voice tinged with annoyance this time. "Every native thing, anyway. Fairies get nothing since we just burrowed in here to eat, but spirits and humans like Victor all have their own little niches carved out in the sea floor. For spirits like the DFZ that have millions of people shoving magic at them, these niches are enormous and are called vessels. The magic that fills that vessel is what makes a spirit a spirit, like water filling up a jar. Following so far?"

"Pretty sure," Lola said, walking over to poke at the bloody

317

fire. "So this place is Victor's vessel?"

"Sort of," the queen said. "Even the greatest humans are infinitely smaller than spirits. The hollows made by mortal lives are simply too tiny to qualify as vessels. They're also where human souls go after their physical body dies, which is why they're called 'deaths.'"

"Morbid but cool," Lola said, holding her hand over the flames, which gave no warmth at all.

"This chamber is the hollow carved out by Victor Conrath's life," the queen went on. "When he eventually dies, as all mortals must, this is where he will wait for one of the death spirits to come and claim him. But, and this is the important part, most humans— mages and nonmages—can only enter their deaths when they *die*. But blood magic is all about the manipulation of human souls, both other people's and the mage's own, which means—"

"Victor can enter his own death whenever he chooses," Lola said, moving away from the flames, which no longer seemed so intriguing.

"Precisely," the queen said, shifting against Lola's back as she peeked through the crack in the zipper. "It's the perfect hiding place! So far as I'm aware, no fairy has ever been able to breach the Sea of Magic, much less navigate to a specific human's death. My knight could have searched for centuries and never found me here."

"And I fell in because Victor drowned me in his blood," said Lola, suddenly feeling dirty. "Even when I bleed him out, I can't get rid of him."

"Well, here's your chance," Morgan said. "Look up."

Lola tilted her head as far back as it would go. There, above the red chandelier at the very top of the crimson room's curved ceiling, was a hole. It was so black, Lola's eyes had a hard time staying on it. If she squinted, though, she could see things moving

318

out in the darkness, almost like she was looking through a porthole on a submarine.

"Is that the Sea of Magic?"

"Yes," Morgan whispered, her voice shaking with anticipation, or perhaps fear. "If we want to escape, that is where we must go."

Lola frowned. A hole in the ceiling didn't look like much of an exit, but unless she wanted to climb the fireplace's chimney, there weren't any other ways out.

"You could grow wings," Morgan suggested.

Lola shook her head and balled her hand into a fist. When she opened it again, she was holding a Batman-style grapple gun with a hook at the end.

"Really?" the queen said, her lovely voice disgusted. "All the possibilities in the universe, and *that's* what you chose?"

"Wings are hard," Lola replied as she aimed the grapple gun at the chandelier. "This isn't. Now hold on."

"I don't have hands."

"Then bite something."

The queen made an indignant sound as Lola fired the grapple straight at the chandelier's biggest arm. When the hook caught, she grabbed the gun with both hands, holding on tight as the flywheel inside took hold and lifted her up to the ceiling.

"See?" she said when they were dangling fifty feet off the ground. "Simple and effective."

Morgan harrumphed, but she didn't complain again as Lola hooked a leg over the chandelier's arm and hauled herself up.

Even up here, there were photos. Aside from Simon at the bottom, Lola didn't recognize any of their faces, but every one of them had the red string hanging straight down off the bottom of its frame. The thread was swollen and heavy-looking, as if it were wet. It made her skin crawl to look at, so Lola kept her eyes on her work, hauling her body onto the chandelier until she was sitting

319

on the red-metal arm directly below the hole.

"Whoa," she said, craning her neck back to look at the darkness above her. "That's intense."

It was *insane*. Lola had always been able to sense when Victor or Simon or any human mage pulled in magic by the pressure it put on her gossamer and, in Victor's case, the strong scent of blood. The magic outside the black hole had no smell, but she could already feel its strength.

Sitting under the portal felt like sitting by an open window during a tornado. She'd never felt magic move that fast in her life, and there was *tons* of it out there. It really was like a stormy sea: huge and black and full of churning currents.

Just poking a finger into it was enough to rip the tip right off her gossamer, making her wonder if this even qualified as an escape. It looked more like instant death. She was turning to ask the queen if there was a trick to traveling through it without being torn apart when she caught sight of her sister's thread.

It was still wrapped around her wrist like always, but the tail that normally vanished a few inches from her skin was no longer invisible. Lola could see it clearly: a long, shimmering line running straight up into the blackness above her head.

"I see it," she whispered excitedly, running her hand up the taut string. "I see the way to my sister! We just have to follow this line!"

"I wouldn't suggest it," the queen said nervously. "Your sister is human and alive, so, technically, she must be somewhere in the Sea of Magic. If we follow that line to her soul, though, we'll end up at her body, which I'm sure is buried deep in Alberich's barrow. That's not where we want to be."

"Maybe not," Lola said, standing up on the chandelier's arm. "But it's where I'm going."

The queen's voice grew furious. "Did you not hear what I

320

just—"

"You're the one who told me my devotion to my sister is what kept me together," Lola snapped. "Do you really think I'm going to see a lead like this and not take it? Alberich is busy with his Wild Hunt. This could be my only chance to set her free!"

"But—"

"I'm going," Lola said firmly. "And unless you want me to leave you here, you're coming with me."

"*Fine*," Morgan huffed. "One exit's as good as another, I suppose. Just remember to keep your gossamer tight. The Sea of Magic is normally only traversable by spirits, but there's billions of humans cowering in mortal terror of Fenrir right now, which means you're as close to a spirit as anything made of gossamer is ever going to get. That *should* be enough to allow us to leave this place without being instantly torn apart. If it's not, well, at least we died on our feet. Your feet, anyway. I don't have any."

"Better to die out there than sit here rotting in Victor's creepy death," Lola said, grabbing onto her sister's thread. "Here goes nothing."

With a huge breath as if she was diving into the actual sea, Lola grabbed the portal's edge and hauled herself up, plunging out of the crushing quiet of Victor's red death into the black chaos beyond. As expected, the torrents of wild magic instantly ripped her away, sending Lola tumbling through the darkness like a leaf in a storm. They didn't tear her apart, though. She held together, clenching her gossamer tight as a fist around her body and the backpack that held the fairy queen.

"I don't believe it!" Morgan cried over the gale. "It's really working!"

"Why do you sound so surprised?" Lola yelled back. "You're the one who told me to do it!"

"Yes, well, there's theory and there's practice," the queen said.

Then her voice grew wondrous. "You really *are* like a spirit."

Lola looked out into the swirling void. She hadn't felt any different back in Victor's death, but now that she was tumbling through raw magic, she could feel the collective fear of millions pushing down on her. Their belief was an iron mold around her gossamer, squeezing her into the unkillable beast they saw on the screen. But while it was that belief that kept her from being torn apart by the chaos, Lola didn't want to be a monster. She just wanted to be Lola, the girl who saved her sister, so that was what she focused on, holding her dream like a candle as she tightened her fist around her sister's thread and yanked.

As ever, the shining line didn't budge when she touched it, but Lola did. The moment she pulled on the silver thread, her body stopped spinning like a top hitting a wall. The jerk at the end would have torn her arm off if humanity's expectations hadn't been clenching her gossamer so tight. Somehow, though, it all came together, leaving Lola standing in the swirling dark with her sister's thread running ahead of her like a shining road into the blackness.

It was as clear a path as anyone could have asked, so Lola started forward, hauling herself hand over hand along the silver string into the void. She'd only made it a few hand-lengths when Morgan whispered from her backpack.

"I'm afraid you're going to have to do this next part on your own," she said, her voice noticeably weaker. "There's too much magic here. Even with your gossamer acting as a shield, I'm barely holding together. If I don't conserve the gossamer I have left, I really will die."

"Do what you have to," Lola said, prying one hand off the thread to reach over her shoulder and zip the backpack all the way closed. "I'll get us through."

"Don't forget... your promise..." the queen wheezed, her voice falling softly as a petal as the weight in Lola's pack grew lighter.

Hoping that was normal, Lola grabbed her sister's thread again, climbing sideways through the swirling magic and deeper into the Sea.

~~~

There was no telling how long she traveled. Similar to a fairy barrow, time and distance felt like illusions here. She could have hauled herself six feet or a million miles, traveled for years or seconds. The shining thread was the only thing she had to mark her progress, and it seemed to run off into the distance forever.

Other shapes flew past her in the darkness. Some were tiny as minnows, others huge as ancient sharks. None of them stopped to bother her, though, so Lola kept going, hauling on and on until, after what felt like an eternity but could have been no time at all, the thread stopped going straight ahead and began to curve downward.

Lola paused, spinning her gossamer into a floodlight as she peered through the dark. This whole time, she really had felt as if she was swimming through a deep sea. Not only did it have pulses and currents and even other inhabitants, it also had what looked like an ocean floor full of cracks and holes. She'd passed over several on her way here, some as big as mountains turned upside down, but nothing compared to what was beneath her now.

Directly below her was a fissure bigger than any Lola had ever seen. Its edges were riddled with tiny gouges, as if the hole had been dug by a billion frantically clawing hands. It was impossible to say how deep it went. Even with her biggest searchlight, Lola couldn't glimpse the bottom. Her sister's silver line went straight down into it, though, so that was what Lola followed, sliding down the thread like a stone bead into the dark.

As with everything down here, it was impossible to say how far she fell, but it *felt* like a long time. The swirling magic got thicker the deeper she went, its pressure increasing as if she were diving into a real trench. But while the power was definitely stronger here, it was also less chaotic. Where the sea above had been every sort of magic flying by at sheering speeds, this pit had only one flavor: a horrible, terrifying, *familiar* feeling.

By the time Lola's feet touched the bottom, she knew where she was. This was Fenrir's vessel, the hole carved out just now by humanity's fear of her monster. She could feel the magic pouring into it as the sides stretched wider, because this was her vessel, too.

Down here more than ever, Lola could feel the monster that was also her on the other side. Its mind was crushed under the weight of humanity's expectations, but it *was* there, and it was afraid. So, *so* afraid of what was happening as it rampaged out of control.

Fenrir's pathetic whimpers almost made her cry, but Lola didn't have time for that. Her sister's thread was floating right in front of her, the only light in the darkness. It was the monster's treasure, too, she realized with a start. Even when it lost control, even when it could no longer think, the monster had kept her sister close to its heart. Kept her safe.

Lola did cry then, scrubbing furiously at her eyes as she followed the thread down the sloping ground toward the deepest part of the pit. Fenrir's vessel was enormous, but hauling herself around down here was actually easier than it had been up top, probably because this was her home. She might not be able to control it yet, but Lola *was* Fenrir. This was her heart, too, and she used that familiarity to dart ahead, kicking off the ground in huge steps with her hands running along the thread like a rail until she saw something glittering ahead of her.

She skidded to a stop, eyes going wide. The monster's vessel was muddy and fresh, a featureless hole dug at the bottom of a dark sea, but the place ahead was different. It rose from the blackness like a shimmering palace, a perfect circle of gold-veined stone spires dotted with gemstones the size of pumpkins. The ground beneath them looked different as well. Where everything else here was the same dull, matte black, the rock beneath the spires looked like expensive marble. Even the magic felt different as she got closer: a hollow, echoey chill, as if she'd stepped into a tunnel.

Lola recognized it at once. That was Alberich's magic. She was looking at a piece of the Underground King's barrow stuck right in the middle of Fenrir's vessel.

That shocked her for a moment before Lola realized it only made sense. She was made of his gossamer, after all. Wherever she was, there could he build his kingdom. Lola didn't know if it had happened by accident when she'd changed or if he was using her as a loophole to wheedle himself into the Sea of Magic, but her sister's thread ran straight ahead into the circle of glittering rocks.

Lola ran after it, keeping her fingers tight on the humming silver as she dove out of the monster's terrified magic and into Alberich's terrifying one. The patch of barrow turned out to be only twenty feet across, just enough to fit a dozen or so of the gold-veined spires standing in a rough circle, like an old-fashioned fairy ring.

And there, lying in the center on a bed of gold and glowing jewels, was a human woman with a silver thread tied around her wrist.

Chapter 16

Strangely, Lola's first thought was that the woman lying on the golden bed looked like the lady from the yogurt ad. Not exactly alike, obviously, but they both had the same thick black hair and up-tilted nose. Her skin was light brown and slightly freckled, just like Lola's was right now, and her closed eyes looked like they'd be friendly when she opened them.

The longer Lola looked, the more familiar things she saw, enough to make her heart clench. No wonder she felt so at home in her yogurt-lady face! It was practically her sister's, which meant it was the closest to her own.

Her own real face.

Lola stumbled forward, her hands sliding up the silver thread so fast that the strand cut her gossamer. She didn't care. She didn't care about rocks, either. Normally, stepping into fairy rings was a top-ten terrible idea, but Lola was too excited to be cautious. She rushed recklessly forward, letting go of the thread to reach out toward her sister—her very own sister, found at last!—as she crossed the stone circle.

Straight into a wall of blood.

Lola jumped back with a retch, rubbing her hands frantically over her face like she'd walked into a spider web, but her fingers came away clean. There was no actual blood. Like everything else in this place, it was magic. Victor's horrible magic scribbled all over the ground.

She hadn't noticed in the rush to get to her sister, but now that she'd been forced to stop, Lola saw that the inside of the fairy ring was covered in bloody spellwork. Victor had never shared enough of his secrets to allow her to read what it did, but there was *tons* of it. Enough to cover the floor in a spiral of densely written red symbols that ran from the edge of the gold-veined stones all the way to the bed where her sister lay.

No wonder Victor had been gone so long! It must have taken days for him to write this much. But while Lola could see the faint glow that meant the spell was active and likely dangerous, she still didn't care. Her sister was right in front of her, and magic never bothered changelings anyway, so she screwed up her courage and stepped back in.

As the bloody magic slapped her in the face again, Lola had a moment of panic. Unless they were aimed at her specifically, Victor's spells normally slid right over her because of her pills, but that wasn't the case anymore. All the blood he'd put into her had been drained out, which meant she might have just made a fatal mistake.

Too late now. Lola already had both feet inside the circle. But while Victor's magic definitely felt more menacing than it used to, she was still a changeling. No one's magic knew what to do with her, not even Victor's. She could feel the bloody magic like humidity on her skin, but it didn't actually stop her, so she pushed right through, running straight over the spiraling red symbols to her sister's side.

She stopped again at the golden bed's edge. From outside the circle, her sister had looked like the yogurt lady. Now that Lola was standing next to her, though, her sister just looked like herself. That shouldn't have been possible for someone she was seeing for the first time, but Lola already felt as if she'd known the woman her whole life, which was how she also knew that something was wrong. She had the very strong impression that her sister should be smiling, but the woman's face was set in a grimace, the muscles around her eyes twitching as if she was having a nightmare.

"Shh, it's okay," Lola whispered, reaching out. "I'm here now. I—"

She stopped, her silver-looped hand hovering just above her sister's. Could she touch her? Would something bad happen? She didn't know, but she hadn't come this far to stop now. She'd never get her sister out of here if they couldn't touch, so Lola took a chance, lowering her fingers the last inch to wrap around her sister's.

Her eyes closed in relief. She hadn't realized how terrified she'd been that Victor's spell would snap down on her, or worse, that her sister would feel cold and dead. Morgan had said that was the only way humans got into the Sea of Magic, but it clearly wasn't the case here. Lola didn't know what a ghost felt like, but her sister's hand felt warm and alive, her pulse pounding like a frightened fist against Lola's fingers.

"It's going to be all right," she promised, clutching her panicking sister's hand. "The nightmare is over. I'm going to get you out."

The woman's face relaxed a fraction, making Lola's hopes soar. She was so happy, her gossamer changed all by itself, rearranging her features until Lola's face was a mirror of her sister's. Just like the first time she'd copied the yogurt lady, it felt instantly right. Even if it was just a copy, wearing her sister's face made Lola feel like more than a pile of stolen details. She felt like a person. A real, true person for the very first time.

"Thank you," she whispered, not even caring that she was crying as she leaned down to kiss her sister's cheek. "Now, let's get you free."

That proved easier said than done. There were no restraints on the golden bed, but when Lola tried to lift her sister off of it, the girl stuck fast. Victor's disgusting spellwork stopped at the bed's base, so Lola assumed the sticking must be Alberich's doing, only she didn't know how to *undo* it. She couldn't wake her sister up, either. No matter how hard she shook her or how loudly she shouted, the sleeping woman stayed trapped in her nightmare.

All out of options, Lola decided to get help. "Morgan!" she yelled, taking off her backpack and giving it a shake. "*Morgan, wake up!*"

"That is not how you address a queen," the head said grumpily, her lovely voice slurring like a drunk's. "I told you I needed to rest. I'm in a weakened state, and the magic of this place is..."

Her words trailed off as Lola unzipped the backpack, and the fairy queen got her first puzzled look at where they were.

"Is this Alberich's barrow?"

"Sort of," Lola said, lifting the pack up and turning it around so the fairy queen could see the circle of stones and the yawning darkness above them. "I followed my thread here through the Sea of Magic. I think we're in Fenrir's version of that vessel thing you were talking about. I found this bit of Alberich's barrow at the bottom, and look what's in it."

She turned the pack toward the bed at the fairy ring's center, and the queen gasped.

"Is that—?"

"My sister," Lola said, grinning at the surge of happiness that came from just being able to say those words. "But she's stuck to that bed, and I can't get her off."

"Of course you can't," Morgan said, pushing her nose out through the gap in the zipper to get a better look. "If Alberich's minions switched the two of you at her birth, then she's been within the Underground King's dominion for her entire life. He's probably had her dreaming there the entire time."

Lola's hands tightened on the backpack's straps. "You mean she's been asleep like that for *twenty-seven years?*"

"I certainly wouldn't have let her wake," the queen said matter-

329

of-factly. "Humans are easy to ensnare, but they get unmanageable once they realize they're trapped. Even I couldn't keep a waking mortal fooled her entire life, and Alberich's magic is far less subtle than mine. He'd have to keep her asleep, or she would have rebelled against him ages ago."

Lola grinned at the idea of her sister kicking Alberich to the curb. But, "How do we wake her up now?"

"She should wake in her own time once she's out of Alberich's power," the queen replied, turning in the backpack. "I'm far more concerned about *that*."

She nodded down at the bloody spellwork, and Lola scowled. "What does it do?"

"I don't know," Morgan replied, sounding very upset about that. "I used to make it a point to know every human language, including spellwork. But Victor's logic has always been difficult to decipher, and I haven't read any of his work for a long time."

She squinted her green eyes at the glowing spell. "I think it's a control of some sort. Living humans shouldn't be able to exist in this place. Alberich must have used his connection to you—and your connection to Fenrir—to get around that by inserting a piece of barrow, but he wouldn't have risked bringing his mortal here unless he had a very good reason."

"I know why!" Lola cried. "I mean, I can't read his spellwork, but I can guess what it does. I thought from the start that it was strange for Victor to create a monster he didn't control. He *hates* anything he can't control, but what if he could?"

She pointed at her sister. "If I was supposed to die, that would leave Fenrir without a head, but the monster was never just me. I've already felt how Fenrir treasures my sister just like I do, and Victor's always used the silver thread to jerk me around."

She ran her fingers down the silver thread. "Maybe he *wasn't* being foolish when he used sisterhood to bind me," she said.

330

"Maybe creating that link was his plan all along. Even when I used to worship him as my hero, Victor couldn't control my mind like he did everyone else's because I wasn't human, but she is. What if *that's* the reason she's here? The reason for all of this!"

It all made sense. Victor was the master of monsters. He'd never make a weapon he couldn't control, but a woman who'd spent her entire life lost inside a fairy dream would be easy to manipulate, and Lola herself had built the leash. She'd tied her sister to the monster with a silver thread! With her gone, all Victor had to do was yank the string and—

"Can you bring back the TV?" she asked in a panic.

"Of course not," Morgan scoffed. "You think I'd be riding in your backpack if I could make things on my own?"

"You haven't been able to spin gossamer this whole time?" Lola asked, astonished. "Then how—"

"I nudged a bit of your gossamer while you were coming to," the queen told her confidentially. "You were the one with the connection to the monster, so it made sense that you should be the one to show it. I might have also borrowed a teensy-weensy bit to make the flowers. It'd just been *so* long since I'd seen anything besides my own hair, and I wanted to make a good first impression."

That was such a bald-faced confession, Lola gaped at the queen for a good ten seconds before shaking her head. Setting her backpack down on the ground, Lola cupped her hands and imagined what she wanted. A second later, a lump of gossamer rose from her palms to form an exact replica of the old TV they'd watched inside Morgan's prison.

The screen clicked on as soon as it appeared. Just like the keycard she'd made to get herself out of prison, Lola didn't understand how the TV worked, and she didn't have to. All she had to do was believe it would show her what was happening outside, and there it was, playing on the screen like a monster movie.

The journey through the Sea of Magic must not have taken as long as she'd thought, because Fenrir had only chewed through a few more blocks since the last time Lola looked. It had grown bigger, though. The monster wolf's shoulders were now several stories above the Skyway bridges, and its teeth were the size of telephone poles.

From the wreckage all around, the city had continued its attack. With some success, apparently, because the monster was bleeding from several cuts across its chest and legs. Lola winced at the bright-red blood rolling through its thick black fur. She was trying to figure out what had finally hurt the unstoppable Fenrir when she saw it.

There, standing like a statue at the edge of a broken bridge, was a man with a golden sword. He was lit up like a torch from the spotlights of the helicopters swarming overhead, but his face was so dazzlingly handsome, Lola didn't recognize it at first. It wasn't until she zoomed the TV's picture in that she finally realized it was Victor.

The man on the screen looked nothing like the one who'd told her he'd take care of Frank just a few days ago. He didn't even look like the stranger who'd taken her from the hospital twenty years ago. This was Victor as Lola had never seen him: a dazzling illusion of his best possible self, concocted for the cameras swarming overhead. He lifted his sword as they swung by, turning the golden blade to show them the red blood dripping from its point. To show them who he was.

He was the hero.

And he was here to slay the monster.

A cold, heavy dread settled over Lola's gossamer. Up in the yawning pit that was Fenrir, she could already feel the terrified magic that had dug the monster's vessel draining away. Draining into *him*.

The Victor on the screen grew brighter as it happened, his handsome face lighting up with the very real power of their belief, which was, Lola realized at last, the entire point. He hadn't brought Fenrir into the world so it could destroy. It was there for him to defeat. He was doing to himself what he'd done to the Black Rider. He was making himself a legend: the man who killed the unkillable and saved the world.

"Huh," Morgan said, watching through the crack in the backpack at Lola's feet. "He's cleverer than I gave him credit for."

"He's a *monster*," Lola snarled, looking at the glowing spellwork under her feet. "He's using my sister to control Fenrir so he can kill it! We have to stop him!"

"The simplest thing would be to kill the human allowing his control," the queen said. Then she caught a glimpse of Lola's face. "Which is clearly *not* an option, so let's move on."

She looked down at the bloody markings on the ground, then up at Lola's sister, and then she shook her head. "There's not a lot to work with. We could destroy the spellwork, but that might trigger a backlash that could fry your sister's brain. Same for dragging her out of the circle, which is also impossible because of Alberich's hold on her."

The queen sighed, a very strange sound from someone without a chest. "There's nothing else for it. If you want to stop Victor, you're going to have to take back control of your monster yourself."

Lola would have normally balked at that idea, but she was feeling pretty monstrous right now. "How?"

"The blood mage's spell is only the second layer at play here," Morgan explained. "Long before Victor came meddling, her soul was trapped in Alberich's dream."

"Does that mean you can get her out?" Lola asked hopefully.

The queen shook her head. "If I had my body, maybe, but she's been in there so long now, the Underground King's magic is her entire world. Even if I could reach her, she'd never accept my hand, but I bet she'll accept yours."

Lola's eyes went wide. "You want me to go into her dream?"

"That's where Fenrir is," Morgan said, but Lola was already shaking her head.

"I can't! I'm not a real fairy. I can't just insert myself into people's dreams."

"You went into Valente's."

"He had a fairy's head," she said, narrowing her eyes. "Also, I know you went through my memories, but there's this thing called *privacy*."

Morgan looked utterly unapologetic. "I was trapped in a box without food for two decades! You can't expect me to turn down such delicious desire, especially when it was *right there*."

Lola rolled her eyes and got back to the matter at hand. "How do I get into my sister's dream?"

"I don't know," the queen said. "You're the changeling, not me. The two of you are deeply connected, though, so just do whatever you normally do. Make sure you pick me up before you start, though. We're treading into completely unknown territory here, and I do *not* want to be left behind in some unstable god's vessel."

The ground *was* starting to shake. Above them, bits of Fenrir's vessel were cracking off as Victor fought the monster. He hadn't gotten anything close to a killing blow yet—his sword was simply too small for that, and Fenrir too big—but it didn't matter. People were starting to believe he could win, and that was enough to collapse the delicate new vessel their fear had dug.

"Hurry," the queen urged as Lola picked up the backpack. "*Hurry!*"

334

Lola zipped the pack shut, throwing the queen onto her back as she got down on her knees beside her sister.

"Hey," she whispered, reaching out to grab her hand again. "I know what he's doing, and I'm coming to help. If you can hear me, come toward my voice. We'll do this together."

As ever, Lola had no idea if her sister could hear her, but the woman's twitching eased when she spoke, filling Lola with hope as she leaned forward to rest her forehead against her sister's.

Their connection really must have been strong. Either that, or her sister had been reaching just as hard as Lola, because the moment she closed her eyes, the dream exploded over her. There was no slow drifting like with Tristan or even Valente's violent grab. Lola was simply *there*, standing on the wolf's huge legs in the middle of the destroyed city.

She jerked in surprise, shaking the ground as her paws slipped on the broken shards of a crushed Skyway bridge. A bridge she could see in perfect clarity, because this wasn't her bleary-eyed monster. This was her sister's dream, the same Fenrir dream all of the DFZ had been having, but her sister wasn't the only one here. Lola's monster was present as well, mewling and panicked as it fought desperately to protect its treasure.

They were *all* fighting to protect each other, Lola realized. She, her sister, and the monster were three panicked faces of the same person. When Lola tried to pull them all together, though, another force shoved back. There was a presence in her head. A horrible, bloody hand she knew as well as her own scream.

Lola raised Fenrir's red eyes to the man on the bridge. The hand in her head twitched as she did, and Fenrir lurched forward, throwing itself onto the Hero's sword like a mad dog. Victor made a show of fighting it off, cutting a bloody chunk out of the monster's foreleg in the process.

Fenrir howled in pain, but Lola howled in rage. Above them in the bright TV lights, the Hero raised his sword again, and she felt even more of Fenrir's magic drain away, but Lola wasn't angry about that. She was furious for the monster's sake, because this wasn't even a fight.

With Victor's hand shoved inside her sister's mind, Fenrir hadn't even been able to snap at him. This whole thing was a sham, a set-up! The Hero could have come to the fight barehanded and it wouldn't have made a difference. The outcome was preordained, controlled by Victor's spell. All he had to do was twitch his fingers, and the monster did whatever he wanted.

But while it was clear how this was supposed to end, her sister and the monster were no longer fighting him alone. Lola was here too now. Lola was free, and she'd die before she let that bastard hurt them anymore.

With a roar that shook the city, she rolled Fenrir to its feet and turned its dripping fangs on the man she'd once called master. She saw Victor's eyes flicker the moment he noticed something was wrong. His poker face had always been flawless, so she doubted the cameras saw anything, but Lola knew. Even if she'd never seen his real face beneath the illusions, she'd lived in fear of Victor for twenty years. She knew his every tell because she'd had to watch them all so hard. It was the only way she'd been able to see his wrath coming, but it was also how she was able to spot what was different now. Because beneath his hero's smile, there was a new emotion on Victor's face. One she'd never seen on him before.

He was surprised.

"You?"

His voice spoke to her through the blood he'd wrapped around her sister, and the hero's shining face fell into a scowl.

"Stop."

It was clearly meant to be an order, but Lola wasn't taking those anymore.

"Why should I stop?" she growled through Fenrir's teeth, her voice huge and inhuman as it echoed off the burning buildings. For the first time, though, Lola didn't mind the monstrousness, because it was powerful. *She* was powerful, and Victor was about to find out how much.

"Why should I stop?" she said again, paying his tiny sword no mind as she crushed the bridge he'd been standing on. He fell to the ground with a Hero's grace, but her paw was already there, pinning him beneath one of Fenrir's freight truck-sized claws.

"Why should I listen to a word you say?" she growled as the helicopters swirled around them. "All you've ever done is hurt us."

"You will stop," Victor said, his face calm despite the giant claw digging into his chest. "Because I have *her*."

Back in Fenrir's vessel, Lola felt her sister jerk as Victor tightened his grip. Meanwhile, in the city, the Hero's face curved into a cruel smile.

"You never did know when to die, did you?" he whispered through the spell. "But your survival changes nothing. I've still got your precious sister. Disobey me, and I'll kill her."

"Not if I kill you first," Lola snarled, pressing Fenrir's giant claw harder against his oh-so-human chest. "Release her now!"

"That's not how this works," the blood mage replied. "Do you have any concept of how long I've worked to arrange this? How much I've sacrificed? I've already staked my life on tonight's outcome, but you just found something to lose. That makes you the one who's weak, my monster."

"I'm not your monster!" Lola roared.

"But you are," he insisted. "That's what you've always been: my monster to slay. I just had to set the stage."

He lifted his arm with a flourish, gesturing with his golden sword at the helicopters swarming overhead. Showing them the Hero was alive.

337

"Stop that," Lola snarled, smacking the sword out of his hand.

"But this is what you're for," Victor explained patiently. "When I slay Fenrir, I'll kill fear itself. When that happens, all the power they gave you will transfer to me. I'll be the hero of the story, the man who saved humanity from the monster not even the DFZ could kill!"

He was grinning as he finished, and Fenrir's red eyes grew huge as Lola remembered Morgan's words from earlier.

"You're trying to become a god."

"Hero," Victor corrected. "Gods are subject to the whims of their believers. I had no interest in those walls, which is why I chose to do things this way. Even the great DFZ could never escape her nature, but a hero is still a *person*. A man with the power of a god."

Lola snorted. "You're no one's hero."

"Yes, I am," Victor said with absolute surety. "I'm the man who will lead his people out of weakness. No longer will we cower in the shadows of dragons and spirits. I will teach humanity how to embrace their true magic, and then *we* will be the masters! I'll make this back into a world where men are gods, and all you have to do is die."

"Not going to happen," Lola said, leaning over him with her dripping teeth.

"You don't get a choice," Victor replied, pointing at the swarm of helicopters circling overhead. "Every eye in the world is watching us right now. If you go through with this, if the monster kills the Hero, then you really will become the undefeatable Fenrir. The wolf that ends the world. Even if you get your precious sister back, humanity's fear will take you over, and you won't be able to stop until everything is destroyed."

Lola wanted to call him a liar, but she could already feel it. When Victor had attacked Fenrir, he'd broken his own spell. He'd

338

shown people that the monster could be hurt, and their terror had eased. That drop in pressure was part of what had allowed Lola to take control, but now that she had the Hero down, she could feel humanity's panic surging back in, squeezing her once again in the vise of their expectations.

"You feel it, don't you?" Victor said as her paw began to shake. "That's the problem with gods. No matter how powerful they get, they can't escape the beliefs that formed them. The only reason you're still in control is because humanity hasn't given up hope that the Hero can win. If you kill me, though, that hope is forever lost. Their fear will flood you until you drown in it, and you'll go back to being the monster you always were. The whole world will be your victim then, including your precious sister, and it will be all your fault. If you let me slay you, though, you're the only one who has to die."

"Why should I trust anything you say?" Lola snarled. "You've never kept a promise in your life!"

"You can trust this because it was what I intended from the start," Victor said, pushing up beneath her claw. "It was never my plan to harm your sister. Alberich wouldn't have let me use her if that was the case, but this was always a partnership of convenience. Fairies are useful, but nothing that feeds on humanity can be permitted to survive in the Hero's world."

He lowered his voice to a whisper. "Let my plan unfold as intended, and I'll crush them all beneath my heel. When Alberich and his kind are gone, your sister will finally be free. Isn't that what you've always wanted?"

Lola growled deep in Fenrir's throat. "That's an easy promise for you to make since I'll be dead too."

"Everything has a price," Victor said, lying back on the broken pavement. "You should know better than anyone that I don't lose. Whether you decide to kill me or not, my legend is already secure.

I'm Victor Conrath, the hero blood mage who went toe to toe with Fenrir for the sake of all humanity! No matter how hard the Paladins crack down after this, they'll never be able to stop the blood magic revolution my actions have started tonight, which means I've already won. The only one who has anything left to lose is you, so what's it going to be, my monster? Will you let Fenrir eat the world to spite me? Or will you do the right thing?"

Fenrir's red eyes narrowed, and then Lola pulled back her claw. Not so much that he could wiggle free, but enough to avoid accidentally impaling him while she figured this out.

There *had* to be a way. Victor was the master of false choices. He only ever presented the paths he wanted you to take while making it seem as if any other decision was doomed, but Lola was no longer his victim. She'd already broken free. Now she just had to figure out how to stay that way.

Easier said than done. The fear of Fenrir pushed down harder on her with every second she kept Victor pinned. People were losing faith in the Hero, and her control over the monster was buckling as a result.

It really did feel like she was drowning in their fear, but that couldn't be the whole story. Both the fairy queen and Victor had likened her to a spirit. But while spirits *were* bound by their natures, they weren't slaves to them. The God of Noodles made noodles, but he ran his restaurant however he wanted. Even the DFZ, city of rampant capitalism, had a museum that was free for everyone to enjoy.

Clearly, there was wiggle room. Victor was doing his best to make it sound hopeless so Lola would give up and die like he wanted, but he'd been right about one thing: she *was* the monster. He and Alberich had slapped Fenrir's image on top of hers, but the wolf was just another face. Another role to play, like the leggy model she'd put on to visit poor, dead Frank. Victor was playing

340

his role too, but if all of this depended on what people saw, then Lola knew what to do.

With a final growl at Victor, she lifted her paw to set him free. He rolled to his feet at once, the Hero's golden sword at the ready. There was nothing for him to swing at, though, because the monster was walking away.

"What are you doing?" he roared in her head. "You can't walk away from this!"

"Try and stop me," Lola said, looking over her shoulder at his little figure, already far in the distance thanks to Fenrir's long legs. "You talk like you're the only actor in this story, but a hero without a monster is just a man with a sword."

"Where will you go?" he demanded. "The whole world fears you!"

"Because of you," she said, forcing herself to remain calm. "They're afraid because *you* made Fenrir rampage, but a monster is only a monster if it acts monstrously."

She said the words as much for herself as for him. He'd taught the world to panic at the sight of her, but Lola was the one who'd always feared her monster the most. She was part of that terrible pressure, that fear that threatened to drown her. Even now, the feel of Fenrir's giant fangs in her mouth was making her panic, but Lola forced it down.

She couldn't be afraid. Her sister was still in her arms at the bottom of Fenrir's vessel. If she lost control now, the surging magic would crush them both.

It was hard to be brave for herself against the monster she'd feared for so long, but Lola could always be brave for her sister. It was the truth that had carried her through her whole life, and it kept her together now, holding her giant breaths steady as Fenrir padded peacefully through the destruction.

"Arrogant creature!"

Victor's voice was a roar in her ear. She couldn't even see him anymore, but his rage was wrapped like a noose around her neck. Around her sister's neck, more precisely, because even though Lola had taken control, this was still her sister's dream, and Victor still had her in his bloody grasp.

"I'll kill her," he promised, making the girl thrash as his bloody hand tightened on her skull. "You think I fear the fairy king? I fear nothing! Now *come back.*"

Lola's paws stopped. Victor sounded pretty scared for a man who claimed to be afraid of nothing, but that was actually more frightening than if he'd been telling the truth. She'd never heard him sound afraid before, and cornered animals were always the most dangerous.

"That's right," he said when he saw her hesitate. "Turn around."

"No," Lola snarled, planting her feet. "I'm not doing what you say anymore."

"You will if you want your sister to live. Or have you grown so monstrous that you don't care about her anymore?"

He spat the threat like poison, squeezing her sister so hard that Lola could feel her pain in her own gossamer. That had never happened before. But just when Lola thought Victor had them cornered, she remembered the fairy queen's words.

You're the most powerful thing in the world.

Lola blinked Fenrir's huge eyes. That was right. She was powerful, so much so that even Victor was trying to kill her to steal it. But if he was trying to take it, that must mean that she had the power *right now.*

The simplicity of that made Lola smile. A toothy, monstrous grin that sent the circling helicopters fleeing. What a fool she was. All this time, she'd been playing by their rules, but monsters didn't follow rules. That was what made them so scary. They bit and smashed and took what they wanted, so that was exactly what Lola did.

Laying Fenrir down on top of a wrecked building, she stepped back into her own gossamer under the Sea of Magic. Her sister was right on the golden bed where she'd left her, thrashing in pain from Victor's grip. Lola couldn't stand the sight, so she opened her mouth and bit down.

Not with Fenrir's teeth. These were her own fangs, the same jagged ones she used to be so afraid of. She'd never tried to pull them out voluntarily before, but they appeared the instant she beckoned, transforming her face in a flash.

After the horror of Fenrir, her little monster seemed almost cute with its shaggy fur and blind eyes. It could still bite, though, and that was what Lola did, chewing straight through the bloody hand that held her sister down.

"No!"

Victor's panicked shout vanished the second her teeth clicked together for the final bite. As the red-glowing spellwork went dark on the ground, a stillness fell over Lola. It was so quiet, it took her a moment to realize this was what it felt like to be empty. The last of the blood was gone. For the first time since he'd stepped into her hospital room, Victor's presence was completely removed from her life, leaving her alone with her sister.

Lola could have wept then. She could have laughed just as easily, rolling on the floor with her sister in the glorious, glorious quiet, but there was too much left to do. She was already back at it, chewing through the golden gossamer that stuck her sister to the bed. Her monster's teeth made quick work of the soft metal and glittering gemstones. The core of stone beneath was trickier, but she kept at it, gnawing and snapping and clawing until she'd cut her sister free.

The woman went limp in her arms as she finished, her body

falling into what Lola hoped was the same stillness she felt. There was no way to know for sure since she still hadn't woken up, but that was fine. She was free, too, now. Lola trusted her to wake up in her own time. Meanwhile, she would keep her promise and get them somewhere safe.

Pulling the backpack with the queen's head tight across her shoulders, Lola scooped her sister into her arms and closed her eyes again, flitting back to Fenrir. The transition was even faster now that she knew where she was going. In less time than it took to blink, she was back in the wolf, looking down at Victor, who was yelling at her in the distance.

He looked so small standing under the spotlights that, for the first time in her life, Lola wasn't afraid of him. He was still dangerous, his face red with screaming rage, but Fenrir was bigger, and she was too far away to hear him. He had no power to stop her anymore. No power at all.

With that, Lola stood her wolf up and walked away. She didn't look back, didn't look at the cameras or the tanks someone had finally rolled up from the Michigan armory. She *did* look at the destruction, but there was nothing she could do about that.

She hated seeing what Fenrir's rampage had done to her city, but that was Victor's evil, not hers. If she let herself feel guilty for what he'd made the monster do while she wasn't even here, she'd drown in the grief. But Lola wasn't carrying his water anymore, so she let it go. She let it all go—the rage, the fear, the resentful sadness that had dominated her life—and as she released each pent-up fury, the monster got smaller.

It'd been doing that for a while, actually. From the moment she'd stopped trying to kill the Hero, the fear had started to shrink. Fenrir had shrunk with it, collapsing down to the size of the two-story buildings she paused to tip back onto their foundations, resulting in a great deal of confusion.

People didn't seem to know what to think about her anymore. The helicopters had left the Hero and started swirling around her, their lights blinding her eyes as the need for a scoop emboldened the pilots. She could feel their scrutiny like knives in her magic, but while that would have been enough to melt Lola back when she was just gossamer, all that attention just dug Fenrir's vessel wider.

The wolf was no longer the simple monster from the movie. Her retreat had turned it into something else: a creature capable of mercy, speech, and thought. No one seemed quite sure what that meant yet, but Lola liked their confusion far more than the fear. The baffled grip wasn't nearly as crushing as the terrified one, letting her shrink the wolf down smaller still as she climbed back into the Rentfree pit.

By the time she reached the ruined stadium at the bottom, she was no bigger than her normal monster. And when her feet hit the bottom of Alberich's ripped-open barrow, she wasn't a monster at all. She was Lola, standing triumphantly with her sister—her real, flesh-and-blood sister—cradled in her arms.

She fell to her knees after it happened, bending over her sister with a laugh of disbelief. She'd done it! She'd come back from the monster without her pills. She'd gotten free of Victor. She'd saved her sister. She'd done it *all* and come out the other side alive! She—

"Lola!"

Her head shot up. The cry was so frantic it was hard to tell, but it sounded like Tristan. Sure enough, when Lola looked over her shoulder at the trashed underground barrow where it had all started, there he was, and across from him was the Black Rider.

They both looked terrible, bloody and battered like they'd been through a war. Her first thought was that Alberich's knight must have been a true monster. Then the Black Rider made a play for Tristan's head, and she realized they'd been fighting *each other*.

345

"What are you doing?" she yelled at Valente. "*Stop!*"

"He can't!" Tristan yelled as his sword sliced through the invisible wall of the Rider's gossamer. "I told you, he's Victor's knight! He can't disobey."

Lola knew that wasn't true. Valente had disobeyed plenty when he'd been with her, but that had been when Victor was gone. Things were clearly different now, because even though the Rider's helmet was off, Valente's blue-glowing eyes didn't so much as flick her direction as he continued his attack on Tristan.

"I don't know how you got back, but you have to get out of here!" Tristan yelled as he parried the Rider's blows. "He only has orders to stop me, so he shouldn't—"

His shouting cut off as the Rider's attacks suddenly ceased. For a moment, Valente stood frozen. Then he turned and bolted. He vanished through the hole in the top of the barrow a second later, jumping so high it almost looked like he was flying. Lola hadn't known he could do that, but she was happy the violence had stopped as she ran over to Tristan.

"What happened?"

"What do you think?" the fairy snapped, his face much sharper and paler than usual as he leaned heavily on his sword. "Victor returned, and the dog obeyed his master. That wouldn't have been a problem ten years ago, but I've been a knight without a queen for too long. It's getting harder and harder to..."

His voice trailed off, sea-blue eyes flying wide as he whipped his head around to stare at Lola. She was about to ask him what was wrong when Tristan fell to one knee, hand on his sword as he whispered, "My lady."

"You have done well, loyal knight," said a sweet voice from Lola's back.

Lola set her sleeping sister gently on the ground and took off the backpack that had traveled with her all the way from the Sea of

Magic. Tristan snatched the pack from her the moment the straps were off her shoulders, unzipping the central pocket to remove Morgan's head.

"My queen," he whispered, breaking into a tearful smile. "You return!"

"You always knew I would," Morgan replied, smiling back. "Of all my court, you alone remained loyal. I will remember that when we teach those traitors a lesson. For now, though, take me away quickly. He's coming."

"Who's coming?" Lola asked, but Tristan had already vanished, fleeing down one of the roads only fairies knew with his queen's head hidden deep inside his gossamer. Lola was still staring at the place he'd been when she felt the cold blast of Valente's winter gossamer.

Snatching her sister back into her arms, Lola whirled around just in time to see the Black Rider jump his bike down the hole Fenrir had left in the ceiling. It looked like he was going to crash straight into the rocky ground. As ever, though, Valente landed perfectly, and on the seat behind him was Victor.

Despite all her progress, Lola cringed when she saw him. He was still dressed as the handsome Hero, but his face was that of the monster she remembered from her childhood. Worse, actually, because she never would have dared to make him this angry back then.

He didn't say anything pithy as the Rider's bike rolled to a stop. There were no lectures, no demands of surrender or poisoned offers of truce. He just looked her straight in the eyes and spat out two hate-filled words.

"Kill her."

The Black Rider jerked. He sat on his bike as still as a stone, his whole body fighting not to—

"Kill her!"

347

The command hit the Rider like a landslide, breaking his resistance as he shot straight at Lola.

"*No!*" she yelled, but it was too late. The Black Rider was already on top of her, his hand reaching out to melt her gossamer just like he had the troll's. She curled over her sister on instinct, closing her eyes in panic, but the attack never landed.

For a soaring moment, she thought Valente had defied Victor's control. Then Lola opened her eyes and saw the truth. The Rider's hit *had* landed, it just hadn't made it to her, because Tristan's blade had gotten there first, stopping the blow less than an inch from her shoulder.

"Get to the door!" Tristan yelled, throwing the Rider back with so much force, he flew across the cavern. "*Now!*"

Lola was about to ask what he was talking about when she saw it. There, standing on the bloody stone directly behind her, was a white-painted wooden door. It was still swinging on its hinge from where Tristan had come through, showing Lola the long, freshly painted hallway on the other side.

It was the same one she'd seen when she'd gone to his apartment: a low road. Normally, those terrified her, but Lola didn't have time to worry about that now. She just grabbed her sister and ran. Tristan darted through right behind her, slamming the door shut just before the Rider crashed into it. Lola felt the impact all the way down the hall, followed by Victor's roar of fury.

His shout was still echoing when something else hit the closed door. It was softer than the Rider's impact, but something about the wet, heavy sound struck Lola as far more terrifying. She was wondering what in the world could have caused such a hideous noise when a red stain began to bleed through the fresh white paint.

Directly ahead of her, two bloody handprints appeared on the door's surface. They were large, a man's hands, but not as big as

Valente's. They got more distinct as Lola watched, the blood welling through the painted wood in beads. Huge drips began to form on the door's surface, but they didn't slide down to the carpet like liquid should. Instead, they dripped sideways, the bright-red droplets letting go to fly straight at Lola.

Tristan's sword blocked them just before they hit. He scowled at the blood on his blade, and then he turned to slash the door. It split in two the moment his sword touched it, falling forward into the hallway to reveal the solid white wall behind it, but the bloody handprints didn't go away.

"Come on," Tristan said, grabbing Lola's shoulder as he sheathed his sword. "Stay close to me, and keep away from the walls. I didn't have time to secure this one."

Lola nodded, sticking to him like glue as they walked straight down the center of the blue-carpeted low road—which was much longer than she remembered—to Tristan's apartment.

Chapter 17

The last time she'd visited Tristan's barrow, he'd been in San Francisco. This time, the huge windows showed a sweeping vista of pine forests and snowy mountains rolling off into the distance.

"Where are we?"

"Denali National Park in Alaska," Tristan replied as he shut the door.

"Isn't that a little excessive?"

Tristan arched an eyebrow and motioned for Lola to follow as he walked through his spacious modern apartment to a door on the back wall.

She did so with trepidation. All the times she'd visited Tristan's barrow before, she'd only ever been in the front room. He'd never taken her into the back, and even after everything that had happened, she was a little frightened to see it now. She was already imagining a cauldron with a hanged man being stewed inside or a pile of barley and millet grains she'd have to sort by hand before he agreed to help her, but the truth turned out to be a perfectly-normal looking guest bedroom with a nice view of the mountains.

"Lay her there," Tristan said, gesturing at the large bed.

Lola nodded and carried her sister inside. She was about to ask Tristan if he could move some of the decorative pillows out of the way when they suddenly moved all on their own. Lola jumped at the sight, eyes wide in wonder.

The pillows weren't moving by themselves. They were being carried by low creatures. Unlike goblins and trolls—which were magical beings in their own right who could someday turn into fairies if they ate enough of their fellows—low creatures were lumps of gossamer given limited life and intelligence in order to perform a specific task. They weren't too different from

350

changelings, actually, though Lola had never seen Tristan's before.

In keeping with their master's samurai kick, these low creatures looked like little Japanese soot spirits. The black poofs bopped and floated like ash thrown up by a fire, but they didn't leave any marks on the crisp white sheets as they moved the pillows and the giant comforter out of the way so Lola could lay her sister on the bed.

She did so with great care, placing the woman's sleeping body on the mattress as if she were a piece of dandelion fluff. Her sister gave a little sigh as Lola let her go but otherwise showed no sign that she was aware of what was going on. Her face was no longer twitching from the nightmare, though, and the thread around her wrist shone as bright as the one around Lola's, which seemed like a good sign.

"Do you know how long it takes people stolen by fairies to wake up?" she asked Tristan as she pulled the comforter over her sister's shoulders.

"Depends on how long they've been asleep," he replied, walking over to peer curiously at the human. "Most fairies who steal children either eat them or send them back to their parents within a few months, but..."

"But she's been like this for twenty-seven years," Lola finished, reaching down to squeeze her sister's hand. "It's going to be okay," she whispered. "You were always there for me. I'll always be here for you. As long as you need, as long as it takes, I'll keep you safe until you wake up."

It could have been wishful thinking, but Lola swore her sister's mouth twitched at that. She grinned right back, grabbing a padded chair from the corner and dragging it over so she could sit at her sister's side. When she was comfortable, she looked up at Tristan.

"So how much is the hotel treatment going to cost me?"

It was bound to be astronomical. Even if she was the one

351

who'd brought back his queen, that had been part of the deal between her and Morgan. Fairies didn't let technicalities like that slide, *and* Tristan had just saved her life. That put her dangerously deep in his debt. But to Lola's great surprise, Tristan shook his head.

"The price has already been paid," he said, giving her a sad smile. "I have not dealt fairly with you, Lola-cat. I promised I would help you, but I have been sorry assistance indeed. Another time, I'd have said saving you from the blood mage's black knight balances our scales, but I was recently reminded of the stain of oath-breaking, and with the return of my queen, I am in a generous mood."

He flashed her a dazzling smile as he waved his hand at the bedroom with its gorgeous mountain view. "You and your sister are now my guests. My home is yours for so long as you wish to keep it."

By the time he finished, Lola was dangerously close to tears. She hadn't realized just how much she'd needed somewhere she could feel safe until Tristan offered it.

"Thank you," she whispered.

The fairy wagged his finger at her. "That's a dangerous word, Lola-cat. Have I taught you nothing?"

Lola shook her head, but she didn't take the words back. She just scooted her chair closer to her sister. When she was settled, the knight gave a little bow and left, closing the door softly behind him.

Alone at last, Lola brought her legs up so she could sit cross-legged in the big chair and watch her sister sleep. It wasn't quite the happy, rain-soaked cabin she'd dreamed about the last time she was in Tristan's barrow, but she still felt peace falling over her like a blanket. Her sister must have felt it, too, because the silver thread on Lola's wrist was quiet as a sleeping child, its glittering length moving only with the rise and fall of her sister's deep, slow breaths. Lola was shifting her own breathing to match when something inside her began to vibrate.

The sensation made her jump. Her magic had been rock solid since Victor's blood had drained out, but it wasn't her gossamer that was shaking. It was Simon's phone, which was somehow still in her pocket.

How she'd held onto it through so many changes, Lola had no idea, but she'd never been so happy to take a call. She leaped on the buzzing device, sliding her fingers through the unlock sequence so fast, she had to do it three times before it was actually accepted. When the screen finally came up, though, it wasn't a call from Simon or Valente or anyone else she cared about. It was a news alert.

Lola almost didn't click it. She doubted there was any news she wanted to hear right now, and she was loath to surrender the peace she'd just found. There weren't any other notifications on the screen, though, and this *was* Simon's private phone. Maybe he was trying to send her a message?

That was the only reason Lola touched it. When she tapped her finger against the screen, the alert spawned a floating video in her AR that began playing immediately, dumping Lola into the middle of what looked like a live interview between Chloe Spark, one of the DFZ's biggest media personalities and Victor's long-term client, and a man listed only as The Hero.

He looked so different from the furious tyrant screaming at her from the back of the Black Rider's bike that it took Lola several moments to recognize her former master. He was covered in more illusions than she'd ever seen. He'd even found the golden sword she'd tossed away. He sat with it glittering in his lap, making sure the shining blade caught the TV lights as he listened intently to Chloe's fawning softball question.

"…obvious every survivor in the city owes you their lives," she was saying in her concerned-interviewer voice. "Tell us, Mr. Conrath, how did you get Fenrir to retreat like that?"

"It was the only way," Victor replied in the Hero's compassionate voice. "When I saw the damage our fight was doing to the city, I knew I had to find a less destructive path to victory, so I used my magic to invade the monster's mind and force it to retreat."

The whole studio burst into applause at this stroke of brilliance. Meanwhile, Lola's hands tightened so hard on the phone, the metal case started to creak.

"Tell us more about your magic," Chloe pleaded. "There are many who'd call what you do 'blood magic,' but that didn't look like anything so awful to me."

"It's not," Victor said, turning to speak directly into the camera. "I did nothing but use the magic I was born with. Those in power have always feared our true strength, calling it 'blood magic' and 'mind control' and other names designed to frighten people away from their full potential. But there can't be anything inherently evil about a power every human has. *All* magic can be misused, but if I hadn't defied the laws designed to keep us weak, I never could have saved the city. My 'blood magic' is the only effective weapon against monsters like Fenrir. It's not evil or dirty or shameful. It's *our* power—humanity's true magic!—and it's one we must all master if we're to survive what's coming."

"And what is that?" Chloe asked, not even trying to pretend that question wasn't staged.

The cameras zoomed in on Victor as he leaned forward.

"War," he whispered, his magically enhanced face so bluntly concerned for the safety of all humanity that it made Lola gag. "Horrible as it was, the Fenrir Disaster was merely a distraction, a horrifying diversion to keep us from seeing the main attack. The

354

truth is, we are already in the midst of a full-scale invasion by the fae, parasitic hunters who feed on humanity's fear. I'm sure you've already heard the reports of riders flying through the skies all over the world. They're not hallucinations or Halloween trickery. That's the *real* Wild Hunt. It's come back to haunt us just as it did a thousand years ago, and all of humanity will be its prey if we do not arm ourselves."

"With blood magic?"

"With *our* magic," Victor said fiercely, never taking his eyes off the camera. "This is humanity's moment to rise above our petty differences. I've already made progress on this front. In gratitude for saving her city, the DFZ has agreed to lift her ban on blood magic. She recognizes that this power is our right, and that it has been kept from us for far too long."

He held out his hand to the camera.

"I speak now to every mage in the world," he said in a ringing voice. "If you want to embrace your true potential, if you want to fight back, then come to the DFZ, and I will teach you. No longer must we live in the shadows and be hunted by self-righteous Paladins. *This* is the moment we stop being prey and take back our world from the monsters that have stolen it from us!"

The studio audience burst into its wildest applause yet. Chloe was actually crying, begging Victor to show them some of his magic on air. He graciously agreed, holding up his long-fingered hands. He was just starting to explain a technique Lola remembered him beating into Simon back when they were kids when she turned off the video.

She sat hunched on her chair in the silent room for a long time after that, shaking with a fury that wouldn't go away. How dare he? How *dare* he steal her triumph and turn it into that... that *lie*! She wanted to say she couldn't believe it, but the problem was that she believed too well. Of *course* Victor had figured out a way to spin his defeat into a victory. Her master never lost. He—

Lola stopped herself right there. He wasn't her master anymore. He was just a liar. A selfish con artist who'd exploited a frightened girl too desperate for salvation to realize he wasn't the hero he pretended to be. Now he was pulling the same trick on the rest of the world, using the disaster *he'd* created to trick everyone into believing his abusive power was the only solution to the Wild Hunt *he'd* unleashed. He didn't care about the damage he caused or the lives lost. All he cared about was doing his bloody magic out in the open with no one to stop him.

"We won't let it happen," she whispered, clutching her sister's hand. "We'll stop him. Him and Alberich. We won't let them do to anyone else what they did to us."

Even as she said it, the old hopelessness rose up inside her like a viper, whispering that she was stupid. She couldn't beat Victor. He was the miracle worker, the master of monsters. Even Simon hadn't been able to escape him in the end. What hope did she have?

The old refrain was swirling through her like poison when Lola stomped it down. She wasn't his scared little monster anymore. She was her own master now, and if Victor thought he could lie and say he'd won just because she'd chosen not to play his game, he had another think coming.

"We'll beat him," she promised, wrapping both hands around her sister's limp fingers. "We'll beat them both and take it back, Valente and Simon and everything else they've stolen from us! We'll show the world what Victor *really* is, and then we'll see who they call monster."

She was still shaking from the fury of the promise when Lola felt her sister squeeze her hand.

Thank you for reading!

Thank you for reading *By a Silver Thread*! If you enjoyed the story, I hope you'll consider leaving a review. Reviews, good and bad, are vital to any author's career, and I would be extremely appreciative if you'd consider writing one for me.

If you want to be the first to know when I put out new books, sign up for my New Release Mailing List. List members are always the first to know about everything I do *and* they get exclusive bonus content like the list-only Heartstriker short story, *Mother of the Year*. Signing up is free, and I promise never to spam you, so come join us!

If you need more books *right now*, you can always check out one of other my completed series, including eight more novels set in the DFZ! Just keep paging forward or select "Want More Books?" in your e-reader's table of contents. You can also visit www.rachelaaron.net for a full list of all my books, high-rez covers, and free sample chapters. If you want to know more about me IRL, follow me on Twitter @Rachel_Aaron!

Thank you so, *so* much for reading! I couldn't do any of this without you!

Yours always and sincerely,
Rachel Aaron

Want More Books?

By a Silver Thread is only the latest addition to my library. I have plenty more titles for you to enjoy! Keep paging forward to see my top picks for new readers or visit www.rachelaaron.net for the full list. Thank you for reading!

Minimum Wage Magic

The DFZ, the metropolis formerly known as Detroit, is the world's most magical city with a population of nine million and zero public safety laws. That's a lot of mages, cybernetically enhanced chrome heads, and mythical beasties who die, get into debt, and otherwise fail to pay their rent. When they can't pay their bills, their stuff gets sold to the highest bidder to cover the tab.

That's when they call me. My name is Opal Yong-ae, and I'm a Cleaner: a freelance mage with an art history degree who's employed by the DFZ to sort through the mountains of magical junk people leave behind. It's not a pretty job, or a safe one-- there's a reason I wear bite-proof gloves--but when you're deep in debt in a lawless city where gods are real, dragons are traffic hazards, and buildings move around on their own, you don't get to be picky about where your money comes from. You just have to make it work, even when the only thing of value in your latest repossessed apartment is the dead body of the mage who used to live there.

"A catchy title, a plucky protagonist and a maximum effort by the author, honestly readers can't ask for more in the urban fantasy genre."- **Fantasy Book Critic**

"I love what Rachel Aaron has done with this novel to expand her stories within this unique world of her creation. I have developed a trust in her ability to write engaging stories of great characters which I feel most comfortable and eager to spend time with, and this book is no exception." - **TS Chan**

Nice Dragons Finish Last

As the smallest dragon in the Heartstriker clan, Julius survives by a simple code: stay quiet, don't cause trouble, and keep out of the way of bigger dragons. But this meek behavior doesn't cut it in a family of ambitious predators, and his mother, Bethesda the Heartstriker, has finally reached the end of her patience.

Now, sealed in human form and banished to the DFZ--a vertical metropolis built on the ruins of Old Detroit--Julius has one month to prove to his mother that he can be a ruthless dragon or lose his true shape forever. But in a city of modern mages and vengeful spirits where dragons are seen as monsters to be exterminated, he's going to need some serious help to survive this test.

He just hopes humans are more trustworthy than dragons.

"Super fun, fast paced, urban fantasy full of heart, and plenty of magic, charm and humor to spare, this self published gem was one of my favorite discoveries this year!" - **The Midnight Garden**

"A deliriously smart and funny beginning to a new urban fantasy series about dragons in the ruins of Detroit...inventive, uproariously clever, and completely un-put-down-able!" - **SF Signal**

The first and most popular DFZ series, complete at 5 books.

The Last Stand of Mary Good Crow

A gaslamp epic fantasy featuring a sprawling cast of colorful Western characters, crystal-mad bandits, ambitious necromancers, and cursed gunmen. Welcome to the Crystal Calamity!

The Montana Territory, 1876, and the discovery of magical crystal has sparked a rush that makes gold a thing of the past. The US Cavalry, the Sioux tribes, and the criminal underworld will stop at nothing to control the mines that produce the new miracle stone, but the beautiful crystals bring a darkness, a madness, and a horror that threatens to consume all who seek their power.

Mary Good Crow, a half-Lakota guide, can hear the crystal's song. She makes her living leading miners to fortune, but there's trouble brewing in the depths of the crystal caves that even she can't navigate. Bandits with crystal-augmented strength, ghosts that roam the living darkness, and madmen driven by the crystals' power to destroy all who seek their prize.

With Josephine Price, a mining heiress with secrets to hide, and Tyrel Reiner, a gunslinger haunted by a necromancer's legacy, Mary must navigate the dangerous world of the new Magical West. The beautiful song of the crystal has never led her false so far, but with war brewing on the plains and enemies in every shadow, embracing the power that's driven so many mad before her might just be Mary's only shot at survival.

What people are saying about Mary

"Possibly the best alternate historical fantasy that you will read." - **Fantasy Book Critic**

"Brimming with imagination, wonderful characters and captivating magic." - **Novel Notions**

"I very much enjoyed the twists and turns throughout this book and strongly recommend it. No one's allegiances are entirely set and the only genuinely good person in the story is Mary Good Crow. Even she has a dark side that she struggles to keep suppressed as a matter of sheer survival. I think fans of the Weird West and urban fantasy both will enjoy this novel." - **Grimdark Magazine**

Forever Fantasy Online

Forever Fantasy Online is the gritty, battle-filled tale of a raiding guild vs the world featuring rules-driven combat, incredible tanking, and the good side of guild drama!

In the real world, twenty-one-year-old library sciences student Tina is invisible and under-appreciated, but in the VR-game Forever Fantasy Online, she's Roxxy--fearsome warrior, respected leader, and main tank of a top-tier raiding guild.

In the real world, James is a college drop-out drowning in debt, but in FFO he's famous--an explorer who's collected every item, gotten every achievement, and done every quest.

Both Tina and James need the game more than they care to admit, but their favorite escape turns into a trap when FFO becomes a living world. Wounds are no longer virtual, stupid monsters become cunning, NPCs start acting like actual people, and death might be forever.

In the real world, everyone said being good at video games was a waste of time. Now, stranded and separated across thousands of miles of new, deadly terrain, Tina and James's skill at FFO is the only thing keeping them alive. It's going to take every bit of their expertise--and hoarded loot--to find each other and get back home, but as the stakes get higher and the damage adds up, being the best in the game may no longer be enough.

"Rachel Aaron and Travis Bach have written an amazing story and a realistic LitRPG." - **The Fantasy Inn**

"Forever Fantasy Online is definitely a book for the gamers among us." - **Fantasy Book Critic**

"Excellent characters, an engaging story and geek humour. What more can one ask for?" - **TS Chan**

About the Author

Rachel Aaron is the author of over twenty novels both self-published and through Orbit Books. When she's not holed up in her writing cave, Rachel lives a nerdy, bookish life in Broomfield, CO, with her perpetual-motion son, long-suffering husband, and far too many  plants. To learn more about Rachel and read samples of all her books, visit rachelaaron.net!

Cover Illustration by Luisa Preissler
Cover Design by Rachel Aaron
Editing provided by Red Adept Editing

As always, this book would not have been nearly as good without my amazing beta readers. Thank you so, so much, Christina Vlinder, Linda Hall, Sarah Braun, Aria Andrea, LJ Andrews, Spencer Albrecht, Javier Rentas, Julia, Robert Ying, K Stoker, Regina Dowling, Sally Jenkins, and Nancy Wise.

Y'all are the BEST!

CPSIA information can be obtained
at www.ICGtesting.com
Printed in the USA
BVHW050947010523
663343BV00010B/172

9 781952 367212